MW01491326

MRS. WYNIFRED STAPLES SMITH
Author of "Pines and Pioneers"

Pines and Pioneers

by

Wynifred Staples Smith

Keim Publications
RR1 Box 725
Weld, Maine 04285
207-585-2466

© 1965 by Wynifred Staples Smith

ACKNOWLEDGMENTS

If I were to give credit to those to whom credit is due, for encouragement that made this publication possible I would need another whole volume. Churches, teachers' clubs, almost every library in Maine, almost every School Union Superintendent in out State, patriotic organizations, both of our U. S. Senators, have given moral support. Newspapers for their publicity, particularly the Bath and Rumford publications have our sincerest thanks. Every summer resident around Webb Lake, every resident of Weld, of Carthage, of Dixfield; in fact almost every town of Oxford and Franklin Counties deserves a large share of thanks.

For Source Material the author is very thankful to Edgar P. Judkins, great grandson of Philip Judkins and to Mrs. Austin Willoughby great-great-granddaughter of Samuel White. Also to Mrs. Gertrude Owen great-great-granddaughter of Amos Trask, Thanks is extended to Lee G. Hutchinson of Carthage for the loan of ancient news clippings and to Dorothy Berry Mason of Carthage great granddaughter of Eldridge Berry who figured prominently in the earliest history of the region.

Especial thanks goes to Donald and Bessie McIntire of Weld and Eugene Norton, without whose help this book never would have been published. And to Rachel Kidder, Librarian of Ludden Library, at Dixfield, thanks for untiring labor and publicity. And to Julian Israelson for publicity. Also special thanks for the cooperation and encouragement of the Bartash Book and Gift Shop at Rumford, Maine.

Printed in the United States of America
Reprinted 1999 with permission

Affectionately Dedicated to my

Beloved Husband

The late Frederick W. Smith

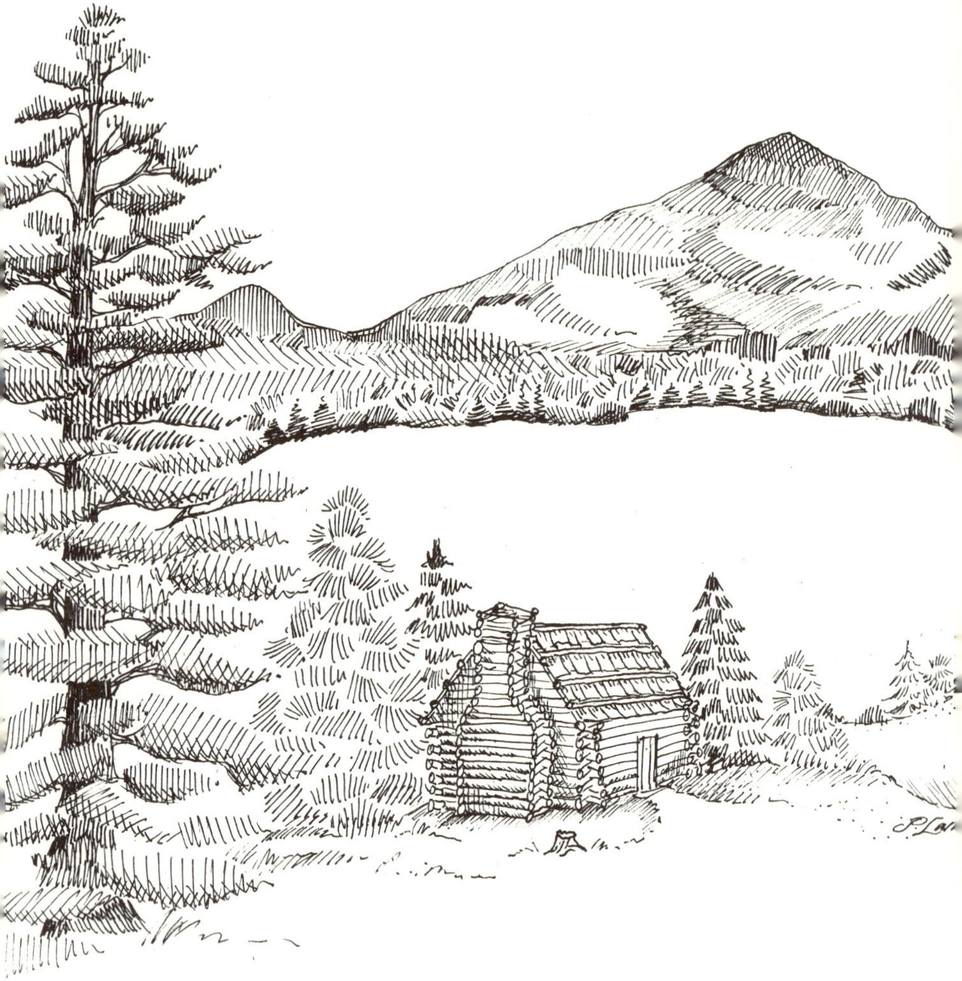

FOREWORD

Oh Webb Lake, lying like a sapphire in the sun, reflecting in your bosom fair, Mt. Blue; Treasuring in your memory the pals of other days—The bear, the salmon and brave people too, who loved your shores! They strip you of your pine, that our fair flag might lifted be on high, and float from mastheads higher than their kind; so men of foreign shores might see, and sigh—"Oh tiny nation, choosing to be Free"! We were an infant country then, who valued Liberty as worth the cost. Our lives invested in Her cause were just invested, never lost.

Webb's crystal waters now reflect the tourist's raptured face and bathe the flesh of myriad children's feet. White sails of tiny boats skim on with dainty grace. This book salutes you with each true tale we here repeat, Oh Fair Lake Webb.

ABBIE F. NORTON

TABLE OF CONTENTS

Chapter
- I. "Taller Timber" 3
- II. "Up-River" 11
- III. When Giants Beckon, Mortals Move 26
- IV. "The Toils of the Road Will Seem Nothing—" 39
- V. "When We Get to the End of the Way" 48
- VI. Little Naomi Learns Some Bear Facts 59
- VII. Of Chairs and Chips and Knitting Socks, and Also Cupid's Wings. 69
- VIII. A Neighbor of Philip's Enlists 80
- IX. Neighbors Are "Near" and So Is An Epidemic of Diphtheria. 83
- X. "An Angel Unawares" Brings a New Settler 93
- XI. Growing Pains, Which Include Social and Religious Activities, Indian Scare and War of 1812 105
- XII. A Rippling Symphony of Ripping Claws 122
- XIII. "Wars, and Rumors of Wars," With Sunshine Filtering Thru. 136
- XIV. Black Accents, "Peter 'n Rhody" 148
- XV. Great Day in the Morning 154
- XVI. Unbelievably Hazardous Travel Conditions in 1814. 173
- XVII. End of the War and Advent of Wolves to Central Maine 176
- XVIII. "Eighteen-Hundred-and-Froze to Death." Plans Completed for the Great Drive 179
- XIX. Giants in Transit 197
- XX. "Safe in the Androscoggin" 212
- XXI. Safe in the Bath Booms 216
- XXII. "Tick-Tock, Old Clock" 230

PINES AND PIONEERS

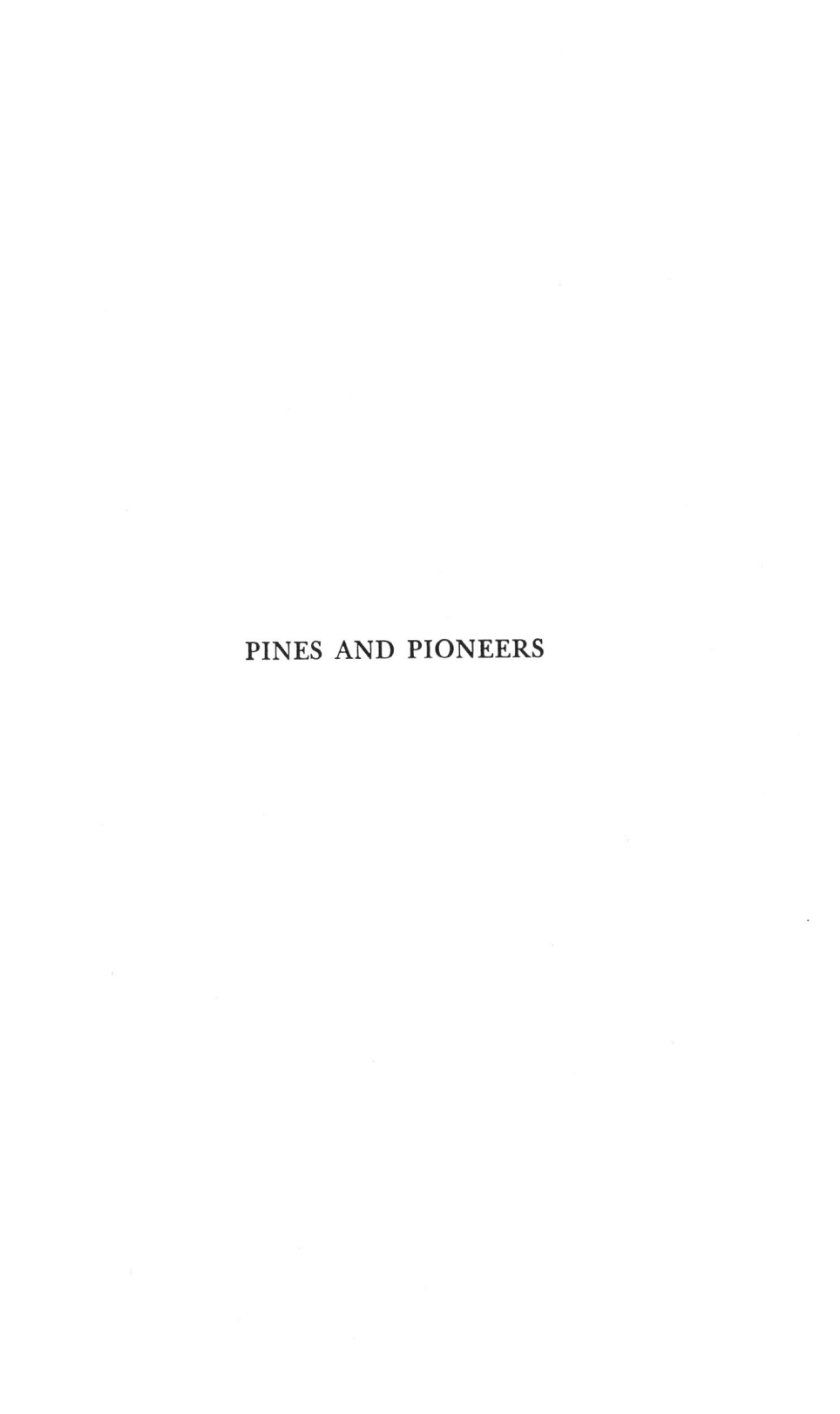

CHAPTER I.

"TALLER TIMBER"

Philip Judkins was born in Charleston, New Hampshire in 1754. He was a joiner by trade, worked in the shipyard in Bath before and after the Revolutionary War. He took a very active part in that struggle, was taken prisoner by the Indians and was carried off to Canada. But it took more than a few Indians to hold Philip for long in one place, and he soon escaped. He worked his way down through the forest living on roots, leaves, berries, and anything he could capture with his hands, for the Indians had taken his gun. He finally joined a small company of American soldiers at Champlain. Under Philip's direction, they soon built a fort and, in time, a goodly number of men were added to the company, which later did valiant service in the cause of liberty.

In 1783, when peace was finally declared, Philip returned to New Hampshire, married Hannah, and worked in Charleston as a joiner, doing any other odd jobs that would help him to support his family. This venture paid fairly well, but after a few years, he decided to try farming. So in 1788, he and Hannah with their two children, their oxen and all their worldly goods, went to Greene, Province of Maine, where Philip believed the soil along the great Amariscoggin River would be very productive, easier cultivated and more desirable in many ways. With the remaining paper money which the Government had supplied its soldiers at the close of the war, from the Pejebscot proprietors, the couple bought a strip of fine land on the banks of the Amariscoggin, later called Androscoggin. Times were hard, frightfully so. As more children came, Philip was forced again to work at the shipyard, whenever he could possibly leave his farm for a few weeks or months. His two boys were too young to be of much assistance to their mother. In Philip's absence, she had to do a man's work on the farm, besides feeding and generally caring for her family. Philip was a man of good judgment, had seen enough of the world to know there was a way for a man to provide for his family and give them a much better living than was possible for him to do under the present plan. Whenever he worked at the shipyard, he availed himself of every opportunity to listen to what men were saying about other parts of the country.

He often heard the owners of the yard express a desire for taller trees to use for ship's masts. Whenever he had a chance, he would inquire of strangers what they knew about the growth of pine farther north. He wondered if all the best timber came from over East, up the Kennebec and Penobscot Rivers. "What grew further up the Androscoggin, what had ever been heard about that?" he would ask. Nobody seemed to know much about the country above Turner and Canton. A few poor settlers had reported Indians were plentiful up Rumford way. They had left their half-cleared lands and returned to New Gloucester. There were later reports that the Rumford settlers had returned to resume the clearing of their lands. The Anasigunticook Indians were a cruel tribe and their name struck terror in the hearts of any who thought of venturing beyond Canton. The Indians, led by chief Tecumseh, were making trouble for the settlers in Ohio. Everywhere there was trouble throughout the nation.

Philip tried to be reconciled to his lot, pitched in and worked like a slave, trying to make things a little better for his rapidly increasing family. Once, when he realized how the years were slipping by, and he was not breaking even, he discussed with one of his neighbors the idea of selling his farm and going "up country". But nothing came of it. For the young man, William Parker, with whom he talked, was a sea-faring man, unmarried, living with his parents, Jane and Benjamin. He was soon off on a trip to the Orient, perhaps never to return. So, Philip dismissed the thought from his mind.

A year later, softly humming a tune, a man from the town of Lisbon came into the shipyard at Bath, where Philip was working on the keel of a great ship. The man marvelled at the extreme efficiency of Philip's work.

Philip said, "It's a pity we can't get masts ten feet longer. Trees don't seem to grow long enough nowadays. It's getting about impossible to find pines tall enough to answer the demand of the trade. If a man could spare the time to leave his work, I believe there is a possibility of finding better timber up the Androscoggin."

The man whose name was Samuel White, asked Philip if the Bath Shipbuilding Company would pay enough more for the very long timber to make profitable such a venture. Philip thought there was no question about that.

Sam White went back to his home and pondered on Philip's proposition. For a week he deliberated. Times were growing worse. The British were bribing the Indians all over the country. They were constantly attacking the settlers from the Canadian border to Georgia. The American sailors were taken from their ships and carried away by the British. All around the section there was talk of another war. They couldn't live unless their foreign trade could go on, their ships go unmolested and the young colony given a chance. Yes, they did need ship timbers, no question about that, for they would soon be building more man-of-war type, if not merchant ships. Maine was the greatest shipbuilding section in the country, and would certainly need all the tall timber there was, whichever way things went.

The next morning, bright and early, Sam saddled his horse and rode to Bath, found his friend Philip and told him he had come to discuss more fully the subject in which they were both interested. That night after work, Philip met Sam by appointment at the Tavern, they had supper together and then went to Philip's room, where they talked most of the night. They tried to plan a trip up the river Androscoggin, but they couldn't keep their minds on it. The national situation was uppermost in their thoughts. Philip felt sure the country would be at war with Great Britain before long. He had heard there were many men throughout the country who felt our American fleet was so small it should never be sent out against the splendid ships of the British Navy.

Congress passed an embargo law with the idea that the stopping of all foreign trade would force England and France to come to agreeable terms with the United States. In this they were wrong and so was the thought of building too many Merchant ships. Already our ports were lined with idle ships whose owners were afraid to send them on a voyage, even along our own New England coast. So there was some danger that the shipbuilding industry was not going to see very soon its former prosperity. Philip might soon be obliged to leave Bath and go back to his farm. He did not dare to use the time it might take to go on this trip "up-river". Philip felt they shouldn't do it then, but Sam White, who hadn't as large a family as Philip, seemed almost possessed by the idea. Before they separated that night, they agreed to wait until the following spring, and if things looked favorable enough to warrant it, they would go on a trip of exploration and at least learn if the great timber regions of the central part of the state on the east, extended across the country toward the west, and if the Androscoggin River flowed through this timber belt. Both Sam and Philip now had sons nearly grown and young Sam and young Philip, as they were called, could certainly carry on by Spring, helped and guided by their mothers, while Philip and Sam went "up-river".

Philip, who was much more conservative and cautious than Sam, won out for the time. Sam went back to his farm in Lisbon, and Philip alternated between the farm and shipyard. But sometimes he would have an opportunity to build a house, or little shop for some of the pioneers, who were fast coming into the town now called Greene. His education was superior to the general run of men round about him, and his advice was often sought. Once a committee was formed in Green with Philip Judkins chairman, to improve their school system. Philip was capable of teaching school and his neighbors begged him to find time for this, but it was impossible.

In the days before the Revolution, the State of New Hampshire offered much greater educational privileges than did the Province of Maine, and until the beginning of the 19th Century this condition prevailed, Maine having almost no schools except in seacoast towns. In the country, private schools were carried on in the homes. At Brunswick, on the Androcoggin, Bowdoin College, the first in the state, was opened in 1802. At Waterville, on the Kennebec, Colby College in 1818 was the second to offer its advantages to our Maine youth. Again on the Androscoggin, at Lewiston, in 1863, Bates Colleges was founded. Two years later, in 1865, on the Penobscot at Orono, by an act of the legislature, the Maine State College was established. All during these years academies and preparatory schools were slowly coming into being throughout the state.

With academies at Hallowell and Berwick in 1791, 1792, Fryeburg and Washington, 1794, Portland was not left behind. By 1825, there had been twenty-five of these schools established in

Maine. Greene was incorporated as a town in 1788, second town to incorporate in Androscoggin County. In 1792, with John Larrabee chairman, a committee of three was chosen to define the limits of school districts and the town voted 12 pounds for schools, the tax to be paid in produce, wheat at six shillings a bushel, rye, six shillings, Indian Corn four shillings. In 1793, 20 pounds were voted for the support of the schools, and in 1794, 30 pounds.

The school committee for 1802 was Benjamin Thomas, Thomas Stevens, Simon Rose, Moses Harris, Zebedee Shaw, Bartholomew Coburn, Cyrus Deane, Philip Judkins, and Dr. Ami R. Cutter. This year they voted to raise $250.00 for schools. In 1805, they voted to build a school-house in the fifth district. With school privileges so limited, it would seem strange, perhaps, that the youth of that period would have much incentive to try to gain an education. But there were some ambitious and determined young people who wished to improve themselves in spite of all obstacles. Ami Parker, son of William, walked from Greene to Brunswick weekly, carrying his provisions. He graduated from Bowdoin College in 1838, receiving his degree as an M.D.

Sam White, of Sharon, Massachusetts, full of pioneer spirit inherited from his Mayflower ancestors, who had the courage to come to America in 1620, could not be content to live on White Hill where he had brought his bride in 1780. He must push on. Those tall trees beckoned him with hands he could almost see. He often asked himself why it was that Philip thought there could be better and greater trees farther on "up-river" somewhere. Night after night while he lay in his bed beside his sleeping wife, he thought over the things Philip had told him.

Finally one night, the whole scene seemed to appear before him. He felt so convinced of the existence of those giant timbers "up-river" that he absolutely forgot where he was, and at the top of his voice, burst out saying, "There ain't no two ways 'bout it, I've gut t' go, I've gut t' go, I tell ye."

Poor Rachel, his wife, was beside herself with fear.

"Oh Sam, Sam," she cried. "Where is it ye be a-goin'? Can't be ye'd be a-leavin' of us. 'Tain't possible, ain't I worked hard ever since I married of ye? Ain't I been faithful? Can it be ye've seen another woman that looks better to ye'n I do? P'r'aps I don't keep my hair 's tidy as some. Ye know I ain't had no bear's oil this summer t' keep it good. By th' way ye eat I'd say my cookin' suited ye well enough. Sam what is it that's ailin' of ye?

Sam was so surprised when he heard his own voice there in the darkness, he could hardly think where he was, or what it was all about. Rachel's arms were about him holding his so tightly he could scarcely get breath to say,

"Rachel, Rachel, dear, I ain't goin' no where without ye and the children, but we're all goin' "up-river" later. I'm goin' up fust to find out 'bout things, but I shan't stay long. I've made up my mind to it. It's a wonderful country off up there, nobody knows how wonderful, 'n I've got to find out."

"But, Sam," sobbed Rachel, "There's Injuns up there. I've hearn the Roccamekas and the Anasagunticooks are all round Canton and Sumner. The farther up ye go the thicker they be. There ain't no ro'd beyond Holmantown and Rumford, is they?"

"Lord forbid that ye have an idee of goin' beyent them wilderness towns. Don't ye remember hearin' tell how John Staples' half-sister, Isabella Collins, married a feller up there in Turner more'n fifteen years ago, and them two young folks went "up-river" — seems if 'twas up 'bove Holmantown, but I ain't sure. Anyway, they ain't never been heard from since. Course ye wouldn't be aimin' to go to that part of the world, would ye, Sam? And think of little Phenewel — how could we take him up there with th' Injuns? There wunt be no schools up there fer the children. Think of the money they voted t' raise here — 410 dollars five years ago, and' they keep on raisin' more every year. Think of the mills 'round here, too. Six big sawmills, grist mills, a cardin' mill. Why, people are growin' rich here in Lisbon. Why do ye want to leave? We have everything here that heart could wish. We have West Ingie molasses 'n sal 'n sometimes spice 'n indigo, and think of the lobsters 'n clams ye c'n git at Bath! I bet they don't grow up that river." Rachel argued on, pleaded and coaxed, till she finally realized Sam was sound asleep. Having freed his mind, he could sleep now.

Early the next morning, Sam saddled his horse and rode to the home of his near neighbor, Russell Hinkley, who was quite surprised to receive a call from anyone so early in the morning.

"Mornin' Sam, What's up, any trouble?" asked Hinckley.

"No, no trouble, Russell, I've come on business. I want to talk about sellin' my farm."

"God'lmighty, Sam, ye gone crazy? What ye aimin' to do, ain't goin' west, be ye?"

"No, I'd'n know's I sh'll go west, may go north. Hain't decided fer sure yit that I'll go anywhere, but I gut a notion in my head an' I'm goin' away fer a spell to look into it. I don't want ye should say a word about this t' any livin' soul, but if I find things is like I b'lieve they may be, I sh'll give ye a dam good trade on my land. So ye c'n be a-thinkin' of it over. I'll be back here in ten days, prob'ly, maybe sooner. When ye see smoke in th' mornin' ye'll know my folks is all right — keep an eye on 'em while I'm gone, will ye? Goodby."

Faint snatches of an old tune drifted back to Hinkley as Sam rode away.

"Ah dum dee, Ah dum dee."

"Well, I'll be hornswoggled, ain't that Sam crazy? Wonder what struck him! What in thunder does he want t' leave here fer?" soliloquized the baffled Hinkley.

The next morning before light, Sam left for "up-river". The November winds were cold, but very little snow had fallen. Sam felt he must make every hour count for he must go and return before the heavy snows came. He reached the home of his friend Philip in Greene soon after eight o'clock. The two greeted each other gladly, Philip looking questioningly into the smiling eyes of Sam as he asked,

"Where you bound for, Sam, this early?"

"I'm goin', Philip, and I want ye should go too. I can't wait no longer, and why should you? Come along, git yer horse and some grub. We c'n make Holmantown easy by night, I think. The goin's bad 'nough, but 'twill be worse'n a week and we've gut t' make time. Maybe we'll find our timber 'tween Canton and Holmantown and wunt have t' go beyent there."

Philip was half way through the kitchen door and didn't hear all Sam said but he called to Hannah,

"Put some grub into my saddle bag while I get that old heavy blanket and my sidearm, and you, Philip, get my short handled axe and my big knife. I'm going up-river with Sam. May be gone a week, maybe two, look for me when I come. Don't let the sheep out, Phil, it's too dangerous for 'em to get out of sight now. Storms may come anytime."

In twenty minutes from the time Sam drove into Philip's yard, they were on their way. As they left the place, Philip called back over his shoulder to anyone who might hear.

"Look after things, and Philip, keep your eye on old Dinah, she's apt to calve anytime now. Asol, you know how the old mare gets cast nights. If she should get cast and you couldn't get her up alone, get Jake Parker to come and help you."

A wave of the arm and they were gone.

Chapter II

"UP-RIVER"

The first two hours of their travel was through country where spruce and pine, along the banks of the Androscoggin, grew to ordinary heights, for the best had been culled out and was already part of merchant ships sailing the seven seas. Philip and Sam, well accustomed to such matters, could soon tell that what they sought was much farther on, so they lost no time pushing their horses ahead as fast as the roads would permit. On through Leeds to Livermore, formerly called Port Royal, they decided to stay for the night at the Inn of Abijah Monroe. Their horses were tired and hungry; so were they. The fare at the Inn was said to be the best. Its fame had spread afar.

Sam said, "I cal'late this is the place for us to stop."

Philip nodded his consent, and they gladly released the care of their saddle horses to a stable boy and went inside the spacious, well-heated main room of the Inn. A great fire blazed on the hearth, and Philip and Sam were pleased with the opportunity to warm their benumbed bodies and stretch their stiffened legs in the glorious warmth of those great burning logs. Sam ordered hot buttered rum for them both, and soon the business ahead of them didn't seem quite as forbidding as it had back on the road an hour or so before they reached Livermore. They had agreed that no word concerning their business prospects should be known by anyone.

Soon their good host, Abijah, called them to the next room where they ate their fill. There was an abundance of food on that table. Roasting on a spit at another great open fire, tended by two women, was a fat, juicy loin of beef. In a huge kettle, suspended from a crane, bubbled a ham of just the right size.

Philip said to Sam, "I guess we won't go ta bed hungry."

They enjoyed their fine meal together. There seemed to be no end to the pies, doughnuts, cookies and fried pies the house provided. At last, they declared they could eat no more and so went back to the main room. As they entered, a tall stranger stood near the fire in conversation with Abijah Monroe. He glanced at Philip and Sam, then looked away. With an expression of deep interest on his face, he quickly gave them a second searching glance. At the same moment, Philip thought he had seen the man before and politely said,

"Excuse me, sir, but have we met before? My name's Judkins."

"Mine is Holman," answered the man.

"Didn't you march on Concord the 19th?"

"Yes, sir."

"I thought so. Have you a brother Jonathan, a Colonel?"

"I have, and he owns most of the township up above here."

"I knew him," said Philip, "back there in the early days of the war, but the Injuns carried me off to Canada and I never saw him again, but I heard he was a great fighter."

"Did you say he lives "up-river"? Philip inquired.

"No, I said he owns a township "up-river" called Holmantown. Two of his sons live there."

These three men talked together a long time. Their voices were low, and other men in the room, however curious, were unable to hear what they said. At midnight, Daniel Holman rose to go, saying,

"I live here in this town, you know. My folks will begin to think the Injuns have got me. You know the Roccamekas camp right over on the Island opposite the mouth of Red Brook, but when those Anasagunticooks come down from Canton, they run."

"Ye don't say .Well, Mr. Holman, it's been pleasant to meet ye, and I thank ye for the information ye've given us. Call 'round if ye ever come our way," said Sam.

Philip grasped the hand of his new-found friend, looked straight into his eyes and said,

"I thank you".

After one of the famous Monroe Inn breakfasts, their bill settled, Philip and Sam crossed on Benjamin's ferry to the other side of the river. They rode for some distance without a word, each too deep in his own thoughts to utter any sound. The great Androscoggin River was now on their right. The country to the north of them was dark and forbidding. A succession of great mountains now came into view, so thickly covered with the black growth of spruce and fir trees that no amount of snow on the

(12)

ground could show through them until well toward their summits. They stretched on until they gradually merged and disappeared into the Canadian forests, seventy or eighty miles beyond.

"What a wilderness?" Sam finally broke the silence. "If there ain't tall timbers up there," he said, pointing north, "there ain't none anywhere."

"You can make up your mind there are some up there or Daniel Holman wouldn't have said there were, and if it is half as good as he thinks it is, you'n I don't have to lay awake nights worrying about feedin' our families after this," said Philip.

As they continued on their journey, they found better traveling on the west side of the river. They made good time across the "Corner" and on up to Canton. They passed through the little settlement and over the lowlands beyond.

"He said it was 'bout ten miles to Holmantown from here. Was it Amos Trask he said would tell us where to go beyent there?" asked Sam.

"Yes, Amos Trask. Trask runs the tavern there, so he will be easy to find," replied Philip.

In time they reached the ford in the river, mentioned by Abijah Monroe, crossed over and found themselves in Holmantown. When the two strangers rode up to the tavern, some of the people living in the settlement, whose homes were nearby, came out to look them over. Strangers were not common in this community and it was "well 'nough" to know something of their business, especially in such times as these, when war was threatening.

"But these men ain't English or Injuns," said one. "Let's see if Amos Trask knows 'em. He seems to — they must be all right."

This vital question settled, they went back into their houses. Philip and Sam left their horses in charge of the stable man at the watering tub, then walked into the tap room. They engaged entertainment for the night, and after a fine supper, told Mr. Trask of their quest. They told him how they had come about their knowledge of the wonderful trees growing about ten miles up the little river, which flowed into the Androscoggin there at Holmantown, and was the outlet of a pond. They told him they had heard that all the land around the southern end of the pond grew so thick with tall pine that a man couldn't see through them and could scarcely climb to their tops. Mr. Trask told them he, too, had heard of this and from reliable sources. He kindly directed them which way they should take to find this wonderful country they were seeking. They passed a very pleasant evening with him, and learned that he had come early from Sutton, Massachusetts, and built the tavern — the first frame building in town. He informed them, also, that the town was no longer called Holmantown, but had been renamed. A certain Dr. Dix, from Boston, had come there, purchased several lots of land, and persuaded the inhabitants to allow him to change the name of their town to Dixfield, in his honor. For this privilege, he promised to found a library for them, but, so far, had not done so.

As Philip and Sam had a big day ahead of them, they decided to retire early and were shown to their room on the second floor facing the street. They had been sleeping for some time when they were awakened by the screams of childish voices that seemed to be coming from rooms below. They jumped from their beds, rushed to the head of the stairs to see such a sight as nobody on earth had ever dreamed. Slowly backing toward the door was Mrs. Trask, a cub bear contentedly sucking her fingers, and happily walking along with her through the door and out into the night. Later, after the excitement was partly over, Mr. Trask informed his guests that the two little girls had been awakened from their sleep and screamed. Their mother had gone to their aid and found the young bear by their bedside. She patted his nose, and he accepted her proffered fingers. She had sufficient presence of mind to allow him to continue this pleasant pastime while she carefully drew him out of the house.

"Well, that's the queerest bear story I ever hearn tell of. Are the bears thick around here?" Sam asked.

"Fairly so, fairly so," answered Mr. Trask.

At daylight our travelers were well on their way. For about three miles, their journey was over meadow land. Now and then, they could catch a glimpse of the River on their left, but after this their road, which was very poor, began to wind over hills. Now and then they passed a log house, but soon there was no sign of habitation. The road now bore to the East away from the river, but Mr. Trask had assured them they would see it again much farther on.

Finally, they came to a tremendous hill, a veritable mountain. In time, they reached the top where they could see the surrounding country in all directions. The little river again appeared at the foot of the great hill at least a mile to the west, on their left.

"Now we go down into the valley, cross the river, follow it along a little way till it bears east. Then we follow a poor road through the woods straight north till we reach the ridge that lies on the west side of the pond," said Sam.

"Yes, that's what Trask said, and here we go. We'll soon know whether it's to success or failure," replied Philip. The road from the foot of the hill to the lake was very bad. The horses stumbled, got their hoofs caught between rocks, and sank knee deep into miry holes where they plunged desperately to regain their footing. Sometimes Philip and Sam would dismount and lead their struggling beasts along through the gullies and ravines where it was nearly impossible for man or beast to go.

"Whoever laid out this road had good courage," Philip said.

After two hours of struggle, they suddenly awoke to the fact that the trees were tremendously tall and growing unbelievably straight and close together. Almost simultaneously they shouted at each other, "Here they are — here they are — the trees — the tall trees."

They jumped from their horses' backs, grasped each others hands, and went around and around in a circle.

"We've found 'em, we've found 'em, Philip. Do you hear me, Philip Judkins, we've found 'em," panted Sam.

He tore his cap from his head, threw it on the ground and jumped on it. Picked it up and threw it in the air. Then he slapped Philip on the shoulder so hard he winced with pain. Even the horses turned to look at the wild antics of the men, who such a short time before had plodded along by their sides as docile as sheep.

Philip said, "If there's any Injuns near, Sam, you'll have 'em all 'round us in no time. I'd like to take all of my hair back home with me, wouldn't you, my friend? And if it is all the same to you, I'm goin' t' eat a bite. Here 'tis, three o'clock and we haven't tasted food since six o'clock in the mornin'. Neither have the horses. I'm hungry enough to eat a raw dog. How is it with you, Sam?"

"Well, I wouldn't turn down some o' that beef we saw roastin' down to Monroe's night before last, if they brought it along 'bout now," Sam grinningly replied, as he hummed his tune.

But he seemed well satisfied with his lunch of jerked caribou and cornbread, which Philip offered him from his knapsack, saying,

"Don't bother to get your stuff out now, we'll eat your grub tomorrow. We've got to hitch the ho'ses and make a little shelter where we can spend the night and then do some lookin' around to see how much of this tall stuff there is growin' 'round the pond. We don't want to buy any land that isn't well covered with this wonderful timber, so we must decide just what we do want, run some lines, stake out the corners and mark the stakes the best we can, so there won't be any question when we get surveyors in here. They say this man Abbott, who owns the most of this country, is a hard man to deal with. Holman said they call this great territory of four thousand acres "Abbott's Purchase". But the township that surrounds the lake, is District No. 5, and the river has no name yet. Jacob Abbott and Benjamin Weld bought this together, but they don't like Abbott, so didn't name the town for him. Prob'ly don't like Weld any better. We must find out for sure where Abbott lives and go and buy this from him as soon as we can. Word will get around about this timber and somebody else will pop up and buy it right out from under our noses, if we aren't careful. Strange to me they haven't done it already."

Sam agreed to every word Philip said, he was too happy to question anything. They had now left the road and gone down over the ridge. They led their horses through the deep woods for a distance looking for a place to camp. Suddenly, through the trees, they caught a glimpse of the lake.

"Quite a little pond," remarked Sam, "and there's quite a few settlers up t'other end beyent them hills. S'pose it's over thar somewhere, he said his cousin lives. What d'he say his name was?"

"Lisha, I believe he said. He did say there would be plenty of men up through that section who would be right glad to work with their oxen for us when we want 'em. We're goin' to want 'em alright, but I don't know just when. You know, Sam, when we start this operation we aren't goin' to realize any money on it till our logs are down in the Bath Shipyard, and that's goin' to be a spell of a long time from the day we start cuttin'. I shall have to sell my farm to get the money to pay in on this great territory. In the meantime, my family has to live. I'm earnin' a dollar a day when there's work in the yard, which isn't steady now, but that's big pay, Sam." declared Philip, practical as always.

"Well, that's all right, I've gut t' sell my farm too, and by cripes I'm goin' to, jest as soon as the good Lord will let me after I git home. When Spring comes I'll come up here and bring my family along, 'n we'll settle right up here on this hill somewhere along this side of the pond, and there we'll stay till you c'n come. I'll make the fust payment on this land, so's we c'n hold it. I cal'late t' live in this town the rest of my days. I like it. You Philip, can do as ye please, ye would anyway. If ye want t' work at Bath awhile longer, that is, when ye git a chance, go ahead. A dollar a day is mighty good pay. When ye git ready, ye c'n come, and we'll begin, and, by the livin' smuts, we'll see it through. If ye c'n earn enough in the shipyard to keep ye goin' p'r'aps it's jest as well if ye don't come 'fore another fall, but I tell ye I'm goin' t' clinch this thing. The time t' ketch suckers, Philip, is when they're runnin'."

They found a place beside a great rock that seemed suitable for a camping place for the night. Spruce trees close behind it sheltered them from the northwest wind that swept over the hill. There was ample room for them and their horses and a little brook ran nearby.

"Well, I guess this place was made for us, look at that gordawful rock, it's mor'n ten feet tall. Good place t' go t' git away from wolves if we could climb on top of it," said Sam.

"If I can't contrive a makeshift ladder out of one of these small spruces inside of ten minutes, I'll go home tonight; but I don't think we'd ever use it here. Besides, I aim to keep this fire goin', for I don't intend to freeze to death," Philip said. All the time, as he talked, he was cutting spruces for the leanto, and placing them in front of the giant rock.

Sam found plenty of old dry cedar trees that he chopped into suitable lengths for firewood. This, with hardwood, furnished them with fuel for the night. Quickly, he chopped small boughs from fir trees below them and made beds for themselves and the horses. Then he fed the horses oats and corn that they had brought from the stable of Amos Trask, chopped a hole through the ice in the brook and they drank their fill. It was a simple task for these two men to make themselves and their beasts comfortable for the night, and they did it all with their axes. They were as able to cope with such circumstances as were the Indians, who once lived there beside the same pond, perhaps beside that same rock.

Philip and Sam took turns keeping the fire. Covered by their thick blankets, they slept well. No wolves disturbed them, and, as usual, they awoke before daylight to face whatever task lay before them. Eating hastily of their corn bread toasted over the coals, drinking hot tea Sam had brewed, they were ready for cruising *lumber on the west side of the ridge. In the afternoon, covered most of the southern territory, and found the amount of growing timber far exceeded what they had dared believe possible. Oftimes they were forced to pause at the foot of a giant pine, where they would marvel at its tremendous girth and height. Philip would say,

"Look at that tree, Sam. It's straight as a die and so tall you can't see the top. Oh! What a mast it would make. Must be more than a hundred feet tall."

The second night they spent in the leanto everything went well with them, and in the morning they folded their blankets, put out their fire and started back along the ridge over the road through District No. 4 to Holmantown. Their spirits were high, they talked fast, making their plans as they rode. Occasionally Sam would burst forth with a few measures of his favorite song:—
"Ah, dum, dee. Ah, dum, dee. Ah dum diddle um a di do. Ah, dum, dee. Ah, dum, dee."

As is always the case, the road back did not seem as long as it had coming. They were surprised to so soon see the opening and the river flowing along over the rocks, where they had crossed two days before.

"Looks like a log house down beyent the ford. I didn't notice it when we came up. Did you, Sam?" asked Philip.

"No, I didn't. Who'd ye s'pose lives there? Let's ride over 'n' find out. It's a good plan to git acquainted with these fellers — we may need their help 'fore we're through. The more I think of this job ahead uv us, the harder it looks. This is a nawful narrer crooked river, an' goin' t' be turrible t' git them long logs down through. Hope we ain't bit off more'n we c'n chew."

They drove down river a few rods to the door of the little cabin. A tall man of very dark complexion gave them a friendly greeting. He had a gun in his belt and an axe in his hand.

*Estimating standing timber.

"Mornin', strangers. It's a long time since I've seen a man from outside," said the easy-mannered young man. He looked like a Spaniard, but had the speech of a Yankee.

"Good mornin', Mister. We've a long journey ahead of us and only stopped to pass the time o' day. We were a little curious t' know who lived here so far from any neighbors. My name's Judkins and his is White," said Philip, pointing to Sam.

"My name is Berry. I come here from the coast, Georgetown. My folks settled there more'n a hundred years ago. I'm pleased t' meet ye," he said, as he offered them his strong, brown hand. "I'm cal-latin' t' build a mill here on this stream, a grist mill, and p'r'aps later a saw mill. This's a good country, and I b'lieve there'll be other settlers comin' in here 'fore long."

Philip was reminded of his own youthful days, when to build and operate a saw mill was the height of his ambition. He hoped this young man would have better luck with his undertaking.

"Do you two b'long 'round here? I see you come from No. 5 way," said Berry.

"No, don't live 'round here, but we like the country jest the same," said the enthusiastic Sam.

As they started to turn their horses, Mr. Berry said, "Call ag'in if y're ever 'round this way."

"Thanks," said our travelers as they rode away, crossed the river and started to climb the mile long hill.

"Hold on my friends," shouted Berry, whose long legs soon brought him sufficiently near to tell them there was a very good trail straight past his house that cut out the great hill and eventually joined the road they had come over two days before. He explained he had spotted the trees on this trail himself to save travel up over Potter Hill, as he called it.

"That hill is a hoss killer. Old Potter must a bin crazy when he went off up there to settle, but some folks'll never git over the fear o' floods, and the higher they c'n git, the better it suits 'em. I told Potter once I thought he was a fool t' spend half his natural life climbin' that hill, but he reminded me of a great flood they had in 1785 or ninety, I fergit which, when he lost all his stock and a barn or somep'n, and he said he w'n't goin' t' have all his stuff carried off ag'in in any sech a way. I told him I thought he was purfectly safe where he was."

"That reminds me of an old feller that used t' live down

'round Lisbon where I come from. He lived near the river 'n' lost everything even his old woman. He clim a tree and stayed a day or two, till he like t' starve t' death. Somebody finally went and took him off in a bo't an' he said 'I'd give five dollars to know where Marm is, but I'd give ten t' know where the old sow 'n', her pigs is'."

They had a good laugh with Berry, whose kind suggestion they took, turned their horses, headed them into the trail and disappeared.

They were happily surprised after an hour, to come out onto the road which afforded them a view of the meadow land through which the familiar and friendly little river flowed. In less than an hour, they were entering the settlement of Holmantown. They urged their horses on a bit wishing to put on a little front when they came into town. The clatter of their horses' feet at first prevented them from hearing the noise ahead, but before they rounded the corner at the Tavern, they distinctly heard the sound of a fife and drum. They pulled up their horses just in season to prevent a collision with a man in an old uniform riding a horse, waving his arms and shouting,

"C-l-e-ah the way! C-l-e-ah the way!"

It looked as if every inhabitant of the settlement was out in the Square. They were looking and pointing down the street. A fifer was playing "Yankee Doodle".

"Godfrey mighty! War's bin declared. Let's git home," said Sam.

Their suspense was short-lived, for they soon learned from a bystander that a tremendous she-bear had been killed on the big island over in the River just below the settlement, and four men were now bringing it up the street on a huge pole.

"They think, prob'ly it's the mother o' that cub that visited the little Trask girls in their bedroom a night or two ago," said a willing informant.

Soon the procession came in sight headed by the fife and drum corps, then came the four men carrying the long pole from which was suspended a very large black bear. She was a heavy load for those men of unusual strength. The crowd of men and boys that followed the great exposition shouted and hurrahed, swung their caps in the air. The boy, carrying his father's gun, which had ended the life of the great beast, was proudly flourishing the old musket and shouting a warning to all Britishers and bears who might ever dare to come to Dixfield, where they would share the same fate. Somebody's horse became frightened, tore away from his hitching post and ran wildly up the street toward the direction of No. 4. Amos Trask soon saw this affair was proving a financial success for him, as nearly every man and boy who had come to see the fun crowded into the tap room and practically cleaned out his wares.

Philip and Sam had their dinner there, said goodby to their good friend Trask and headed south. Three hours later, when they reached Monroe's Inn, they found their friend Holman waiting for them.

"Kinda thought you'd show up today," he said.

Sam stuttered and stammered in his enthusiasm, trying to tell him of their success in the woods above Holmantown. Holman urged them to buy this property as soon as they could, told them to communicate with Jacob Abbott, who lived in Concord, New Hampshire, and advised them to learn his price, terms of sale, and the name of his representative in No. 5, if he had one. This Philip agreed to do as soon as he reached home.

"Supper is served, ye better come quick, or 't'will be colder than a dead lamb's tongue," advised the beaming-faced Abijah and Philip and Sam were not slow in seating themselves at that long table.

"We certainly got here in time, Philip. I was doubtful yisterd'y mornin' 'bout gettin' round here in season," Sam said, as they settled themselves at the groaning board.

They had already counted their money and found they had about four dollars between them, enough to pay for this banquet, their lodgings and breakfast, their horses' keep and some besides. The future looked bright to them, and they saw no reason why they should not relax and enjoy that meal. What a meal it was! Abijah had previously told his wife to see to it that these two men, when they returned from "up-country", were given the best the house could afford. The supper for which Philip and Sam each paid twenty-five cents, today would cost at least $2.50 per plate, with servings half the size. So much food was placed on the table it seemed scarcely to have been tasted after Sam and Philip had gorged themselves for an hour. Roast beef, roast pork, roast turkey, were all done to a turn by those capable women of Abijah's kitchen. Boiled ham, hogshead cheese, pearly white onions swimming in cream, a great brown bowl filled with steaming yellow squash, another with boiled purple-tinted potatoes of the Cowhorn variety, highbush cranberry jelly, slices of salted cucumbers brought from the wooden half-barrels in the cellar where Mistress Monroe stored the more perishable treasures of her larder. Butter, cheese, cream, even white sugar was there, with loaves of "rye 'n' Injun" bread. A great apple dumpling boiled in a bag for hours to be eaten with cream and maple sugar; pumpkin, mince, custard, and apple pies, native strawberries that had been preserved "pound for pound" according to the popular rule.

Mrs. Monroe finally appeared from the kitchen, offering them tea and milk to drink, and asked if there was something more she could bring them. With difficulty, Philip and Sam rose from the table, almost staggering to the next room where they sat for a while smoking their long-stemmed pipes in front of the fire; a picture of contentment. It was soldom men of their type were so privileged. With their stomachs full, their business affairs settled for the time, they were able to enjoy themselves, but it was not long before Philip's head began to nod. Sam noticed this, and said,

"Hey, Philip, wake up. We're jest like a couple o' old trees in a mill pond. So waterlogged we're ready t' sink. I never et so much in my life and never spect t' gain. C'mon, let's go t' bed 'n' git a early start termorrer mornin'. I didn't like th' looks o' th' clouds t' th' south t'night when we come down river. Liable t' start in stormin' 'fore mornin'."

As they planned to do, they were on their way by daylight. The wind was cold and raw. Philip shook his grizzled head and pulled his coonskin cap low on his forehead.

"It's comin' right in off the Old Atlantic," he said.

"Glad we ain't up on the shore o' that pond jest startin' fer home," Sam said.

They hurried their horses over that long rough road to Leeds. Philip felt almost condemned for doing so, but it began to snow and they simply must not get caught far from home in the heavy storm that they could see rapidly coming in from the southeast.

Philip said, "You'd better stop over night with me, Sam. I doubt if you'll be able to make Lisbon tonight, the way it's beginning' t' pile down. There'll be a foot o' snow by dark, I think. You see, we're not makin' as good time as we did. The wind is beginnin' to blow, won't be any road left in half an hour. My horse acts tired already. Does yours?"

"Ye us", Sam admitted he thought his did also; but they rode on, covered with snow which began to melt on their leather garments, wetting them through in spots. At Philip's suggestion, they put their blankets over their shoulders.

"Gosh Almighty," said Sam, "Guess this 's th' worst we've struck."

"Wel, it isn't the worst we will strike. By the way we're gettin' it now we'll have a foot of snow long before dark, and it's goin' to be dark early tonight you know."

"Oh! Lord Harry! I know it, and Rachel, how she'll take on. I c'n jest hear her now. She'll have me dead and buried under ten feet o' snow with the Injuns dancin' a war dance over me. For a woman brave as she is, she will make th' greatest touse over little things and borrer more trouble than any two women need t'. I spect I sh'll have t' tie her to a horse 'n' lead him all th' way, if I ever git her up t' No. 5. Prob'ly when I git home she 'n' all the young ones 'cept Sam'll be bawlin' t' th' top o' their voices, she'll have 'em all so worked up an' worried over me. My oldest girl, Rachel, is exactly like her mother that way. Worries 'bout things, but, then, all women folks are a little that way, I guess. Gehosaphat! How the wind blows!"

"Well, I think you may be right, Sam. Women are a little finer-grained than men. Good thing they are, too. They sort of keep us in our places some of the time, I think, don't you?"

"I d'no 'bout that, Philip, but I know I'm freezin' t' death slow but sure. Let's walk fer a spell. The knees o' my britches are wet through and I got t' git warm some way. This wind cuts right through me."

They found the snow reached their knees, and higher where it was beginning to drift. The walking was very difficult now for them, as well as their horses. They trudged on, rather a sorry spectacle in their snow-covered fur caps and blanket capes, resembling, somewhat, a pair of brown and white clad Arabs. Sometimes the horses would stop and turn their heads to look at their masters as if to ask why they were kept out in such a storm. Philip patted the neck of his horse and said,

"We have to keep goin', we have to keep goin', old feller. I'm sorry but you'll get a good meal and a good bed when you get home, and so will I. It won't be long now, only about two miles more."

But those two miles took two hours to travel. It was growing dark and the air was so full of snow it was difficult to see where the road turned into Philip's place. It was a welcome sight to find young Philip waiting in the barn door to take their nearly exhausted horses, for they were so cold they could scarcely get themselves into the house.

"Come in, come in, boys," said Hannah Judkins, "You're lucky to be alive. What a day! I was so in hopes you could get away before this storm came. Hope you've had good luck. How are you anyway?"

Philip answered, "Well, I'm the coldest I ever was in my life, I think. Hannah, is there a drop of rum in the house?"

"Oh, yes, Philip, there is and I'll mix some hot with butter and molasses at once. Shove that poker in the coals, Betsy, while I get the things."

"Don't you bother with any butter, wife. Jest put in plenty o' rum and cayenne with your hot water and molasses," said Philip.

"Ye needn't waste yer kian on me, but don't be sparin' on yer rum," chattered Sam, through his teeth.

Hannah had a kettle of water boiling on the hearth and lost no time in mixing a drink that Sam said "would melt the North Pole right out of its socket". Then she built up the fire, the wind roared in the chimney and made sounds that suggested legions of Arctic monsters in mortal combat. "Hoo — oo — Woo" it wailed, driving the smoke down the chimney into the room and nearly blinding them all. "Hoo —oo — Woo' mockingly answered the now reviving Sam. Blow her old blast. Yer can't git us now."

Soon their clothing began to steam filling the room with the mixed odors of pine, spruce, fir, horse and Medford rum.

"Whew! It's gettin' hot here, Hannah. Gosh, I guess you wern't sparin' of the cayenne in mine," said Philip.

"No, she wan't. She gave you your share and Mr. White's, too," said young Betsy.

"I want to get you thawed out, so you can tell me what you found "up-river", said Philip's wife.

"Great sufferin' Moses!" said Sam, "I darn near fergut them trees fer the minit."

Philip then proceeded to tell his wife and daughter the story

(24)

of their adventures. Hannah, in the meantime, was preparing their supper of baked beans and brown bread. In front of the fire, on the griddle, she fried great rye pancakes the size of a dinner plate, which she heaped on a deep yellow nappy, spreading them thickly with butter and maple syrup. When the pile was about eight inches high, she poured a pint of good heavy cream over it all with more syrup on top of that for luck. Then, cutting it into wedges like a pie, she placed it in front of them. When they had finished their meal, Sam pushed back from the table, tilted his chair at an impossible angle and said,

"Well, I don't see but I'm jest as full o' grub as I was last night at Monroe's Inn."

"Oh, my wife's a fair cook," said Philip.

Young Philip, after giving the two jaded beasts the best possible care, came and sat quietly listening to the report of their findings "up-river". He was much interested in all they told and wished he might have gone with them. Sam noticed how he drank in every word his father said, and finally asked if he would like to go up there later on.

"Oh, yes! exclaimed young Philip.

"Ye know, young feller, I've got a boy 'bout your age, p'r'aps a little older, 'n' I've a girl, too, and a darn good lookin' one, if I do say so. Well, she looks like her mother o' course."

He hesitated for a moment, looked hard at young Philip, then at his mother, and then back to the boy. Seemingly satisfied with his inspection, he asked,

"Why don't ye let this boy come down t' Lisbon and git acquainted with my young folks, Philip?'

"Maybe, maybe. Perhaps he can come later," said Philip.

As they were the previous evening at Monroe's Inn, fully fed and weary, Philip said, "Let's turn in."

Sam slept with young Philip that night who asked, as they were drowsing off,

"What's yer girl's name?"

"Rachel, named for her mother," was the answer.

Chapter III

WHEN GIANTS BECKON, MORTALS MOVE

The awful storm that came up the Androscoggin Valley that last day of November proved to be all Philip had predicted .It snowed all night and the greater part of the next day. More than two feet of snow fell on the level, and the wind blew a gale, piling it into drifts ten and twelve feet deep. Travel to Lisbon was an impossibility and the restless Sam was forced to remain a guest of the Judkins family for four days. During this time, he and Philip had ample opportunity to discuss thoroughly their business prospects. First, they must get a letter off to Mr. Abbott. Philip agreed to attend to that and send the money for the down payment, provided it was not too large. Sam said he would be able to make the second payment in two years, if this, also, was not too great. Many men, at least twenty yokes of oxen and several pairs of horses would be required to land that timber on the banks of the small river. Log camps for the men, also hovels for the oxen and horses must be built, hay and grain provided in large qualtities, and, also, the necessary equipment of axes, cantdogs, saws, chains, ropes and extra sleds, not forgetting the many cooking utensils that would be needed.

Hannah listened to their conversation and, sometimes, added a helpful suggestion. Her judgment was as good as theirs in some matters.

In the late afternoon of the third day, a regular cavalcade of ox teams came up the road from Lewiston way. There were twelve yokes of cattle drawing a huge sled in front of which had been chained a large log, the length of which determined the width of the road it plowed. Several men and boys, glad of the opportunity to thus "work out their taxes", were driving the oxen or shoveling great drifts to the side of the road.

At noon the following day, when Sam reached home, he found Rachel, as he had expected, in a "state of mind". The rest of the day and evening, he spent trying to reconcile her to what was before them. Rachel knew she was expected to want to do what her husband thought best, regardless of whether or not it seemed wise to her. Her erratic Sam had always gone ahead with any of his schemes, and he would with this one, this she knew, but it did not make her any happier, and she dreaded the day when they would leave their comfortable log-house home. The children were wild with enthusiasm over the prospects, but this gave her no comfort.

Sam's patience was nearly exhausted waiting to hear from Philip and learn Mr. Abbott's price for the timberland. After two long weeks, the letter came by Post Rider. Philip wrote he thought the price was high and the seven per cent interest on the loan still higher, but was convinced the venture was worth taking, and so enclosed the papers for Sam to sign and return to him. Then he would send them with the twenty-five dollars as down payment to Jacob Abbott at Concord, New Hampshire. In his letter, Abbott had informed them that hereafter they could transact this business with Caleb Holt, his representative in No. 5, to whom they would make their second payment, due, December 1st, 1811.

The morning after receiving Philip's letter, Sam began to make his arrangements. First, he hurried over to Hinckley's, told him all was settled in his mind, and offered to sell his farm for what, to him, seemed a very low price. Hinckley, with true Yankee shrewdness, argued and haggled for a long time, believing Sam was determined to sell his land, but he underestimated Sam's bargaining qualities. Sam, finally tiring of the long discussion, said,

"Wal, I see ye ain't 'zactly int'rested as I thought ye'd be, our farms joinin', 'n' so I sh'll haf t' sell t' Mr. Thompson, I guess."

With this, he turned his horse's head toward home humming his little "Ah — dum — dee" as he rode out of the yard. When he reached the gate, Hinckley called,

"Sam, I haint 'zactly sayin' 'no' today, but I'll let ye know t'morrer."

Sam grinned, squinted one eye and said under his breath, "I thought so," then continued his humming. This was a case of Greek meeting Greek, and bright and early the following morning Russell Hinckley appeared at Sam's door. The terms of sale and down payment were made, Hinckley agreeing to make the remaining one thousand dollar payment on November 1st, 1811.

Rachel stayed in the butt'ry all through the trying hour it required to make the final arrangements, crying softly to herself, while Sam could scarcely suppress the broad grin that kept threatening to spread over his face. When Hinckley had finally affixed his signature to the crude, but binding, agreement, Sam stepped down the ladder into the cellar hole and brought up a brown tobey full of cider. This they drank slowly, each enjoying the satisfaction of knowing he had "dickered th' best". The smile on Sam's face grew no less as he remembered the cherries he had slyly added to the cider in the summer, unknown to his wife.

To move one's family, with all its possessions, seventy or eighty miles in the spring over poor roads, with ox-drawn sleds, in the Province of Maine was no small undertaking. Only those with inborn pioneer spirit could successfully accomplish such a gargantuan task. Sam's body was not too young, but his heart was youthful. Had there been a modern doctor present, he would have found Sam's arteries very young. Nothing daunted him and his friend Philip had the same make-up. They were a well-mated pair to assume the proposed undertaking. While Sam's wife was naturally a worrier, and Philip's wife, Hannah, the opposite, we shall see that Rachel, in case of emergency, was as efficient and courageous as Hannah. Sam and Philip had both married helpmates in every sense of the word, and they knew it, never entertaining a question of doubt as to the absolute capability of their wives.

Sam's first job was to build two large sled bodies. One must have sides at least six feet high, and the other must be made like a tall hayrack body. Going in the spring as they must, a large amount of hay and grain would necessarily be required to feed the oxen, horses and other animals they would take with them. Much of this would be consumed on their journey, which might be of two weeks duration, and Sam hoped there would be enough left to feed them for a little time after reaching their destination, when he could procure more from the settlers. He must, also, take all their household goods and supplies for his family of six. He wanted to buy another ox team, but dared not spend the money, as he had promised Philip to make the second payment on the timberland, due in three years. Of course, they planned to cut, yard and float to Bath and collect for all the timber before this payment was due, but if there should be a war, and it certainly looked now as if there were no escaping it, there would be no market for the tall trees.

Besides all this, Sam had his family to support. He must raise grain and vegetables of all kinds to feed them, as well as his livestock, this coming year. He decided to take only his two best cows, one with calf and a young bull, from his good-sized herd, and "sell the others to Hinckley.—Prob'ly," he said. He must take both horses, as his wife would ride one and young Rachel the other. Naomi and James would ride on the loads when they did not care to walk. Sheep was his next consideration. As Rachel had wool enough to last through the coming year, he would sell all but the two cosset lambs born the spring before, one a ewe, the other a buck, and these two would eventually mean a good flock, barring accidents. Of course, he could buy a sheep or two up there if necessary. As pigs came in great litters of twelve or thirteen, they were easy to obtain, " 'n' I'll be darned if I'll take any along. But them hens o' Rachel's, what in tarnation c'n I do with them?" he asked himself. "She'll sqwak louder'n they ever did if I leave 'em behind. I'll jest haf t' take some of 'em." So, this meant building a hencoop, besides a sheep pen. Then as an afterthought he said,

" 'Course old Carlo'll go along with us, he'd follow the young-ones wherever they went. Thank the Lord I ain't got to build no doghouse."

He was also thankful they owned so little furniture and wished they could leave part of that behind, but he knew better than to suggest anything of the kind to Rachel. There were two beds — one that he and Rachel slept on, the other occupied by the two girls, Rachel and Naomi. Young Sam and thirteen year old James slept in one of the bunks and baby Phenewel in his hooded cradle, or beside his mother. The chest of drawers, more precious to Rachel than any other of her household possessions, unless it were the few pewter dishes her mother had given her when they were married in Walpole, Massachusetts — they must all go.

"How in the Old Boy be I goin' ter take them spinnin' wheels, swifts, niddy-noddles 'n' all them darn things that go with cardin' 'n' weavin' wool 'n' flax?" he inquired of Rachel one day when he thought she was in a communicative mood.

Sam was delighted with the way she tossed off the answer to his perplexing question.

"Well, two heads is bettern'n one, if one is a punkin head. Ain't it so, Rachel?" Sam asked.

As winter advanced, Sam and young Sam, working from daylight till dark, began to realize they had accomplished a great deal toward preparations for their trip. Finally, Rachel caught the spirit and began making her plans toward the same end.

She said, "There's so many things in a well-furnished home like ours. First, there's my highbeds, my feather beds 'n' bolsters, my quilts 'n' blankets. Them eight fleeces of wool and my flax I must spin before we start, for the way they are now, they'd take up too much room on the load. My two iron kittles, the big arch kittle, my cheese press, hoops n' folla, drain board 'n' all that, my bowls, my churn, butter tray 'n' paddles, wooden spoons 'n' puddin' stick, sap troughs, at least a dozen, 'n' the spiles 'n' sap yoke. Then there's our two chairs, table 'n' six stools, the settle 'n' wheelpeg for spinnin'. The clock, the andirons, fire-dogs, sad irons and skillets, bread shovel, spit 'n' all th' cranes 'n' pothooks 'n' my tin kitchen. I mustn't fergit t' have Sam take the bent hooks out of the log over the fireplace where we put the pole accrost t' dry things like clothes, punkin, apples 'n' sich. An' then there's my whole set o' dyepots, indigo 'n' corprus an', fer Heavens Sake! I like t' fergut the cobblin' tools. That old bench'll take up a nawful lot o' room, but it'll haf t' go, an' that side o' sole leather too. My roots 'n' yarbs 'n' seeds, my dried punkin, apples 'n' peppers 'n' all Sam's seed corn — they'se any amount of that. Phenewel's cradle, Sam's bootjack 'n' o'course Sam'll want to take his hosshave along, so's he c'n make shingles later on for our new home. Then there's our baskets, that my folks used t' call wicker flaskets, same's they used t' call pork barrels powderin' tubs. I most fergut the flales 'n' mortars 'n' pestles. There's all the stuff down in the cellar hole, almost a full barrel o' salt pork, two tubs o' butter, a tub o' pickles, a stone jar half full o' strawb'r's, half a barrel o' vinegar 'n' some cider, not much, I hope, fer it's darn hard now. They'se a lot o' soft soap, some potaters, turnips, beets, a few carrots 'n' a few apples. Don't know as we c'n pack 'em so they won't freeze, but we c'n try. We got a lot o' peas 'n' beans out in th' barn on a scaffle over the sheep. I've bin trying' all winter t' git th' boys t' finish thrashin' 'em out, but they're so taken with the idee of goin' away, that they won't do much but talk till it's too late t' git started this spring."

One day she laughed aloud when she realized how anxious she was to go to the new country, but decided like any woman she would not admit it to her husband, at least for a while. Young Rachel had been secretly watching her mother of late, and decided she was not opposed to the idea of going away, as she pretended. Knowing how troubled her father had been over her mother's reaction to the proposition, she quietly told him what she thought about it. The news made Sam happy, but he kept his own counsel and waited for Rachel to confess, as he knew she would, and before long.

One lovely day during the first week in March, Sam said to Rachel, "You know, it won't be long before th' snow will settle, 'n' when it starts thawin' days, 'n' freezin' nights, so't t' crust will hold mornin's, we c'n start out."

For a few seconds Rachel made no answer, no sound came from her lips. Then suddenly, she gave way to a great sob and started for the buttry. Sam caught her in his arms just before she reached the door of the only room in the house where she could be alone.

"Oh, Rachel, what's the matter — what've I done now?"

"Oh, Sam," she sobbed, "it ain't nothin' ye've done. Yes it is— I mean, I don't mean—yes, I do mean. Ye see, I can't go, I'm afraid, 'n' I wanted to so bad. Ye see, I think I'm on the ro'd agin, 'bout two months gone. Ye know how sick I always am th' first three months, 'n' how could I ever ride a hoss fer seventy or eighty miles?" With this, she buried her face in Sam's old linsey-woolsy jacket and let herself go.

"Now, Marm, in th' fust place, I didn't spose ye wanted t' go. In th' second place, ye c'n ride flat on yer back on top o' one o' them air feather beds any time ye feel sick. Th' girls c'n ride yer hoss 'n' I've a notion t' ask young Philip Judkins t' go along with us t' help out on th' trip. He's a very tol'rable handy young feller 'n' Sam 'n' I's goin' t' have plenty t' do drivin' both them teams. 'Nother hand t' sorta look after the women folks would be pretty good, I'd say, mebbe."

It required only a fraction of a second for Rachel to see through Sam's little scheme, also to make her forget her own troubles. Philip Judkins had been spoken of in her hearing before, once at Hinckley's. It seemed they might have designs upon him as a suitable mate for their daughter, but Rachel had forgotten the matter long since. Now that young Rachel was fifteen, of course it was time to think about such things. They had said at Hinckley's, she remembered, that young Philip was straight and tall and had a way with him. Later she asked Sam about this.

"A tarnation good-lookin' feller, I call him, 'n' one that ain't afraid t' work. Knows how tew. 'F he should happen ter like it up thar, mebee he'd stay 'n' help us build th' log house. His father said if 'twan't fer needin' him so bad on the farm, he'd take 'im down t' th' shipward t' work, fer he said he could handle a broad-axe 'bout's well as he could. Did you know, Rachel, they don't use but four tools t'make a ship with? Th' broad-axe 'n' whip-saw, adz—some calls it a shim-aze—'n' the pod auger. It takes 'bout a year ter build a ship, an' did ye know they're buildin', right now, the biggest ship they ever built, 'n' goin' t' launch it right off 'n' goin' t' call it th' Lapwing. She's a four hundred and fortyone- tonner, they say. They did build th' smallest full-rigged ship ever built anywhere, in 1802. She was named th' Ann, 'n' only a hundred 'n' thirty-two tonner."

Rachel allowed that heretofore he had not taken any special pains to inform her of what he had seen at the shipyards, and let him know she did not like this too well.

He said, "Now, Rachel, don't blame me fer that. In them days, when I was a'goin' t' see Philip at Bath, you was a'devilin' me all the time fer fear I was goin' t' leave this place er somp'n. I thought th' less I said 'bout it, th' better, but now ye want t' go, things is diff'runt, 'n' I'll tell ye anything ye want t' know."

In less than a week, Sam decided the time had come.

"We'll start loadin' soon's we have breakfast. If the crust holds the oxen this mornin', th' sooner we git away, the sooner we'll stand under one o' them tall trees. Godfrey Mighty! What trees!"

That day they loaded everything they possessed except the beds and food for their supper and breakfast. In the half light of dawn, they piled Rachel's featherbeds on top of the loads which were so tall they had to be securely bound with ropes to the sled bodies. The food they would need on their journey, they packed in the rear of one sled; in the other they put the hencoop and sheep pen. Th young bull and one cow were tied to the sled's rear stakes, the second cow and her calf to the stakes of the second sled.

Rachel went back into the long house, stepped into the little buttry for one last look. There were the rows of empty wooden hooks where she had hung things so many years. One old broken noggin, where it had set she couldn't tell how long. A half circle of dried pumpkin somebody had dropped on the floor, was the only evidence of food in the room where she had prepared so many meals for her family. Tears gushed from her eyes as she tenderly ran her hand along the old shelf, beside which she had stood and mixed jonnycakes, doughnuts, seed cookies, pies, and so many things Sam and the children liked. And the children — would they be happy off up in this strange wild country, she wondered.

"C'mon, Rachel, c'mon, Marm. What's holdin' of ye back? We gut t'make Green t'day, if possible. Philip wants we should stay with them t'night."

Wiping her eyes, Rachel came back through the room, glanced over at the stripped bunks, and to her amazement, saw on top, thrown back out of sight as far as possible, the canopy frames of her two beds. This sight brought her out of her crying spell and threw her into a state much harder to reckon with, as Sam well knew. She threw up her head, and sprang into the doorway with the speed and litheness of an angry catamount.

"Sam White, what d'ye think ye're about, leavin' my canopy frames behind? My father made them for mother more'n fifty years ago."

"I c'n make some more fer ye jest like 'em when we git settled a mite up there," faltered Sam.

"Well, yer wunt need t' bother yerself, Sir, for them tops is goin' right along with us."

"But they're s'gormin' 'n' take up s'much room," whined Sam.

"They go, or I don't. Ye c'n take yer own choice, Mr. White."

"Oh! My Godfrey Mighty!" sighed Sam, as he went back into the house and pulled, none too carefully, the great unwieldly frames down from the top bunk and stamped out. He passed them to young Sam, who was already on top of the tremendous load and, reaching down for the cause of all this discussion. He carefully placed them on the hay, saying, "Best place in God's world for 'em."

Rachel, having gloriously won her battle, strode to the side of the horse and mounted without help, disdaining Sam's proffered hand. Young Rachel, holding in her arms the long square-cornered butter tray, in which little Phenewel had been previously bound with a pillow under him, handed the precious bundle to her mother, who, with a jerk of her head, spitefully sniffed an order to her spouse to "tie th' bowl ont' th' back o' my saddle, if ye ain't plannin' t' leave Phenewel behind on top o' th' bunks."

When this rather difficult feat was accomplished, Rachel gave a quick jerk on the bits, which brought the young mare into action and gave Rachel plenty to do to manage her for the first half mile. She rode straight as an Indian, looking neither to right nor left, letting the mare run for a time, but when her anger cooled a little she slowed down the horse and glanced back over her shoulder. There was no sign of her family, so she had to sit and wait a long time before the great loads appeared, coming slowly around the bend in the road. When Sam saw his wife sitting there, he wondered, "s'pose the old settin' hen's gut cooled off yit? Quickest on the trigger of any woman that ever I see."

Oxen are so slow moving and these beasts of Sam's were drawing huge loads over roads partly bare in places. Often, Sam would order a halt to rest. At noon, they came upon a little brook across the road, so Sam said,

"Here's as good place as any fer us t'eat a bite."

He walked over to the side of Rachel's horse, grinned into the now docile face of his wife, and asked,

"Rachel, m'darlin', which one o' th' buckets did ye plan t'eat out of this noon?"

She now accepted his help to dismount and walked with almost queenly grace to the end of the sled, where were all the tubs and jars of food which she graciously dispersed to her hungry family.

The afternoon wore on, twilight was beginning to fall, when they came into the Judkins' dooryard. Waiting there were Philip and young Philip, standing in the barn door. Hannah and Betsy were in the doorway of the frame house which Philip had built a few years after their first home of logs proved too small for his increased family. Sam started shouting his greeting to Philip long before they reached the yard. He could scarcely control his impetuous nature sufficiently to drive those stupidly slow oxen up to the house. He felt like leaving the whole train and running to grasp the hand of his friend. Philip was very fond of Sam and equally anxious for their meeting, but he always had absolute control of his emotions and a reserved manner — a man of poise. Now that Rachel had ridden into the yard, courtesy demanded that he should step forward to greet her and offer his hand in place of the horse-block generally provided at more affluent homes. Rachel graciously accepted this civility, saying,

"I'm pleased t' meet ye, Mr. Judkins."

Philip thanked her and said, "This is my wife and our girl, Betsy."

The wives shook hands, but Betsy was too interested in the driver of the second ox-team now coming toward them to even see Rachel, until her mother sternly said,

"Betsy, show your respect for Mrs. White."

She quickly bobbed a courtesy in Rachel's direction, but her eyes were on young Sam, all the while.

Unnoticed by everyone, young Philip, following the manner of his father, had gone to the side of young Rachel's horse, bowed, offered his hand and waited. Miss Rachel, not to be found wanting in politeness, copied her mother and placed her foot in Philip's hand, touched his shoulder with the tips of her fingers and made a very graceful landing. They looked into each others' eyes, smiled and looked away. No word was spoken.

In a shorter time than would seem possible they were all inside the house, except for the men, who must spend some time caring for the horses, oxen, cows, sheep and hens. Hannah had the supper well started before the Whites arrived, but they began immediately working together, and getting acquainted, although they agreed they felt they had known each other for years. Young Rachel and Betsy were already giggling together, beginning to tell their secrets and comparing their dresses. Betsy, who was supposed to be "settin'" the table, was too excited and preoccupied to properly attend to that important function until her mother mildly reprimanded her for "inattention at such a time". What woman could help but be a little irritated under such circumstances with six extra people and a baby to be fed and entertained for the night, crowded into a small house where there were already four others. This was a situation that required a cool head, and silly girls must learn there were times for all things. This was the time to get supper and Mistress Betsy had better make no mistake in this matter.

Soon, five men and boys filed into the room, which was both kitchen and dining-room. Ten persons gathered around the long table Philip had carefully built years before, when ten was the number to daily sit at his board. His six oldest children were now married and gone to homes of their own. There were benches and stools on which all could sit, chairs not being too common in the homes of the first settlers. Hannah, with womanly pride, had planned this meal several weeks before; now it was being served. A great roast pork, a fat goose, served on shining pewter platters, potatoes, turnips, gravies in brown earthen bowls. There was a large yellow nappy filled with luscious applesauce that had been stewed with cider and molasses. Loaves of ryebread, pats of newly made butter, half a cheese, milk and cider to drink, three large pumpkin pies, squares of gingerbread, the tops covered with a shiny substance that Rachel wished she knew more about, never having seen the likes before. Hannah apparently read her thoughts, and told her it was a new "wrinkle, come from Scituate, Massachusetts. Betsy Staples, our neighbor 'cross the river up in Turner, told me how to make it".

She offered the recipe to Rachel, who thankfully accepted it. They ate from wooden trenchers as was the custom in country families of small means. Their knives and spoons were made of thinly drawn iron. Forks were used only by a few wealthier people in cities like Boston, New York and Philadelphia, never having been seen by the pioneers of Maine. Forks seemed to them a very foolish and expensive luxury, in fact, declared by some to be "very onhandy".

The meal finally over, the men gathered in one end of the room to give the women and girls a chance to wash the dishes at the long wooden sink. Appraising glances were exchanged between the two groups. Out of the corner of his eye, Sam saw more than was dreamed by the young folks, and to fully convince himself he was not mistaken in his surmises, suggested to young Sam and Rachel,

"Prob'ly you young folks would like t' learn how t' play th' new game ye learnt over t' Hinckley's t'other night. Spin th' plate, wa'n't it?"

This was what they needed to break the ice and set them off. From then on, they required no urging toward better acquaintance.

When Sam saw how well his plan had worked, he asked Philip if he would allow his son to accompany them on their trip up country, "T' sorta help out with th' drivin' 'N' p'nouverin' o' th' youngones 'n' women folks. I b'lieve yer said he could do quite a job shoein' oxen 'n' hosses. That's one thing I hate like pizen.

I've brought along some extry shoes fer th' cattle 'n' hosses, my anvil, forge, belluses, harness 'n' things, so 'f we sh'd need anything done on th' way, I'd be mighty glad t' have Philip 'tend to it. Besides, if ye c'n spare him I'd like t' have him stay t' help build our camps."

He knew full well there was little chance of their needing to have any horses or oxen shod, for he had shod both yokes of oxen, as well as both horses, a very short time before they left Lisbon. But he wanted to make some excuse other than the real one for taking Philip along. His scheme had already been discovered by Philip — that transparent Sam couldn't fool him — and Philip wasn't at all opposed to the idea. It looked like a fair arrangement to him, "Of course, time will tell," he said to himself.

He then thought it a proper time to offer Sam some more cider. The boys were all too busy spinning the plate and paying their forfeits to bother with cider drinking. Sam observed young Philip had become suprisingly adept at the game in the short time they had spent playing it. It didn't seem to bother him in the least to pay his forfeit of a kiss to Rachel, but pretty, demure little Rachel showed considerable embarrassment, and that suited Sam. In his eagerness to promote the affair between Rachel and Philip, he was blind to the fact that his own son was paying Betsy Judkins his undivided attention. Heretofore, young Sam, "had sorta courted" Anna Hinckley, but Sam thought it was "a rather shaller affair". He was debating in his mind as to whether young Sam might be one who wore his heart on his sleeve, and he determined that, should this prove to be the case, he would inform that young gentleman there was to be no foolin' 'round with any darter o' Philip Judkins. There, he would draw the line.

Rachel, now very tired from her long day in the saddle, suggested to Hannah that they should all go to bed, offering to have her men sleep in the barn on the hay, but Hannah was not that kind of hostess. To be sure, they were finally packed away like sardines, but this was to promote warmth rather than from lack of room. They were very comfortable, slept well and arose next morning to an early breakfast. Soon, they were on the road again headed "up-river". Young Philip was with them. His father had told him to go and make himself useful, but not obtrusive.

"The Whites are fine people, show them you come from just as good stock, my boy," was all Philip said.

Hannah bustled about and somehow found time to pack his knapsack with extra shirts and stockings, told him to treat the White girls as he would want young Sam to treat Betsy, and not to stay up there too long.

"Prob'ly your father will go up later 'n' lead the old mare for you to ride back on. It would be quite a trip for you to make on foot, I guess."

CHAPTER IV

"THE TOILS OF THE ROAD WILL SEEM NOTHING—"

They could only travel about two miles an hour and the first night found them near the small settlement of Livermore, where they decided to stop. Sam longed to go to Monroe's Tavern and spend the night where those wonderful cooks held forth, but such extravagance could never be considered.

"Marm 'n' I might take our supper there, but, godfrey mighty, I can't afford t' take all them youngones and I wouldn't think o' goin' without 'em."

So he looked once more far up the road where he could see the roofs of Monroe's buildings, heaved a sigh as many a better man has done, turned and went back to his family and collection of animals. They tethered their horses beside the road in the shelter of some thickly growing fir trees, put blankets over them, for the nights were cold, fed them liberally of the shiny oats and yellow corn, gave them plenty of hay, watered them from the nearby brook. Then they fed the cows. The sheep, which they took out of the cramped quarters, they let stand beside the cows as they had often done, for sheep like to be with cows and will almost never leave them. Rachel's hens had to stay in their coop, like it or not.

"They ain't a goin' ter git a chance t' fly all over God's creation here 'n these woods," Sam said.

While all the animal feeding was going on, Rachel and the girls were heating baked beans over a fire Philip had made, buttering brown bread, making tea, cutting gingerbread into squares, and preparing a good, satisfying supper for them all. Little Phenewel was taken out of his butter bowl, bounced around in the arms of first one, then another, fed some warm milk, which Sam had found time to milk from one cow. The baby was in high glee, so glad to be free from that funny cradle. He was five months old and held up his head and crowed "louder than that rooster can".

"Ain't his little back straight and strong?" Sam said.

Before they left Lisbon, Sam had put large wooden pins along the side of one sled body and on these hung a ladder, so it was an easy matter for Rachel and the girls to get themselves and the baby to the top of the load and onto the feather bed. There were plenty of quilts and blankets to cover them and they were as comfortable as could be desired. The men and boys took advantage of the other load, disdaining Rachel's offer of a feather bed.

"The hay's good enough fer us t'night, mar'm," said happy old Sam, apparently having no care in the world.

While he never doubted the dependability of old Carlo, who was beginning to be a little deaf, Sam was particular to sleep where he could always see the fire and the sheep, which were nearest of the animals. He knew before morning there would be hungry wolves back there in the forest whose mouths would slaver as they watched those lambs, and would come silently to steal them away, if the fire were ever allowed to die down. But old Sam wasn't that kind of a pioneer. He could sleep with one eye open, and did. The fire didn't go out and the cosset lambs slept peacefully with their little feet tucked under them, the old dog on one side, their friends the cows on the other, with never a thought of danger. God tempered his wind to those lambs, even though they were not "shorn". He kept them all, animals and humans, in the hollow of His hand, for He neither slumbered nor slept. He had said, "Go ye into all the world — this Gospel must be preached." In no way could it be carried better than by these same pioneers over whom God surely watched.

"The crust's harder 'n flint," announced Sam, as he started yoking the oxen that had been eating for more than an hour and were now ready, with the other well-fed creatures, to start out again.

"Godfrey Mighty, boys, we c'n make time t'day. I spected 'twould thaw durin' th' day and slow us up turrible, but it didn't."

When they passed the Inn, Sam couldn't resist the temptation to stop a minute and greet his good friend Abijah, let him meet his family and see how well equipped he was for his trip. Abijah had wonderful news to tell him.

'Since you been here, they've built a ro'd clear through t' Holmantown on this side o' th' river 'n' ye wunt have t' ford anywhere 'cept mebbe a few small brooks 'sides the one in Jay. 'Course there's been a ro'd part th' way for a long time, but they go right through now all the way, on this side of the river. All

(40)

ye gut t' do is foler the ro'd 'n' ye'll land in front o' Amos Trask's tavern in time. Wonderful weather fer travelin'. Call again. Good-by."

With a flourish of his goad stick and "whoa hish there" from Sam, they started moving. They found the roads in excellent condition for a way, and covered the first ten miles of their journey to Jay, where the river bore sharply to the left, straight west. Here they forded a small stream. They had considerable difficulty crossing the so-called brook. The ice broke through on the farther shore and when they finally landed after very nearly capsizing one of their loads, Sam said,

"If, 'Bijah calls that a brook, wonder what he calls the Androscoggin River! Godfrey, the water come right into both loads, prob'ly wet all the grain. Hope it won't spoil marm's spinning wheels. Mebbe the water'll all drain off 'em. I know what I'll ketch if it don't. What a brook!"

After leaving the settlement of Jay, the roads grew very rough. The oxen began to sweat and so did Sam.

"I d'know's I'd call this a ro'd," Sam finally said. "Guess we can't do no two miles an hour over this traveling."

The oxen, always so faithful, labored on, slipping and stumbling over rocks, bare ground, long stretches of ice, then equally long stretches of ledge.

Sam remarked, "I've never seen such ledges as is in this ro'd. Th' horn-beam runners on them sleds will be all wore through t' nawthin'. I guess th' men who laid out this highway must've hunted fer ledges."

"Ye us, they must of," replied young Sam.

The ox sleds dragged and grated over these enormous flat rocks making an unearthly sound, at times. Often, the horses would actually slide down over the rocky inclines, making it nearly impossible for Rachel and her daughter to stay in their saddles. After enduring about eight hours of this, Sam, trying to keep up the courage of his family, called out,

"There's a cabin ahead, see th' smoke. Guess we better stop fer th' night when we reach it. I'll bet everybody's tired an' so is the oxen. How is it with you, Rachel? You ain't rode on th' hay t'day."

Rachel told him she was all right, and glanced back over her shoulder to see if little Phenewel were riding comfortably. To her horror, she found the butter bowl was gone and her darling baby with it.

She screamed like a hawk, "Oh, Sam, Sam, the baby's gone!"

With a cut of her whip, she turned the young mare and was started back over the road before Sam or any of the others could realize what had happened. The mare, wholly unused to being whipped, jumped like the wild creature she had suddenly become, and went on down over those rocks, ledges and ice, and was soon out of sight of the terrified Sam, who called with all the strength of his powerful voice for Rachel to stop. She heard nothing. her one thought was to find her baby before the Indians or wolves tore him from his butter bowl bed. She thought of the things she's heard about the way Indians tortured white children. She had seen all that was left of one of their sheep, after a wolf had torn and slashed it with his awful fangs. These frightful thoughts drove her into a frenzy. She lashed her horse. "Go— go— you black devil go! Get to my baby in time."

She leaned sideways trying to find a sensitive spot on the mare's side where she could strike a more telling blow. "Go–go–go" — with each word a cruel lash was laid on with the whip. With ears laid back, the now frantic steed ran on, froth dripping from its mouth. Both woman and beast had lost all control, they were wild creatures. Rachel's drawn white face was the face of death. Her lips were shut tightly over her teeth. The mare didn't run through the water-filled gullies, she took them at a leap and was on. Finally, ahead in the road, she saw a brown and white object. Involuntarily she jumped to one side to avoid it, just as Rachel screamed "Stop, stop you fool stop." But the sudden jerk to one side was too much for the old saddle girth, It broke, throwing Rachel to one side and off onto the icy ground. The saddle and blanket at the same time tripped the feet of the mare and threw her on her side with a terrible thud, where she lay helplessly tangled, unable to rise. Rachel made no sound, for she had entered that state of oblivion where fear never comes.

As quickly as he could after Rachel left them, Sam ordered young Rachel to dismount and let him have her mare. Young Sam begged his father to let him go, "You weigh fifty pounds more'n I do, father, and that old mare has been traveling all day. I'm a lighter load fer 'er than you are."

Sam wanted to go, oh how badly he wanted to, but he saw the

wisdom of his son's proposition and, taking off his gun and belt, threw it quickly around young Sam's waist, saying, "Here, take my gun. I know ye gut one o' yer own, but yer might need two 'n' p'raps yer mother'll need one o' 'em. If I hear ye shoot, I'll know there's trouble, and I'll come as fast as I can, anyway. Send that old mare, Sam. I hate t' have ye do it, but what's her life compared t' yer mother's and our poor little boy's?"

Away went young Sam, and old Sam, after pulling another gun, and old musket from under the hay, started as fast as his legs would carry him back down over the road, old Carlo close at his heels.

Young Sam did send that old mare. Never in her life, had she gone so fast. She seemed to sense something terrible had happened. She knew her own black colt had gone over this road. She could not understand why, for she had followed her mother ever since they had left home. In her wise old head she knew Sam wanted her to hurry, and hurry she did. He patted her neck and said, "Good old lady, good old lady, hurry please." But as he rode on and no sight of his mother or the baby met his eyes, he, too, became desperate. He had no whip, the reins were too short for a substitute, and so with all his strength he brought the heels of his boots up against the belly of the old mare. She stumbled, gathered, stumbled again, but found her feet the second time and galloped on, her heavy paunch making queer noises as she swayed from side to side of that awful road. At last, Sam saw something in the road ahead and, starting to pull up his horse, dismounted beside the butter bowl, where little Phenewel lay bawling his head off. His little red face was covered with tears and his wide-open mouth displayed a poor, little trembling tongue and toothless gums. He held up his arms for Sam to take him.

Sam, with tears in his eyes, said, "Oh, darlin' little brother, you're safe. You're safe. Can't ye speak, little boy? The Injuns and wolves didn't git ye after all, but where's our mother? Oh, if only ye could speak."

Just then the mare whinnied a call to her own lost one, and was immediately answered from beyond the bend in the road. With Phenewel still bound in his bowl, Sam ran with all his might toward the place from which the answering whinny had come. On one side of the road lay his mother softly moaning. Across from her, was the beautiful black mare, her legs still

(43)

caught in the saddle and blanket, one leg spurting blood, where the caulk from her shoe had gouged her as she fell.

"Poor girl," Sam said to her and then went to the side of his mother. Setting the bowl down, he took her in his arms.

"Dear Marm, please wake up. Please open yer eyes. Phenewel is safe and wants ye. Can't ye speak, Marm?"

He tried to think what people did to restore a fainting person. The only thing he had ever heard about was holding burning feathers under their noses, but he had none to burn. Then he remembered hearing how somebody had thrown cold water in their faces, and this had worked. As no water was at hand, why would not snow do the trick? He tried the snow, all the time carrying on his pleading.

"Marm, can ye hear me, don't ye know little Phenewel is right here beside ye?"

Then he heard his father's voice in the distance, heard his sturdy old boots thumping over the rocks, Carlo "ki-yi-ing" at his heels.

"Hello, Sam. Hello, Sam. Have ye found 'em?" he shouted. Then he came in sight and when young Sam saw him he grew almost too weak to suport his mother. When Sam reached them, he started slapping Rachel's face and hands, shook her, and put more snow on her face. Soon, she opened her eyes, looked wildly about for a second and gasped, "My baby, my baby."

"He's right here beside ye, Marm, cool as a cucumber. Never hurt him a mite."

He placed the butter bowl, still holding the now happy baby, in the mother's eager arms. She grasped her beloved treasure, now hugging it close as she rocked back and forth, sobbing, crooning, partly to her baby, partly to her God in thankfulness.

"Don't ye worry no more. Soon's ye feel ye c'n ride, ye c'n git right ont' th' old mare an' start back ter yer feather beds. An', by the way, where's th' young mare? Has she gone back t' Lisbon sick o' this country already?"

With a jerk of his head, young Sam motioned down the road, but said nothing. His father knew there was something wrong, but he, too, kept silent. Taking his wife in his arms, he said, 'We'll stay here, Sam, while ye go 'n' fetch the colt. If ye need me, holler, 'n' I'll come."

Young Sam hurried to the side of his beloved mare, freed her from the straps and blankets, pulled on her bridle and brought her to her feet. This exertion caused a greater flow of blood from the wound. He did not know what to do, and called, "Father, come down here a minit. I've found th' mare."

Sam ran down the road and there stood the colt, with her life blood slowly covering the ground with a crimson carpet. For a minute, this resourceful man was unable to decide what was best to do, but his moment of indecision was short.

He said, "Sam, I don't want yer mother should see this hoss or know she's bin hurt. The sight o' blood might be bad fer her th' way she is. Ye know she's—" then he hesitated and looked helplessly at his son, who said, "No, I didn't know, but I thought she acted sorta queer sometimes lately and I wondered if mebbe—."

"Well, she is," declared Sam. "I'll git her 'n' Phenewel ont' th' old mare's back, 'n' lead her up t' th' place where we stopped. You keep outa sight with th' young mare. If she bleeds too hard, ye better stop 'n' cord her leg with th' rein. Pull it jest as hard as ye kin fer yer life. I'll go as fast as I kin 'n' send Philip ahead t' that house we saw jest 'fore we stopped. Mebbe them folk'll have some puff-balls they'll give us t' stop this bleedin'. At least they'll have cobwebs. It's goin' t' be a big loss if we lose this mare."

Then he trudged on, pulling the tired horse along by the reins, trying to keep up Rachel's courage as well as his own. Finally, he reached the waiting ox teams. It only required a very few words to send young Philip up the road on the now jaded old mare's back.

He drove into the yard of the log house where stood a young man. Philip quickly told him of their plight and asked if they had puff-balls or anything that would help. The young man called to his father, who quickly came from the house. He told Philip he had served in the cavalry of the Revolutionary Army, where he had worked with horses all during his enlistment. He said he'd go at once and do all he could. From the house, he brought linen bandages and other things wrapped in cloths and from the barn a coil of rope and a little wooden bucket with a cover. His son had the horse waiting for Mr. Ludden, for this was the man's name. Quickly he and Philip drove back over the road. They found Sam waiting by his ox teams. Mr. Ludden told them to follow with what hay they could on a pitchfork. Proceeding down the road, they were finally at the side of young Sam and the injured colt, who by now had lost so much blood she seemed too weak to walk. Spreading the hay for a bed, Ludden adjusted his rope in the expert way he knew so well, pulling in just the needed manner, and down went the black colt.

"Better straddle her neck, young feller, t' keep her from strugglin'," said Ludden, and, without a moment's hesitation, took pincers from his kit, saying, "The artery is cut in her leg and must be tied up."

This he did with the dexterity of a veterinarian. Then he sewed up the cut, using a long curved needle, threaded with linen his good wife had raised, cured and spun. After this, he took from the little wooden bucket a quantity of swine manure, which he plastered thickly over the wound. Placing a bandage over all, he said,

"That hog manure will stop all bleedin' an' ye needn't worry no more 'bout that. But ye'll have t' keep her quiet fer a spell while it heals, 'cause ye don't want t' rip out the stitches. O'course she'll be weak from loss o' blood, but plenty o' grain'll supply that in a little while."

Sam offered to pay Mr. Ludden for all he had done to help him, but that old-time gentlemen wouldn't accept anything.

He said, "Don't mention a little favor like that. I may be needin' help myself some day."

Then he asked Sam where he was bound for, and learning that Weld was his destination, said, "I've got a neighbor near here and his name's Josiah Newman. His brother Ebenezer lives up there 'n' has bin out here several times t' visit Josiah. Ye'll find him a good man, I think."

Sam said, "I'll look him up soon's I kin," then added, "I've got t' go 'n' tend t' m'wife. She took a nawful ride jest now. Ye know she lost our little boy off'n th' hoss, 'n' when she found it out, she drove back over them ledges fer a couple a miles 'bout's fast, I cal'late as ever a woman rode. Then th' mare shied when she see th' baby there in th' ro'd, 'n' it busted the girt 'n' threw my wife off. An' it looks as if she struck darned hard. She's 'spectin; has been a couple months, mebbe more, 'n' I'm gol-blasted scared. It's a bad place t' be sick, here in these woods."

Ludden looked nearly as worried as Sam, and said, "Doctor Holland lives in this town, but is away now. I'll go right home'n git my wife t' send ye down somethin' fer her t' take. I think what she'll give her'll keep 'er from, from—. I'll bring it right back."

Shortly he returned.

"My wife sez fer ye t' drive up t' my place with yer cattle 'n' everything. She'll take care of yer wife if she does git sick, 'n' ye c'n let yer mare's leg heal 'n' yer oxen rest fer a week er so. We ain't th' kinda folks t' deny help t' pioneers. We've bin in th' same bo't 'n' know how 'tis. Ye come right along Mr. White, 'n' make yerself ter home."

The generous hospitality of the Luddens was not different from that shown by most early settlers of the Androscoggin Valley and throughout New England. The brotherhood that existed between farmers, the kindly ministrations of their wives, who never refused to sit with a sick friend, act as midwife, care for those unfortunates stricken with frightfully contagious diseases, even prepare the dead for burial, demonstrated their innate determination to render aid and comfort, whenever the need arose. Their daily religion influenced them to a constructive interpretation of the precepts of the Golden Rule.

Sam took his family and animals to the comfortable home of his new friend. All Mr. Ludden had promised, he provided and more. From a draught she brewed from Poppy leaves, Mrs. Ludden kept Rachel sleeping for several days. This rest and quiet prevented the abortion they feared. On the sixth day, Rachel, now feeling fully recovered from her accident, was ready to start up river with her family. Sam again tried to make remuneration to Mr. Ludden for the many favors received, but without success. They regretfully left the home of these good Samaritans, and continued on their way.

Chapter V

"WHEN WE GET TO THE END OF THE WAY"

"It's ten miles t' Dixfield from here," Sam announced, "an' we oughta git pretty well up to'ds Berry's b' t'night. I don't think we c'n make that gord awful hill t' day, but mebbe we c'n git t' th' foot of it."

Rachel rode on top of the load with little Phenewel in her arms. Her wild ride had taken a toll from her strength and she realized she must guard her health from now on. Besides, she felt much easier in mind when the baby was in her arms and not behind her. Philip now rode the colt, although young Sam suggested to his father that it "wouldn't hurt Philip t' drive th' oxen part o' th' time 'n' let me ride." But Sam replied, "Guess ye c'n walk if I c'n. Besides Philip's sort o' company."

"Well, whose company, I'd like t' know?" asked the boy.

"Mebbe that's fer us t' find out," replied his father.

Later on, when young Sam glanced back over his shoulder to see why the horses were not more closely following the ox teams, he found out. They had stopped there in the road, apparently unconscious of anyone except themselves in the world. Philip leaned far over and gave Rachel her first real kiss. She smiled at him unabashed.

He said, "Ye aren't mad if I kiss ye, are ye, Rachel? I've grown t' like ye a lot since we started on this trip. I hope ye like me — a little."

She replied, "I liked ye 'fore ever we started. Back there in th' dooryard when ye helped me off'n my hoss."

"Whoa! Hish!" shouted young Sam, and then made a great to-do urging his oxen along. The spell was broken and the young couple rode on to their places behind the load. The mother, from her post of observation, had witnessed the love scene down the road, and hoped her husband had, too, for she knew how he had set his heart on this union of the two families.

That noon, while eating their dinner by the roadside, young

Sam asked his sister what she and Philip were looking for, back there in the road under the pine trees.

"S'pose you's looking' fer roses 'r lilies 'r was it tulips? I've hearn tell they do grow on pine trees."

Philip gave him a push, landing him on his back in the mud and water, as he said, "Some day I'll show ye what grows on pine trees. All's ails you, ye ain't gut nobody t' help ye pick tulips off'n pine trees right now."

They all shouted and laughed at these youthful jokes, as Sam brushed the mud off his backsides, letting Philip's little insinuation pass unnoticed. With an appraising glance at Philip's six foot body, he thought perhaps a wrestling match with him some day would be a lot of fun.

So he asked, "How d'ye like ter wrastle best? Collar 'n' elbow, 'r cetch 's cetch can?"

To which Philip replied, "Make's no difference t' me."

Old Sam gave both boys the once-over. His son was about the same height as Philip, was a year older and looked ten pounds heavier. Philip was seventeen, agile as an eel, straight as an Indian, and nearly as dark of complexion. He decided this would be a good match. He hoped he'd be around to witness it, when the two young fellers decided to "take holt".

With a swing of his goad, Sam started his caravan toward Dixfield, which they sighted in an hour. When they reached the place where he and Philip had forded the river when they came up the fall before, he stopped his oxen and showed them all how fortunate it was they had been able, on account of the new road from Jay to Canton, to stay on the east side of the Androscoggin, for now the river was very high.

* "Spect it looks 'bout's it did when that Grover feller 'n 'his girl, Mary Walker, was waitin' over thar t' git married. Amos Trask tole me 'bout it. Seems they had agreed t' meet th' minister on this side o' th' river. He come up here from Greene and when he gut here, couldn't git acrost 'count o' high water. He could see 'em waitin' on t'other side 'n' hollered acrost 'n' said, "Edsel, dew ye take this woman t' be yer lawful wedded wife?' 'I dew,' sez Edsel. 'Dew ye take this man t' love, honor 'n' obey till death dew ye part, Mary?' I dew,' sez Mary. 'Then I declare ye man 'n' wife. Whom God hath jined t'gether, let no man put asunder. Amen.'

*A similar instance recorded in "Maine, A History," Vol. III, Page 808, Centennial Edition.

An' thy drove off, married, Amos said."

When they reached the Tavern, the genial proprietor, standing in his doorway, greeted them pleasantly and wished them good luck. Sam inquired if his little girls had received more visits from the bears of late and Trask assured him they had not.

He said, "But 'twon't be long 'fore they'll be comin' round agin."

That evening, there was a springlike feeling in the air, and Sam feared it was not likely to freeze that night. Rachel hoped the cold nights would continue till they reached No. 5, where they would tap maple trees and make syrup and sugar. To be sure, she had brought some from Lisbon, of last year's run, but not enough, she feared. She knew all her provisions must be stretched to the limit, for it would be impossible to raise their usual amounts this year. A log house must be built, enough ground cleared to enable them to plant corn, wheat and, she hoped, some beans, and all this had to be done within the next ten weeks. She was so glad Sam had insisted upon their bringing Philip along to help them and had wondered if he would be willing to stay long. Now she knew he wouldn't want to leave. This was a comforting thought.

Young Rachel was happy and sang along the way as gaily as the spring birds that now began to hop among the trees, chirping and twittering. It was spring, the time for singing and love-making. The birds knew it, Rachel knew it. In a few more days, the good old sun would call forth from their winter quarters all the little furry and feathered folk. The woods would lose the fast-thinning mantle of snow, countless streams would add their music to the birds' songs. Lovely May flowers would soon show their pink faces among the dark green, slumbering leaves.

The sun had set, twilight was beginning to fall, when they reached the foot of Potter Hill.

"Here's where we spend our last night on th' ro'd, my dear Rachel," called Sam, as he stepped in front of his oxen, patted their noses and started pulling off their yokes. Young Sam was close behind with his team. Rachel, Naomi, James and little Phenewel were soon down from their nest in the hay.

"I must feed my hens," Rachel said, "or 'twill be s' dark they won't eat t'night."

Sam handed her a small wooden measure full of corn, which she threw into the coop of her beloved chickens.

"Of all things alive!" she exclaimed, "what d'ye think has happened? One o' them hens has laid 'n aig, right here in th' coop."

They all thought this a great joke, and the woods rang with the sounds of their merriment.

"I do declare!" said Sam, "ef that ain't oncommon, 'n' t' think that old hen laid 'n aig 'n' never sed a word 'bout it. Most old hens cackle when they've done suthin' smart. Don't th' Marm?"

Rachel made him no answer, keeping her thoughts to herself, as she started preparing supper. The girls helped fry bacon, butter the jonnycake Mrs. Ludden had given them, and get things ready. Sam asked to have his jonnycake dropped into the hot bacon fat for a few minutes and then to have molasses poured over it.

"Godfrey Mighty! This is good," he remarked, and then all the others wanted some. Strips of jerked caribou meat they also heated and freshened in the hot fat.

"Makes it taste like new," Philip said.

"Goes t' th' right spot," appreciatively mumbled Sam from his bulging mouth.

Rachel confessed she had seed cookies in the stone jar under the hay, and if anybody wanted some enough to dig down, they would find them about middle way of the load. Young Sam was not long in digging down. Little Phenewel had his warm milk and the calf had hers. The cattle and horses had their hay and grain and the little yearling sheep ate their fill beside their friends, the cows.

Tomorrow morning, the boys would give all the animals a drink at the stream just ahead. The left-overs were few, but jonnybread was added to the warm milk to make old Carlo happy with his ration. The wooden trenchers and noggins, iron knives and spoons, were washed at the brook and made clean for breakfast. Now it was dark. The big fire blazing near felt good to them all as they stood around making bets on the time they would have their first glimpse of the pond. Sam had a thousand and one questions to answer regarding the wonderful place they were soon to see. Rachel asked if there would be any maple trees close by their camping place and asked Sam again to assure her that he had brought along all of the sap troughs. After her experience with the canopy bed frames, she didn't have too much faith in Sam's performances.

They found their places for the night in the hay, which was not as high in the air as it had been. With growing anxiety, Sam had seen that his hay was not going to last long after they reached No. 5. He thought perhaps Ebenezer Newman, the friend of Ludden's, might live nearby and would sell him what he needed. This fact remained — the cattle and sheep could forage in the woods, particularly in the springtime, and keep themselves from starving.

"Oh wal, they's always a way. I won't cross th' bridge till I git tewit. Ah—dum—dee. A—dum———." Sleep cut short his musings.

At four o'clock the next morning, every member of the party was brought to a sitting position by the clarion call of the big brown rooster. "Cock-a-doodle-doo, cock-a-doodle-doo." Over the hill and through the valleys echoed his challenge. He flapped his wings against the side of the coop, disturbing the hens who set up a cackle. The bull lowered his head and pawed the ground. The youngsters screamed with delight, until the little valley echoed and re-echoed with sounds resembling a county fair. Young Sam jumped from the load to throw a blanket over the hencoop and stop the voice of the bragging chanticleer, when, to his surprise, he discovered another egg. Rachel reminded Sam, "twan't always the old hens that cackled, sometimes it was the male of the species that was a trafle noisy."

As there was no more sleep for anyone, the men quickly fed and watered the animals, milked the cow, and Rachel and the girls prepared breakfast. By six o'clock they were starting to climb the long hill. In about an hour they had reached the top, traveled along a comparative plateau for a mile, and, to their amazement, realized they had to go down as far, if not farther, over the western slope of the hill. The view to the northwest and south was quite a revelation to all except Sam, who let them enjoy this experience, exclaiming and exulting for several minutes. He told them the region far away to the northeast was called "Dead River Country", and over there was a great mountain named for Colonel Timothy Bigelow, who "clim up tha t' git a look at th' country when they was a'goin' up through t' Canady with Arnold."

"Philip told me all this stuff, 'n' that Bigelow got took captive at Quebec, but got away afterwards. Way off t' th' north is th' great lakes; country's full o' Injuns, but they say they's two, three settlers up there. First one that come is English 'n' his name's Rangeley. Them mountains over west that's covered with snow, is called White Mountains. They's in New Hamsha 'n' stay white on top th' year 'round, Philip sez. Y'know he comes from New Hamsha 'n' he sez them mount'ins is turrible tall. Taller'n any we gut in this Province, but I doubt it some. I don't believe they've gut anything anywhere any better'n we gut here. Suits me."

Then he said, "Let's see, who was it bet we wouldn't see the pond till three o'clock this afternoon?"

Young Sam admitted he was the guilty party.

"Wal then, Philip guessed the nighest, fer he sed 'twould be noon, but yer both purty far out th' way, fer thar she is, right down thar 'bout five miles from th' foot o' this thunderin' great hill. Ye can't see much of it, th' trees is so tall 'round it, but boys boys that's where we're goin' t' make our fortunes; there's where we're goin' t' git rich. Marm, there's where you 'n' I sh'll build our new home 'n' spend our days."

There was no throwing of caps in the air and no hurrahing, for the whole scene had a quieting effect upon them all. Philip walked over and stood beside young Rachel, taking her hand in his.

"Do ye like it?" he whispered.

She nodded her head, looked over at her mother and saw her reach for the gnarled, brown hand of her Sam. A tear ran down her cheek, but he didn't notice it. His eyes were far away at the foot of the pond and he was unconscious of any other thing in the world except the tall trees.

"Wal, if you folks is so spellbound yer gut t' stay here fer th' rest o' yer lives, I guess I'll be movin' along. Whoa Hish!" shouted young Sam.

Such moments are seldom experienced and always short-lived. It only needed the raucous voice of the youth to bring them back to earth and start them down the hill.

"Wal, I b'lieve this hill is longer on th' down side than 'tis on the up. Ye know there's a man livin' over thar t' th' right, 'n' he come up here t' git away from floods. Seems curi's, but then he wunt be bothered with frosts 'n' p'raps that's half he come fer. Everybody t' his liken' I s'pose. Them cattle don't like goin' down hill s' well's th' do up, I bet. One thing, th' loads ain't s' heavy now's they was," said Sam.

On the west side of the hill, the road was still frozen and the sleds slipped easily along — too easily for the speed of those four red and white brutes. They now had to pull backward to prevent the sleds from hitting them. The stout pole pulled at the iron ring of their yokes, bobbing up and down as the loads slipped over icy rocks. At last, they reached the foot of the hill where Sam ordered a halt.

"Here we'll stop 'n' eat our dinner 'n' rest a spell. I want t' see my friend Berry. Won't be gone long. You boys feed up, you girls git dinner, 'n' I'll be with ye b' th' time yer ready."

True to his word, Sam soon appeared, bringing along his tall dark friend, Tom Berry. The men shook hands, the women nodded to the stranger and then went on with their preparations for dinner. Berry talked with them about road conditions ahead, offering Rachel and the girls the use of his home for rest, but they politely declined. Then he left them. The Whites went on with their meal and had nearly finished when Tom Berry reappeared bringing a two-gallon wooden bucket of maple syrup. Handing it to Rachel, he said, "My wife thought mebbe ye wouldn't have much chance t' make syrup this spring 'n' p'raps this would help ye out a little."

Rachel was delighted with the generous gift, thanked him and said, "Ye shouldn't spare yerselves short."

Berry assured her they had not, and said there was not much else to do around there at that time of year except to make syrup and sugar. Rachel decided she couldn't let such generosity pass with just a "thank you" so, as anxious as she was to be on their way, she took time out to go to the little cabin, knock on the door and enter at the summons of a sweet voice from within. On a bunk in the corner, lay a bright-eyed young woman with a tiny infant on her arm.

"Oh! I'm so glad you came in. You're Mrs. White, I know, and you're the first woman I've seen since we came here two years ago."

"D'ye mean t' say ye've had this baby here alone, with no woman t' help ye?" asked the deeply concerned Rachel.

"Oh, I wasn't alone. I had Tom. Couldn't have a woman, there aren't any around here but me. That is, the nearest is five miles up the ro'd, a Mrs. Holt who's just married. She and her man are building' their log house right now, I hear. She's never had children yet, o'course. Tom 'n' I thought she might not be much help if she came. I gut along all right. I'm goin' t' get up t'morrow," declared the young woman.

"How old is yer baby?"

"Week old today," she proudly replied.

Rachel thanked her again for her kind gift, assured her they would meet again, and was off to rejoin the others.

"I'll tell ye one thing, and that ain't two. Th' ro'd ahead is th' wust we've struck. 'f we git them two loads over it t'day, we'll do well." They took a long breath, glanced soberly ahead, and, resolving to let nothing stop them, started the last lap of their journey. The road proved to be all Sam had said of it and more. Long since they had become accustomed to traveling over poor corduroy road. There had been strips of it all along the way, particularly on the awful stretch from Jay to Canton, but this was the limit.

"My Godfrey Mighty! Of all th' rim wrackin', gut bustin', bowel gowelin' highways I ever see, this hez gut 'em all laid b' th' heels. Whoa! Hish! Broad. Whoa! Hish! Star. C'mon ye old sunups. If ever ye pulled, pull now. By th' great livin' smuts, I had no idee this ro'd c'ud be s' bad. When Philip 'n' I cum over it last fall, 'twa'nt s' bad, 'r didn't seem so. 'Course th' ground froze 'n' th' wa'nt none o' these holes that go down t' Chiny. Guess it's lucky we didn't wait no longer to start up here, it's thawed out so t'day this ro'ds all puddiny in places. Them corduroy rails is flippin' 'round like eels in a mill pond. Jerushy Jane Pepper! Let's stop 'n' rest fer a spell. How ye doin', Marm? Ain't this th' gosh darnedest, back-breakin'est flounderin' round ye ever did see in all yer life? If ye don't want t' go no further t'night, we won't. Jest say th' word, Marm, 'n' we'll unyoke."

Thus spoke the nearly exhausted Sam. But Rachel had made up her mind t' see it through that night, and on they went.

Around four o'clock, they reached the top of a small hill, from which they looked down into a gully made by a little brook. On its banks a small cabin was being built. A young man and woman were at the moment struggling to place a morticed log into position on top of its mate. All the party except Sam were entirely absorbed in the doings of the camp builders. Sam had brought his oxen to a dead stop and was gazing off to his right with all the heavenly expression of cherubin and seraphin covering his face. He was so absorbed in the sight upon which he gazed, that, for once, he became speechless. For a full minute no sound came from his lips. Rachel knew what caused the tears that were running unnoticed down his cheeks. She placed a finger over her lips to command silence, pointing to Sam and then to the tremendous black forest beyond them. It was now their turn to stand in silent awe, as they, too, gazed at the magnificient spectacle. Sam, finally sensing the deep silence about him, noted the rapt expression upon their faces and whispered,

"Th' trees, th' trees".

Stilled by the vast grandeur of the scene, both young men remained unusually silent and thoughtful for some time. In after years, its memory would return and, with it, the same wonderment. "What was it?" they would ask themselves. Why were they so strangely impressed by the great forest? To appreciate the emotion they were feeling, one would have to experience the same thing. Words can not adequately express it— for "only God can make a tree'..

"How d'ye do." The Whites were suddenly aware of the presence of the young couple, who had left their labors to come to the top of the hill to greet them.

"Our name's Holt 'n' we've jest started t'build us a home. Are you folks cal'latin' t'settle 'round here?" asked the young man.

Sam told him they had bought the land surrounding the foot of the pond and would be their neighbors. He told young Holt that another family by the name of Judkins would come later to settle there and that he and Judkins had bought the land together.

The Holts expressed their pleasure at the prospect of having new neighbors. Mrs. Holt said she was quite lonely there by the brook-side, especially when her husband had to be away.

"We're glad there's a grist-mill up 'bove here. They had t' carry their grist on their backs, wait t'have it ground, 'n' git home 'fore dark, if they could. Made a mighty long day fer 'em, as at first there wa'nt one near'n Farmington 'n' that's twenty-five miles away. The new one's jest up th' ro'd 'bout four mile," she said.

"Yes," cheerfully added young Holt, " 'n' there's a saw mill there, too. Looks now 'sif folks could git along." He added that there was another settler living just below by the name of Pratt.

"I'm glad yer here 'n' we're goin' t' be neighbors," said Rachel. "C'mon down 'n' see us when ye can."

The girl said they would, but that they had their log house to finish as soon as possible, so they could start working on their land.

Rachel told her she understood, and said, "We're all in th' same bo't, 'n' remember, if ye need help, jest call on."

Then Abel said to Sam, "If ye want, we c'n swap works. I ain't a great joiner m'self, I'm a farmer, but I c'n do what I'm told, 'n' I'd be glad t' have some help, 'n' be glad t' help you, Mr. White."

Sam said, "That's a good idee. C'mon down 'n' we'll talk it over."

"Are we goin' t' sleep on the loads t'night, or are ye goin' t' build a lean to as ye spoke o' doin'?" asked Rachel.

"Well, I planned, ever since I wuz up here last fall, t'have us spend th' fust night down over th' hill t'ds th' pond beside a rock that's there. I guess there's time enough t'build a leanto 'fore dark. "Twould be fun, wouldn't it, folks?" Sam temptingly asked.

They agreed it would be, so, heading the oxen down to the right, where there was no sign of road, but fairly open country, they made one more plunge into the unknown and shortly landed at the side of Sam's "gord orful rock". There it was, tremendous and reassuring. On the pond side, the leanto Philip and Sam had built the fall before was still intact. The uprights and cross pieces stood firmly, supporting the boughs of spruce and fir. The bough bed was undisturbed, though still partly covered with snow. This fact seemed to add courage to the tired old Sam, and he said,

"Seems most 'sif Philip was right here with us, and oh how I wish he wuz."

"Well, I'm here. What's the matter with me?" joked young Philip. "I c'n build a leanto, if that's all ye want."

But Sam shook his head. He was too tired now to shoulder all his responsibilities. Both boys realized this and pitched in with all their youthful energy. In an unbelievably short time they had constructed an addition to the leanto, which was now large enough to house them all. The horses could stay where they had the fall before, and the hencoop they left on the sled, covered with a blanket.

From the sleds, they took food. Then they milked the cow and built a fire. Rachel and the two girls made up bough beds, cooked supper, fed Phenewel his milk and even pulled the table out from under the hay and set the trenchers of food upon it. The hot meal soon revived Sam, and he lost no time after that in keeping up his end of the conversation. Later in the evening, he confessed to Rachel that he was "jest 'bout starved t'death 'fore supper, but now, I'm full as a tick. Y'see that Philip c'n do what he sets out ta. Ain't he a nice, bright boy? Rachel, ye don't s'pose our Sam's thinkin' 'bout Betsy Judkins, dew ye? Prob'ly ye noticed what Philip sed t' him back there in th' ro'd that day he pushed him int' th' mud. I never give it a thought hardly, but, blast my hide, if it ain't worth thinkin' 'bout."

"Sam White, what has gut into ye? Yer gittin' t'be a reg'lar matchmaker. Ye'd better let love take its own course, or ye'll wish ye had," firmly advised Rachel.

"Wal now, who's a'stoppin' of it, I'd like ter know. Guess we all better git t' bed."

"You'd better gone longago," snapped Rachel.

Chapter VI

LITTLE NAOMI LEARNS SOME BEAR FACTS

The hillside awoke, that morning, to sounds never before heard there. Children screamed with delight, hens cackled, a rooster crowed, a dog barked, sheep bleated, the old mare whinnied when they led her colt down to the brook, and the cow mooed when her calf started to wander down over the hill. The clear ring of axes was answered by the wher, wher, wher of a wood saw. The pounding of hammers echoed through the trees. Rachel and the girls had found their sap troughs and spiles and already were starting to tap the maple trees that grew so abundantly up on the hill above the leanto. Rachel congratulated herself on their maple grove. She had to admit it was even better than the one they had down to Lisbon. When she and the girls returned to the leanto, Sam asked where she would like to have them build the log house and said he had at first thought it should be there by the rock, but realizing that time was the great factor in the success of their venture, had decided on living in the leanto until the log house was ready. After that, the leanto could be used as a barn for the animals until they had time to build a regular one. Probably they wouldn't be able to build the barn until after harvesting time. Rachel only asked that he build the cabin as near the brook as deemed wise, for she wished to avoid carrying water any great distance. The rest was entirely up to Sam, who said,

"'Course luggin' water eight 'r ten rods ain't nothin' t' me, but I'll 'blige ye, Marm, 'n' build this log house close t' th' stream."

From then on, sounds of their activities came from all directions. As often as Sam needed him, Abel Holt came and worked with them. Young Sam, at other times, went to help Holt. They worked early and late, like so many ants in a hill. Now and again, as he worked, Sam would glance down across at the magnificent growth of pine that extended along the shore of the pond out of sight down the river.

"I'l be glad when Sund'y comes 'n' we c'n take a trip down over part o' our land. Boys, ye don't have no idee what sight's ahead o' ye. Why, them monstrous trees is goin' t'make yer eyes pop out o' yer heads. Some o' them pine trees is goin' t'make masts tall 'nough fer ladders t' heaven. When our sailors git 'n American flag flyin' from top o' one, it's goin' t'scare the British slouch paunches right off'n their darned old tubs inter th' sea. I c'n see 'em right now a-jumpin' overboard."

"Well, ye better git 'em goin' down th' river, then, yer father thinks there's sure t'be a war. One of th' last things he told me 'fore we left was jest that, 'n' he thinks it's liable t' come most any time," said Philip.

"Shall ye enlist, if war's declared?" queried young Sam.

"Yes siree, I shall. Shan't you?" spiritedly demanded Philip.

"Wal, it all depends," replied the easy going young Sam.

Philip was disturbed by the indecision shown in this statement. Until now, he had never given serious thought to a marriage of Sam and his sister Betsy. In his heart, he had begun to cherish a deep fondness for little Rachel, as he liked to call her, but if her brother was going to shirk his duty to his country in time of need, he wasn't the kind of man he wanted his sister to marry. This thought kept wrangling in his head and he couldn't seem to throw it off, and one day it became so disturbing that he again asked Sam about it. This time, Sam well knew Philip was serious and so confided in him.

"I'll tell ye what, Philip. All th' way up here on this trip, I've had Betsy on my mind. Mebbe she ain't given me a thought. I'm goin' nineteen 'n' I'd like t' marry 'er if she'll have me. I sh'll bring 'er up here 'n' we'll have our own log house 'nother year. If she don't want t' do this, mebbe I'll go t' war, if it comes t' that. We'll go together, p'r'aps."

Philip was surprised. He didn't know whether to be glad or sorry. He had barged into this thing with both eyes shut, but now they were open and he felt almost afraid. His sister Betsy was gay and light-hearted, never had been known to have a serious thought, and wasn't a bit like her mother or father. "Jest like her grandmother" he had once heard his mother say, but this meant little to him, for he had never seen any of his New Hampshire relatives. He wished he were home and could talk with his parents about it all. For two days he seemed unusually reserved, at times

(60)

almost avoiding young Rachel. She failed to understand this new attitude and wondered what she had done to offend him. Her mother noticed the change, too, and hoped Philip wasn't going to get "tetches o' grouch". She had heard of men who had such spells. However, cares slip easily and quickly from youthful shoulders, and the little affair was soon forgotten. The young people romped, ran, laughed and sang through their many tasks. Boredom was unknown to them, mainly because they were given work to do, taught to do it well, taught to obey their parents, and to respect them and all elderly people.

Sam and the boys decided a meal of fish would taste good after all the jerked meat they had eaten during their trip, so they went down to the lake shore, chopped a hole through the ice, baited their hooks with salt pork, and just as fast as they would pull them out, caught a dozen fine trout, none of which weighed less than two pounds. Sam was in high glee over this good luck and constantly hummed his tune as he fished and all the way home, where he exultantly handed his wife the great basket filled with the speckled beauties.

"Don't say no more 'bout salt water fish, nor clams, nor lobsters," he said.

The first five logs had been fitted and placed for the four walls of the commodious log house, which now began to assume the appearance of a dwelling. Sam had built log homes before and knew how it should be done, but Philip's skill and ability to make a perfectly fitting mortise and tenon was a welcome surprise.

He told Rachel, "That critter, Philip, c'n make one end of a log fit another, jest like a duck's foot in th' mud. It's so gol durn tight a wood tick can't crawl through it. Ye know them fellers down t' Bath said his father c'd build a ship with a broad axe s'tight it didn't need caulkin'. Seein' his son's work now, I half b'lieve it."

Rachel smiled as she watched the expression of affection and enthusiasm on Sam's face.

"Ye jest love Philip Judkins, don't ye, Sam?" she asked.

The look Sam gave his wife at this moment would be hard to describe, but he said, "Gosh all hemlock! Wha'd'ye think?"

The cabin grew fast, being thirty-five by twenty-four feet, with a door and one window facing the lake. As fast as possible the men covered the roof with bark and the floor with split poles.

It was quite amazing to see their accomplishments from day to day. In a huge iron kettle outside, set over two short logs between which a fire was kept, Rachel and the girls were almost constantly boiling down sap into syrup and sugar. The men had pitched the hay from both loads into one pile, giving Rachel access to her numerous boxes, bundles, buckets, baskets and bureau drawers. The space in front of the leanto now resembled an out-door living and dining room, with kitchen thrown in.

One morning when Rachel and the girls were gathering the sap that had overflowed the troughs, Naomi, having finished her task, wandered from the others up over the hill toward the road. She was curious to see the log house the Holt's were building with Sam's help. It had seemed such a short distance from the road to their stopping place by the rock, Naomi believed she could skip up there in five minutes. She found, to her disappointment, after walking much longer, that the brook and log house were still nowhere in sight. This was a beautiful, sunny morning in the last week of March. As the sun climbed higher, pools of water began to gather in the little hollows, overflow and start running down hill. Water dripped from an old leaning treetop where snow had lodged. She saw a rabbit jump from behind an old stump and disappear behind another. She stood still, watching for a time, and hoped he would dart out again further on. As she waited, something drew her attention to a peculiar sight just ahead. By a great up-rooted tree, which gave the appearance of a huge, snow-covered fan, there seemed to be smoke rising from a tiny hole in the snow and brush which made a pile about five feet high against the tree roots. She watched it for a while and wondered if the fairies lived down there and if that was smoke from their fireplaces. She was not entirely sure that she believed in fairies, but if there were "hants" there must be fairies, and they just had to have fireplaces, and fireplaces had to have smoke. What harm would it do to look down that chimney and see for herself. Fairies never hurt anyone. "Hants" only worked during the night, and never in daylight.

In the distance, she could hear the boisterous laugh of her father and the boys at their work on the cabin. This gave her assurance and she tiptoed to the edge of the blowdown and watched the steam rising from the brush and snow. She gathered her courage and ventured to the top of the pile and looked down into the hole. She couldn't see any fireplace, she could only see a small bottomless hole. Maybe there were no fairies or "hants" down there. If she only had a long stick, she could at least learn how deep the hole was. If she had her father's ox goad that would be just the thing to use, but he would never allow her to play with it. Of course, it would be wrong to take it without asking, but could it be very wrong if she only kept it five minutes and then put it right back in its place.

"N A-O-M-I, N-A-O-M-I. Where are ye, Naomi child?" called her mother.

"Right here. I'm comin', mother." and away ran the little girl from her enchanted retreat to join her mother and sister as they returned to their practical duties. All through the noon hour and later on, when helping her sister wash the dinner dishes, Naomi dreamed of the beautiful fairy home down under the snow by the old tree roots. The more she dreamed, the more she saw it all. There were dozens of them living down there, tiny baby fairies in snowwhite cradles, fairy kittens, fairy puppies, yes, and fairy lambs all skipping around among the Mayflowers and partridge vines. Probably they ate boxberry plums for food. Of course, their beds were made from the beautiful soft green moss, like she had seen appear each spring at Lisbon from under the melting snow. Maybe the fairies made bands for their hair of the lovely gold thread her mother gathered in summer to use for medicine. Then there were the acorns to use for cups and saucers. Common folks didn't use saucers, but probably fairies did.

"What on airth be ye dreamin' 'bout Naomi? Ye've held that noggin in yer hand, starin' into space, fer th' last ten minutes. Fer heaven's sake set it down on th' table 'n' go out 'n' feed th' sheep. Father told ye that was yer job from now on," ordered young Rachel.

Dutifully, Naomi trudged over to the new leanto a little beyond their own living quarters, taking in her arms a small quantity of hay as she passed the fast diminishing stack. The four oxen stood in a row, then came the cows, calf and bull. The little sheep were by themselves in a small pen at the further end of the leanto. As she passed the oxen, stuck into the fir boughs and slabs that filled the side of the shelter where they stood, were the two long goad sticks, ready for use whenever the oxen were needed. Yes, there they were with a sharp brad in the end of each.

If she should push one of these down into the chimney, she must be very careful not to hit a fairy. But, what was she thinking of, there wouldn't be a fairy at the end of the chimney, there'd be a fireplace and maybe a kettle boiling, and a brad couldn't hurt an iron kettle. Perhaps it would slop the water in it and put out the fire, but fairies could build fires with just a wave of their wands. They didn't even need to use flint. Perhaps when they saw their upset kettle, they'd come up to see who had done it, and she, Naomi White, would see a really truly, cross my heart, stone dead, fairy.

The conclusion was too much. She was tempted beyond what she was able to bear. Those two goad sticks, there in plain sight, settled the question. After looking carefully in all directions, to make sure nobody could see her, she threw her hay into the sheep pen, rushed back to the oxen, grasped a goad and ran with the speed of a fawn up over the hill and out of sight. As she approached her fairy land, the steam was still rising from the spot at the foot of the old tree, just as it had earlier. Stepping forward as daintily as any fairy she had pictured in her mind, she carefully pushed the long brad-tipped goad down into the chimney. Then something prompted her to give the goad a sudden hard push to upset the fairy kettle in the fireplace. So, with all her strength, and using both hands, she jabbed that goad into————. With a ferocious snarl and growl, the whole pile of brush and snow arose like an erupting volcano, spilling out, not lava, not fairies, but a young black bear, throwing Naomi on her back, where she struggled, half buried in snow, arms and legs waving in all directions. Dead branches snapped sending clouds of snow into the air. After a tremendous effort, the bear extricated himself and began plunging and jumping out of the flying debris, and lumbered away as fast as his clumsy legs could propel his logy body. Naomi screamed with all her might and finally scrambled to her feet. For a moment, she stood and watched the bear waddle straight down toward the leanto, apparently too dazed from his long winter's hibernation to quite sense the nearness of other creatures, until he was well in sight of the men working on the roof of the log house. Naomi's screams attracted their attention just in season for them to catch a glimpse of the shaggy beast as he sidled into a hemlock thicket near the brook.

Philip and young Sam left the roof in nothing flat. Sam

wasn't far behind them, shouting, "Godfrey Mighty! Godfrey Mighty! Where's m' gun? Where's m' gun? Marm, bring m' flint 'n' powder. There's th' gord orflest great b'ar right over thar thet ennybody ever see 'n this world. Marm, marm, go t' Naomi. She's been et up I know. She's right up thar where he come from a-screamin' her head off. Go! Go! Git m' gun, I tell yer. Oh! Heavens t' Betsy, Whar is that gun? Will ye go t' that youngone, Rachel White, will ye go?" Sam's great blue eyes were nearly bursting from their sockets. His face was so red he seemed on the verge of apoplexy as he waved his arms and ran back and forth from the sleds to the leanto, tripping over the dog, who was barking and jumping.

"Git out o' m' way, Carlo, 'n' go git m' gun."

Philip and young Sam snatched their guns and ammunition from the blanket roll where thy kept them and were halfway down to the thicket before Sam could get started. Carefully they entered the thick growth with their loaded guns in their hands, expecting every moment to have the opportunity to test their marksmanship, only to find that the bear had slipped through the heavy underbrush and disappeared. Here and there, they could see his tracks in the soft snow. Sometimes he walked along old mossy logs and left no trace of his footsteps. When they had followed him about ten minutes, Sam caught up with them, sweat running down his face in rivers.

"After I see Naomi come straddle-buggin' down over that side hill and knew she wa'nt hurt a mite, I started 'n' I run so that I like ter busted m'in'nards. 'N' now I'don' know's I care a tinker's dam 'f I never see that old brute agin. But then, we orter git 'im, fer he'll kill our sheep th' minit we turn 'em out, 'n' besides, in 'bout five days, he'll be almighty hungry 'n' come right back here 'n' git 'em, anyway. I don't b'lieve old Carlo c'd fight 'em off, he's too old now," sadly admitted Sam.

For a minute the three men paused, considering what to do. Philip, the youngest of the party, kept silent waiting for Sam's orders, which seemed delayed. Finally, he said, "Would it be a good plan t' go back t' camp fer some food 'n' then start trackin' this old feller? Prob'ly he's still logy, and, as ye say, won't be hungry fer 'bout five days. He won't be dangerous 'n' won't travel very fast till he sorta comes to. I'd think now was our best time t' capture 'im."

Young Sam felt the same and showed his admiration for Philip's good planning. The three of them returned to the leanto, put a generous amount of food and ammunition into their knapsacks, took a blanket apiece and started out again.

They had been following the bear tracks for half an hour when they saw a large blowndown ahead and soon learned the bear tracks led entirely around it.

"Wal, I swan! That old slouch-paunch is huntin' fer another place t' den up. Want's t' sleep some more, but this blowndown didn't suit 'em. Guess he's a fussy cuss," Sam said.

The tracks led on and they followed. One hour, two hours. The sun was beginning to drop behind the hill at their right. They passed the outlet of the pond and followed along the riverbank a mile or more, but saw no further indication that the bear was seeking a den.

Young Sam ventured, "I ain't seen no good places where he could stop since we left that old blowndown back there. If we have t' camp down here t'night, we oughter git 'nawful early start 'r he'll git way ahead o' us. I don't know if bears travel nights this time o' year, same's they do later on when they prowl 'round killin' sheep, skinnin' 'em, rollin' up their hides and tuckin' 'em under rocks t' hide 'em."

"Ye'us boys, we oughter git this old b'ar t'night. We can't afford t' lose no time on th' cabin. They's a powerful lot o' work t' do on it yit," declared Sam, as he trudged along through the snow and water.

"What's th' fust thing b'rs eat after they come out in th' spring?" asked young Sam of his father.

"Wal, I don't think's I zactly know, but I've hern tell they did like wild cabbage roots t'eat fer th' fust few days. They's somethin' 'bout them roots that gives 'em 'n appetite, 'n' by godfrey mighty after they git that ye want t' look out, I tell ye," warned Sam.

They now went along on higher ground where there was less snow, and the ground was bare in the openings. Suddenly Philip pointed ahead where, on a large spot of mossy ground free of snow, lay the object of their search evidently having given up hope of finding a place that night in which to finish his nap. The wind, coming from the south had blown the scent of the men away from him. He had not heard them and so had gone to sleep.

Sam White had hunted and killed bears many times during his

fifty odd years; was a good shot, as was his son. Chances were that Philip also knew his gun, but they had come upon the bear so suddenly that Sam had made no plans as to who should fire the first shot. Quick-thinking Philip, with a nod towards Sam, decided that question. Sam raised his old musket, took careful aim and fired, the bullet hitting a trifle above the bear's heart. The beast, with a fearful snarl, raised himself on his haunches, looking wildly about, and, as his head swung toward the men, Sam put a bullet into his neck just under the ear, and bruin entered his last long sleep.

After being sure the bear was dead, young Sam slit its throat with the knife he carried in his belt and then joined his father and Philip, who had seated themselves on an old log.

"Ye better dress 'im off, father, I ain't no expert at that business."

Sam found the bear was not too thin, as he feared he might be after his long fast, and his meat would feed them for many days to come. His capture meant an added degree of safety for sheep along the shores of the pond.

It was too late in the day to try to get the great carcass home that night. Sam knew of only one way to put the bear out of reach of wolves and other animals that would soon be drawn to the spot by the scent of blood. He believed the young bear would weigh 150 pounds when dressed. When he had found a tree of suitable height, they dragged the bear to the foot of it. Both boys climbed to within seven or eight feet of its top when it began to bend over, and the higher they climbed, the nearer the tree top came to the ground. When the distance between top and ground was satisfactory to Sam, he buckled one end of his belt around the neck of the bear and fastened the other end to the tree near its top.

"Now, let 'er go," he said to the boys, who released their holds on the tree and dropped to the ground. Up went bruin dangling by the neck far from the reach of night prowlers.

"Godfrey Mighty! We gut t' toenail it home now, boys, 'r be caught in th' dark. Must be four miles t' home. Sufferin' ol' tom-cats, we gut t' hurry," spluttered Sam, and hurry they did. Old Sam White knew his points of the compass, day or night. When in the woods at night, if stars were out, he would climb a tall tree and read the heavens like a mariner. He was too heavy for much tree climbing, but it could be done. In daylight, he could use the good old sun for his guide and so nothing bothered him. The boys were "trappy" and could have traveled twice as fast, but respectfully walked behind Sam and let him set the pace as he softly hummed his tune. Keeping the river always on the right, they soon came within sight of the pond, then all was easy for them. It was practically dark when they reached home. Rachel and the girls had fed the animals, milked the cows and had supper waiting for them, Afterward, as they sat around the fire, Sam gave them a detailed account of the bear's downfall and painted a vivid picture of his sleeping quarters for the night.

Early the next morning, the two boys went down river, cut down the tree and released the bear from his perch. They tied his feet together, ran a pole through his legs, and brought him on their shoulders back to the log house. This meat added to their larder and gave them a great lift. With block and tackle, it was an easy matter to suspend the bear from a tree near the door, where they skinned him. As long as the cool weather lasted, the meat would keep sweet, but when the warm days of May came, Rachel would be obliged to smoke all that remained of "Naomi's Fairy", as they called him.

Chapter VII

OF CHAIRS AND CHIPS AND KNITTING SOCKS,
AND ALSO CUPID'S WINGS.

April showers now began wasting the snow away. The brook rose and overflowed its banks. Little rivulets ran down over the hill sides. The ice in the pond began to look dark in places. The boys were glad to see it would soon break up, giving them a chance to fish from the shore. The lake was alive with trout and salmon as also was the river.

"Course there'll be no end o' pickerel fer t' make chowder. Rachel thinks they be nawthin' up here t' take th' place o' th' fish 'n' lobsters we got down t' Merrymeetin' Bay. I tell 'er she ain't never et a fish till she eats one o' them trouts, 'n' she's found already how they taste when thy're fried in pork fat," Sam said, as he winked a wicked eye at Rachel. " 'F I had time, I'd build a bo't so't we c'd go out on that pond 'n' dew a little fishin' but 'twunt take long t' build a raft, 'n' that'll work fer this year. 'Nother year we'll have more time. 'Course I promised t' build Marm a loom, but, godfrey, I'v gut t'build a house fust. Where d'ye s'pose ye'll want t' have th' house built, anyway, Marm? Right here b' th' rock?" he asked Rachel.

"No sir, not by this rock. I want it up on th' ro'd where I c'n see a passer-by. It's alright here b' th' rock fer now, but not fer always," Rachel declared.

As she gave Sam her ideas regarding the place she would choose for a building site, Philip watched the expression on young Rachel's face. He wondered if she would be as positive as her mother now was, when she grew up. His mother was always quiet and willing to leave the settling of most questions to his father.

By the middle of April, the log house was ready for occupancy. A log fireplace had been built on the center of the back wall. There were two bunks for men on one side of the room and two for women on the opposite side, and room for one bed, this for Rachel and Sam. They set Rachel's chest of drawers beside her bed, the table in the middle of the floor. The settle beside the fireplace, and the two chairs and six stools with the spinning wheel filled the room. They were crowded, of course, but didn't mind that. As soon as the ground thawed sufficiently, the boys would dig a cellar hole, for there were many and various containers filled with food brought from Lisbon, still in the sled bodies. Rachel was happy as a young bride, settling her new home. Little Phenewel could now enjoy himself in one of the lower bunks, 'round which had been built a little fence. He was beginning to roll and tried to pull himself along. He couldn't be left alone now, on top of the high bed. He would soon begin to creep when it would be warm enough for him to try his luck on the pole floor.

Now that there was a place to sit and candles out of the wind would stay lighted, they could work in the evening on many things required in the home. They managed to find a little space where they could squeeze the shoe-maker's bench into the house, and now Sam could make or repair the shoes for the family. In those days, men, as well as women, worked evenings by candlelight. Men fashioned things of wood, cooking utensils, tubs, buckets, pieces of furniture, and all kinds of articles needed for the home, while the women, then as now, spent their evenings making all sorts of wearing apparel for the family.

They were not the kind to sit idle with folded hands, they enjoyed keeping busy. The boys preferred to be whittling or carving something with the fine sharp knives they carried with them, generally in leather cases suspended from their belts. Philip wished to make something for little Rachel that she could enjoy as her own, so while Sam and his father were busy making pegs and hooks from crooked limbs to put in the log walls so they could hang their clothing, Philip decided to try his luck at making a chair. There were only two in the house. Rachel sat on one and generally Sam used the other. He felt he would like to see his Rachel sitting on a chair of her very own. There was no dry material. It must be made from green timber now standing in the woods. He would cut out the necessary strips of either maple or birch into short lengths and hang them over the fireplace to dry. He knew there wasn't much time for them to get very dry in the short time he'd be staying with the Whites. Any day now, he could expect to see his father come riding into the yard, but he wanted so much to make Rachel a present before he left and had nothing he could give her unless he made it, so decided to take a chance. He knew just how he would make it. It would be like one his father had made for Philip's mother years before. She called it a "ladder-back chair".

This kind required two round long uprights, and two short ones, eleven rungs and three or four slats for the back. The uprights were only about two inches in diameter, the rungs not more than one when they were finished. It couldn't take long for them to dry, so he went about his task happily whistling a tune. In no time, he had his pieces of wood drying over the fireplace. Each evening he would take down a stick and start working it down to the size he wanted. Then he put it back to dry until the next evening. He refused to tell anyone what he was making. but Sam mistrusted before anyone else that it was some sort of a chair or stool for young Rachel. One rainy day, when he found Philip feverishly working with his old draw shave trying to make narrow strips from a lovely piece of poplar, Sam knew then it was a chair and those white strips of wood would sometime make a lovely basket bottom for a chair. Sam felt sorry for young Philip because the tools with which he had to work were so crude, but there was no help for it and it made his admiration for the boy all the greater. He admired his determination. He hoped his daughter would appreciate Philip's efforts. For fear she might not, he spoke privately to his wife on the subject, telling her he was convinced the boy was making a chair for Rachel, so between them they hatched a little scheme for the furtherance of the cause so dear to them both.

As soon as the men had left the cabin to work on the hovel and make it more secure against bears or wolves that from now on would always be lurking near, Rachel called her daughter to one side. She told her Philip was, undoubtedly making something for her, and asked her if she would like to return the compliment and knit him a pair of stockings.

"I've kept his mended so far, but they'se gettin' awful thin on the heels and I'll bet he'd jest love a pair ye'd make him".

No sooner said than done. Out came soft natural brown yarn from one of Rachel's innumerable baskets. The precious bone needles that had been treasured by several generations of women in Rachel's family were taken from their linen case. Rachel counted the stitches on a pair of stockings she had just that morning washed for Philip, and the knitting began. Every spare moment young Rachel could get, she spent on those stockings. Her needles flew in and out like lightning. Her mother warned her that his father might come most any day and take young Philip away to their home in Greene. Little Rachel almost cried when she allowed herself to think of what it would be like when Philip left her. She hadn't realized until very lately how much she loved him and how lonely she would be without him. To be sure, he hadn't asked her in so many words to marry him, but, young and inexperienced as she was, she felt he would do this before he left. If he didn't, she just knew she would die. She couldn't bear the thought when she allowed her mind to dwell on this too long. She found herself staring into space, her hands lying idle in her lap, the stocking neglected.

When her mother observed this absentmindedness, she would ask, "Tired of yer knittin', dear?"

"Oh, no, oh no, mother," the flustered girl would reply, and away she would go, needles clicking, eyes snapping, as she raced round that stocking.

Once her father remarked, "Why daughter, ye go round that stockin' like a copper 'round a keg. Must be ye're in a hurry."

"Sh-sh-sh! Father, don't talk so loud," would caution the bashful maid.

Every day the welcome signs of spring were more evident. Each new day seemed warmer than the previous one. The occupants of the log house were happy and full of the mere joy of living. A pair of robins discovered there were people living on that sunny hillside. Never before had this happened. For several days they hopped about the yard, inspecting the corners of the hovel roof, trying to decide whether to build their nests in one of the sheltered nooks, or in the crotch of a large maple tree nearby. Friendly litte chick-a-dees and little sapsuckers had been there when the Whites arrived, but after Sam had hung the bear in the tree they were almost too friendly and made many a meal from the strips of fat along the opening of his body. Now the bluejays and woodpeckers had learned about the great banquet provided for them in the tree and their screams filled the air. Flashes of blue were continually meeting the eye. Little Naomi was kept busy running to frighten the birds away. Rachel finally decided she must do something about this condition, so, with the men assisting, they soon had the meat cut into small sections, packed in wooden firkins with covers and the whole placed on the roof of the hovel. As fast as she could Rachel smoked and salted the meat, preparing it for storage.

"Ye must git me some hemlock bark right away, so I c'n start tannin' his hide. It's a beautiful skin and will make a lovely warm rug, or we c'n keep it till ye c'n git aonther 'n' th' two would be 'nough fer a co't fer ye, Sam," Rachel said.

"Now, Marm, that'd be grand, but ye've gut 'nough ter do without makin' any fur co'ts. I 'spected nothin' but that scare ye gut over the b'ar would upset ye," said the solicitous husband.

The month of April seemed short to them all, particularly to young Rachel and Philip. The chair was beginning to take on shape, and bid fair to being a success. The knitting was progressing well, too. One stocking was finished, the other half done. Philip felt certain that if his father came now he would give him a lift and together they could finish the chair before they went home. He wished very much to do all the work himself, but knew his father could give it a finish impossible for him to accomplish. He kept his thin white poplar strips pliable in a tub of water, ready to start weaving into the seat as soon as the last rung and slat was solidly placed. Just one more evening would finish the job and tomorrow would be May Day and Saturday. His father, he felt, would be sure to want him home to start working on the land the first of the week. There was one thing he must decide for himself — he couldn't ask his father if he should marry Rachel. That was a man's own business, but he would like to please his father and, of course, his mother. What was it she had said to him when he left her two months ago? He remembered now. "Treat the White girls as you would want young Sam to treat Betsy." That was what she had said. It suddenly dawned on him that his mother and father both favored the idea of his marriage to Rachel, perhaps that was one reason they had let him go with the Whites. He was so filled with happiness at the thought of the whole thing that he hardly knew what to do. What do men generally do at such times, he asked himself. He had heard how some fools fell on their knees and begged for the hand of the girl they wished to marry. The idea was so disgusting he spat on the ground. Then he remembered hearing someone say the right thing to do was to ask the girl's father first. That didn't appeal to him either, for he wanted to know what Rachel thought of it. Of course, that was it, and all there was to it. The thing for him to do was go and find out and go now and go he did.

He found Rachel alone in the cabin knitting furiously on a brown stocking. He heistated a moment, swallowed hard, straightened up to his full height of six feet and asked, "Rachel, what yer knittin'?"

"Stockin'," answered Rachel.

"Who fer?"

"You."

"Why?"

"Cause,"

"Cause what?" he asked.

By this time, he stood very near to her looking intently into the lovely blue eyes.

"Cause what?" he repeated.

The little fluttering heart wouldn't permit her to speak. She could only sigh and look helplessly into the great brown eyes of the handsome boy so near to her now. She could feel his hot breath on her check.

"Rachel," he whispered, "Ye're makin' that stockin' fer th' same reason I'm makin' that chair. I'm makin' it fer ye 'cause I love ye."

He drew her to her feet and clasped her in his arms. She was so short he could only kiss the top of her head at first, but he lifted her easily, as one would a doll, till her pretty red mouth was even with his, and their lips met as they sealed their troth.

He set her gently on her feet and asked, "Will ye marry me someday, Rachel?"

"Ye'us I will," the sweet voice answered.

Philip turned and left the happy girl, going straight to Sam, who had started to feed the oxen. Now that he had learned where he stood with young Rachel, he must finish things with her father. No half-way business suited Philip.

"Sam, I've bin talkin' t' Rachel jest now. We've decided t' git married when we're old enough 'n' I've earned some money. I hope you 'n' yer wife have no objection t' this. I love Rachel 'n' sh'll try hard t' make her happy."

Old Sam simply floundered in his joy. All the things he had

planned to say if ever he had the opportunity fled from his mind like dew before the morning sun. All he could do was grasp Philip's hand, and, as his blue eyes started to overflow, said "My boy, my boy, godfrey might, m'boy. Ain't I glad, ain't I glad. Gosh all hemlock, let me go 'n' tell Marm. Don't I wish yer father wuz here now."

He rushed past Philip, stepped on Carlo's toes, who let out a howl, entirely unnoticed by Sam, as he dashed on, almost falling over the doorsill in his hurry to impart the joyful news to his wife.

"Marm, Marm," he gasped, "Philip's asked her, 'n' she's goin ter."

"Thank th' Lord," said Rachel.

Rachel laid herself out to get them a good supper that night. To the roast bear meat, she added a generous supply of the best her larder afforded, even serving some of her 'pound for pound' strawberries brought from Lisbon. Sam slyly suggested they might have a drink they had also brought from Lisbon, but that idea was nipped in the bud instantly.

"Sam White, they ain't no cider, I put it in with th' vinegar long ago. It wa'n't fit ter drink 'n' hadn't bin fer six months. What ails ye, anyway. Don't think fer a minit I'm goin' ter feed out that devil's kindlin' wood t' my boys. Ye c'n git that idee out'n yer head right now, Mr. Sam White," snorted the angry Rachel.

"Now Marm, now Marm, don't start ravin' t'night. I didn't mean nothin', nothin' 'tall," said the penitent Sam.

After the bountiful supper, Rachel told Naomi she would help her wash the dishes, "so't th' young folks c'n spend their time t'gether, what's left."

Young Rachel and Philip walked out in front of the cabin, arm in arm, discussing their future plans. The night was lovely. They were happy. No cares, no worries came to torment them. A few kisses there in the moonlight and they were content to return to the cabin. For some reason, every member of the family had gone to bed. Only the dim light from a tiny candle lighted the room. Philip wondered if this was the proper thing to do on such an occasion. When his older brothers and sisters got engaged, he was too young to notice what did happen in their home, but at least, he thought, it was kind of them to let Rachel and him have the entire use of one end of the room. He thought of the unfinished chair. Rachel thought of that last stocking, all ready to "toe out". Somebody had kindly placed the two chairs side by side at the end of the fireplace. Since Philip had been there he had never sat on one of those chairs, always taking a stool. He had never seen young Rachel sitting in a chair, for she, too, always used a stool. But — how did this happen — the settle built for two had been moved to the opposite side of the fireplace with its back to the beds. This struck Philip as very comical, for he plainly saw Sam's hand in this change, and he laughed aloud.

"Come, Rachel," he whispered. "Guess yer father meant fer us t' set here."

It is safe to gamble that neither chair nor stocking changed one whit during the rest of the evening. Early to bed and early to rise, was a precept generally followed closely by the people of that day, but the two young people clasped in each others arms had no idea of time which slipped by unnoticed, until Philip suddenly was all too forcibly reminded by the old tall clock, then one long kiss and good-night. Rachel retired behind her bunk curtains, as Philip snuffed the candle. Very soon all was quiet. Only Sam's contented snore now and then proclaimed the fact there were people in the room.

May first was another beautiful day, as the White household awoke to action. Great fleecy clouds sailed by in a sea of blue. The whole earth seemed new. To the young lovers, it seemed to be made for them. The ice on the lake had now thawed in many places and showed water all along the shore. The ice appeared to be breaking and would soon go out. Philip hoped against hope that this might happen before he left for home, as he longed to see that beautiful body of water free from ice. He and Rachel walked down through the woods to the shore to have their first view of the lake together. Opposite them on the east, a great cone-shaped mountain of sapphire stood.

"Just the color of yer eyes," Philip told the girl.

At the head of the lake, directly north, majestically rose several giant snowcapped piles that had the appearance of having been shaken apart by some master hand. For several moments, the young people stood gazing at the inspiring sight.

"How beautiful," sighed Rachel.

"It's a grand country, isn't it?" asked Philip.

He then told her his father had said there were fifteen or twenty families living along the west shore and beyond away into the hills. Told her a man had built a saw mill somewhere up here. The man's name was Holman and was a cousin to a friend of his father.

"Some day I intend to find them. Some day he may saw the boards for our home," he said.

As they walked along the narrow strip of sand that edged the shore, they felt sure that, in the summer, when the water was lower, there would be a lovely bathing beach for their use. Rachel hoped lilies would grow near the shore. She had never seen pond lilies, but her mother had described their beauty to her. As they walked along, they came to an old log that long ago had washed upon the shore.

As they sat down on it, Philip took Rachel's hand in his and said, "I'm wonderin', Rachel, if ye realize the serious condition our country is in at th' present time. My father thinks we may soon be at war again with th' British. Also th' Injuns. I feel I sh'd tell ye that if this happens, I sh'll enlist in the service of my country."

"Oh, no, no," gasped Rachel. "What'd I do if anythin' sh'd happen t' ye? I couldn't let ye go, dear."

He patted her hand and assured her that nothing would happen to him.

"Nothin' happened to father, 'n' he fought the British 'n Injuns fer eight years. If men use their heads, they don't git killed," he told her. "Ye mustn't worry 'bout this, Rachel, jest wait fer me t' come back. 'Course, I may not go. There might not be a war. I'm only tellin' ye what father thinks, for I b'lieve it's only fair that ye sh'd know."

Quickly they rose to their feet, looked into each other's eyes for a moment, and then Rachel said, "I don't want ye sh'd shirk yer duty on my account, 'n' I appreciate yer tellin' me this. If ye decide ye must go, remember I sh'll always be waitin' fer ye, always waitin' fer ye."

He kissed her, held her close to his heart and kissed her again. They went back over the hill to the cabin and started to finish their presents to each other.

About noon, Old Carlo set up a dreadful barking. At the same time, Philip Judkins rode into the yard, leading his old mare.

Sam was in seventh heaven when he saw his dearest friend. He talked so fast and so loud, no one knew what he said, but the expression on his face told them all he was trying to say, and more. Young Philip's greeting of his father was exactly opposite to that of Sam's. He walked slowly to his side, took his father's hand, and they smiled at each other.

"Father" was all young Philip said.

After a moment, Philip said, "Well, son?" and young Philip nodded his head. The three words spoken by father and son were sufficient. If their greeting seemed cold to the emotional Whites, it mattered not. From then on, pandemonium reigned. Young Philip managed to find an opportunity to inquire for the health of his mother and sister and was satisfied to let other subjects rest until he and his father should be alone, away from the noise and confusion of the happy-go-lucky, kind-hearted Whites.

The dinner that day, in the little cabin was a happy affair. Rachel again brought out the best the house afforded. She had managed to keep a goodly amount of bear steak packed in the now fast disappearing snow, waiting for the day when their good friend Philip should appear. This she broiled to perfection over the coals in the fireplace. Here she roasted potatoes, which somehow they had kept from freezing all the way from Lisbon. They had been wrapped separately in cloths, packed in wooden buckets and deeply buried within the hay. It seemed a miracle, but there they were. Pumpkin pies, doughnuts, and, to their suprise, cheese. Sam had more than once questioned Rachel about that. It seemed to him there should be a little left, but Rachel had managed to evade the issue and now here it was, but as Sam said, nothing was too good for Philip.

When the meal was finished, the last joke cracked, the young lovers sufficiently jollied, Philip said, "I want t' make as much time as possible 'n' would like t' reach Dixfield t'night, so I think we best be on our way, Philip."

Sam begged him to stay overnight with them, but time was precious and Philip needed to begin at once on the arduous duties that springtime brought.

Young Sam managed to get an opportunity to inquire for the health of Betsy, but Philip, apparently blind to the situation, only replied, "Oh all right, she's all right."

Young Philip and Rachel had already exchanged their gifts,

(78)

which they had somehow managed to finish, and said their goodbys in secret, far from spying eyes. They had repeated their vows, and expressed their love for each other. Now with the swing of their long legs, both Philips, father and son, mounted their horses and rode away. All the Whites waved their arms and called goodby until the men and their horses disappeared over the brow of the hill.

The road to Berry's, as we know, was very poor. The condition prohibited much conversation. Young Philip felt too depressed at leaving Rachel to speak of their engagement. Sam had no doubt already informed his father of the fact. Tomorrow would be soon enough for him to talk, he thought.

When they reached Berry's, they saw Tom and his wife sitting in their little cabin door, a picture of contentment.

"They know we must keep on if we're t' reach Dixfield 'fore dark," was all Philip said.

They took the trail through the woods instead of climbing the long hill, and in another hour came out into the road. Familiar scenes now reminded young Philip of the happy hours he had spent with the Whites as they slowly wended their way over this same road nearly two months earlier.

They reached Trask Tavern for a late supper. Young Philip enjoyed the stories told that evening around the fire. Amos Trask was a gifted narrator and before the evening was half spent, young Philip was convulsed with laughter so often that he went to bed in a much happier frame of mind than he had thought possible a few hours ago.

Taking the advice of several people, who seemed to know, Philip and his son remained on the east side of the Androscoggin River and continued their trip through Jay to Livermore. Noon brought them to Abijah Munroe's and a good dinner. The rest of their journey through Leeds and Greene was over roads much easier to travel than those they had known the day before. Home looked good to young Philip, better than he had expected. His mother and sister Betsy looked sweet to him. Yes, it was good to see them again. All the things in the house seemed so nice and clean. Everything smelled so good, nobody could cook just like his mother. A bed felt good after all those weeks of sleeping in a bunk. His mother understood just how tired he was, and urged him to go right to bed and tell them all his news the next day.

Chapter VIII

A NEIGHBOR OF PHILIP'S ENLISTS

On an adjoining farm down river from Philip Judkins' place in Greene, lived Benjamin and Rebecca Parker. They were natives of North Yarmouth, their parents having come to that settlement very late in the sixteen hundreds. Benjamin, when a mere boy, was a soldier in the War of the Revolution. At its close, he married Rebecca Royal and settled in Freeport where ship building was the main industry. But in all towns the men were engaged in farming on a greater or lesser scale. Land in Greene was rapidly being bought from the Pejepscot Proprietors and word reached Benjamin that the fertile strips along the banks of the Androscoggin River were much more desirable than land in Freeport. He and Rebecca decided to sell their place there and went at once where prospects seemed better.

Their eldest son, William, spent much of his time at sea, going on long voyages on sailing ships that sometimes never saw home ports for three or four years. He was engaged to marry Hannah, daughter of Deacon John and Jane Brown Larrabee, who had come from North Yarmouth. Theirs was one of the very first families to settle in the unorganized township of Lewiston, later called Greene.

In the spring of 1808, William returned from a long voyage and he and Hannah Larrabee were married. After spending a few weeks with his bride, and helping plant the crops on his father's farm, he began to get uneasy. His family very much desired him to remain at home, buy the farm above them owned by Philip Judkins and engage in the all important business of agriculture.

William's life for years at sea had "gut into his blood" his father said. The arduous tasks necessary to successful farming seemed too much for such small compensation as could be realized, or so William thought. Also he believed his father's methods most primitive. A man must be made of iron to cope with farm conditions, and Benjamin found himself nearing the breaking point.

One evening when the family gathered for a few moments of relaxation, Benjamin asked William if he would go down to Bath Ship Yard where Philip Judkins was working, and have a serious talk with him, and learn positively if he would sell his farm to them, and at what price. William agreed to start early the next morning. His father urged him to ride a horse, but William said he wished to be free to cut across country where there were no trails, and besides a horse would be expensive to feed. Benjamin asked him when he thought he might return.

"Hard tellin'" he replied.

William kissed his beautiful wife, holding her close to his breast for several minutes. His heart was heavy. He had done his best to leave them with a cheerful face, for he wanted them to remain ignorant of his plans as long as possible.

It was late afternoon when he came in sight of the falls at Lisbon. Swollen by the melting snows, the big river was bank full. The roar of the falls below could be heard for nearly a mile. William blew a long blast on the cow horn hanging from a tree by the ferry slip to call the ferryman to set him across. This all took time and it was almost six o'clock when he walked into the Inn at Bath and inquired for Philip Judkins.

That evening they spent in the taproom listening to tales the travelers told of conditions they had known or heard in different parts of the country. There were sailors there, awaiting their call to man the outgoing ships. There were several owners of merchantmen and others who were waiting for their ships to be completed. Some of these men favored the Sedition Act, passed by Congress, while others hated it because they believed it deprived honest men of the right to speak their minds when laws were made that they thought improper, particularly that of two years before, forbidding foreign trade. This was causing more and more dissatisfaction. While some claimed it would force England and France to cease interference with our shipping, others could only see the distress caused to the people of our nation. All sorts of schemes were being launched to evade the law. There was much smuggling of goods across the Canadian border at Eastport. The English, of course, favored this and aided in every possible way, even sending armed ships into Passamaquoddy Bay to protect the smugglers. Our government did everything possible to enforce the law and ordered some of its naval vessels to Eastport, the

Chesapeake being one of them. The land guards, numerous and dishonest, accepted with alacrity all bribes offered them. The whole performance was fast becoming a serious situation. Everything was confusion and seemed to be leading to war.

"What do you say, William, let's have a drink of hot buttered rum and turn in. You must be dog tired. We might as well sleep on the question for we can't settle it tonight. One thing is sure, the British can't come into this bay and get us 'fore mornin', unless they can sink several ships out there that's guardin' the town," said Philip.

"Wal, I don't know 'bout that, but I do know I wish I was on one o' them air ships right now. P'h'aps ye ain't thought of it, but I'm on my way now t' enlist. Called here t'see if ye'd let me buy yer farm later on 'f ye ever git 'round t' sell it. Jest give me th' fust chance. That's all I ask. 'Course if we ever declare war, I may not come back. Then ye won't be pestered any more by me, but I'm plannin' t' come back, 'n' I ain't plannin' t'be killed by any British, French, or Injun vermin," William declared.

"You're a good man, William Parker, and I'd rather sell my farm to you than any man I know," said Philip, as he grasped the hand of his young friend. "You're the kind that never gives up, and probably if you ever own it, you'll make more money with it than I ever have. It's a mighty fine farm. Never saw better soil, but I don't believe a man can be a farmer and a joiner at the same time."

"Thank ye, Philip, thank ye. I know ye'll keep yer word 'bout th' farm, 'n' I also know ye're th' best j'iner in this Province. I don't see any trouble with yer farmin' either."

For two or three days these two men, one young, the other nearing sixty, met in the evening, either in the taproom or up in Philip's bedroom, to discuss the things they had heard during the day. The third evening, when Philip returned from work, William did not appear and Philip knew he had gone — but where?

CHAPTER IX

NEIGHBORS ARE "NEAR" AND SO IS AN EPIDEMIC OF DIPHTHERIA.

The first few days after young Philip left No. 5, the Whites felt something had gone out of their lives, and young Rachel was very lonely. Her mother realized this and tried to cheer her, but they all had difficulty in keeping up their own spirits. Rachel decided that she and her daughters would go up and visit Mrs. Holt. At this time of year, there were opportunities now and then to take an hour off. Sam thought this would be a good time to get acquainted with some of his neighbors on the west side of the pond. Leaving young Sam to guard the livestock from bears and wolves, he took James along to ride the old mare. He mounted the young colt, who had now fully recovered from her accident. There were several log houses along the way and he inquired at one for the home of Ebenezer Newman, which proved to be two miles up the road. They rode to the door of the log barn and were cordially greeted by Mr. Newman. He and Sam were friends the moment they met. Ebenezer Newman, an old soldier who walked with a limp, had a jovial manner and gave Sam a handshake equal to the one he in turn receievd. Sam told him of his experiences with the Luddens of Jay and how he had learned of him through them.

A life-long friendship started that day and Sam was happy to find that Ebenezer was the same sort of generous man as Ludden. Thankful to find that he could depend upon him for extra hay, grain and seed and other things they would need to buy that first year, Sam turned to other topics. Newman eagerly inquired for news of the national situation, and was deeply concerned over the probability of another war with England. He said he had a son, Ebenezer, nearly eighteen, and didn't want him to experience the suffering he had in the other war. His eleven year old son, Oliver, had by this time shown his finely-matched pair of calves to James, and demonstrated how well he had taught them to "Whoa, Hish,

Back, Haw and Gee'..

Newman said, "There's a peculiar epidemic here in this town, 'n' it's spreadin' fast among th' children. There's a family livin' up 'bove here 'bout four miles. They've lost two children a'ready 'n' th' third is very sick now. Th' man has jest built a sawmill 'n' gristmall, and fine house and barn fer these parts. I hope th' death o' these children won't discourage th' Holmans. Some folks think it will 'n' they may move away."

"What's th' name, did ye say?" queried Sam.

"Elisha Holman."

"Oh! I'm sorry. I'm mighty sorry. I know his cousin, Daniel Homan of Livermore. He's a mighty good friend t' me," said Sam, and hesitating a minute, asked what kind of disease was afflicting the children.

"They call it dipthery. Their throats fill up 'n' th' poor children choke t' death. Nawthin' c'n be done t' save 'em. Sam Gordon, who lives above here, told me he built th' coffins fer th' Holman children, 'n' said th' two little pine boxes settin' side b' side was a pitiful sight. He's used t' sech things, makes coffins fer th' whole town, lays out th' dead 'n' never seems afraid o' any diseases. Never refuses t' go when he's sent fer. A mighty good man, Sam Gordon. We've got some good men in this town. When I left New Hampshire I was a little shy I might be makin' a mistake, but my wife want t' come along with her sister, Hannah Masterman, so's all three girls c'd be t'gether. Ye see, her sister Marthy married Nathaniel Kittredge. They were the fust settlers here, in 1800. Then come Caleb Holt 'n' his wife that same spring, haulin' every blessed thing they owned on a sled. Next come John Phelps from Groton, Vermont, and I'll be blessed if his wife didn't bring a spinnin' wheel th' whole way on her back. After this they come in here thick 'n' fast. There was Joseph 'n' Abel Russell, 'n' that Abel was the strongest darned man. He went over t' Temple through th' woods 'n' brought back a grindstone on his back that weighed a hundred pounds, 'n' some claim it weighed a hundred 'n' ten. 'Bout this time, James Houghton settled cross th' pond. Then Abel Holt, yer neighbor, 'n' Ebenezer Hutchinson who lives over back o' him came. Jere Foster, Jacob Coburn live over near Masterman's on th' hill. Oh! they's a number o' other settlers around. Jonathan Pratt, who lives near ye, has bought a nawful lot o' territory off north o' Masterman Hill. He's a great worker 'n' so's his wife. Then there's th' Phinneys, they live way up on th' side o' that mountain t' th' right o' th' big blue one, 'n' th' Barretts, they live up near 'em somewhere. The Storers live jest above here, big family, eight or nine o' 'em, four or five boys, all great workers, can do anything. John's smart in books 'n' that Daniel has built a good part of that gristmill alone, fer Lish Holman. He c'n build anything from a bridge to a barn. Oh! we gut some fine men in this town. Now, ye take this Thomas Russell, he was an officer in the war from Massachusetts 'n' had a colored slave 'n' called him 'Pomp'. Wherever Russell went, that 'Pomp' jest shaddered him. After a while th' darky learned a few tricks 'n' found he could git through th' British lines without a might o' trouble. He gut t' be a valuable spy, but finally they caught him 'n' sentenced him to be shot. 'Pomp' was too smart fer 'em, though, 'n' broke away 'n' finally gut back t' th' American lines. Russell wouldn't let him go again, but give him his name 'n' his freedom. After th' war, Russell come here with his family 'n' Pomp, is treated jest as well as if he was white. He worships th' ground Russell walks on, 'n' all the Russells use 'Pomp' like one o' th' family."

"But now, speakin' o' this dipthery that's come t' us, they sait don't make no difference if ye don't go near anybody that's got it. It'll sorta come right to ye. Children have it worse'n grown folks, but grown folks do get it. I want ye t' know that my folks are keepin' away from Holman's jest th' same."

"My godfrey mighty! I'd say they better. I've got two young ones, younger'n this boy here 'n' 'nother one comin' this fall. I hope t' God ther won't any o' 'em take it." As fear gripped Sam's heart, he could hardly take time to bid his new friend good-by. He rushed James toward home, stopped at the door of Holt's log house and ordered Rachel to get home just as fast as the Lord'd let her.

It was many days before any of Sam's family ventured forth again. Rachel was frightened half out of her wits and watched the children with an eagle eye for any signs of a sore throat. She fed sulphur and molasses three days running, skipped three days according to prescribed rule, then began again. She forced them to drink great quantities of "sulphur water". This she made by pouring water over sulphur and letting it stand overnight. The children drank quarts of the evil-tasting draught. If one sneezed, it was put to bed and made to drink tansy tea to induce sweat. The Whites lived in mortal terror for two months and well they might, for across the pond the settlers were losing their little children at such a rate that they were panic-stricken. They buried them at night by the light of perforated tin lanterns that held one tallow candle. Sam resumed the family prayers they had been neglecting in the confusion of their trip and life in the leanto. Now each morning, with breakfast over, they knelt and prayed for deliverance from the frightful pestilence and God heard, and answered their prayers.

As soon as the ground thawed sufficiently, Sam and his boys began work on the land, preparing to plant their crops. They had brought from Lisbon a home-manufactured plow. On the plowshare were fastened strips of old iron, broken saw plates, even pieces of old tin which Sam had collected, mostly from the shipyard at Bath. The implement was crude as could be imagined, but with two yokes of oxen drawing it and Sam White holding the handles to keep the thing in line, much was accomplished. They had to plow around stumps, which they had been unable to remove and, in places, were forced to break the ground with spades.

It was back-breaking work for man and beast, but nothing could kill the courage of these pioneers. The virgin soil would produce fine crops, Sam knew. For fertilizer, which was necessary in spots, he used a fish or two, and in every hill of corn there was placed a lovely trout or pickerel, alternated with two fat chubs or three small suckers. One good-sized eel would do the trick, Sam thought, for he hated "like pizen to put them good trout in the ground". He kept James and Naomi busy fishing for two whole weeks. They just despised the task, but that made no difference. They must raise a great amount of grain and vegetables for the coming year. Sam often sighed in vain for the help young Philip would have given them if he could have remained. But he cheered himself with the thought that some day he would come back and hoped that day would be soon. If only there would not be another war, then Philip would come to stay. Young Rachel breathed this prayer ever night of her life as she knelt beside the lovely ladder back chair he had made for her. Sam knew the warm June sun would make his crops grow fast. He, also, knew the danger of disease was greatly lessened, and no new cases of diphtheria had been reported. They all felt relieved, their taut nerves began to relax, and Sam could now hum on endlessly: So far, no bears had come to disturb the sheep that fed on the grass that grew in the yard near the log house. The cows and oxen grazed early and late on the side hill along the brook. Often in late afternoon, lulled by the sound of droning bees, they would lie down, close their eyes and chew their cuds for a long time, the picture of contentment.

Rachel, now well along in her pregnancy, spent many pleasant hours sitting at the door of the cabin knitting and sewing for her family. Sometimes she worked on tiny things for the baby who should appear in October.

"This ought t' be th' last one, th' child of m' old age," she told her daughter.

Now that young Rachel was thinking of marriage at some future day, it seemed fitting that intimate subjects should be discussed between mother and daughter. If the baby was to be born in October or, possibly, in November, there were many plans to be made in the meantime. Rachel reminded her daughter there would be no Mrs. Hinckly to come in to help this time. So far as they knew, there were no women in the neighborhood who would act as mid-wife. Young Rachel, not yet sixteen, must take her place at her mother's bedside. Her mother dreaded the day, not for herself, but for the innocent young girl, who must assume the cares and duties of a pioneer's daughter. There could be no shirking from this serious, coming event. When the discussion was finished, Rachel gathered her daughter in her arms and soothingly said, "Don't let this worry ye too much. I've been through it all five times before. There won't be no trouble. I'll tell ye jest what t' do. We'll have everything ready when th' time comes. Our Savior was born in a stable with nobody but Joseph t' help, 'n' I guess I c'n git 'long here in our nice new log house with you 'n' yer father waitin' on me."

The second week in July, they had their first green peas. Now their crops were growing abundantly. They cut quite a quantity of hay along the hillsides where no trees grew and where the animals were not allowed to graze. Sam engaged from Eben Newman whatever hay and grain would be required for the winter and things looked promising to the courageous Sam, who was just where he wanted to be. The only thing lacking for his absolute contentment was the presence of his friend Philip with his family.

The silks in the tasseled corn began to grow dark in August, and soon they could roast or boil the golden ears. The delicious string beans, the baked trout, wild strawberries, all swimming in cream, provided these Whites with food unequalled on tables of that day. September ripened the corn, beans no longer picked green would soon be ready to stack and dry. Later the flails would beat out of their pods the yellow-eyed beans to stew or bake with pork. Golden pumpkins were getting good-sized, also squashes and carrots. Beets and turnips could soon be stored in the cellar hole with the cabbages.

"Next week we c'n dig our taters, I think, fer I want t' git th' fall work done up in season t' go down t' Greene for a day 'r two, before yer mother gits down," Sam said to his eldest son, who replied, "Wal, I want t' go t' Greene myself. I got a little business t' tend t' down there 'n' besides I want t' learn about this war everybody's talking' 'bout. Philip's goin' t'jine up 'f th' thing keeps on, 'n' he thinks I ought ter, but I can't say's I 'zactly agree with him. What d'ye think 'bout it, Pa?'"

Poor Sam had never given it a thought. The idea nearly floored him, and he exclaimed, "Godfrey mighty, Sam, what'd I do without ye? 'Course I could git along durin' th' winter, but swampin' Moses! another spring I'd be bound hand 'n' foot. What in tarnation did young Philip put that idee in yer head fer? How does he think his father's goin' t' git along without him? By Godfrey! I guess it's time I went t' Greene. What on airth ye gut t' attend t' down there, anyway?"

Sam looked questioningly at his son. He had forgotten the little episode of the spring before, when they were wending their way over the Jay road. Now he remembered it all.

"Thunderation! It's that little crazy-headed Betsy Judkins that's gut under yer skin — course t'is — I like t' fergut her. Good Lord! Sam d'ye like her? Dew ye, or don't ye? If ye don't, ye c'n keep away from Greene, but if ye do, ye better start grainin' th' old mare t' day, 'n' we'll go t' Greene jest as quick as these crops is in."

That night, after the others had gone to bed, Sam very cautiously started to question his wife concerning the time she expected to be confined. At first, she talked as if there were no question but that her baby would arrive the first week in October, but, after her palavering old mate built up his side of the argument with much flattery and honeyed words, he finally believed he had convinced her she was mistaken in her reckoning.

"M'darlin'," he said, "I don't have no idee ye'll be holdin' no young one in yer arms 'fore November. Ye know, Old Peppermint, yer quite a hand t' worry, 'n' quite apt t' look on th' dark side o' things. 'Course I don't mean ye always dew, fer ye don't. Gen'rally ye come 'round t' my way o' thinkin' in th' end. Yer one oncommon sweet woman. I ain't a questionin' yer judgment, but really ye don't 'pear t' me t' be goin' t' lay in 'fore November. Sam 'n' I's plannin' on takin' a little trip down river next week, if we git th' taters dug, 'n' really 'twunt do no harm if we don't git 'em all dug till we git back. We shan't be gone more'n two night, wal, three at th' most, 'n' James 'n' Naomi c'n put th' cattle 'n' sheep in early nights, 'n' now that we gut doors on t' th' leanto, b'ars 'n' wolves 'n' no wild animals c'n git to 'em."

Carefully watching his wife's expression change in favor of his proposition he waited until he had no doubt that she sanctioned his plan, and then said, " 'Course I wouldn't go off down thar 'n' leave ye, Marm, if ye think there's a ghost of a show that ye'll need me 'round here. But as long as ye don't 'spect 'fore November, I think we better go. Ye see, Sam wants t' find out 'bout Betsy Judkins. He wants me t' sorter help 'im." He didn't fool Rachel one bit, she could read Sam like a book. Not feeling too sure of her dates, she decided to let him go and take a chance.

Sam and his boys made the dirt fly as they dug potatoes early and late. Naomi picked them up, and Sam estimated there were thirty bushels of them.

"Not s'many's I hoped, but more'n I 'spected," he said.

They had already harvested their oats and corn. Later they would take the corn and wheat to Holman's mill to be ground. On Wednesday morning, October third, the two Sams headed down river.

"Ah-dum-dee, Ah-dum-dee. A-dum-diddle-una-di do", hummed old Sam half way to Berry's. When they reached the ford, they found a fine new sawmill ready for business. Tom Berry had built it all himself, with the exception of a few weeks labor he had been obliged to hire for raising the walls and roof timbers and the construction of a dam. Daniel Storer had come down from No. 5 to help him. He lived with his father, Joseph Storer, near the Holman place. The family had come from Hopkinton, New Hampshire, in 1806. Daniel told them he and James Masterman had come from Hopkinton with one horse.

"We come ride 'n' tie. It takes longer, but it's better'n walkin' all th' way" he said. He told them he had lately bought land on that side of the great hill, his land joined the Potters, and he was clearing it as fast as he could. He said that someday, when he got married, he'd settle there. Sam was glad to make the acquaintance of this man, who had several brothers who owned oxen. He hoped they would want to work in the great pine forests when he and Philip started to cut their tract of land at the foot of the pond.

When they reached the Monroe Tavern at Livermore, it was too late for them to go farther that night. Sam thought his boy really deserved a little pleasure after all his hard work, besides he wanted him to see how men lived outside their own homes. He may have craved a little of Mistress Monroe's cooking, but, of course, he would not admit this, particularly to Marm. In fact, he had once said a little more in praise of it than he intended, and Rachel had lost no time in putting him in his place.

The meal that night was up to standard. Young Sam literally stuffed himself. Never before had he seen so much food on one table, and observed that Mrs. Monroe was the best cook he had ever seen.

His father cautioned him not to repeat the statement, and said, "I think Mis' Monroe is one o' th' best cooks I ever see, but o' course can't hold a candle t' yer mother."

Young Sam gave the subject serious consideration, but kept his conclusions to himself.

As they passed the night at the Inn, they again enjoyed Mrs. Monroe's excellent cooking for an early breakfast, and sunrise found them on the road. In about four hours, they were greeting Philip with undisguised affection. He said he had been looking for them for a week. Young Philip appeared glad to see them, particularly Old Sam. Mrs. Judkins and Betsy were pleasantly surprised to receive a visit from their friends, but Betsy showed no particular cordiality in greeting young Sam. The day passed mostly in conversation regarding the coming war. Neither Philip nor his son had any doubt of its being just around the corner. They had worked from dawn to dark on their large farm. During the summer, young Philip had become quite proficient as a joiner, assisting his father whenever there was an opportunity in odd jobs around the town. But there was so little money in the country and so much poverty that both men could scarcely earn enough to carry on.

To start operations on the No. 5 tract would be out of the question, Philip said. In fact, he could not see a chance ahead for them ever to begin. Their discussion continued through the evening. The young people seemed to disappear after supper. Young Sam asked Betsy to take a walk with him and she rather reluctantly accepted his invitation. They strolled along the river bank, the harvest moon making the whole country nearly as light as day. A muskrat plunged from the bank into the cool dark water, leaving a widening wake that shimmered in the moonlight startling Betsy and causing her to move closer to Sam.

He eagerly caught her in his arms, saying, "Oh! Betsy, don't pull away from me. I love ye, 'n' have ever since that night we spent here last spring. Don't ye love me at all? I thought, that is —I hoped — ye might. Please say ye do. That's a wonderful country up there. Come up 'n' see it. You'n' I c'd be so happy up there t'gether. Wunt ye marry me, Betsy? I'm nineteen now 'n' able t' make a home fer ye. Father said I c'd buy all th' land I want, fer after th' trees are cut off there'll be any amount o' farmin land. Say ye love me 'n' ye'll marry me."

"Sam, I'm sorry. I can't tell you how sorry I am, but I don't love you, and I can't marry a man I don't love. You wouldn't want that."

"Is there anybody else?" asked the desperate Sam.

"Oh no. Nobody else. I guess I'm not old enough to fall in love," Betsy said.

Sam knew this was not the reason. He released her and they walked back to the house in silence. When they entered, Sam knew by his son's expression that Betsy had refused to marry him. He was sorry that his son must have the heartaches this affair would cause, and suggested they should go to bed. He wished to spare young Sam all possible embarrassment.

Inside their room, behind closed doors, Sam asked, "T'Tain't no use, is it, Sam?"

The boy shook his head, but said no word.

After a few moments silence, old Sam said, " 'Member there's jest as good fish in th' sea as ever was caught. We'll start fer home early in th' mornin'."

(91)

Betsy did not appear for breakfast, but her mother had a package to send to young Rachel. This was a gift of cochineal bugs that she had bought from Hannah Parker, whose husband William often brought such things from the West Indies. The bugs when ground and steeped produced a vivid red dye. Young Rachel had greatly admired the red dress worn by Betsy in the spring when they spent the night there. Young Philip had urged his mother to obtain the dye stuff and was delighted to know Rachel could soon have the coveted dress of red. What young Philip did not know, was how sad of heart young Sam was as he rode away. Later in the day, Betsy confessed to her handsome brother that no man could marry her who considered his country second to anything. Philip decided his sister was not such a scatterbrain as he had once feared.

Chapter X

"AN ANGEL UNAWARES" BRINGS A NEW SETTLER

As soon as the two Sams had left the yard that day for Greene, Rachel called her three children together, explained to them, "Now yer father 'n' Sam are gone, we folks hev gut t' look after things. Fust time we've been alone here. Let's do up all th' chores 'n' make things as nice as we can. James, ye better sweep out th' linter with that old cedar bough broom 'n' make th' hovel look good. Yer father sed ye must git th' sheep in early. I think 'twould be well 'nough to git th' cows 'n' oxen in 'bout th' same time. No later than four o'clock, I'd say. Might's well be on th' safe side. If you 'n' Naomi want t' ketch us a couple o' fish er so fer dinner, we'll have 'em 't eat 'long with some o' th' new taters, 'n' I'll cook some beets t' go with 'em. We'll have a good time here t'day 'n' t'morrer, even if we are a little lonesome. Don't ye young ones go where I can't see ye. You c'n ketch all th' fish we need right down there on th' shore where I c'n call ye if I want ye, 'n' don't dare t' step foot on that raft."

The two Rachels then set about to put the cabin's one room in fine order. They scrubbed the split pole floor with soft soap. The floor was rough and splinters stuck in their fingers, but that did not deter them. The table was scoured with soap and sand, also the trenchers and noggins and the odor of soap and water pleasantly penetrated the room. Rachel was so pleased with their work, she decided to take down her canopy top cover and wash that, and when this was done and the lovely piece of linen back in place, Rachel said, "I guess we might 'bout's well call this fall house cleanin' 'n' I'm glad it's done. Flies're most gone now, 'n' we might jest as well be done with things. I wish yer father could bring us home some winda glass, but I s'pose 'twould be hard t' carry on horseback. He'd be sure t' break it gormin' 'round. Prob'ly wouldn't let Sam fetch it. This old sheepskin don't let much light in. This afternoon I want t' finish that little woolen blanket 'n' then I'll be ready fer whatever comes — next month."

They had a hilarious time eating their dinner. Naomi had caught, with a little help from James, a five pound trout that made a meal for them. They told the story of their experience with just as much enthusiasm as was ever shown by any fisherman of their day or since, insisting that their mother weigh it with her balance scales. The cabin rang with sounds of their mirth as they stuffed themselves with the good food their mother had prepared.

After the dishes had been washed, little Phenewel put in his bed for his afternoon nap, every one settled down to some pleasant task. Young Rachel started knitting on another brown stocking, James and Naomi were picking hazel nuts to dry for winter, from bushes growing near the cabin. The very air breathed contentment. Now and then, a crow would call to his mates to gather for a conference. It was drawing near the time when they must go south for the winter. Already that day, James had seen two flocks of geese fly over the pond, led by the old gander who kept them in an even triangular formation headed for warmer climes. James hoped they would settle down and light on the pond. If they had done so, he intended, if he could sneak his father's gun out of the cabin, to take a shot at them. But they sailed by, crying "Honkle—honkle—honkle" and finally became a mere speck in the distant sky.

Rachel began her sewing and to herself said how lucky she was to have such a nice family and the best home a person could wish for. When she had left Lisbon, she had never thought she would be so happy again. Just then, she felt a little twinge in her back, but that was nothing. She had felt them often ever since her accident last spring when she was thrown from her horse. Now the pain seemed a little different, sharper perhaps. She soon forgot it, as her fingers flew, hemming the last side of the baby blanket. She was reminded of the beautiful sheep they had owned in Lisbon, from which the wool had been sheared to make this blanket possible. She wondered how long it would take to raise another flock as good as the one they had sold to Hinckley. She greatly regretted their inability to bring those sheep to No. 5. Next spring there would be another lamb. The two cossets had grown wonderfully well that summer and were really sheep now.

"Lucky Naomi routed out that old b'ar last spring so th' boys c'd shoot him. Mebbe they wouldn't be any sheep now. Oh' Oh" she exclaimed.

"What's th' trouble, mother?" asked young Rachel.

"Nawthin', I guess. Jest one o' my little pains, or else I et too much dinner. M'stomach aches's well as m' back. Prob'ly I'm tryin' t' carry too much o' a load. Didn't that trout 'n' them beet pickles taste good? I'm glad I put yer father's old cider int' th' vinegar barrel, so't we c'n have all th' vinegar we want fer pickles this fall. We ain't got no apples t' make cider now, but they's a lot o'mother in that barrel 'n' I c'n add a lot o' sweetened water t' that 'n' in no time 'twill be vinegar. In that way, I'll piecen' of it along fer quite a spell, dewin' of it that way. Takes a good many years t' grow apple trees, p'r'aps we c'n buy some apples later on t' dry fer pies 'n' sass. Yer father sez Eben Newman has set out a big orchard. Them Newmans come here eight years ago, they say. It seems they was quite a party of folks livin' in Deerin', New Hampshire, that come across here t' Andover some twenty miles west o' us. They was plannin' t' come t' No. 5, but found there wa'nt no ro'd from Andover across, jest a trail made earlier by th' Injuns. They call it Coos Trail. So they all stayed there in Andover at Merrill's Tavern till March. The men folks worked out what they could 'n' managed t' git through th' winter. So they started out with th'r ox teams t' break ro'ds through t' this town. Andover men helped 'em some with their teams, 'n' they finally got through, but Eben told yer father they had t' spend one night in th' woods, stuck in a snow drift. His wife, Sarah, was a Dowse from Billerica, Massachusetts. 'n' her sister Hannah, with her husband, James Masterman, was part o' th' crowd 'n' these Dowse girls had a sister Marthy, who had married Nathaniel Kittredge, 'n' they was th' fust settlers here — come years before. That's how the others happened t' come , I 'spose. Yer father said Ebenezer told him this Hannah that married Masterman was an oncommon woman, 'n' she made a stew outer a deer they shot there in them woods. She made it right there in th' middle o' th' night in that snow drift, 'n' fed twenty-seven on 'em, 'n' kep' up their spirits so's they c'd start out agin early in th' mornin'. When they all gut here 'n' found this sister Marthy they hadn't seen fer years, Eben said there was a turrible takin' on fer a spell. Fust them Dowse girl'sd laugh, 'n' then they'd cry. Said he begun t' think his wife was a-goin' crazy."

"My soul, how my stomach aches. I thought that thing had stopped pesterin' of me, but I see it's come on agin. 'Twas more'n hour ago it took me afore—Oh, my Lord in Heaven! Ye don't 'spose."

"Don't 'spose what?" asked young Rachel.

"Oh, nawthin', I guess. Here I've talked th' whole afternoon away 'n' only hemmed this little blanket, while ye've gut yer stockin' ready t' set th' heel. What's gut into me t'day, t' make me s' lazy? Must be 'bout four o'clock 'n' time fer James t' git th' cattle in."

It was not long before James and Naomi appeared with a bucket filled with hazel nuts. After taking them into the cabin and hanging them on one of Sam's crooked wooden hooks to dry, the children drove the cows, calves and oxen into the hovel and closed the door.

James, imitating his father, heaved a sigh and said, "B' godfrey mighty, they're safe now."

Rachel rose from her chair and went into the cabin, young Rachel knitted on, her thoughts centered on her lover. Would her father bring a message from him, she wondered. Would Betsy Judkins be nice to brother Sam? She felt quite certain Sam loved Betsy and she believed he had gone down there to tell her so. Father was always hinting at such things, but father, was a matchmaker, anyway, so mother said. She knitted on for half an hour, dreaming of her handsome Philip, not realizing how the time was flying.

Suddenly, she heard her mother cry out, "Oh dear! Oh dear!"

This was an unusual thing to come from her mother, the woman who was never ill and always seemed able to face anything, no matter how difficult. Young Rachel quickly gathered her knitting and put it into her basket as she rushed to her mother's side.

"What's th' matter, mother. Ye don't look right. Are ye still in pain?" asked the frightened girl.

"I might's well tell ye girl, bad's I hate t'. I'm goin' t' have the baby some time t'night. Ye needn't be scairt. They's nawthin' t' be scairt of. I sh'l stay on m' feet as long as I c'n. O' course I'll have t' stop now 'n' then t' have a pain, but we'll git some supper, right off, 'n' git th' young ones t' bed soon's we can afterwards. I don't want them t' know nawthin' 'bout it. They'll soon be asleep. Naomi 'n' James slept right through when Phenewel wuz born. 'Course you went over t' Hinckley's that night 'n' Mis' Hinckley come over t' our house, same as I allus went over t' her's when her children wuz born."

The two women set supper on the table as quickly as they could. James brought in the milk, a large bucket full. Rachel strained it into earthen pans and set them in the fine cupboard Sam had somehow found time to build. Its doors were mere frames over which thin linen cloth had been tightly drawn and fastened with wooden pegs. Soon all were eating except Rachel, who told her children her dinner had upset her stomach. Young Rachel, attempting to eat, admitted she, too, had overeaten at noon. The tall clock, brought from Lisbon, struck seven, the signal for Naomi and James to go to bed. It was well, for Rachel could no longer sit quietly as she had earlier, but paced the floor, back and forth over those split poles. Her lips were shut tightly over her teeth, an expression of grim determination on her face. Young Rachel, realizing her mother was suffering acutely, asked what she could do to help.

"Nawthin', darlin', nawthin' anybody c'n do, but I wish I'd never let yer father leave."

It was nine o'clock now and Rachel still walked the floor. Ten o'clock, and the pacing continued, but often the woman would stop and grasp, with both hands, the heavy doorpost, pulling with all her strength. When the pain subsided, she would start again, over and back, over and back, from one end of the room to the other. When the faithful clock struck eleven, Rachel said to her daughter,

"I'm goin' t' bed now. We'd better git th' poppy leaves out o' m'box that Mis' Ludden give me. She said if I needed 'em, to steep 'bout half a cup full in a pint o' water, 'n' take a swaller now 'n' then. I don't intend t' use 'em less I have t', but ye might's well have 'em ready. They's plenty hot water there on th' crane 'n' 'twont take long t' steep 'em if we need t'. Everything else is ready in th' top drawer."

As she said this, she slipped off her clothes, put her linen nightgown on, and lay down on her bed. A great sigh escaped her lips, but nothing more.

"Fix me th' poppy leaves, daughter, I can't stand it no longer."

Groans now came through her white lips. She was beside herself. It mattered not who heard now.

"Drink this, mother. Drink it quick. "Dear God, help my poor mother. Oh, please help her," prayed the frantic girl.

From the opposite bunk, Naomi began to cry aloud, awakening little Phenewel, who added his lamentations to hers. James, from his bunk, gave his mother one frantic glance, then threw the bed quilts over his head and began to sob. Old Carlo, from just outside the door, sensed with canine instinct, the anguish of his mistress and howled dismally in sympathy, there in the darkness, while far below in the deep woods near the lake, the scream of a wildcat answered back.

The poppy-leaf tea now began to take effect and the suffering woman grew quieter. Young Rachel, whispering in her mother's ear, asked how long this was supposed to last.

"Never been like this afore. Can't understand it. Must be it'll end afore long. Have plenty o' tea, in case I need it," said Rachel.

It was nearly an hour before she spoke again. In the meantime, young Rachel had managed to quiet Naomi's fears, stroking her head with one hand, and patting the cheek of little Phenewel with the other, and she rocked his cradle with her foot.

But now the effect of the drug was wearing off, and Rachel's agony was fast returning. Something must be done.

Young Rachel went to the bedside of her young brother and, gently uncovering his head, said, "James, ye're only a boy, I know, but ye're th' only man in th' house t'night. We've gut t' have help fer mother, I'm afraid shes' goin' ter die. Can't ye go up t' Holts 'n' ask them what t' do? They must know o' some woman in this neighborhood who goes out t' help at sech times. Won't ye go, little brother?"

"I'm scairt t'. I'm scairt o' that blow down whar th' b'ar was," he whimpered.

"There's no b'ar there now. Father killed him."

"I know, but p'r'aps they's another one come by now. I can't go till daylight. Then I'll go."

Rachel just could not force the boy to go out into the night and take that deardful walk through the dark woods, where she knew wild animals lurked. She had the courage to go herself, but could not leave her mother.

"Gimme some more tea. Please, quick!"

Again the opium from the poppy leaves gave Rachel relief.

She relaxed and almost slept, the girl thought. She decided then to keep her mother comfortable until daylight regardless of the amount of "tea" it required. Then she would send James for help. Surely there must be someone who could come.

Streaks of dawn were now coming from the east across the pond.

Rachel grasped her brother's shoulders. "It's daylight now. Wake up 'n' go t' th' Holts jest as fast as ye c'n. Tell them if we don't have help our mother will die. Tell them the baby is due, but won't come. Tell them t' hurry."

James went up over the hill in record time, buttoning his jacket as he ran. He knocked on the doors of Holt's house and walked in. He was crying hysterically now, almost too frightened to deliver his message.

"Mis' Holt, Mis' Holt!" he screamed. "My mother, she's dyin'. Is ennybuddy livin' round here that c'n come down 'n' git her baby fer her? She can't do nothin' 'bout it herself. She's most dead." James started jumping up and down, waving his arms.

He screeched, "My father's gone t' Greene. We ain't got nobuddy t' help us."

"Run t' that house jest above here. Mis' Pratt lives there. She'll go." said Mrs. Holt.

James soon reached the door of the Pratt cabin, frantically pounded on the door and pushed it open.

"Mis' Pratt, Mis' Pratt," he shouted, "Come Quick. My mother she's a dyin'. Mis' Holt said ye'd come."

Just then a tall, middle-aged woman, in a long nightgown, stepped from one of the bunks. She seemed to appear from nowhere.

She walked to the side of the frantic boy, laid her hand on his head and said, "Be quiet, m'boy. Yer mother won't die. I'll go home with ye. I'll find her baby fer her. I've found lots o' 'em in my day. Some fer myself 'n' a lot fer other women."

She quickly dressed and started down over the hill with the boy, whose hysteria had subsided, but whose body still shook with dry sobs as they hurried along.

Before they reached the cabin, Rachel's frightful groans could be heard. The woman feared there was trouble ahead, but she walked into the house with a brave, sweet smile on her face. Young Rachel was so thankful to see her, that she could only bow her head as tears ran down her cheeks.

"I'm Mis' Pratt from above here," said the woman. "I've come t' help ye. Don't cry, dear, I think we c'n manage."

She thoroughly washed her hands and arms at the wooden sink and asked where various things were kept, as she set more poppy leaves to steep before the fire.

"How long has yer mother bin in labor?" she asked.

When Rachel told her, she only shook her head. Then she told Rachel she had better take the children outside and said she would call if she needed her, suggesting that they go out under the trees and eat a picnic breakfast, after they had done their chores.

Mrs. Pratt was an experienced midwife. She soon found, upon examination, that Rachel White's case was not ordinary. It was many hours before that baby was brought into the world, more dead than alive, but alive just the same. The ministrations of the strong old midwife, although eventually successful, took the last ounce of strength remaining in the body of the pioneer mother. The instant the first cry of the baby was heard, she sank into the sleep of complete exhaustion.

"If things had gone on much longer, yer little sister wouldn't a lived; ner yer mother neither I'm afraid. Has yer mother ever had an accident t' her back?" suddenly inquired Mrs. Pratt.

Rachel told how her mother had been thrown from her horse in March and had struck on her back on the icy ground. "That's it" said the midwife.

All that night the competent, but frightfully tired old woman stood at her post. She watched tenderly at the bedside of the prostrate mother, never allowing herself a momen'ts sleep. Occasionally, the tiny baby would cry, but this was a natural consequence and gave wise old Mrs. Pratt no concern. It was for Rachel's condition she feared, but there was very little she could do now. She had done her work. At times during that day, she had almost despaired of saving either mother or child, but she had prayed as she worked, even though the mother was a stranger to her. The God she tried to serve had never failed her in times of trouble, and she had labored on, firmly believing He would answer her prayer and save the woman and her child. Now, as she sat there, she thought of her own experiences there in the wilderness in the years gone past, and how her own children had been born in the little log house. Nobody but God and her husband had watched over her, and, after all, they were enough. She smiled at this thought, then suddenly her expression changed. She stood on her feet and looked about her, as if expecting some one other than Rachel and the sleeping children would be there. She almost spoke aloud, before she realized her imagination had run away with her. To herself she said, "If I had a man that'd leave me alone at such a time, I'd —." She sat down and continued her vigil.

All day Friday and through that night, Mrs. Pratt nursed the mother and child. Saturday morning there was a marked improvement in Rachel's condition. The baby seemed out of danger now.

Rachel said, " Did I hear ye say yer name's Pratt? I've heard th' name before, somewhere. I'm mighty thankful ye live 'round here. I'm obliged t' ye, no end. Hope I c'n do somethin' fer you some day. Ye've been here quite a spell, 'n' I don't want t' ride a free horse t' death. I guess we c'n git along now."

"I guess ye can too, they'll both pull thru. I promised Jonathan I'd be home t'day, so if ye feel it's alright, I'll go 'long. I want t' git things ready fer Sund'y."

Sam and young Sam had made an early start from Monroe's Tavern. Sam planned to reach Dixfield in season to call on his friend Amos and give young Sam an opportunity to become acquainted with the jovial proprietor of the Inn.

"Let's cross t' th' other side o' th' river. Ye ain't never bin on th' west side o' th' Androscoggin. It's a grand river 'n' I think it looks better from that side. Water ain't deep now 'n' we c'n ford at Dixfield well's not," Sam said to his lovelorn son, who wasn't interested in scenery. It made no difference to him on which side of the river they were. Sam pointed out various interesting spots, particularly the view of the lofty mountains away to the north.

Handsome country, wide river, good soil, fair ro'd, good weather."

No response.

Young Sam was so quiet as they rode along, his father was disturbed and regretted that he had encouraged his going to Greene. The miles dragged and they rode on in silence. Sam cudgeled his brain for some cheerful topic of conversation, but failed to think of one. They journeyed on through Jay and Plantation No. 1, later called Peru. As they neared the place where he and Philip had crossed to Dixfield nearly a year ago, they came to a log house on their left. Sam rode up to the door and was cordially received by the man of the place whose name was William Walker. Sam told him they had come from Greene and were bound for Plantation No. 5 up in Abbott's Purchase, where they had settled the previous year. He told him of their various experiences coming up the river on the other side and they conversed together for about an hour.

Sam said, "When we come up river last year, we run into a lot o' trouble. Lost our baby off'n a hoss 'n' my wife raced back t' find him. Her saddle girth busted 'n' it throwed her off ont' th' ground 'n' like t' broke her back. Th' mare went down 'n' cut her leg 'n' dam near bled t' death, 'n' th' Luddens that live over there took us in 'n' fixed us up. Awful kind folks."

"Yes, they are," said Walker, "Levi Ludden, a brother, lives jest above here. Merrill Knight, the fust settler, lives down below near th' brook. Yer musta passed his place. An' Major William Brackett, one o' th' proprietors, 'n' our town's only Revoluntiary soldier, lives jest this side o' Knight's." This contact was a pleasant and lasting one, for Sam's genial nature won him many friends.

The water was now low at the ford just above the village where they crossed. At the Trask hostelry Sam felt quite at home. It had been his intention from the start to spend the night there and that was one reason he had taken his time at Walker's. The supper was good and the time passed quickly. Young Sam's spirits were lifted by the humorous anecdotes of Amos Trask and others who came into the Tavern for a night cap, and altogether the evening in Dixfield proved a success.

It was early that Saturday morning when the Sams started for home. Sam wanted to stop and visit with Tom Berry, but young Sam said, "Oh, let's git home, father. I've bin away long 'nough. We've bin gone most four days 'n' I want t' git t' work."

The woods were still beautiful with maple, oak and beech leaves that remained on many trees in locations where the frost had not fallen so heavily. Soon, every leaf would fall on its mossy bed to be covered later with a blanket of snow. Sam, at peace with the world, hummed his tune and thought his own thoughts. It was not worth while to try to engage his son in conversation. As they left the main road, and started down over the hill to their cabin, they saw a woman approaching, which was an unusual sight on that road.

"Who d'ye spose 'tis?" asked Sam.

"Dunno," was the reply.

The woman stepped in front of Sam's horse and stopped. "Be ye Sam White?" she asked, as she squared her shoulders. "Well, I'm tellin' ye now, 'f I had a man that would go gallivantin' off t' Greene fer four days 'n' leave me t' have a baby with only a young girl t' tend out, I sh'd hope he'd have his haslet pulled out by th' roots 'fore he got home. That's what oughter happen t' men like you." She jerked her head a trifle higher and marched on.

Sam rode on to his house, all the while trying to think of what he could say to make his peace with Marm. James took his horse at the door and he tiptoed into the quiet room where lay his wanfaced wife with a tiny girl baby asleep beside her.

Rachel looked at Sam. She was almost too weak to speak, but managed, "Well, yer here."

"Marm, Oh Marm. I din't 'spose, or I'd never left ye. How be ye, anyway- Did ye have a hard time? Is it a boy, or—"

"It's jest one more poor female born into th' world t' breed young ones fer some man t' leave alone t' suffer, jest when she needs him th' most. Jest one more poor fool born."

"Oh, Rachel, don't talk so. What's happened t' ye, anyway? Ye never had no great trouble afore, did ye?"

"No great trouble. No. I don't spose you'd call it much, but all I wish in this world right now is that you'n all th' other men in it would have jest one baby. There woudn't be no more born. I c'n tell ye that. Right now I sh'd like t' see ye lay here on this bed 'n' suffer one hour, the way I did fer twenty-four. Ye wouldn't be standin' there now, grinnin' like a Chesshire cat. If't hadn't been fer Mis' Pratt, the babyn' I'd both be dead now."

"Oh, that's how 'tis. I wondered what had come over that old biddy. She like t' blowed me right off'n th' ro'd. What's the old she-wolf's name, anyway?"

"Mis' Pratt, I told ye, 'n' I sh'll always think of her as an angel. From now out, I intend t' go out th' way she does 'n' help all th' women o' this section whenever I c'n. She told me she never refused t' go at sech times 'n' had brought more'n two dozen children into th' world, besides havin' nine 'r ten o' her own. Y'know, Sam, th' Bible tells of entertainin' angels unawares. Wal, we've had an angel right here in this house a-visitin' us, but ye've bin away 'n' wa'nt here t' do no entertainin'. Porr Little Rachel was 'bout scairt t' death 'n' so was James and Naomi."

(103)

With this, Rachel began to cry, in spite of her determination to fight her Sam to a finish. She now broke down completely and reached toward him with her marble white arms. Sam gathered her to his penitent heart, crooning his regrets, admitting his neglect and swearing never to leave her again. The comforting over, Sam wanted to know what name she had given the baby.

"Yer don't spose I'd name her 'thout your help. Ye've always named th' girls 'n' I've named th' boys."

"Wal, let's call her Cynthy. Shall we, Marm?"

"Yes, it suits me if it does you," replied the now smiling, proud mother. So Cynthia she was named.

"Come t' dinner, father," called young Rachel. Sam left the bedside of his wife humming his "Ah-—dum—dee". He was happy once more. There had been a little storm, but the rainbow now shone through the clouds. God was in His Heaven and all was right with the world.

After dinner, Sam remembered to give young Rachel the package Mrs. Judkins had sent her. The girl was delighted. The new dress she would make and color with the bright red dye would be wonderful. In the bundle with the dye was a letter from her Philip. This was far more precious to her than all the dresses in the world. It informed her that he would come to spend a few days with them in about a month.

Chapter XI

GROWING PAINS, WHICH INCLUDE SOCIAL AND RELIGIOUS ACTIVITIES, INDIAN SCARE AND WAR OF 1812

For some time after the birth of Cynthia White, in the fall of 1809, her mother was in delicate health. The frightful ordeal she had endured took a great deal of her vitality. It was several months before she had either the courage or strength to assume the heavy tasks that fell to all mothers in the wilderness of the Androscoggin Valley. Young Rachel took her place at her mother's side and soon proved that she, too, was a pioneer. Both mother and father were proud of their capable daughter and each day were astonished at her accomplishments. The first of November, when Philip came to visit her, he, too, was pleased with the marked ability she demonstrated.

One day he said to her, "Rachel, you've grown up since last May. When I went away you were a little girl. Now you're a woman, and a very pretty one. Don't blush, dear, it's the truth."

"Well, the truth shouldn't be spoken at all times, I've heard," replied the happy girl.

Philip remained with them for two weeks. The young people enjoyed every moment of his visit. One day, young Eben Newman rode into the yard. He came to invite them all to his father's home for a supper and dance. This was the first time any of them, except Sam, had seen young Ebenezer. He had his father's jovial manner. Everyone in the log house was charmed with him, and an hour later, when he rose to leave, they urged him to remain longer with them. As soon as he had gone, Rachel asked her mother if it were possible to get the cloth for her new dress dyed and made up to wear to the Newman's the following week. Her mother said it was, if they both worked on it all of their spare time. It is needless to say they accomplished the feat, making her an Empire gown in the fashion of the day. Around the square low-cut neck of the dress, the mother fastened a narrow ruffle of fine lace she had knitted years before in Lisbon.

On that lovely Indian Summer evening, when young Rachel, on the arm of Philip Judkins, stepped into the Newman house, they attracted the eyes of all and the red dress created a sensation. There were other lovely girls present, who hoped for a dance later on with the handsome young stranger. Susan and Martha Newman, whose mother Sarah had come from the wealthy and aristocratic Dowse family in Billerica, had been well-trained in genteel deportment. This is an accomplishment not often found among young women in a wilderness town. The two daughters of James and Hannah Masterman, Hannah and Sarah, with their brothers Marmaduke and Benjamin, also belonged, through their mother, to the Dowse family. Nancy, daughter of Martha (Dowse) Kittredge, was also, like her cousins, a young lady of refinement.

Daniel Storer brought his sister, Lois, a tall, graceful girl. These young people had lately come with their parents from Hopkinton, New Hampshire, to settle in the neighborhood. There were other young people from nearly every home in the locality. Mrs. Newman graciously greeted young Sam, Rachel and their friend Philip. She was a charming hostess, making the young people feel at ease. This was an unusual affair for them, the first time they had ever been invited to a real party. The regular "kitchen breakdown", as country parties were generally called, was not just like this. Tonight, they sat at a long table in a dining-room. Few farmers boasted of such a room. The meal was well served. There was a snowy linen cloth on the table and napkins for all, which the girls daintily spread across their knees, imitating Susan and Martha Newman. The boys, after casting one disdainful look toward the napkins, decided to leave them in their peaceful folded whiteness. At first, the conversation was limited and sketchy. Young Ebenezer and Philip exchanged their ideas about the distance across the pond at its widest place, which fish was more delicious, trout or salmon, and touched on other subjects. Finally, Philip asked him how he felt regarding the affairs of the nation. Eben did not appear to be greatly interested at first, but when Philip said they were certainly in for another war, be allowed he didn't think there was anything sure about it. Philip very emphatically informed him it unquestionably was a sure thing. After this, for some minutes, all the young men were quiet and thoughtful.

Mrs. Newman, who with the help of her sister, Mrs. Kittredge, was serving the meal, realized the bashfulness of her young lady guests, and took matters into her own capable hands. Complimenting Rachel on the shade of her beautiful gown, she told her it was the first she had seen of this color. This opened the way, and was all they needed to start an animated conversation. Compliments flew and the chattering was incessant from then on. The food was excellent. Wonderfully roasted turkey, stewed high-bush cranberries sweetened with honey; potatoes, turnips, pickles, deep custard, pumpkin and mince pies, fruit cake, doughnuts and cheese. The table was loaded with the best that part of the country afforded. By the time the meal was finished, they all felt well-acquainted and anxious to clear the room for dancing. Mrs. Newman proudly told them that some day they would build a two-story addition onto this new room, which would then be used for a kitchen.

Ebenezer Newman was a fiddler and greatly enjoyed playing for others to dance the jigs and reels they loved. No other instrument was necessary to make them the happiest crowd of young people in the Province of Maine. Later, from the log house adjoining the dining-room, Mrs. Newman, Mr. and Mrs. Kittredge with Mr. and Mrs. James Masterman, who had come earlier on horseback from the other side of the pond, joined the young people and added greatly to the success of the party. They needed no jazz orchestra or other stimulant to pep them up, youth and the joy of living, human companionship and a clear conscience were all that was necessary. "Take yer partners fer Lady o' th' Lake"—and they rushed for first place. Rachel danced with every man present. Philip never sat down the whole evening. Sam almost forgot his longing for the girl down in Greene, he was so busy dancing with the tall Storer girl.

They swung their partners in Lady of the Lake, till the girls resembled great pinwheels of varied colors. Rachel's red skirt was a whirling blaze there among the indigo blues and hemlock bark browns. Again squeaked the old fiddle with the tune for Boston Fancy, and it proved to be very fancy indeed as the boys lifted their heels in a double shuffle. Money Musk was another popular dance. Roy's Wife, Speed the Plow, Chorus Jig, these they raced and chased through. The girls pivoted and courtseyed, while the boys stamped their cowhide boots, making the new floor tremble. All these they danced and more, and not until the wee, small hours of the morning came, did the host decide he had played enough.

Then, at Mrs. Newman's invitation, they went out into the log house where the long table had again been spread with more food. This time there was no lack of table talk and pandemonium reigned as they all ate their fill for a second time. Regretting that the night was not longer, they thanked their hostess for the best time they had had ever in their lives, and rode off into the darkness.

The next morning at breakfast, the young people graphically described all that had taken place at the Newman's. Rachel asked her mother why they all crooked their little fingers when they held their teacups. Mrs. White said she supposed it was the style now, but showed surprise to learn that the Newman's owned teacups, living as they did so far back in the woods.

"But, oh, mother, they've got a whole set of chiny, 'n' th' loveliest long white tablecloth in the world. And, mother, they had forks on the table, but nobody used 'em 'cept the Newman girls. I didn't dast, fer fear I'd spill somethin' ,'n' mother, Mis' Newman sent her respects t' ye, 'n' said she was comin' t' see ye very soon. She heard 'bout yer awful sickness when Cynthy was born. Said she wisht' she'd known 'bout it, but she said Mis' Pratt was th' best woman 'round here at such times, anyway. Oh, mother, we did have such a good time. I wish I could go t' a party like that every night."

"Wal, Marm, I cal'late it's our turn t' entertain," said Sam. " 'Course we ain't got no place t' dance, but we c'n have a party 'u' show 'em how t' spin th' plate. I'll bet they ain't never heard o' that up here in these woods. Ye c'n give 'em somethin' t' eat, can't ye, Marm?"

"I c'n make some maple candy 'n' fix some snap corn 'n' doughnuts, 'n' we've got plenty o' milk t' drink. 'Course that ain't much, compared t' all th' vitals they giv' you," said Rachel, half apologizing.

"Oh, some day we'll have a good house," Sam said, "place t' dance 'n' everythin'."

"Don't ye fergit, Sam White, ye're goin' t' have a room in it fer my loom," snapped Rachel.

"M'darlin', I never fergit nawthin'. But set yer mind easy, I heard t'other day th' Storers are fixin' t' build one. Prob'ly ye c'n git them t' weave yer cloth when ye git some wool. I was up t'

(108)

Storers t'other day 'n' Daniel was out side th' ro'd cuttin' timber fer t'make th' loom. Spoke as if he was goin' t'make it hisself. Quite a feller, that Dan'l. Ah—dum—dee. Ahn—dum—dee. Ah—Dumdiddlum—. Ain't you folks goin' t' ask th' Storers down here t' th' party?" he asked.

"Course we are. What d'ye spose? What's gut inter yer head now, Sam?"

"There ain't nawthin' gut inter m' head. Ah—dum—"

But before he could finish, Rachel cut him short, saying, "Don't tell me ye ain't a-schemin'. But ye don't have t' git upset 'bout them young Storer folks, fer Mis' Holt told me Dan'l's got a girl down t' Chesterville 'n' his sister Lois's got some young feller round here. Ye needn't start makin' no more matches in this family. Th' last one ye tried didn't work out very well.

The Whites now busied themselves making preparations for the party. The Newmans and Storers were duly invited and on the appointed evening, the young people arrived. They spun the plate, played blind man's bluff, hide the thimble, cat's cradle, told riddles and stories and sang songs. They ate maple candy and snap corn covered with butter. Sam played his Jew's Harp and they managed to dance a little on the split pole floor, but it wasn't much fun, and they soon tired of it. The new game, spin the plate, was more popular. The kissing forfeits especially appealed to the boys. The girls pretended not to like it and squealed and squirmed, but they got kissed just the same.

Philip's two week vacation was about over. He must return to Greene. He had promised his mother he would leave No. 5 before the heavy storms set in. Both mother and father had warned him regarding this. They did not want their son to experience what Philip and Sam had endured the previous fall.

All during his visit, he had felt he should like to persuade young Sam to enlist in the American Army of Resistance, though he well knew his aversion to it. He knew Sam was unhappy over Betsy's refusal to marry him and felt sorry for him, but he would have been sorrier had she consented, for he knew she had no real love in her heart for Sam. He felt that if he would only enlist, he would soon forget about Betsy. So, here was another good reason for urging Sam to join him later on, when they would go to Portland and offer their services to their country.

The following day, which was Saturday, Philip determined to

settle the matter. He asked young Sam if he could spare the time to go fishing for a while. Sam said he could. They begged some salt pork from Rachel to use for bait, took their few hooks from out the woolen cloth where they were kept, and made ready to go. A fish hook was a scarce article, and, when obtainable, cost sixteen cents. They made their lines of double-twisted, heavily waxed, linen thread and they were carefully treasured. For a rod, they cut a sapling when they went down to the lake shore. Their preparations made, they hurried down through the woods to the pond. The raft Sam had built earlier in the season was well up on the beach and it took no time for them to float it and get aboard. They poled their craft up the lake a short distance and anchored off the mouth of a brook. Almost before those small pieces of pork struck the water, the hungry fish snapped them up. First a four pound trout, then a five pound salmon rose to their bait. Philip began to wish the fish wouldn't bite so fast, for in no time at all they had caught more fish than they needed and there hadn't been a moment in which to talk to Sam. The opportunity for the planned conversation was already lost, but he squared his shoulders as they drew the raft up on the shore and asked,

"Sam, have you ever changed yer mind about enlistin'? I thought p'r'aps by now, ye might be thinkin' of goin' down country somewhere with me and joinin' up. I want t' see some of th' country before I come up here t' settle, 'n' I thought maybe you might, too. My father says travel is a great educator, 'n' I think he knows, but there's more to it than that. I tell ye, Sam, the British are plannin' agin t' take America."

"Wal, they can't never do it," said Sam.

"Mebbe they can't, and mebbe they can. I don't feel sure, but I do know they'll try before long if we don't have more protection fer our coast 'n' Canadian border."

"What's th' matter with our Navy protectin' our sea coast?" asked Sam.

"Our Navy?" Philip scornfully retorted. "Sam, we've got just twenty fightin' ships 'n' th' English have a thousand, and as fer our Army — it's jest a joke, 'n' old Madison sets there on his beam-end down t' Washington, drummin' his fingers, worryin' fer fear he won't be elected President a second time. I wouldn't vote fer him more'n I'd vote fer one o' yer father's oxen, even if I was old enough t' vote, which I'm not. I guess he's done one good thing, though. Father thinks he has."

"What's that?" asked Sam.

"Well, he's made William Henry Harrison commander of the whole Northwestern Army, but father says the other officers he's appointed don't amount t' nothin'. I tell ye, Sam, I'm worried. Come on down this spring 'n' we'll go t'gether. Come on, won't ye, Sam?"

"Oh, I d'know," replied the procrastinating Sam.

When the boys reached the log house with their catch, they found one of the Gordon boys, who lived beyond the head of the pond near Holman's, had come to bring an invitation from Nathaniel Kittredge to the Whites to attend a religious service at his home the following morning. Philip decided to stay over another day and go to church with Rachel and her family. He was acquainted with Mr. Wyman and would be glad to meet him again. Mr. Wyman was a godly man, who traveled on horseback through the Androscoggin Valley towns, preaching the gospel of Jesus Christ. For many years, the good man continued this service to the early settlers. He and Elder Lemuel Jackson, the first traveling preacher to visit No. 5, conducted services thru the towns of the valley.

In District No. 5, the summer of 1809 was called the "Time of the Baptist Reformation". In August of that year, the Congregational Church had been organized with eighteen members. Services were held at private homes on Sunday until 1826, when a meeting was calld to take action regarding the building of a Meeting House. That year $920.00 was subscribed and in 1828 the edifice was completed. October 22nd of that year the settlers of the District dedicated the first church which was built on Center Hill, overlooking the present village.

After young Gordon left the White homestead, Rachel said, "I want you boys t' start bringin' in th' bath water so I c'n be heatin' it. Ye better fill up th' old big kittle 'n' heat part o' it outdoor, 'n' I c'n heat th' rest o' it in th' house. Naomi, bring in th' two tubs 'n' we'll give th' children their baths right now. There'll be time 'nough 'fore supper fer you 'n' Rachel t' take yers. I'll take mine while you girls're gittin' supper on. Too cold now fer the men folks t' go t' th' pond. They'll have t' take theirs there in th' corner by th' sink. James, ye go 'n' git the big old blanket 'n' hang it up there fer a curtain. When ye git t' washin', use plenty o' soap, 'n' see that ye do a good job."

The Whites, as usual, rose early that Sunday morning, happy to have the opportunity to attend a religious service in the company of their new neighbors. As soon as the barn chores were done, Sam started clamoring for Rachel to clear out while he and the boys shifted "their duds" and got themselves "ready for meetin' ".

"S'pose ye think us women folks ain't got no shiftin' t' do? But I guess we c'n wait till you've done your'n," said Rachel.

In time, they all donned their Sunday best, mounted their horses and started to travel the four miles to Kittredge's home. Sam rode the young mare with Naomi behind him seated on a folded blanket. Rachel, with Cynthia on one arm, drove the old mare with the other. Young Rachel rode Philip's horse, with Phenewel in front of her, tied to the pommel of her saddle, where she could watch him. He no longer reposed in his journeying, but sat erect, his fat little hands grasping the saddle horn. Young Sam, Philip and James had to walk, and started a full hour ahead of the others. When Sam left the cabin with the females of his flock, they resembled a tribe of moving gypsies, not an uncommon sight in those days. They were cordially received by the Kittredges and the good Elder Wyman welcomed them all with fatherly kindness. They were provided with seats of various kinds. Daniel Storer shared his hymn book with Rachel. The book was "Hymns and Songs by Isaac Watts, D.D." Elder Wyman opened the service by resquesting his congregation to sing the following hymn, number 22:

> "Terrible God who reign'st on high,
> How awful is thy thundering hand.
> Thy firey bolts how fierce they fly,
> Nor can all earth nor hell withstand.
>
> And ye blessed saints that love him too,
> With reverence bow before his name.
> This all His Heavenly servants do,
> God is a bright and burning flame."

After this disturbing hymn, the good people gladly listened for three long hours to what must have been a somewhat comforting sermon, if one can judge from the text, Proverbs VIII-17th—"I love them that love me. And those that seek me early shall find me."

By sunrise Monday morning, Philip, after thanking the Whites for their hospitality and promising Rachel he would come again in the spring, if he didn't enlist, waved a good-by and left.

For young Rachel, the winter of 1809 and ten was long, but she kept busy as did all the members of her family. The two Sams with James resumed the clearing of their land. Sam, not having fully decided where he would build his house, but knowing it would be on higher ground, gradually continued working toward the top of the ridge, preparing the land as he progressed, for what some day would make him a fine farm. The best trees, he saved and would later haul to Holman's mill to be sawed into joists, boards and lumber of smaller dimensions suitable for use in the construction he planned. Other timber he burned or left in piles for fuel, of which they would consume many cords during the year. Rachel and her daughters, like all pioneer women, cooked, scrubbed, spun, knitted, sewed and mended early and late. This was their life. Often, but not always, they attended a religious service at the home of a neighbor. Sometimes a traveling parson officiated, but often the meeting was just a service of prayer led by one of the neighbors. One such service was held at the White homestead, conducted by Mr. Kittredge.

In the spring, Philip came again and once more asked young Sam to go with him and join Captain Herrick's Company at Lewiston, but Sam refused.

Philip and young Rachel declared their love for each other, promised to be faithful until they met again, and this time really said good-by. She knew he would enlist as soon as his father's crops were planted and that she would not see him for a long time.

The spring of 1810 found the Whites with quite a large area of cleared land. They were able to plant larger crops, which would be greatly needed for now they had two more calves, another sheep and Sam had bought a pig from Eben Newman. He was encouraged to see all his possessions increasing, his flocks and herds growing in number, even Rachel's six hens had multiplied to over forty. Foxes were so numerous and bold that it was next to impossible to raise a full flock of chickens. Some one had always to stand watch over them during the day, and even then, out of the sky, would swoop a hawk to snatch a chicken before their very eyes. Naomi was official chicken girl and was good at it, except when she got dreaming of fairies, her mother said. This year when Rachel and the girls made their maple syrup, Naomi seldom left her mother's side. She had no desire to witness a repeat performance of a bear disturbed in his nap.

James, now fourteen, and beginning to grow tall, was expected to act his size, if not his age, and many were the tasks put upon him. Of course, he and Naomi had a certain amount of fishing to do, but this year not as many fish would be required for fertilizer. Through the winter the animals had produced a good supply of that.

Caleb Holt had come, at Sam's request, to view and discuss boundary lines of the land purchased from Abbott. Caleb lived on the east side of the pond nearly opposite Sam's place. His farm, largely of meadow land, produced large quantities of hay. Holt was glad to make arrangements to sell any extra he might not need, to Sam. Holt agreed to haul the same on sleds across the pond in winter over the road the settlers used during that season.

Berries grow abundantly on newly cleared land, and Sam's place was rich with strawberries, raspberries, blueberries, elderberries, and all these Rachel "Put by" in one way or another. The strawberries, raspberries and blackberries she did pound for pound. The blueberries she dried on cloth covered frames in the sun. These she used like currants or raisins in cakes and cookies, or soaked them overnight, making them like fresh berries and fine for pies. The elderberries, Sam said, made a fair pie, but better wine.

"Ye know, Marm, our Lord told Timothy t' make a little wine fer his stomach's sake."

Rachel would reply, "If I make any wine outer them berries, it won't be fer your stomach's sake, I'll tell ye that, Sam White. Prob'ly shan't make no wine anyway." But she always did make a little just the same and Sam somehow always managed to get his share.

The Whites were a happy family. Summer produced fine crops, which they harvested in the fall. They built another hovel in which to store them. After this, the endless job of land clearing began. Sam, by now, had become acquainted with most of the settlers in the Plantation, and enjoyed an occasional hour of pleasant conversation with them.

The following spring, as he and his son were felling great trees, burning brush and doing the many necessary things in their operations, Jonathan Pratt and his son Seth appeared and said they were on their way to the pond for fish. After catching all they could carry on a pole across their shoulders, they started for home. Soon a large bear appeared. He had been following them for some distance, but gave no sign of trouble except to show that he wanted the fish. As they were unarmed, they were obliged, as they went along, to toss the bear a large trout, when upon devouring same, he would return for more. This performance continued until they were within sight of their home and their fine catch practically exhausted. After the recital of this unusual episode, the Pratts left, Sam telling them he hoped they'd see plenty of fish, but no bears.

As the summer advanced, Sam began to plan his trip to Lisbon. The $500.00 payment on the farm he sold to Hinckley two years before would be due the first of November. He must go and collect the money and have it ready to pay Caleb Holt, Abbott's agent. People had said one must be on time in any business dealings with this Abbott, but Sam felt entirely different about Caleb Holt. However, he had no idea of neglecting anything regarding his obligation to that land owner. He would give him no opportunity to take advantage of him.

The harvesting finished, Sam started for Lisbon the last week in October. He looked forward to his return to the town where he had lived with his family from 1780 to 1809. Of course, he would spend one night at least with Philip and possibly another with the Hinckleys. It gave him much satisfaction to know his wife would not be having another baby while he was away from home this time. His son, now twenty years old, had become thoroughly dependable. As he left his home that morning, he felt a comfortable sense of security for his family and looked forward with anticipation to a visit with his old friends.

He spent half an hour with Berry in District No. 4, and learned he was sawing boards at his mill for Robert Potter's barn. Berry told him a man named Joseph Winter had settled that spring on another great hill a mile or two beyond Potters. They discussed Daniel Storer's prospects.

Berry said, "He's moved down here, bag and baggage, neighbor to Potter. Jest another man who wants t' live on th' highest hill he c'n find, but he's sech a worker, he'll git ahead wherever he is. Even on a desert island."

Sam's next stop was Trask's Tavern, where he only stopped for a few words with Amos and went on.

"An evenin' with 'Bijah at Livermore was somethin' t' look forward t'," and tomorrow would find him once more with his dear friend Philip. However, when he reached Greene, he was surprised to learn how the spirit of war was everywhere. The hatred of the British had so magnified in the hearts of the people nearer the coast, they could speak of nothing else. Young Philip was somewhere with the western armies; Nathaniel Larrabee, brother of Hannah Parker, in parts unknown. Several companies were in Lewiston, two of militia and one of cavalry. All farmers of Turner and surrounding towns were being trained by Captain Seth Staples of Turner. Nearly every day brought news of new companies being formed in other towns on or near the Androscoggin. Nearly every county boasted of a regiment. Excitement was at fever pitch. The peaceful little town he had known scarcely seemed familiar now. After staying one night with Philip, Sam decided to go on to Lisbon and find out how things were there. The extremely high prices of all necessities were effecting everyone and Sam feared that Hinckley might not be able to pay the whole $500.00 due him.

"What then?" he asked Philip.

"If he hasn't saved all of it, try to persuade him to borrow what he lacks. Tell him we must have it all in order to meet our obligation to Abbott, or we are ruined."

Sam did not sing a note on his way to Lisbon. All along the way were constant reminders of the approaching conflict. He met several recruiting officers, more than once saw groups of men drilling in fields. When he finally reached the home of Russell Hinckley, he learned that both of his sons were with companies guarding the town of Bath. Hinckley was trying alone to manage his large farm, which included that formerly owned by Sam. Owing to the unsettled situation, Sam felt almost certain that the $500.00 would not be forthcoming, but to his surprise found Hicknley was able to make the full payment.

That evening he passed over the money, all in gold. Sam hardly slept that night and when morning came was thankful to start back to Greene. In those days, five hundred dollars was a large sum of money. To Sam, every stranger he met on the way, appeared like a bandit. Still no humming of the familiar tune could be heard. Instead, when any passer-by gave him a searching glance, a cold sweat would start on his forehead and he would whip up his horse. The road back to Greene seemed twice as long as ever before and the gold he was carrying inside his boots became heavier every mile.

When he reached Philip's door, he excitedly exclaimed, "Godfrey mighty! Philip, take this filthy lucre. I never understood afore what the Bible meant 'bout money bein' th' root o' all evil. But now I do. I've sweat a gallon sence I left Lisbon, worryin' 'bout this dam money. Take it quick, 'n' send it t' Abbott. I ain't a-goin t'lug it t' Number 5 t' give t' no agent. I'd drop dead 'fore I got there."

Philip was amused at Sam's recital of his experiences, but he said, "If you don't take the money to Caleb Holt you'll have to go to Concord, New Hampshire and pay it to Abbott."

"I'll be cow-kicked fust," said the wild-eyed Sam. "Philip, I'd ruther walk all th' way home with this money, than ride one mile to'ds th' coast, th' way things is now."

Philip calmed his fears and persuaded him he would have no trouble taking the money up-river. The time had passed when a man could spend a pleasant hour conversing with acquaintances along the way. Sam's only desire seemed to be to get as far away from people as possible. The money in his boot legs was a constant worry. He had ridden all the way on the east side of the river, spent the night with the Luddens, where he knew his money would not be stolen from him, and didn't even dare sleep at Trask's Tavern, which sometimes housed strangers for the night. Late the next afternoon he rode thankfully into his own dooryard. His home never looked so good. The people up here in the woods concerned themselves little with the talk of war, and believed it would never come.

Sam and his boys resumed their land clearing. Occasionally someone would bring stories from the outside of atrocities committed on the high seas by the "damn British", but these wild tales were soon forgotten. These happenings were too far away to disturb the dwellers in the wilderness a hundred miles from the coast.

The spring of 1812 brought the usual cheer of the season. Rachel and her girls were as busy inside the house as Sam and the boys were outside. On March 23rd, a meeting of the inhabitants was called at the home of David Wheeler, for the purpose of incorporating and naming the District. The people petitioned the Commonwealth of Massachusetts to grant them permission to call the 15 square miles that surrounded the lake, Webb Pond Plantation.

In 1782, a party of men had set out to explore the country from the Kennebec to the Connecticut, intending to build a connecting road between the two rivers. In passing through, they discovered a pond about six miles long, near which were the remains of a cabin. On a tree nearby, was carved a name, "THOMAS WEBB". At the foot of the tree they found an old musket and some traps. Now in 1812, the eighty inhabitants desired to name their town Webb in honor of the first settler. Their petition was granted that year, and the town, the lake and its outlet river were all named for Thomas Webb.

The last week in March, 1812, a stranger came into the settlement. He was dressed like a scout and had apparently traveled many miles. He informed the settlers that a great catastrophe was about to befall the people of Webb Pond Plantation. Through sources he could not disclose, and, having felt such pity for the people of this isolated community, he had traveled for many days, to come and warn them. He felt they should pay him for the time he had spent in coming and considered this to be worth $60.00. He said he would, upon receipt of this money, divulge the all-important secret, and this would give them time to protect themselves. After much discussion and planning, the settlers collected the needed amount, which meant almost every dollar in the community. Then they were told the frightful news, that, on a certain day late in July, the Indians were coming to destroy the settlement. The stranger told them he had obtained this information from a friendly Indian he had met on a hunting trip many miles from this vicinity. He then went his way north to warn other settlements of the approaching danger.

As quickly as possible, the men of Webb called a meeting and voted to ask the great Commonwealth of Massachusetts to provide them with sixty-four guns equipped with bayonets, also ammunition, to protect themselves from the Indian raid. A committee was formed of men from Avon, Phillips and Webb to patrol the woods, the towns voting to pay them two dollars per day for this service and the payment to be made in produce as there was no money left in the Plantation. They decided to build a fort on the side of Masterman Hill. James Kittredge, Benjamin Masterman, Jr., Stephen Webster, Emerson Storer, Jacob Coburn, Joseph and Abel Russell were to do the building. Caleb Holt gave them the boards to cover the roof and the use of his ox team to draw them from the Bowley Mill, which had lately been built on the river near the foot of the pond. However, before their plans could be executed, word came causing greater consternation.

One afternoon in June, Eben Newman went riding fast down over the road from Abel Holt's, his horse wet with sweat and showing other signs of having been driven hard. He jumped from his mount and inquired at the log house door for the men folks.

Learning they were some distance away in a lower field hoeing corn, he said to Naomi, "Go as quick as God'll let ye 'n' tell yer father war's bin declared," then turned his horse and galloped away.

The girl made a fast trip to that corn field. Only once before had she run like this. That was when she drove the bear from his den. She was considerably more frightened now than she had been then, for there was going to be war and her brother Sam would go. He had said when news of Philip's enlistment had reached them, that it would be time enough to go when war was declared. He didn't believe that day would ever come, but if it did, he would certainly go.

There was no more hoeing corn that day. Both Sams saddled their horses and rode toward the home of Eben Newman. Reaching there, Mrs. Newman informed them that her men had all gone to Center Hill to learn what they could about conditions and perhaps organize a Company which would later join a Regiment down river. Both Sams set out to find their friends on the hill.

When they returned to the cabin that night, young Sam informed his mother that a dozen young men of Webb would soon be going to the front. He said he and Eben Newman had decided they were needed more for home defense and would stay to fight the Indians who were soon due to attack them. Of the two evils, this seemed the lesser to the over-wrought mother. She would at least have the comfort of knowing where her boy died, if die he must, and there was always the chance he might save his life and theirs too if he stayed there.

The people of New England had forced a repeal of the embargo, but a non-intercourse Act with France and England had been enacted in its place which was no improvement.

President Madison had not favored another war, but he had wished to be re-elected for a second term. His friends, who wanted the United States to declare war, had told him that unless he joined with the majority, he would never be re-elected. This had frightened him into calling a secret session of the Congress behind closed doors. The bill, proposing war was discussed and passed on June 19th, 1812, and the war was on. President Madison appointed William Henry Harrison as Commander of the northwestern armies, and he advised the government to build a fleet on Lake Erie, which later acquired great glory for our country. The declaration caused stagnation of business everywhere. Along the coast and throughout the Province of Maine, there were no markets for home produce. Articles of necessity could only be procured at enormous prices.

The British had won the service of the Indian Chief Tecumseh before war was ever declared. Now he would have his chance to try to incite every tribe along the Atlantic seaboard and drive the Americans back south of the Ohio. The British were equally as cruel as the Indians and allowed them to scalp and torture defenseless women and children, as well as men, from the Canadian border to the Gulf of Mexico. Although the ships of the American Navy were few, they were often victorious in encounters with the British. From all points of the compass came reports of battles on land and on sea. One day a victory for the Americans, the next day another victory for the British. Sometimes the Maine people would take courage. Then the report of a man-of-war being taken by the enemy would drive them back into the depths of despair.

The fort in Webb was built in two stories. The first of rocks, 28 by 56 feet and 12 feet high. The wall was four feet thick. The upper story was of hewn logs 14 inches square and 32 by 62 feet high. The upper story projected beyond the lower on all sides. Inside the fort, or garrison, huge iron kettles were arranged over arches for boiling water, which the women, from the over-hanging upper story, would pour upon the heads of the attacking savages, in case the men failed to stop them with their musket fire.

The settlers moved into the fort with the exception of the Ebenezer Hutchinson family and James Kittredge and his wife. She was very ill and couldn't be moved from her home over the rough road the short distance to the fort. The road ran directly past the Kittredge home. It was arranged that Kittredge should watch through the night and when the Indians appeared discharge his musket and thus warn the inmates of the fort. He sat all night at the door of his cabin with musket in hand, but no Indians came.

The settlers remained in the fort for about six weeks. The men, meanwhile, went out in armed squads to work on their farms.

At the expiration of this time, when no Indians had made their appearance, the settlers decided they had been the victims of a swindler and thankfully journeyed to their respective homes.

CHAPTER XII

A RIPPLING SYMPHONY OF RIPPING CLAWS

The remainder of that summer of 1812 was a nightmare for the frightened settlers of Webb Plantation. Men continued to carry their muskets when on the road or in the fields, and women kept their guns loaded and within reach at all times. Little children were not allowed to leave the door steps of their homes.

Everywhere hearts were heavy. No word from Greene had reached the Whites since Sam left that town the fall before. They felt out of the world. No government protection, no standing army to guard them. Just a pitifully few men and boys with sixty-four muskets in addition to those they had brought with them. These guns had been used for defense in that other war with the British. Ammunition was one great factor. They could run bullets when lead was available, but they could not make gun powder. What they had was so precious. They almost knew how many grains there were in their powder horns. There was never a moment of their day or nights, when they could feel at ease. When from sheer exhaustion they fell asleep at night their rest was inadequate. Ofttimes the imaginary war whoop of the Red men resounding through their dreams, brought them from their beds, prohibiting further sleep.

Rachel deeply regretted their ever having left Lisbon, but Sam repeatedly assured her conditions were even worse down there, reminding her of the constant fear of Bath and Brunswick citizens, of British war vessels entering the bay and invading the towns on the Kennebec and Androscoggin.

"Of course, its bin nough t' be spectin' Injuns any minute day r' night, but Godfrey Mighty, a ship full o' British cannon sailin' up th' river, would look worse t'me than a pack o' painted Injuns. I cal'late I n' James could do quite a butcherin' job on them fellers 'f they should come round here. Ye 'member when I got a bead on that old b'ar, he didn't go fur. I've laid awake nights a worryin' jest long 'nough t' be cocked 'n' primed t' put a bullet through one o' them Injun snakes. My conshunce won't trouble me a might, if I ever git th' chance. An' you, Rachel, don't want t' be chicken-hearted, if ever ye see one of them devils come round here, ye want to shoot fust. If I knew they was going t' carry you'n the young'uns off, I'd rather shoot ye all myself now."

"Oh, Sam, what be ye talkin' 'bout?" asked Rachel.

Somehow the crops were gathered, somehow they carried on through the winter.

Spring came. They planted, they hoed, cut their hay and harvested. It was September 1813. They received little news from the outside. Even though disturbing, news of any kind helped break the monotony of their lives. Sam decided to ride to Dixfield and learn what he might of affairs down river and of the country. Amos Trask welcomed him, introducing him to several men, mostly inhabitants of the little village which had grown noticeably larger since he and Philip spent that first night at the Tavern almost five years before. Two of the men, Joseph Eustis and Peter, son of Amos Trask, were earnestly discussing the latest war news. Eustis, who had come from Rutland Vermont, in 1803 to settle on a long hill west of the village, a part of Holmantown, later named Mexico, was giving an account of the battle off Pemaquid Point between the American brig Enterprise and the British brig, Boxer. He told them, gathered there in the tap room, how after a bloody encounter, in which both Captains were killed, the victorious Enterprise towed the battered Boxer in to Portland where the two captains were buried side by side. Eustis told them he had that day ridden from Lewiston where he had heard the news. Excitement ran high.

Peter Trask, "Only think of it boys, just last week a battle off our own coast. We begun to think we'd never see any fightin' this far north."

William Waite and John Marble, both veterans of the other war, had ridden in from their farms just outside the village and joined the others in the tap room.

Marble said, "Peter, ye don't want t' fool yerself. Them Red Coats 're stubborn critters, they'll hang on like a dog to a woodchuck."

" 'f they don't come int' this Province afore ther through, I'll be surprised," added Waite.

Sam said "Godfrey mighty, m'friends, Pemaquid 's less 'n

thirty mile from th' place where I uster live. Sufferin' old tom cats, d' ye s'pose they's any more o' them British ships lurkin' 'round Merrymeetin' Bay, waitin' fer a chance t' sail up the Kennebec? Thank God, they can't git up th' Androscoggin very far. Th' falls at Brunswick 'uld stop th' buzzards."

As Sam finished his statement, Captain Walter Carpenter, a near neighbor of Eustis, asked him about the Indian scare they had the year before at Webb. He inquired if they had ever been able to learn where the imposter came from who took their money, and caused so much trouble. Sam told them nothing had been heard of "The' yeller-bellied skunk".

"He ain't never been back fer a'nuther visit, but if he ever shows his head about them parts agin, th' men o' Webb Plantation'll string him from Masterman Hill t' th' Androscoggin River."

Eustis' son, Charles, who kept the store across from the Tavern said, "If ye ain't got men 'nough in Webb Plantation, let us know, 'n' we'll come up 'n' help ye. A feller like that's worse than any Injun, and I'd like t' tend t' th' brute."

Captain Carpenter, a man of more than average education, asked the men gathered there to state their views regarding the possibility of establishing a separate peace between Great Britain and New England. There was little understanding of the question among these men, some of whom had not heard of it previous to that evening. As they discussed the problem, they soon agreed there was no chance of its accomplishment.

The next morning at Eustis' store, Sam bought a quarter pound of tea, half a pound of saleratus, and ten pounds of salt to take home to Rachel.

The news of the first battle of the Province, off the coast of Maine, spread like wild fire. Sam stopped at every house along the way, telling the welcome story of victory for the Americans. Few people understood the reasons for burying British Captain Blythe beside Captain Burrows of the Enterprise, but there were many things, then, as now, hard to understand.

Rainy days, and occasionally on a Sunday afternoon, little groups of men gathered to discuss the questions of the day. Probably due to the fear of an Indian raid, which some still believed might come to them, there were but few young men who had left Webb to join the American forces. Young Sam and young Ebenezer were always on the verge of enlisting, but usually something occurred to prevent. The endless demand for their time and strength to help support their families, continually faced them. There were few enough men in the settlement, some like Ebenezer Newman still suffering from wounds received in the Revolutionary War.

One day Sam said to his wife, "If t'want fer **our tall trees, I'd** favor startin' north ag'in. Wonder how fur a person 'uld have t' travel to git away from trouble?"

Rachel informed him there was no such spot on this earth.

"How'd ye 'spose tis up t' th' North Pole?" he asked her.

"Wall, I cal'late th' only trouble ye'd find up thar, would be freezin' t' death, 'n' that wouldn't last long, 'n' painless, so th' say. Be ye thinkin' a-goin'?"

"No, I ain't thinkin' a-goin' nowhere, but I'll tell ye one thing though, Sam 'n' I's gt t' fix up th' hovel 'fore winter. Fust place 'taint really warm 'nough fer th' cattle, 'n' ye know them slabs in this end next tha oxen aint very strong. A b'ar, or a good big wildcat cud tear 'em off if they's hungry 'nough. I've hear'n they've seen an awful big wildcat's tracks tother side th' pond."

"I should think ye'd better tend t' it then. That 'ud be one less thing fer ye t' worry 'bout."

"Guess yer right, Marm, I think we better build in some good log sides, soon's we git th' taters dug."

They dismissed the subject from their minds. While Sam was never lighthearted as in former days, he was not "worried t' death", and sometimes hummed a little. Rachel, judging from the way he snored nights, believed he was getting more sleep. One cool night in late October, when the only sound to disturb the stillness was an occasional rattling of the chains around the necks of the cattle, the inhabitants of the log house were sleeping. Old Carlo was curled up in front of the door, not hearing the sound of a great grey, velvet-footed panther who padded up the path from the pond where he had been to take a drink and look for a possible woodchuck or coon for a midnight snack. He caught the scent of warm flesh. A few years before, when he had been in this vicinity, there had been no sign of any living creature. Now, as he came further up the hill, he knew there were many of them near, not of his kind, but the sort who could not fight, for they had no claws or sharp teeth. Their soft warm bodies were full of blood, and their flesh would tear easily. **The taste of it was** sweeter to him than any other. He now smelled that hateful thing that barked and called those human creatures with fire in their hands who came to kill. Once, one had killed his mate. That awful fire had blinded him, but he had escaped. Now this stupid thing that barked, but was not good to eat, lay guarding those delicious ones he desired. Without a sound, he crept nearer. He could plainly tell now, the hateful thing there by the door was old and deaf. There was little danger of his awakening the fire-carriers. Boldly now he walked to the hovel where the scent of those great luscious bodies made water drip from his tongue. What a feast was in store for him! Those human creatures had placed a silly barricade around his banquet table, but it was nothing to him. With one wrench of his powerful paw, he clutched the heavy slab, tearing it from the side of the hovel, raking four deep gashes along the side of old "Broad". The noise of the cracking slabs wakened Sam and the others, Carlo sang out with all the power of his old throat as he ran toward the hovel. The scent of fresh blood infuriated the panther as he tore a piece of flesh from the rump of the ox, which bellowed with pain and fear as he plunged and strained for freedom from his chain. Sam and his sons were now on their feet, snatching their guns, Rachel lighting the candle in the tin lantern from a live coal from the fireplace.

"It's b'ars or wildcats after the cattle. Have ye got yer flint, Sam? Light 'nother lantern, Rachel. James, put a charge into that musket 'n' come quick 's ye can. Daughter, set somethin' afire, a sheet 'r somethin' that'll burn, 'n' bring it out 't scare off th' animal, whatever 'tis. Oh, my God! hear them cattle beller."

Out through the door those two men went, no shoes on their feet, nothing but their night clothes covering their bodies. The moonlight shown on the beast, disclosing his whereabouts at the end of the hovel, where he had torn away part of the side, and where he was slashing and tearing at the fallen ox. "Star", his mate, was fearfully straining at his stanchion post, bellowing frightfully as was the other yoke of oxen, the bull and cows that stood beyond. The poor sheep, huddled together, were pitiful in their helplessness. Sam fired. The shot went wild. Young Sam fired, this time crippling the great cat, but he was not giving up that feast. He jumped inside the hovel, landing on the back of the helpless ox, tearing at its flesh with both teeth and claws. By this time, James had the old musket loaded with a powerful charge of powder and two bullets. His mother was close behind him with both lanterns in her hands, at her side Rachel holding the flaming sheet with the tongs, its light affording great assistance to James, showing him exactly where to aim. Bang! went the old musket, kicking back and landing James sprawling on the ground, but the bullets had gone home. The blood of the catamount now mingled with that of old "Broad", and its head lay in the great wound it had made in the back of the ox.

"Open the door back o' th' hosses, James, 'n' let th' old mare out, then p'raps you c'n crawl through her crib' n' reach in t' cut th' young mare's halter. She's goin' t' ruin herself, th' way she's jumpin' 'n' plungin'. She's scairt t' death o' th' smell o' blood. Them poor cows, too, hear them beller. Git 'em out o' there soon's ye can, boys. Prob'ly they'll all lose their calves. Godfrey! what a mess we're in," Sam said, as he worked desperately to free the three struggling oxen who were threatening to pull the hovel down over their heads.

"There aint no chance o' old Broad gittin' over this. I got t' kill 'em. But there aint no room t' knock 'im in th' head, where he lays. I doubt if he's got strength t' git up ont' his feet, so's we c'n git him outen here. 'd hat mightily t' hafta cut his thro't; but we got to save his meat, 'n' th' sooner we bleed 'im out, th' better," said the provident man. Rachel asked her husband if he was sure the injured ox would not recover with good care.

He replied, "No use, Marm, half th' muscles in his rump is tore out of this side. You women folks better build a fire beyent th' hovel 'n' anuther one this side, near 'nough so we c'n see **Old Broad.**"

"What ye want one built beyent th' barn fer?" asked Rachel.

"That's t' keep any more panthers from comin'. They don't very often travel in pairs, but sometimes they dew. When I told ye t' set a sheet afire, I thought it might be wolves out here after th' sheep. We know they allus go in packs, but these old cats roam round alone. Prob'ly they aint no more round here. Hope they aint."

When young Sam had pulled the panther away from the ox, Sam went in beside his faithful, but now conquered and mortally wounded beast. Tears were slowly trickling down his brown cheeks.

"Good old Broad," he said. "How I hate t' do it, but ye'r sufferin' 'n' ye'r 'spectin' me t' help ye. Ye've helped me fer a good many years; you've never stopped, even when ye's tired 'nough t'

(127)

die, ye kept ploddin' on. Broad, don't ye hear me? Can't ye git up now? Whoah Hish, Broad? No use, Marm, he can't lift that old body ag'in," sobbed Sam.

Rachel called her eldest son. "Sam, taint fit fer yer father t' have t' kill that ox. It'll take too much out er him. Mind ye, he raised old Broad from a calf, the same spring Star come. Funny, too, they was pretty well matched. He made that little ox yoke fer them two calves. They was awful little when you begun t' yoke 'em up 'n' drive 'em round th' door yard. I c'n see now, jest how proud he was, cause you c'd leave 'em to gee 'n' haw. Yes, I know you love 'em, jest like he does, same's we all do. But Sam, ye're younger than yer father. Why don't ye shoot th' poor critter? It's no use t' try t' git 'im outer thar till he's dead. Don't wait. Go 'n' do it now. Yer father'll never ask ye to. I can't bear t' have ye stick 'im. He won't know nothin' 'bout it, when ye shoot."

Sam waited only long enough to reload his gun, He walked past his parents, head erect, stepped through the gaping hole to the side of the suffering animal, placed his gun barrel just under the ear of the old red ox — a flash — a deafening roar. Old Broad's head dropped to the floor of the hovel.

Sam, without a word, walked slowly back to the cabin. He was willing to let his son finish his task with the sharp knife always carried in his belt. As he waited in his doorway for the carcass of the ox to drain of its blood, he sat quietly, living over the past. Rachel looked with pitying eye at her forlorn spouse, her own heart aching unbearably, now overflowed. She went to her cupboard, where safely hidden deep within the meal bucket, was a bottle of Medford rum—"fer medicine". Making sure she was unobserved, she poured a generous quantity of the encouraging element into a noggin, added a little hot water and molasses, and offered it to her husband.

"No, Marm, No. I guess I can't drink it. My heart's tew heavy."

"Drink it, Sam, it'll do ye good," said his wife.

And he took it, his courage beginning to return almost with the first swallow.

By the time young Sam, with James' help, had removed the few remaining slabs from the end of the hovel, and had the other yoke of oxen ready to pull old Broad out upon the ground, the father had revived, and took his place once more as master of the situation.

He said, "Fust thing t' do is skin 'im. Soon's we've got 'im half skun, 'll put th' gambril stick into his hind legs, an' hitch th' rope to it. When we git this done, James, you drive th' oxen round here 'n' we'll tie the other end o' this rope t' th' ring in th' yoke. Now then, James, if yer ready, start 'm a mite."

"Whoa Hish Turk, Whoa Hish Swan," called the clear voice of the boy.

The mountain of beef began to move slowly along the grass toward the tree. Now it lifted ever so slightly.

"Don't haul 'im up too high, James," said the father. "If ye do, I can't reach to take out his entrails—there, right there. Whoa back-hold it. That's jest right."

Sam quickly finished the job, and his son drove the oxen along till their burden had been hoisted the sufficient distance from the ground.

"Put more wood on yer fires, girls. We can't let 'em go out. Every darned wildcat in th' Province 'll be here fore mornin' 'n' kill off everying we own. We shall have t' set up th' rest o' th' night, 'n' keep watch. The powwow we've made, 'n' the smell o' this blood'll call every kind o' wild animil ye ever heard of. Oh, how sorry I am, Sam, that we hadn't found time somehow, t' build a long barn!" "But Godfrey Mighty, how could we?" asked the tired, young man?"

"Sam White, ye couldn't either of ye done more'n ye have. Don't blame yerselves one mite. Ye can't do more'n work every minute. Come, darter, let's git 'em a bite t' eat. If they've got t' set up all night -awatchin', the least we kin do, is t' feed 'em," said the mother.

"James, ye lo'd all th' guns we got 'n' have 'em ready, while Sam'n I eat somethin'. Then you c'n eat. I guess Marm 'n' Rachel better watch with us, 'n' if it come t' it, Naomi c'n take your place if you sh'ld have t' lo'd up ag'in. We've got t' keep our eye peeled, cause we got t' watch th' cattle 'n' things. The poor critters won't come back nigh this hovel t'night; they're too scairt. I callate you 'n' I better stay down over th' hill near where they're huddled under them fir trees; fer that's jest where th' beasts'll come, unless th' smell o' this blood call 'em here fust. So ye see, we got ter watch both places. I've heard th' wolves are thick over

(129)

'round Masterman Hill acrost th' pond down country. Funny we ain't never seen any round here. Eben Newman told me th' feller that lives beyent Holman's mill, got two last year, that had killed some o' their sheep, but since then they aint seen a one. S'me folks say the reason they don't bother worse, is becuz they live on th' deer. When I was out t' Dixfield last year, a feller there in th' tavern, by the name o' Norcross, said if they didn't git these wolves killed off in this country 'fore long, thar wouldn't be a deer left. Fer what they didn't eat, they'd scare off to Canady er somewhere."

The remainder of that night the Whites watched with loaded guns in their hand, but nothing occurred to alarm them. Carlo barked at intervals until daylight, a sign, Sam said, that there were wild creatures back in the woods waiting for the fires to go out. If this was true, they waited in vain, for those fires were kept brightly burning through the night. As soon as it was light, Sam rode up to engage Abel Holt to come and help them build a new log barn.

When word reached the other settlers of the destructive visit of the panther, they decided to "Make a Bee' and build this barn for Sam. Young Eben Newman rode to the home of every settler on the west side of the pond. soliciting as many hours as they could give to erect a suitable barn to safely house their neighbor's live stock. This must be erected as quickly as possible, for now the danger of attack was much greater, and the Whites could not be expected to continue their all night vigil indefinitely.

Early the following morning came Abel Holt, Jonathan Pratt, James Swett, who had just come from Brunswick to build wagon wheels for Joseph Storer; Daniel Storer, his two brothers, Isaac and John, each came with a yoke of oxen. Their father, Joseph, rode a horse, carrying a short handled axe which he stated he brought for making wooden pins, explaining he was getting rather old and could no longer do the hardest of work.

"But I c'n set all day makin' pegs."

He told Sam their neighbors, the Newmans, were on their way; that Ebenezer was having "another bad spell with his leg, but he wants t' help make pegs, 'n' I'll warrant ye, we c'n make all ye'll want t' use on this barn 'n' some besides."

During the preceeding winter, Sam and his boys had yarded out more than sixty spruce logs intending to use them for a barn, but had been unable to take time from their other duties to do this. The delay had cost them dearly.

Sam was greatly encouraged by the friendship shown by his neighbors as they drove into the yard.

"Didn't 'spose I had so many friends," he said.

For the second time the hillside resounded with the music from axe and saw. It was amazing to watch the rapid accomplishments of those twelve men. Sam regretted not having Philip there 't' take charge, but being no novice, he soon learned there were many fine joiners present, and each seemed to know exactly what to do.

The Sams had decided to build the new barn as near to the old one as possible. The men who had brought the oxen started to haul the logs toward the building spot as others hewed and sawed them into proper lengths. James Swett proved to be an expert in fitting the mortices and tenons. Daniel Storer, though young, was nearly as good at it, and shortly the first logs were laid, and the hovel, 40 x 60 feet was outlined; then sooner than it would seem possible, the second tier of logs was in place. Sam gave his orders and the others obeyed. He was so busy and excited the first hour that he failed to realize that these men must be fed.

When he finally thought of this, he called to James, "Go tell yer mother t' start a big biled dinner, tell her there's twelve out here workin' 'n' they've got t' eat."

A little later, James said, "Mother told me to tell ye not t' worry 'bout her end o' this job; that she c'n 'tend t' it, 'thout any yer help." "Mis' Newman's in th' house workin'. She says Mis' Pratt's comin' t'morrer 'n' somebuddy else th' next day. Th' women folks o' this neighborhood ain't goin' t' let mother work herself t' death feed'n all these men. We've let old Broad's carcass down outen th' tree, 'n' sawed him half 'n two. They plan on th' men eatin' th' best of one hindquarter t'day. They said they'd have steak fer dinner, with taters 'n' things, 'n' use th' rest fer soup 'n' dumplin's fer supper. Marm's makin' a rousin' big Injun puddin'. Don't look 'sif ye need t' worry 'bout ennybuddy goin' hungry t'day er t'morrer."

The log barn grew, and by night the walls were four feet high. Two of the Pratt boys offered to stay, keep the fires and watch for wild animals that might come, so Sam and his boys could get a much needed rest.

In four days the barn was completed, and the roof covered with bark, and the kind neighbors had returned to their homes, leaving only James Swett and Ebenezer Hutchinson to set stanchion posts and build stalls. A door of hewn logs had also to be constructed, and a pen for the sheep. When Sam and his boys drove their live stock into the shelter of the new barn, happy as a child with a new toy, he again gave vent to his thankfulness with many an "Ah — Dum — Dee". There was not a happier family in the Province of Maine than the one nestled beside the great rock on the side of Webb Pond.

Through the winter of 1813 and 1814, the same task of clearing the land continued, but the feeling of security for his animals which Sam enjoyed, helped greatly to ease the anxiety he experienced for the welfare of his family. In the evening, the men, for now James was considered one of them, made "Stanshil Bows", for the tie up. Sam had brought enough from Lisbon for eight cattle he had brought with them, but now these two cows having calves every year, had produced four heifers, and this year, two of those heifers had given him calves. Now he had six cows and two calves. The bull calves that had come, were fattened, killed and used for food.

Up until now, Rachel and her girls had felt obliged to spend their evenings knitting, sewing or mending.

Rachel said, "We're all caught up with everything. Th're aint nawthin' left t' make. If we only had a loom, I c'd be weavin' cloth 'n' things fer Rachel when she gits married; but as 'tis, all we c'n do is knit, knit, knit. We got s'much woolen underwear, 'n' s'many stockin's I can't hardly find room t' put 'em."

She finally decided to knit some lace, and her daughter Rachel, began to make plans for embroidering a sampler.

Her mother said, "If I's you, I know what I'd make at th' top of it, 'n' that's a ship with sails set."

"What for?" asked the daughter.

"Wel, I don't 'spose ye ever heard o' that ship, th' Mayflower. But down in Walpole, Massachusetts, when I was a girl, they was a deal o' talk 'bout it. Seems some folks years back in England, didn't like th' way they done things over there. Didn't like th' way they run th' church. Quite a lot of 'em was what they called Papists, 'n' some wan't. Fust, a Papist King 'ud order a few heads chopped off, 'n' th' next thing he'd know, he'd lost his head 'n' he wouldn't know nawthin'. Then t'ther side u'd start choppin' off heads, stick 'em up on poles so't th' birds c'd pick th' eyes out. Some lived with th' King, 'n' some didn't; but they all argured 'n' argured. The thing didn't come t' nawthin'. No peace fer nobuddy. So finally, a crowd of 'em, they called theirselves "Pilgrims", crossed over t' Holland; stayed awhile there, 'n' then they all come over t' this country on that ship, Mayflower. Yer father's great gran'father 'n' gran'mother come with 'em, 'n' she had a baby right on that ship, jest afore they landed there in Plymouth Harbor th' fall o' 1620. They called 'im Peregrine. Queer name, wan't it?"

"No queerer than Phenewel, I'd say."

"Wall, anyway, seems these Puritans was looked up to, more or less. Yer gran'mother White used t' tell that these Whites uster visit th' King sometimes fore they left England, 'n' they had a boy more'n five years old, and once they had 'im set in th' King's chair so's they c'ld tell 'im 'bout it years afterwards."

"What was that boy's name?"

"I ain't 'xactly sure, but I think 'twas Samuel. Ye're father swears 'twas. He's jest like evrybuddy else, 'n' thinks it's a great feather in yer cap if yer folks come over on that Mayflower. Mebbe 'tis. Ye might as well draw out a picture of a ship on yer sampler. Seems t' me I should, 'n' why don't ye have a flag on it, with th' word Mayflower on it? Ye know they copy all th' family records from th' Bible, 'n' broidre 'em on. Sometimes, they have a Bible verse tew. I'd like that, wouldn't yew?"

"Then they make all th' letters in th' alphabet, t' fill up what space is left, but ye want t' be sure t' leave 'nough room at th' bottom fer yer own name, 'n' th' year ye make it. Its gittin' t'be th' style t' have one o' them samplers hangin' in yer best room. Yer father said when he was out t' Dixfield last year, Susan, Amos Trask's daughter, was a-startin' t' make one. 'Course, we aint got no parlor yit, but some day we're goin t', so yer father says. If this war would only stop, mebbee we could git started."

"If this war would only end, Philip would come home 'n' we could git married. Its been so long since he went away. If we only had a chance t' git mail like they do in Greene! Won't there ever be a post rider come to Webb?" asked the girl.

"Some day when 'nough settlers come in here t' make it worthwhile, ther'll be one, no doubt."

"If father or Sam would only go to Greene, there might be a

letter there. Philip said he would send one to his mother, and she would find some way to send it here to me. If things was different with Sam and Betsy Judkins, I'd ask him to go down and find out what they have heard about things."

"Little good t'would do ye to ask yer brother t' go t' Greene. Y'r father's th' man thet likes t' go down thar; but Rachel, don't ye worry so much. I been a-thinkin' lately. This war can't keep on forever. That old English King aint goin' t' spare himself short by keepin' on sendin' ships full o' men, 'n' provisions over here fer us t' sink. They got sick of it in seventy-five, 'n' will agin'. I'll bet they won't hang on another year. What'd ye say? Let's start makin' y'r weddin' clothes! Ye know, I'm a-knittin' o' this lace t' put on some o' y'r things when ye do git married."

"Oh, mother dear, is that true? Oh, I'm so glad. I've been wishin' fer th' longest time that we could start somethin', but what in th' world could we use t' make th' dress of? Of course, th' only dress I've got is my red one. I could be married in that."

"Well, not 'f I know it. No daughter is goin' 't stand up in no sech a rig as that. 'Taint modest. Ye'r goin't be married in white, same's I was. Ye know I've got that lace weddin' veil y'r grandmother White said was among th' things that belonged t' y'r great grandmother Susanna."

"Who was she?"

"Aint I jest told ye? She come over on th' Mayflower. Y'r jest like all young folks. Can't 'member nothin' 'bout y'r ancestors; but ye better try 'n' keep this in y'r head. O'course, it's all set down in th' Bible, but 'twould be well 'nough fer ye to 'member somethin."

"Now, speakin' o' weddin' clothes, I got a number a yards o' fine linen I spun 'fore I was ever married. Thought prob'ly I'd use it all t' make dresses fer my babies, but I didn't. I made a Christ'nin dress fer my fust one, same's I done fer all o' ye, 'cept Cynthy, 'n' I must tend t' it right away 'n' have her Christened 'fore cold weather. I don't b'lieve in baptis'n pore young ones in th' winter. Aint I hearn' tell how they use t' put them little shiverin', screamin' babies int' cold water, in an ice cold church 'n' all they'd have on 'em was a little short sleeved dress. Course, they didn't put 'em in all over, 'less they was Baptists, 'n' sometimes them little critters wouldn't live no time at all afterwards. You c'n never make me b'lieve God Almighty's goin' t' hold any mother guilty fer waitin' fer warm weather to git her baby baptised, if it didn't happen t' be born in th' summer! " 'N' when I heard a minister say that 'Hell is lined with infant's sculls a span wide', meaning them little things that didn't git baptised, I c'n tell ye, I have all I c'n do t' keep my settin'. Some folks dew have th' queerest notions 'bout God's love. He said, 'Suffer little children to come unto Me' but he didn't mean we was t' make th' children suffer when we was a-bringin' them to Him. We're th' ones t' dew th' suff'rin 'pears t'me, 'n' some of us dew plenty of it, seem's if."

Chapter XIII

"WARS, AND RUMORS OF WARS," WITH SUNSHINE FILTERING THRU.

In Greene, Hannah Parker's little boy, Ingerson, was about a year old and learning to walk. He had taken three steps that day. Hannah was on her knees, back to the open door, her hands held toward him, encouraging him to take one more step.

"Come to mother, come to mother, darlin',"

"Come to father, darlin'," a husky voice said, coming from the doorway.

"Oh! William, William, is it you?" cried Hannah.

"Yes," he said, as he clasped her in his arms. Tears of joy ran down his cheeks, as he kissed first Hannah, then the little Ingerson, who was crying, too, frightened at the sight of a stranger.

"Oh, William, where have ye been so long? Was there no way t' let us know? We feared so fer yer life. Are ye well? Have ye been hungry? Hav ye been fightin' on land or sea? D'ye think th' Injuns'll attack us here and will they come from up river, the Anasagunticooks, or have they joined the British and gone northwest, or what d'ye think?"

One question at a time, please. First, I'm well. I have never been hungry. Most of th' time I've been on board th' Chesapeake. Didn't ye git a letter from me, Hannah?" he asked. "I sent one last fall, 'n' ye knew I'd gone t' sea for I sent word from Bath by Philip. I'm on a furlough now, been given a month t' work on th' farm 'n' help git some crops in. This country needs food jest as it needs ships, guns 'n' ammunition. Is Jake still here? I've worried fer fear he'd run away 'n' enlist as a drummer or a cabin boy on some old ship. Ther're mighty few goin' out 'n' I doubt if he c'd git aboard one in any of our home ports. He ain't old enough t' go anyway, 'n' father needs him here. Time enough fer him t' go later."

From daylight till dark during the four weeks of his furlough,

William worked on the land with his father, who was beginning to show his age.

"Jacob is a likely lad," he told William, "I'd hate t' see him git inter this war. Fer th' Britishers are jest as cruel, 'n' th' Injuns jest as treach'rous as when we fit 'em in '75. But Jake's crazy t' go. Keeps talkin' 'bout it all th' time, pesterin' th' daylights out o' me. I 'spect every day he'll light out. He uster sneak out 'cross th' river 'n' go up to Turner t' th' Stapleses, t' see Seth, 'n' its' my 'pinion that air Seth put idees in his head. But Seth's bin gone fer more'n a year. We heard they've already sent him out as a recruitin' officer, but he ain't bin up here yit."

William was at a loss to know what to say. He wanted to comfort his father somehow, but what was there for anyone to say. After this conversation, they worked on in silence, planting corn, Benjamin dropping the seed and William covering it.

Finally Benjamin said, "Wal, I s'pose this is th' last day ye'll be here t' help me—fer a spell anyway. I sh'll hat t' see ye go, but, there's one thing, I don't want ye should go again 'n' not tell Hannah where ye be gon'. If ye do be goin' back t' th' Chesapeake, say so, 'n' if ye aint', say so tew."

"I'm goin' back t' th' Chesapeake, Father. I'm obliged t' do that, fer I b'long t' th' Navy now 'n' ther' ain't no choice. It's orders. Th' Chesapeake's a man o' war, not a merchant ship. Ye'll know where I am as long as she stays afloat."

During the time William had been away, Hannah and Rebecca had woven linen for making feather ticks, as covering for feather mattresses were then called. Hannah had made a fine one for her bed. William was delighted to have the opportunity of sleeping on the live geese feathers and told Hannah he could still picture the great stretch of Labrador coast alive with wild geese where he had gathered the feathers.

"When this trouble's settled 'n' it's safe t' go t' sea once more, I'll go up there 'n' bring back feathers enough fer a bed fer every one o' our children and one for Philip and Hannah Judkins."

"Ye won't need t' make yer trip very soon, fer it don't look like ye c'n stay home long enough t' raise a very large family," Hannah laughingly said.

"Wal now, Hannah, ye never c'n tell by th' looks of a to'd, how far he'll hop," countered William.

The next day, William left early, but this time when he said good-by, everyone knew where he was going and that he might be long in returning. He had tried to save them some heartaches the first time he had left, but now the situation had changed. They all stood around the little kitchen trying to be brave for his sake. He kissed them all, Hannah last. Then he walked silently through the doorway. A dry sob caught in Hannah's throat, but there was no other sound. Benjamin pitied his sweet daughter-in-law. She deserved so much and had so little. He decided right then, regardless of the expense, to buy the shiny new thorough-brace carriage he had seen the week before for sale in Lewiston. The next day, he purchased it ,also a new harness and, bringing to Greene the first carriage in town, he presented it to Hannah, who cried with delight. She and the Parkers enjoyed that carriage together for many years.

Spring passed into summer, summer to fall, then the cold winter added more trouble to the over-burdened families, not only along the Androscoggin, but all over New England. People were going hungry and cold, there was no ship-building and very little business of any kind.

Hannah sought for news of the Chesapeake. While William was at home, he had told her that the United States Navy had only twenty ships, while the British had over one thousand. She wondered what would happen to the Chesapeake, should she ever be attacked by a fleet of those great boats that carried so many guns. Some actually boasted of one hundred sixty, while the largest American ship carried only forty-four.

Before war had been declared, Captain Seth Staples had ridden up both sides of the river, urging all men of suitable age to enlist. Now he came again. This time both old and young were called. At last Jacob had his chance. Captain Seth was his friend and a great hero in his eyes.

"Men ain't made Captains fer nothin'," he said, and away he went, crossed the river on a raft, walked and ran six miles to Turner and joined a company of Infantry.

About this time, word reached the people that frightful battles were being fought in Ohio, and that thousands of our soldiers were being slaughtered by the British and Indians, who had come down from Canada. The Americans were losing in nearly every territory, in every encounter, or so they feared, not realizing the great strategical ability of General Harrison. The whole Northwestern Army would soon be lost, they thought. A dozen men from Greene and Turner were then with that army. Most of the territory beyond Ohio was in the hands of the enemy. Fear gripped the hearts of the people. Deacon John Larrabee, whose son Nathaniel was somewhere in the northwest with Captain Herrick, thought they should hold a season of fasting and prayer in the Parish. He traveled from house to house talking and praying with his neighbors, who knelt with him, sometimes in their kitchens. Sometimes in the fields, a group of old men would fall to their knees, pleading with God to save their country. Several times during the' week, the Reverend John Daggett held sessions of prayer at the little church which Deacon John and his brother Stephen had built in 1794. The Sunday morning services were three and four hours in length. An hour out for lunch, if it had not been appointed a "Fast Day", then back for several hours more. At these times, the services had one hundred per cent attendance. Holy Communion was served every Sabbath, some people were greatly sustained by their faith, while the courage of others was at its lowest ebb. They felt their God had forsaken them and there was no longer efficacy in prayer. Philip Judkins, with heavy heart, worked unceasingly on his farm, never unmindful of young Philip, now with the northwestern armies. He wished it were possible for him to join the American forces. He was now past sixty, but were it not for leaving his wife and daughter to do all the work at home, he would certainly have a try at some of those redskins with his old musket.

He knew their ways, he had learned them in a hard school, where they had tried every torture they could invent except scalping, but he had outwitted them in the end and sometimes, even now, nearly thirty years later, he would think of how he had balanced the score. He didn't dare think about how many he had killed, although somehow it didn't seem like murder to kill an Indian. He wondered if it looked that way to God. He hoped so, in fact, he mostly believed it did, but, sometimes, when he thought of the Sixth Commandment, it troubled him and he was glad he couldn't take part in this war. He would vow not to fight again in any war, but he was fighting a battle of nerves, and it was harder for him in a way than any he had known. However, the stalwart old war horse was not giving up yet. The faster calamities befell him, the harder he braced himself to meet and overcome them. His good wife, Hannah, was made of the same rugged material, trained in the same school of hardship and self-denial. Her children had all married and gone with the exception of Betsy and Philip, and Philip — was he alive? One letter the year before had told them his company was on its way north, but no further word had ever come. Philip, with Hannah and the others, clung tenaciously to their Faith and continually asked God to spare their dear ones. They believed He would hear their prayers and so carried on.

On Upper Street in Turner, conditions were no better. Seth, training Turner boys to fight, was ready, at a moment's notice, to march in defense of any place along the coast or river. He was unable to spend much time with John and Betsy, his brother and wife, with whom he lived. His short visits were a comfort to them, but they daily expected he would be ordered away. John hoped and prayed that in this event his brother would not be sent out of the Province. Seth's efforts as a recruiting officer had proved very successful and there were men and boys now in service from every town bordering on the river. Little groups coming from Rumford, Dixfield, Peru, Livermore, Jay, Leeds, Hartford, Sumner, North Auburn, and all the towns below.

John's health was still good, but the fear of another lung hemorrhage was always in the back of his mind and prevented both him and Betsy from fully enjoying their life together. Betsy was one to look on the bright side and it was well she could, for she was expecting another baby and this time it must also be a boy.

"John must raise boys t' help him," she would often say to Aunt Abigail, but when she said the same to John, he would reply, "I don't know as I want t' bring another boy into th' world t' have t' jine armies 'n' fight fer existence. That's th' way it's been in our family as fur back's anybody knows. Father used t' say, all his grandfathers had fit somebody, either Injuns or white men, ever since th' fust one come over from England on th' Mayflower. What on airth ails everybuddy 'n' this world, always wantin' t' fight. I s'pect some o' our neighbors think I oughter be down on th' coast with a gun in m'hand, but they ought t' know I ain't able."

When he finished this remark, he would look askance at Betsy, hoping she would agree with him, but she always had her eyes turned in another direction, and sometimes poor neurotic

John would wonder if she felt the same as he feared others did.

During the year of 1812, it was anybody's guess which was faring worse, the land forces or those on the sea. Reports came from London that the British laughingly claimed our ships were mere pine boxes, while they boasted of their wonderful oak Men of War.

The American brig Nautilus was captured her first day out from New York by the British brig, the Shannon. It was not long, however, before good news drifted up to the people of Maine. The Constitution, commanded by Captain Hull, had won a great race against eleven British warships that had tried to catch her for nearly two days, when she escaped and was off for parts unknown. The news that came brought the account of a second victory for the Constitution in a ghastly battle with the Guerriere, Captain Dacres, commanding. The people of Boston went wild with joy. The Guerriere had gone down and they began to think England could not have everything her own way. Captain Hull and his officers were feted. Six hundred people sat at dinner with them. In New York he was wined and dined and presented with snuff boxes and swords. Poets wrote verses and set them to music. Soon all the boys in Boston and up the coast to Portland were singing an improvised ballad of great length.

Very shortly came a new dance tune called "Hull's Victory", and soon at every kitchen breakdown held in New England, the fiddlers, as they sawed off the tune, called "Right hand to partner. Swing half-round. Balance four in line, swing partner in center, down the outside, back and down the center, return, cast off one couple and swing contra corners".

Down in Delaware Bay in October, came the report of another sea battle. The American ship Wasp, carrying eighteen guns, Captain Jones in command, sighted six English merchant ships, each carrying sixteen and eighteen guns. One of these was the Frolic. Captain Jones succeeded in smashing the Frolic to splinters and killed or wounded one hundred ninety-two of her men, while his own crew was only lessened by five killed and as many wounded. Just then a French ship, Poictiers, with seventy-four guns heaved in sight and Captain Jones was forced to give up his prize, the Frolic, and haul down his own flag. So it went on. Victory, then defeat. One followed the other. Next, came word that on December 26th, Old Ironsides, for that was the name they now called the Constitution, had wrecked the Java, off the coast of Brazil. Taking the Governor of India and all of his officers prisoners of war, she again sailed proudly into Boston Harbor. The cannons on the shore saluted — Old Ironsides had done it again. England began to wonder if her supremacy of the seas could possible be disputed by that weak little nation across the ocean.

The year 1813 began with terrible land disasters, although the American Navy was still wining victories. At Monroe, Michigan, eleven hundred British and Indians, commanded by Proctor and Tecumseh, with five cannon, crossed the Detroit River on the ice and attacked the Americans, the Indians tomahawking and scalping the wounded. Proctor made no effort to stop this inhuman treatment and for this treachery, even Tecumseh looked upon him scornfully. Then, in May, came good news of the retreat and great mortification of the British at Sackets Harbor.

Late one afternoon in early fall, Captain Seth Staples rode up to the door of the Parker homestead. He dismounted and walked into the barn, as countrymen always do when serious affairs are at hand. Old Benjamin stood just inside the "tie-up" and had a low stool in one hand, a bucket in the other. He was about to start milking, when he saw some one come into the barn. His sight was none too good now, and to himself he said, "Wonder who this c'n be. Didn't s'pose there was an able-bodied man left around here. Who's there?" he called.

"Seth Staples," was the answer. "Are ye alone, Mr. Parker?"

"I be, sir. Come in. Any news?" asked the already suspecting man.

"I'm afraid there is, and it isn't good. The Chesapeake has been captured 'n' taken t' Halifax."

"God in Heaven!" said Benjamin, and he quickly sat down on the milking stool. "Poor William. How I wish I knew how it went with him."

Seth felt there was nothing helpful he could do or say, so bade Benjamin good night and rode away. Poor old Benjamin. How could he tell Hannah, and how could he tell Rebecca, now getting old as he. Well, he would do the milking first, and perhaps in the meantime he could think of just the right thing to say to them. So, he finished his task and, with a deep sigh, stood up, squaring his stooped old shoulders. He walked slowly into the kitchen carrying his bucket of milk. There he found Hannah and Rebecca sitting in silence. He set his pail on the table, cleared his throat twice, and said, "Wal, girls, I've got some bad news o' th' Chesapeake."

Rebecca interrupted saying, "Ye needn't repeat it, Benjamin. Hannah saw Seth Staples goin' into th' barn, so she went out 'n' listened t' what he said."

Rebecca rose from her chair and strained the milk into an earthen pan, saving a little for the cat. Then she set the pan away in the pantry, washed the milk bucket and strainer, took her knitting from a basket and started to knit on a half-finished sock for William, still believing he would come back some day to wear it. Hannah went into her bedroom, knelt at the bedside of her sleeping child and prayed with all her soul for the safe keeping of her William.

"Dear Lord, please don't let him go hungry. If he's a prisoner in Halifax in one of their foul dens, give him courage and strength to endure. Don't let them torture him. Please, Oh! Please. And dear God, bring him back to me."

For a few minutes she allowed her tears to flow unrestrainedly, then she composed herself, wiped her eyes and returned to the kitchen taking along with her the tiny linen dress she was making for the new baby she was expecting. This second one would come in February. She must have everything ready.

To herself she said, "And William doesn't even know it's comin'. Oh! dear, maybe he never will."

Over one hundred thirty years ago, when the people of this country were passing through their second struggle for liberty, news traveled so slowly that it sometimes took several weeks for the account of a battle to reach the Province of Maine. The poor souls waiting for news of their loved ones, were nearly distracted at times. Finally came the encouraging report that General Proctor and his entire force of white men and Indians had been badly beaten by Major Croghan and his men, under the direction of General Harrison at Fort Stevenson on the Sandusky River in Ohio, and were driven back after two days and nights of fighting. This raised great hopes in the hearts of the people. What a pity it was they could not have known then that never again would a British soldier set foot in Michigan or Ohio except as a prisoner!

Later came a report that Admiral Hardy had been ordered to destroy Stonington, Connecticut and had sailed with four ships near the town. He had sent a messenger with a white flag to tell the Selectmen he would give the inhabitants just one hour in which to leave Stonington. They asked themselves what they had done that their towns must be burned. Nothing. However, the Selectmen had great courage and they sent back word to Admiral Hardy that they would fight to the end. Sending their aged men, women and children back into the country, the young and able-bodied men dragged to the top of a hill overlooking the harbor, two old eighteen pounder cannon, two six pounders and one four pounder. They had only a small amount of powder and but few balls. Lieutenant Hough was in command. Admiral Hardy could not get his ships near enough to use his cannon, but at sunset when the sea was calm, he had his bomb vessel towed close to shore and began shelling the town under cover of night. The Stonington men quickly dragged one of their cannon out upon a point, threw up some breastworks, rammed two balls into the muzzle with a heavy charge of powder behind them, and sent the charge crashing into the British ships. This drove them away for a while, but, when morning dawned, back came the Dispatch, an English ship, and opened fire on them. Jeremiah Holmes, an elderly man, who had been a prisoner on a British man of war, knew how to manage guns and was in charge of that old cannon. He sighted and fired a charge plumb into the side of the Dispatch, and kept up his good work until his ammunition was exhausted.

"Shall we surrender?" asked a faint-hearted citizen.

"Not while I live," shouted Holmes, driving a spike into the vent of the cannon, while shots of the enemy flew thick and fast.

Later, they obtained six more kegs of powder. The Stonington men dragged the cannon down off the hill to the blacksmith's shop, drew the spike from the vent hole, then dragged it back onto the hill again, where Holmes sent shot after shot into the Dispatch and damaged it so badly that its Captain was obliged to order it back out of reach. Two more ships sailed up and opened fire, but the old cannon sent back its reply. The British fired shell after shell into Stonington, setting homes on fire, but the brave men of the town put out the fires and fought on. After three days, the British gave up and sailed away with twenty men killed and fifty wounded. Only one man from Stonington was killed. The whole country rang with praise for Jeremiah Holmes. This incident gave renewed courage to the people of New England. Even Hannah took heart and often hummed a line or two of "A drop of brandy, Oh", the song all the young boys were singing around the town.

As winter advanced, the cold and the poor condition of the roads prevented much travel or communication from coast to inland towns. In February, the second child, Lois, arrived in the Parker family. Hannah's father and mother, Deacon and Jane Larrabee, came over to see the little girl and tried to cheer their forlorn daughter. Poor Hannah mourned the fact that William had not known little Lois was on the way and would probably never see her now.

"What's to become of us all, father?"

"We are in God's hands. He will never leave nor forsake us. You know, dear child, 'not a sparrow falleth, but the Father knows'", replied the good old Deacon, whose faith had been sorely tried many times before.

"Come, let's eat a bite, folks, and get cheered up a little," said Rebecca. "Let's have a cup o' hot tea 'n' some gingerbread. I know tea's mighty expensive and mighty scarce, but I've got a little put by fer a special occasion. Some William brought from Chiny, and I've made some gingerbread from a rule Betsy Staples sent down to us. She calls it "Muster gingerbread". It's cheap t' make," and proudly offering them a plate full of good generous squares, she explained, "Th' shiny stuff on top is made by bilin' t'gether half a cup o' molasses with half a cup o' cream till it's fairly thick. Put in a little butter 'n' let it cool. Then spread it on top o' th' gingerbread." Then as an after-thought, she added, "I call it tol'rable."

"How d'ye make the gingerbread?" asked Jane Larrabee.

"Let's see, now. Ye take a cup o' molasses, or ye c'n use maple syrup, half a cup o' sour milk, half a cup o' good thick cream, big pinch o' salleratus, yes a big one. 'Bout two, really. She said she put in a heapin' teaspoon full. Then — well, there, — where was I?"

"Ye jest got t' th' salleratus," replied Jane.

"Oh, yes," said Rebecca. "When ye put in a good pinch o' salt 'n' another o' ginger. She said almost as much ginger as salleratus, that is, if ye had it. Ye see, the ain't none o' th' Stapleses ever gone t' sea, so they don't have much spice, same's we do. I'm goin' t' send some o' ourn up t' her soon's anybuddy goes up th' river. S'pose ye got all you need, ain't ye, Jane? Ye see, William always brings back a lot when he comes home from a trip. Th' last time he come, he brought ginger, nutmeg, cashey, cloves, 'n' th' greatest lot o' indigo. I told him we had enough o' that now t' do all our colorin' fer th' next five years."

"Mebbe it's lucky ye have, Bec," said Benjamin, "fer William may not go t' India agin very soon. If this blasted war keeps up, ther won't be nobuddy goin' nowhere."

"Oh, Benjamin, don't talk that way. 'Course he'll be goin' t' sea agin, if he wants t', but I hope he'll be content t' farm it, after this. This war can't last much longer. Oh yes, 'n' there's more t' th' gingerbread. I got off th' track a little. Ye want t' put in enough flour t' make it so't ye can handle it, but jest as soft as possible. Softern doughnut dough, a mite, but so's ye c'n flip it right off th' cake board right on t' yer baker sheet, 'n' not break it if ye c'n help it, but if ye do, jest pat it t'gether a little. 'Twon't hurt it any. An' don't have yer oven too hot. Bake it when th' bricks are cooled off a little. Then, as I said, when it's cool, spread on that biled 'lasses 'n' cream. Yes, there ain't no question that William's a-doin' alright somewhere," said Rebecca. Slyly winking at Jane, she continued, "Hannah must cheer up, I say. You'n I've seen worse'n this in our day, 'n' I tell her we mustn't b'lieve but William's safe 'n' sound wherever he is. He's always bin able t' crawl out through a mighty small hole, 'n' my opinion is that he ain't changed yit."

Hannah then smilingly said, "Let's drink our tea from my Chelsea cups, my wedding present from William, in his honor. I know 'twould please him, if he knew."

"You women c'n have yer tea, but me 'n' th' Deacon will have our gingerbread with a pitcher o' cider," said Benjamin.

About this time, Captain Seth was ordered to Portland, where he remained several weeks. Upon his return to Upper Street, he related a story he had heard that greatly amused John and Betsy.

He said, "Things have been happening up in grandfather's town in Scituate lately. A feller told me a British ship come into th' harbor, plannin' t' burn two vessels loaded with flour. The Scituate men were all back in th' fields workin', but th' Bates girls Abigail 'n' Rebecca, saw th' ship 'n' knew what it was up to. They thought the'd see what they could do t' save th' flour. Rebecca is eighteen 'n' Abigail fourteen. Rebecca c'n play th' fife 'u' Abigail c'n beat th' drum, th' feller said. Th' ship put out her small bo'ts 'n' they was movin' to'ds th' shore. Th' girls hid behind some rocks 'n' Rebecca struck up Yankee Doodle 'n' Abigail beat hell out o' that drum 'n' shouted "Right face, March". Wal sir, he said them men heard it 'n' stopped rowin'. The officers listened, then turned right 'round 'n' went back t' th' ship, jest in season, too, fer Captain Bates was rushin' in from th' field t' open up his old six pounder on 'em. That feller told me them two girls c'n have anything they want in Scituate, or Boston, either. He laughed fit t' kill hisself, said he'd known 'em all his life 'n' they was sure likely girls."

This story of the Scituate girls made John and Betsy laugh for weeks, in fact all winter. They passed the good story along and half the people in Turner and Greene were laughing with them inside a week.

For more than a year, the war had continued and there had been no fighting on Maine soil or along the coast. People began to take courage. There was much political disturbance and other troubles, but the Indians had remained quiet through the Province. Due to rumors without any foundation in truth, the people had been dreadfully worried at times. Women and children kept close to their homes, where loaded muskets stood in handy corners, ready to be used if necessary. The women knew how to use them, and a boy must be very young indeed not to know how to shoot. Men took their guns along with their hoes, scythes, rakes and other farming tools, as they had since the first white man stepped foot on American soil. But the Androscoggin folk began to believe they were well out of danger from both the Indians and the British.

CHAPTER XIV

BLACK ACCENTS, "PETER 'N RHODY"

On May 3, 1813, at Fort Meigs, the gallant Harrison defended an embankment and enclosure against four times his own numbers. The tyrant Proctor, with his English and blood-thirsty Indians, were forced to retire. Harrison victoriously led his army into Fort Malden, and recaptured Detroit.

One night after the Parkers were asleep, a light tap sounded on the door of Benjamin's kitchen. At first no one inside the house heard it, but, the second time it sounded, Hannah, a light sleeper, was awakened. Quickly throwing a light shawl over her shoulders, she crept to the bedroom of Benjamin and Rebecca. On her way she had to pass a window that looked out upon the yard in front of the door, and she could see two human forms standing there. Their faces looked very dark in the moonlight. Her heart froze in her breast. She put one hand on Benjamin's shoulder, lightly shaking him, the other she placed over his mouth.

"Sh—, Father Parker, there's some one at the door. Two of them. I think they're Indians. They've knocked twice," she whispered.

Old Benjamin came out of his bed with a leap, but without a sound. As he stepped into his boots, he whispered, "Hannah, give me my musket, there in th' corner."

He was wearing a linsey-woolsey night shirt. Straightening to his full height, squaring his shoulders, he stepped to the door, unbarred it and looked into two black faces. In the uncertain light, he did not know what or who it could be standing there, but after what seemed an age, a deep voice said,

"Oh, please massa. Please help us'ns. We is pore cullud folks. Run away and tired. Come all th' way from Virginny. Some folks below heah done tell us you's kind to everybody, an' me an' my wife Rhody done walk all de way heah. We uns'll work h'ad fer you all. Work in de fiels, work in de house. We uns don' ask no money. Jes food an' clo'se. Please Suh, cain't we cum in?"

This was the queerest situation Benjamin had ever had to face.

To be sure, they did need help, but they had so little to eat these days. If they divided with these two, would there be enough to go around?

For a moment he hesitated, then he said, "Come in. Come in 'n' rest fer th' night, anyway."

As they managed to drag their tired bodies in through the door, Rebecca appeared fully dressed, apparently ready for any emergency.

She said, "Good evenin', folks. Have a chair. What's yer names?"

"We ain't got no names 'cept Peter an' Rhody," the man replied.

Rebecca brought bread, milk, cheese and gingerbread from the pantry and placed it on the table for them. They ate ravenously, their great eyes rolling from side to side. When they had eaten every last crumb, Rebecca said, as she gave them a lighted candle, "Now you two go up that ladder into th' loft 'n' git some rest. Be careful o' that candle 'n' don't set th' house afire."

After the colored people had climbed the ladder and closed the trap door, Hannah came from the darkness of her bedroom and, throwing her arms around Rebecca, said,

"Oh, I'm so glad you took those poor creatures in and fed them. All this time I've been just prayin' you would, for, who knows, p'raps if we're kind to them, somebody'll be good to William wherever he is."

They said good night and soon the house was silent once more. Rebecca remained awake for a while, planning how she could manage to feed them all. She was comforted by remembering the words of her Lord, "Tis more blessed to give, than to receive".

The following morning, Benjamin had a long talk with Peter. He learned that the day he and Rhoda were married, his master sold him to a man in Tennessee, but he escaped, taking Rhoda with him. Benjamin decided he had good cause for running away, and told him, as long as he was a good honest boy, he and his wife could stay with them. Also, that he would give them a name, and hereafter they would be Peter and Rhoda Freeman. Benjamin and Rebecca never regretted this act of theirs. The Freemans stayd with them as long as they lived, afterward going with William and his family, whom they served faithfully all of their lives.

On September 5th, 1813, about thirty miles east of Portland, a bloody encounter off Pemaquid Point between the American brig Enterprise and the British brig Boxer occured. Captain Burrows, with four men of the Enterprise, and Captain Blythe, with seven of his crew on the Boxer, were killed. Both ships suffered tremendous damage and it was with great difficulty that the victorius Enterprise sailed into Portland Harbor with her prize. Much credit can be given to the Americans for their chivalry as they buried both Captains side by side and erected a fine monument for each on Munjoy Hill in Portland. There were those, of course, who did not feel as kindly disposed toward the English Captain, and, as usual, somebody wrote a song entitled "The Sons of Liberty".

There were ten men wounded on the Enterprise, one of them William Parker. A piece of iron shot from the cannon of the enemy tore through the flesh of his upper left arm, lacerating it horribly. It was a close call. The ship's surgeon was as good as any of his day, but this was not too good. It was several weeks before William was able to go home on "Sick leave." The people of Greene heard the news of the victory off Pemaquid, little realizing William Parker was aboard the Enterprise.

One afternoon in late October, when Rebecca saw a man with his arm in a sling coming slowly up the road, she said, "Well, here comes some poor soul that's been wounded by them wicked men from 'cross th' seas. Come Hannah 'n' see if ye can see who 'tis."

"Jest let me lay the baby in her cradle 'n' I will," answered the obedient girl.

"As she walked toward the open door, they both heard a familiar voice lustily singing, "We boxed her up t' Portland 'n' moored her off th' town, jest t' show th' Sons o' Liberty the Boxer of renown."

"Oh, Mother! 'Tis William. 'Tis William!" she screamed, as she ran like the wind down the hill and threw her arms around him. What's happened t' ye?" she cried.

"Jest a scratch from a British tom cat," he replied, but later, when he showed her his wound, Hannah fainted.

After supper, when the family, which now included Peter and Rhoda, were gathered in the kitchen, Benjamin asked William if he went to Halifax aboard the Chesapeake.

"No, thank God, I didn't. I was lucky, too. Prob'ly ye didn't hear of it, but the Chesapeake was tied up in Boston Harbor fer a week or so after we come back from cruise. When they wouldn't divide up with us sailors the prize money due us from several ships we'd taken, there was a pile o' trouble on board 'n' darn near mutiny. Lots o' th' boys got drunk, left th' ship 'n' fergot t' come back. Cap'n Lawrence was new t' us. Jest been appointed t' c'mand th' Chesapeake. Good feller, too, but a little too thin-skinned t' stand bein' laughed at. So, when Cap'n Broke of the Shannon, anchored jest outside Boston Harbor he sent a letter by boat t' Cap'n Lawrence, challengin' him t' fight. He accepted the dare. The Shannon carried more guns than th' Chesapeake 'n' our sailors never had a chance t' learn what Cap'n Lawrence would do in time o' battle. As th' time drew nearer t' go out t' meet th' Shannon, th' boys drank more'n more. Their dissatisfaction o' losin' their prize money 'n' not having much confidence in Cap'n Lawrence made 'em desp'rate. I happened t' be one sailor sober enough t' go on errand fer th' Cap'n. He wanted t' send a message t' his friend who lived in Boston to tell him 'bout th' comin' battle with th' Shannon. His friend lived quite a distance from th' wharf, 'n' 'twas more'n an hour 'fore I found his house. He took some time t' answer Cap'n Lawrence's letter 'n' when I reached th' dock, there wa'nt any Chesapeake there 'n' she was well out o' th' harbor. A strong wind had come up in her favor 'n' whether it was fer that reason or perhaps th' Cap'n forgot he'd sent me ashore, he left afore he planned, I don't know. Anyway, there I was. No ship, no nuthin'. The Enterprise had been docked side ' us fer two days. Once I had talked with Cap'n Burrows, her commander. I stood there watchin' th' Chesapeake goin' out o' sight 'n' Cap'n hailed me from his forred deck 'n' asked me where I'd been. I told him 'n' he offered me a place on th' Enterprise. I've been ther ever since 'n' thought I was mighty lucky I was left behind, fer th' poor old Chesapeake is now rottin' in Halifax. So are all her crew that escaped death in th' battle with th' Shannon, 'n' I guess they wish they'd died then, too. I heard that poor Cap'n Lawrence said, as he was a-dyin', 'Boys, don't give up th' ship". He was a brave man, I think'."

"What about the battle off Pemaquid?" asked Hannah. "That's what I want t' hear 'bout."

William replied, "I don't want t' talk 'bout it, Hannah. I've seen plenty o' bloodshed sence I enlisted, saw plenty afore, but this slaughterin' o' human lives on both th' Enterprise 'n' Boxer is somethin' I don't want t' think about.

Finally Benjamin said, " 'Pears t' me we ain't gittin' much peace

(151)

on airth yit, that kind th' angels sung 'bout s'long ago. Seems 'sif things is growin' worse 'n' worse ev'ry day."

"They ain't growin' wusser fer us, Marssa Benjamin, Me 'n' Rhody is gittin' betterer 'n' betterer. No use talkin', de good Lord sent us up here alright. You all been so good to us, we both rather be daid than go back to Virginny. You all s'pose dey ever fin' us up here, Sir? asked poor Peter.

"No danger, Peter. No danger o' that. They's altogether too busy fightin' th' British t' trouble 'bout you," replied Benjamin.

As the beautiful days of early November began to turn cold and a chill crept into the air, William decided his arm would not allow him to return to service that winter. He would be of no use if he went. So he comforted himself with the fact that he could remain at home with his family till spring. His mother took charge of the treatment of his wound. She was, like all women of her time, fairly well skilled in such matters. The home remedies they used, often did help. Sometimes they hindered the progress of recovery, but there was no alternative, and those who used them were at least benefited mentally, which also probably helped physically. Women of the Androscoggin Valley were no exception and they had remedies for all ills. One was a salve they made by simmering together beeswax, beebalm and mutton tallow. The beebalm, an herb resembling mint with red or lavender blossoms is often seen in Perrenial gardens of today. This salve, Rebecca used on William's arm, kept the still-sloughing wound clean, and good old mother nature did the rest.

"It was difficult for William Parker to content himself there in Greene doing the little he was able to accomplish with one hand. When he found fault because he could do so little Peter would say, "Massah William, I do work for three hands. You all jes' let yo' pore arm get well. Then you all kin go fight."

The long winter of trial came gradually to an end. With the passing of March the snow disappeared. One sunny April morning William gathered his belongings, bade his dear ones good bye and rode away. Peter rode with him as far as Brunswick to bring back the horses.

The British wished to acquire a direct land route from Halifax to Quebec. Sir John Sherbrook, Governor of Nova Scotia, was ordered to occupy the Province of Maine as far as the Penobscot.

Through his generosity, an order was given not to burn Bangor.

However, the banks at Bath and Wiscasset ordered all coin removed to places of safety.

By the fall of 1814 all land east of the Penobscot had fallen into the hands of the enemy, Bangor and Hampden included. Bath people voted to pay its soldiers eight dollars per month payable when the money was available. Prices soared with business failures everywhere. In many cases actual want existed. Shipping news reeked with murderous depredations of pirates. Bath seamen were often pirate targets, but still courageously managed to "Sail on and on, and on!"

Chapter XV

GREAT DAY IN THE MORNING

Up in District No. 4, the Whites always so active, learned at that season there wasn't enough to do to keep them busy so began to make plans. For several days after Rachel and her daughter had decided to begin the making of the trousseau, young Rachel was unusually quiet and her mother feared something was troubling her. All through the long months she had waited to hear from Philip, she had never complained; but now it was evident to the mother that she was becoming discouraged.

"Don't ye want y'r weddin' dress made o' th' fine linen, or would ye rather wait, 'n' try t' git somethin' different from down country later on?" asked the mother.

"Oh, yes, mother, I shall love to have my dress of the linen you've spun, and if I ever wear it, I'll always treasure it 'n' keep it for my daughters to wear—but—"

"But what, daughter?"

"Lately, mother, I can't help thinkin' I shall never wear the dress. Maybe Philip will never come back. I have always felt sure he would, till lately—but now—now."

She covered her face with her tiny hands and cried softly.

"Don't cry, little lady. Y'r man'll come back. I'm sure he will. Ye've been a patient, good little girl all through these years, 'n' don't ye give up now. I know its hard. Life is always hard, 'n' sometimes when th' night looks th' blackest, they's a wonderful sunrise jest beyent. Soon's yer father 'n' th' boys gits th' crops in, yer father'll go down t' Dixfield, 'n' mebbe he'll hear some good news. Let's we make ourselves b'lieve its so 'n' twill be lots easier. I've done this more'n once in my life 'n' it helped me over some rough places tew."

"Did it always turn out th' way ye wanted?"

"Well, not always, but sometimes it did. I was a deal happier while I was believin' of it anyway."

When Sam learned from his wife of their daughter's growing

uneasiness, he decided to go at once and get what information he could.

"The' plantin' c'n jest as well wait a day or two. There won't nawthin' come up fer two weeks any way. Th' last o' May is jest as cold up here, as th' middle o' th' month down t' Lisbon. I 'spect th' wind comin' off them old icebugs up north, is what does it. They's all o' two weeks' diff'rence in this part o' th' country, 'n' that on th' coast."

True to his word, Sam saddled the young mare whose black satin coat gleamed in the bright sunlight. She reared several times, nearly unseating him before he could pull her down and get started up the hill. Sam's animals were always well fed and full of life. Men of his happy, generous nature are always good providers. Sam ate well and saw to it that all around him did the same.

At noon, when he walked into the Tavern after a fine ride in the wonderfully invigorating air, he was ready to eat a good dinner, and he hoped to learn encouraging news of war conditions. He too had been playing Rachel's game of "Makin' b'lieve", and now expected to learn the truth. Amos, as usual, greeted him with a smile as did the other men gathered there; but Sam immediately sensed somthing was wrong.

"Wal, boys, how is things?" he asked.

For a few moments nobody spoke.

Then Amos said, "Have a swaller o' rum on me, Sam, while we wait for dinner, 'n' we'll tell ye; for ye might's well know things aint goin' right."

Sam dreaded to hear more, but he had come for this purpose, so must listen as Amos mixed the drink. John Eustis, a lively young son of the Deacon, not wanting to keep Sam longer in suspense, told him, Great Britain, realizing there was no chance for peace with New England, had the week before, on April 25th, blockaded its port and all others in the country. They had seized Eastport and a serious invasion of the eastern part of the Province seemed imminent. Word had been received, that Sir John Sherbrook, Governor of Nova Scotia, had been ordered to occupy all territory east of the Penobscot; but nobody could be sure that this could be true or just rumor.

As the inhabitants of the little town came and went, Sam soon realized conditions were too serious to allow of any light conversation. The visit which he had "b'l'eved" would be such a pleasant one, had proved to be entirely opposite. As he paid for his dinner, Amos remembered to hand him a letter addressed to "Miss Rachel White, c/o Mr. Amos Trask, Dixfield, Province of Maine". It had arrived by Post Rider at Christmas time nearly six months before, but there had been no opportunity to send it to Webb, a circumstance Amos regretted.

Sam lost no time in starting for home. The letter would make Rachel happy and he hoped would give them all a better understanding of national affairs. The grave conditions that threatened the Province, that he must report to his family and neighbors, caused him to question whether it would have been better, if he had never left home. Before there was always the possibility of improvement; but now the dreadful question of whether the enemy would continue its march westward and perhaps be accompanied by Indians, was too much for Sam. He could not think of it all without a shudder. Heretofore they had felt some degree of security from Indians; but with those wild men of the forest and the King's well fed and splendidly equipped soldiers, what chance had a handful of settlers in the woods, living miles apart, untrained and unequipped?

The first three miles, Sam hurried the mare along over a fair road, but from there on the hills made any speed impossible and Sam rode slumped in his saddle, a picture of dejection. When he reached the top of Potter Hill, he was surprised to come upon a family moving toward Webb. There were five of them. The father, mother, a daughter about fifteen years of age and two younger children. The man said his name was Whitney and they had driven their ox teams and horse from Lewiston. Through correspondence with Caleb Holt he had bought a piece of land west of the ridge upon which Sam and his family lived. Said he had visited the place the year before, seen Ebenezer Hutchinson, who was settled near, learned from him the names of several nearby settlers, and from his description had decided it was a good location in which to settle. Whitney said he had become so concerned living within the town of Lewiston, which was so accessible to an invading army, that he had decided to go further into the woods where he hoped they would be safe. Sam related their experience of the year before, with "Th' feller who cried 'Injun'. He took our money 'n' skeedadled". Whitney agreed with Sam that Webb was not far enough north to insure any great degree of safety, after all.

As they traveled along together it was satisfying to Sam to hear news of Lewiston and Greene folk. Whitney had stopped at the home of Philip Judkins to inquire if it were best to remain on the east side of the river and had learned of Philip's and Sam's prospective logging venture. He was glad to know there would be an opportunity to find work for himself and oxen later on. Their advancement over the road to Webb was very slow, but the low condition of Sam's spirits did not seem to warrant his hurrying, even though he bore Philip's letter to Rachel.

They had traveled together for over two hours, when Whitney said, "Jest as we was leavin' Judkin's door yard, a tall young feller, looked like a soldier, come along, 'n' by th' way th' women folks kissed 'im 'n' carried on, I jedged he must be one o' th' family. They called 'im Philip too. So I 'sposed—"

"Wal, sufferin' old tom cats. Ye s'posed right. Godfrey Mighty, let me git by y'r team. I want t' go faster'n yew do. Now was that boy all right? Wa'n't hurt 'r nawthin', was he?"

"Wal, he had his arm in a sling, but he walked along, smart as a cricket," replied Whitney.

In less than an hour Sam galloped into his yard, never stopping to remove saddle or bridle from the black mare, but with a cheerful "Hello!" rushed into the log house, his face beaming.

"Rachel, Marm, Rachel daughter, look at this; but before ye read it, let me tell ye' Philip's home. Philip's home 'n' must be in fair shape, fer he walked in on his two feet. I've seen a man jest t'day, that seen 'im yest'day when he come to his father's house with his arm in a sling. Whitney didn't think he was hurt bad, 'n' ye better be thankin' God, he was hurt. 'Cause he's home now, where he's goin' t'be needed 'n' soon p'r'aps. Fer the enemy have come over th' line from th' east. Moved right int' th' Province, clear t' th' Penobscot, 'n' God knows how much further b' this time. This man Whitney, I told ye 'bout, is jest movin' in. Is goin' t' settle over back o' this hill, down near Eben Hutchinson's, 'n' he says half he come up here fer, was t' git away from Lewiston, 'cause he b'ieves th' English is goin' t' march right in on 'em down thar. He says he thinks I'm right. Th' only place we'd all be safe, would be right round th' North Pole settin' on 'n' icebug."

Young Sam, who had taken care of the mare and had come in

(157)

to hear the news, asked "When ye want t' start movin', father? Shall I bring th' sled bodies around here 'n' start packin'?"

Sam grinned knowingly and said, "No ye needn't do no sech thing, but if I's you, I'd happen down th' back side o' this ridge some day 'fore long, 'n' offer t' help Whitney build his log house. Ye might think 'twas worthwhile."

So intent were they in their thoughts of a possible invasion west of the Penobscot, that young Sam entirely forgot his father's suggestion that he offer his services to the new settler Whitney. He had recovered from his loss of Betsy Judkins and was not especially interested in any matrimonial schemes of his father's.

Rachel and her daughter now made their needles fly. There were yards of lace to be knitted, long seams to be sewn, embroideries to be stitched, as well as tiny hems. Rachel was an expert with her needle and insisted that her daughter make every stitch a perfect one. The shirts and all underwear were made of the snow white linen. Young Rachel was so thrilled and happy. The prospects of a visit from Philip caused the hours to speed on wings. Every unusual sound from outside would send her running to the door. One morning when a rider did come into the yard, she rushed out so suddenly, meeting him near the door, that she almost threw herself into the arms of a man who proved to be Whitney. He had come to ask for help in building his log house.

The next morning Sam and each of his boys with axes on their shoulders went over the ridge. Young Sam never regretted that trip, for he loved at first sight, pretty little Lydia Whitney. Every day he went to help her father, not only to build a log house, but also a log barn and induced several of his friends to aid in the project. Every day he became firmer in the hope and determination that Lydia would become his wife. He was twenty-three years old and his time was his own. In the past he had only worked for himself when his father did not need his services, but now he had an incentive that would drive him harder than ever before. A steady worker, he went quietly about his tasks, leaving most of the conversation to his father, but of late he had changed and his loquaciousness became noticeable to the family.

One evening his mother called her husband aside, saying, "What's come over Sam? That Whitney aint been a bringin' no rum into th' settlement, has he?"

"No Marm, he haint. Ye c'n smooth ye'r feathers right down.

Whitney don't bring no rum up here, but he brought somethin' that's cheered up our Sam, more'n that ever would. I kep my mouth shet 'bout it, 'cause ye allus carry on so 'f I ever mention sech a thing; but I'll tell ye now Marm, I never see no duck take t' th' water any fastern'n Sam's takin' t' this Lydie Whitney, 'n' by gosh, she's arousin', good lookin' gal, smart's a whip, 'n' — Ah—Dum—Dee, Ah—Dum—Dee."

"Wal, I'm glad t' hear it. Sam's mooned round ever sence Betsy give 'im th' mitten. I've pitied th' poor feller, but wa'n't nawthin' I c'ld do. All these girls up here was spoke for. How old is this Lydie?" asked the mother.

"Old 'nough," replied Sam.

"Guess we better dig some dandelion greens t'day, girls," announced the thrifty mother. "The're gitten t'be 'bout th' right size, 'n' I see there's a bud er two showin' on some that's growin' over near th' barn. If we git more'n we want t' eat now, I think I'll salt down some. Marthy Kittredge told me last year, she salts all she c'n git. That is, she does if she c'n git th' salt. I wish we had a store in Webb. Somebuddy said a feller by the name o' Morrison was goin' t' set up one on t'other side, in a log house James Houghton owns. Hope t' th' Lord he does. Yer father went t' Dixfield 'n' never brought back a grain o' salt. Don't 'spose he c'ld think o' nawthin' that day but th' British a-comin', 'n' I'd know as I wonder. But they don't seem t' be comin' though, dew they? I 'spect they're makin' some awful big preparations down country t' meet 'em, if they dew. Prob'ly that's why Philip don't get hisself up here, or mebbe his arm's worse'n what Whitney claimed—Well, speak of the devil 'n' ye'll hear his chains rattle. Look up th' hill Rachel 'n' see who's a-comin'."

Down the road he came. A man now. No longer a boy. He rode to the side of the beautiful girl who had so patiently waited through the years.

He folded her in his arms and said, "Thank God, dear Rachel, you are safe and well. Thank God we have both lived to see this day."

He kissed her over and over, looking into the sweet face as though fearing it might vanish from his sight.

"But you. How is it with you darling? How about your arm? I thought you had it in a sling. Is it well so soon?" asked the worried girl.

(159)

"Its very nearly well, but my right arm is all right. See?" said he as he crushed her to his side again, smothering her with his kisses. "What made you think it wasn't?"

"That man, Whitney, said you had it in a sling when he came through Greene, 'n' we thought, we was afraid, ye see we didn't know."

"There wasn't much to know, my girl. I got a bullet through it that splintered the bone and it took so long to heal, my commander sent me home. Told me to stay this summer and fall. Use it what I could to get the strength back and if necessary, wait till spring before I joined my regiment. We drove the British and Injuns out of the northwest country last year. That's when I wrote you."

"And I got it last month," laughed Rachel.

"Well, I've been in the hospital at Buffalo since, trying to get this arm healed up. Our troops were there all last winter drilling under General Brown. I expect there's goin' to be some awful fightin' this summer, for they plan to take Fort Erie. I wanted to be in on it, but I guess I can't."

"Thank God ye can't," said the mother. She already loved Philip like a son and was thankful he had come home, even at the cost of a severe injury.

That evening Rachel and her lover were again allowed the privacy of the high backed settle by the fire. As she sat, tightly held by his good arm, she bashfully confided the fact that her wedding dress was nearly finished.

"You darling," he said. "Its June. There's still another week left. Can't you finish it in season? You once said you'd like to be married in June. I've saved every penny I possibly could since the day I left you, the fall of 1811. I could make a holdin' payment on some of this land, same as your brother Sam has done. In time we can pay for it all. Go wake up your mother and father. See what they say. Let's settle it tonight."

"Ye aint got t' wake us up," said Sam, stepping into his boots and pulling his jacket on over his night shirt. "We couldn't help a hearin' what ye said. Pile out o' that bed, Marm, 'n' put a blankit around ye. Le's talk it over."

"Oh mother," cried Rachel, "do ye think we could finish that dress this week?"

"Of course ,darter. We c'n sit up a little later nights t' work, if we have t'."

"Wal, that's all settled. Tell ye what we'll do Philip. I had plenty o' logs left from th' barn, 'n' we'll build on a room fer ye. A little bed room. An' ye c'n stay here with us till ye git ye'r own log house built. Godfrey Mighty! Marm, aint this a goin' t' be good t' have 'em right here with us? Ah—Dum—I'm hungry, Marm. Git out some jonny bread 'n' milk. You young ones lay down 'n' go t' sleep. No 'taint mornin'. Ye can't git up now. What are we doin'? Wal, we're gittin' ready for a weddin'. No, not t'night, next week."

Just then Phenewel bounced out of the bunk beside Naomi and called for bread and milk. Cynthia, awakened by the hullabaloo, started to cry. Inside of fifteen minutes Mother Rachel had slipped a dress over her nightgown and placed noggins of bread and milk on the table for them all, young Sam and James sleepily joining the rest.

Pandemonium reigned for an hour. Gradually the family returned to their beds; with the exception of father and mother, Rachel and Philip, who sat making their plans until the good old sun took a hand and started lighting the eastern sky.

"What's the use of goin' to bed now?" asked Philip. "The thing for me to do, is go back to Greene and get my best clothes. I don't think I'll stand up in these old things to get married to you, in all that lace and fine linen."

"Wal, if that's what ye'r goin' to dew. Ye c'n ask your folks t' come up t' th' weddin'," said the mother.

After a good breakfast of bacon, corn bread, "rye and Injun coffee", Philip went back down river. He reached Monroe's Tavern too late to go further that night and passed a pleasant evening reminiscing with the jovial host, and describing some of his experiences with the Northwestern Army. At Greene the following late forenoon, where he had seen the family up in arms over the coming event, it was decided that Hannah and Philip would accept Rachel's invitation to be present at the wedding ceremony; but Betsy declined with thanks and asked her mother to convey her regrets to the Whites.

That afternoon, at Parker's store, Philip bought a gold wedding ring for his bride, then he went to the home of Reverend Wyman and engaged him to come to Webb the following Sunday to officiate at the wedding.

Hannah carefully sponged and pressed Philip's "best close". She had made them from wool she had spun, woven and colored a very dark blue just before he went with the Army and was quite fearful that they would be too small for him now; but they proved to be no tighter than the fashion of the day demanded and when he tried them on, his appearance made his mother justly proud, both of her achievement and of him, for he was a handsome young man. She washed, starched and ironed to a surprising degree of perfection his "boiled shirt" and stock collar. His boots were blackened with mutton tallow and lamp black and then polished until they shone. With his black silk tie and handkerchief of linen, she had made from her own flax, he certainly would look "well 'nough".

The third day he returned to Webb with not only his wedding clothes but all his other worldly goods which were not many compared with the outfit of a young man of today. It included his underwear for both winter and summer, several pairs of woolen stockings, a deerskin jacket, coonskin cap, four woolen shirts and as many made of linsey-woolsey, his razor and comb, his broad axe, small axe, adze, and a whip saw. His father told him to take only his side arms and he would bring his army musket when he and Hannah came a few days later.

While Philip was away, young Sam conceived the idea of adding a bedroom to the log house before the wedding. His father thought it could not be done within a week; but the young man was so fired with enthusiasm and thoughts of his own wedding at some distant day, no amount of hard work could frighten him. So he rode to the home of his friend, young Eben Newman, told his story and the fun began.

When Philip came back down over the hill, to his amazement a half-built room appeared on the back side of Sam White's log hous.e

"This is our weddin' present t' ye," cried young Sam. "Trouble is, ye've got t' help finish it, now ye've come. If ye'd stayed away a day or two longer, I guess we could of finished it."

"Well, I guess I shall be mighty glad to help do the rest of it, boys," said the prospective bridegroom, then added, " I wish I had time to make a bed. I think that would please Rachel."

"Mother's goin' t' let ye have her other one for a while. Ye know she's got two. Thing I wish ye'd do, is finish cuttin' th' door through. Father says he'll go up t' Holman's mill an' git boards fer a door. S'pose ye could make one that 'ud shet?"

"I s'pose I could," answered Philip.

When young Eben told his mother, Sarah, of the approaching marriage of Rachel to the Judkins boy, she said, "Well, Eben, that young fellow has used his eyes, while you don't appear to be seeing anything but crops. I can't imagine how you could allow such a beauty as Rachel to be carried away by a man who has not been near her in three years."

"Mother, my chances with that girl wouldn't have been any better if he had stayed away thirty years. That question was all settled 'fore they ever came to this town—so young Sam told me."

"Well, Eben, I want to send over a couple of fat geese to help out with the dinner. You'd better kill a pair right away and we'll hang them up to age till the day before the weddin'. Then you can take them over. You can tell Mrs. White so she can depend upon havin' them."

The evening after Philip arrived, he took young Rachel for a walk along the ridge, thinking it might be a good plan for her to have some fresh air. She had sewed nearly every moment for more than a week and admitted she was a little tired.

"Let's walk up toward Naomi's bear den," suggested Philip.

They had walked only a few rods when a large doe stepped into the road above. She did not see them so Philip ran back to the cabin, took Sam's gun from the hooks above the fireplace, snatched the powder horn, loaded the old fowling piece and rushed back up the hill. When he reached Rachel's side there was no deer in sight, but she told him where it had disappeared. Very quietly they walked on, entered the open space beside the road where the deer was last seen and followed. As they both wore moccasins, they made no sound. Soon through the maples and other hardwoods that grew in a strip along the hillside, they saw the mother deer, and with her two fawns. Philip raised his gun, took careful aim, fired, and down fell one of the fawns. The other one with its mother ran, their white tails waving as they disappeared. Philip reloaded as quickly as possible and started toward the dead deer, when a tremendous buck stepped into view. His great antlers were in the velvet stage, making them appear larger than usual. He lifted his magnificent head, stamped a fore foot and blew a challenge. Philip's training and marksmanship had not been in vain. The gun he carried was of ancient manufacture but there was in the defiance of this handsome forest creature a quality to bring forth the best effort in any man. With a little smile on his face, he accepted the dare of the courageous buck, aimed for the spot just below the ear and fired. The huge animal jumped forward as if to charge his antagonist, but the bullet had taken effect. Philip's aim had been true. The monarch of the woods fell prone beside his offspring.

"You better call your brothers and tell them to bring along their knives if they want some meat for the wedding," Philip told the excited girl. Soon two deer hung in the tree waiting to be cooked for the marriage feast.

"Too bad to kill such a young deer," the elder Rachel said, "but it will be just as tender as chicken. I'll salt down what we don't use of the big one. No use talkin', I'v got t' have more salt t' use, an' what's more, I must burn some corn cobs to git the ashes to use for raisin'. I want t' make some strawb'ry short cake for th' weddin'. I think I gut 'nough white flour that Sarah Newman give me last fall, t' make a good big one. Naomi, you must see 'bout gittin' th' strawb'ries. They're jest right t' pick now on th' side hill. Them I put down last week was jest fine. They'll taste awful good next winter."

Every hour of every day was filled with pleasant tasks for the inhabitants of the log house. Somehow word spread through the neighborhood that young Rachel White was to be married the coming Sabbath. The two fat geese were delivered at the home along with a pair of linen sheets. Young Eben brought them to Rachel and said "Mother told me t' tell ye, these sheets come from Billerica an' her mother made 'em for her weddin' in 1782. My Aunt, Marthy Kittredge, sent over these piller cases t' go with 'em. They sent their best wishes for your happiness, tew, an' said t' tell ye, if they's anything ye want 'em t' dew t' help, jest send word."

Collins Pratt, now a young man about twenty, called to leave a pair of live-goose feather pillows, a present from his mother. John Storer brought on a wagon, the wheels just having been made by James Swett, a pine blanket chest, a gift from his parents. The boards from which the chest was made, had been sawed at Elisha

Holman's mill from trees grown on the Storer farm. The Holts, their nearest neighbors, brought a strip of home woven carpet for the bride. Eben Hutchinson's wife sent a pewter platter. The Whitney's though new-comers to the neighborhood, having a little personal interest in the Whites, believed it warranted their sending Sam's sister a pair of brass candle sticks, a possession long treasured by Mrs. Whitney. Her family had once lived in Boston where they had bought them soon after the close of that other war, from a man named Paul Revere, who kept a shop and foundry where he made many articles from silver and brass. James Swett being informed of the approaching marriage of Sam White's daughter, sent a message that he was making a spinning wheel for her. There would not be time to finish it before the wedding, but she would reecive it soon after.

On Friday, late afternoon, Rachel declared her daughter's trousseau finished, and said "For a pioneer's darter, I think 'twill dew". She tenderly fondled the square lace-edged neck of the white gown which had now almost become a part of her beloved child.

"Bring her happiness, little dress. Bring long life, health and security. Don't let her pathway be as rough as mine has been; but let her man be as good to her as Sam has been to me." A tear dropped from the eyes of this grand New England mother as she returned to the practical duties of cooking, scrubbing and making ready for what is to every mother after her own wedding has passed, the greatest event in her life, the wedding of her own daughter.

Saturday brought more activities to the little home than it had ever known. Everything everywhere was put in the best possible order. Naomi and James had gathered spruce boughs and long strings of Princess Pine with which they decorated the doorway to the new bedroom, making a lovely arch under which the bridal couple would stand. They filled wooden buckets with branches of belated cherry blossoms which they found in the woods and placed them at either side of the door. On the table, on top of the cupboard and on the sill of the open window, they set smaller buckets filled with painted trillium.

About four o'clock, Philip and Hannah Judkins, accompanied by Reverend Thomas Wyman arrived. They had left Green the day before, stayed overnight at Trask Tavern and driven leisurely along since morning. Hannah was not accustomed to riding long distances and her husband thought best for them to take their time and enjoy the hospitality so graciously afforded at the little Inn at Dixfield.

Rachel's supper for her guests and family was typical of all Saturday night suppers in the Province. She served baked beans and brown bread, pickles, Indian pudding with cream, custard pie, seed cookies and tansy cheese; raspberry leaf tea for the grown-ups and milk for the children. The long table was filled to over-flowing, and all had stools or chairs. Reverend Wyman asked a long blessing. After this general conversation began. It was a great event in more ways than one. It was Hannah's first visit to the Whites, the first time she had seen the town where she would eventually come with her husband as they approached the sunset of their lives, to try for the third time to make their fortune. It was also here that her son Philip would settle with his bride and probably spend his days. Hannah wondered if she would again be contented to live in the wilderness. She well knew what it meant. The early days for her and Philip in Wayne had brought many trials; but life in Greene had been easier. Now at sixty, she asked herself if she really felt equal to assume again the strenuous tasks of the wife of a pioneer.

The national situation was the principal topic of conversation among the men. Reverend Wyman, always an optimist, encouraged them with words of assurance including the quotation "The Lord is my light and my salvation. Whom then shall I fear. The Lord is the strength of my life. Of whom then shall I be afraid—" from Psalm XXVII.

After the nourishing meal had been eaten, the young people went outside to enjoy the beautiful June night, while the five elderly people discussed affairs at hand. Reverend Wyman, after obtaining from the two mothers the dates of birth of their children, of their admission to the church and all other questions pertaining to the coming marriage, Rachel informed her guests that the men folks would sleep on the hay in the new barn. The women and little children would remain in the cabin. Then Sam lighted the tin lantern, escorted Reverend Wyman, Philip, young Philip, Sam and James to the hay mow. They were all provided with quilts and pillows and soon slept as peacefully as did Phenewell and little Cynthia inside the log house.

Rachel's second canopy bed now standing in the new bedroom

had been freshly made and the snow white canopy cover adjusted. The chair, Philip's first gift to young Rachel, set beside the chest, her present from the Storers. On the chest, the pair of brass candle sticks. When Hannah was offered the use of the room, she graciously declined the favor, saying it should be first used by the bridal couple. Then going to her traveling bag, she brought out a handsome little gold framed mirror and told Rachel it was to hang over the chest.

"It's one I brought from New Hampshire to my first home in Wayne many years ago," she said.

"Happy is the bride that the sun shines on," quoted Rachel as she kissed her daughter good morning. "It's time you was up. This is one of the loveliest days th' Lord ever made. We must be up 'n a-dewin'. Mr. Wyman's goin' t' preach over t'other side at 'leven o'clock, and he wants ye t' be married at nine sharp, so he c'n git away."

It was then only five o'clock and four hours would seem enough for eating breakfast and dressing for any occasion with some time to spare; but there were many last things to attend to in preparation for a wedding even in those days. Thirteen people to be given breakfast was something of a proposition. Two children, washed, dressed and kept in order, was another. The two Sams and James always needed a once over from the mother, and last, but not least, the wedding feast must be prepared, with all the cooking done at the fireplace. These two geese must be 'cooked to a turn' on the long spit that would hold them both. On another, the hind quarters of the fawn must be roasted. Some one must stand watch over these, turning them very often to prevent burning. Fiddlehead greens was to be one vegetable, served along with carrots and cowhorn potatoes. In her tin kitchen, brought from Lisbon, Rachel would bake the shortcake.

She decided to send the men, including the minister outside the cabin as soon as breakfast was over.

"Ye'll have t' shift fer yerselves for a while. Take ye'r best clothes t' th' barn and change into 'em out there, while we git the children dressed 'n Rachel gits herself ready. I'll call ye 'xactly on th' minute, 'n' don't ye come a mite sooner."

Rachel White's wedding day was typical of June days in Maine. The warm sun brought forth the scent of pine trees mingled with that of the wild cherry blossoms. No sweeter bridal chorus was ever chanted than the martins caroled as they flew back and forth past the log house. The soft breeze from the south rustled the waters of the lake till it sparkled like diamonds. Across on the opposite shore, the long stretch of cleared land lay like a huge emerald in the sunshine, while beyond, silent and majestic, the great sapphire mountain stood guard. Young Philip pointed out the beauties of the place as he stood with his father waiting.

"This place ought to be good enough for a young couple to settle in, hadn't it, father?"

"It looks like a Garden of Eden to me this morning," replied the father.

Inside the log house there were other things to do than admire the scenery. Rachel was stuffing the geese with dressing flavored wtih chives and sage she had grown the previous year. Hannah was cleaning fiddlehead greens. Naomi, after finishing the breakfast dishes, had begun to wash and dress the children, when the mother with a horrified expression announced,

"If there ever was a numbskull in this world, I am it. Here I have been frettin' for over four years, 'cause Elder Wyman didn't seem t' git up here only in cold weather, and I didn't want Cynthy christened at that time o' year. Now here he is, on one of th' loveliest June days one ever did see, and me so taken up with Rachel's weddin', I couldn't think of my poor little Cynthy's soul's salvation. I must say 'Pride goeth before destruction 'n' a haughty spirit before a fall'. I don't know what punishment's ahead for me for bein' so vain; but I deserve all I s'll git. Go quick, Naomi, and git th' little christ'nin' dress out o' that chest and see 'f twill dew t' put on t' her without washin'. I'll bet its yeller as saffron 'n' I don't know as it'll even go round her. She's lots older 'an Phenewel 'n' the rest of ye was when ye wore it. She'll prob'ly look jest like a skun cat in it."

When the dress was brought forth, Hannah assured Rachel "it was perfectly all right. A beautiful dress," she said.

This made Rachel much happier and she decided "It will have t' dew." Then she went back to her cooking, all the time keeping watch through the bedroom door to see if Rachel was properly donning her wedding clothes.

"Ye can ask Hannah t' fasten yer weddin' veil if ye like. I thought mebbe, ye'd like t' have a few of these white violets on it near ye'r face. I picked 'em at daybreak this mornin', 'fore you was awake. They are there in the bowl."

Hannah said "Rachel you are the one who should have that privilege. I appreciate the honor, but I want you to have it. Let me attend to the deer meat. I'l git it onto the spit and have it already to start turning the minute the wedding is over."

It was eight forty-five by the tall clock when Rachel called the men to come in.

"Ye see, since ye went, I've come t' my senses. We're goin' t' have Cynthy christened before th' weddin'. Elder Wyman, this blue bowl was my mother's and I want ye should use it. I've put water in it and it's warm. I'd like t' have Hannah 'n' Philip stand up with me 'n' Sam while ye baptise our baby girl."

No more simple or beautiful christening service was ever held than for this child of the wilderness. The lovely little girl seemed almost to sense the sacredness of it all, when she smiled into the face of that man of God.

Taking her in his arms he said, "In the name of the Father, the Son and the Holy Ghost, I christen thee Cynthia."

The elderly people stepped back, Rachel now holding her child in her arms, as Sam brought his daughter from the little room into the flowered archway, where Philip met her. They made a picture as they stood, those happy young people. They had no fear for the future, no doubts assailed them. Absolute confidence in each other's love, gave them the assurance they needed to face any situation that could arise.

"Philip, wilt thou have this woman to thy wedded wife, to live together after God's ordinance in the Holy Estate of Matrimony? Will thou love her, comfort her, honor and keep her in sickness and in health; and forsaking all others, keep thee only unto her, for as long as ye both shall live?"

"I will."

"Rachel, wilt thou have this man to thy wedded husband, to live together after God's ordinance, in the Holy Estate of Matrimony? Will thou obey him and serve him, love, honor and keep him in sickness and health; and forsaking all others, keep thee only unto him, for long as ye both shall live?"

"I will."

As Philip placed the ring upon Rachel's forefingers, he repeated after Mr. Wyman—"With this ring I thee wed. and with all my worldly goods I thee endow."

And Mr. Wyman then said, "I now pronounce thee Man and Wife, in the name of the Father, and of the Son, and of the Holy Ghost. Amen."

As usual, the two mothers shed a few tears during the ceremony, but as soon as Philip had kissed the bride, Sam saved the situation by not only kissing the bride, but all the females present including Hannah Judkins.

After the noise and confusion had subsided, young Philip called Reverend Wyman aside and handed him a dollar, which was a generous amount in that day for performing a wedding ceremony. Reverend Wyman was most grateful and after wishing the young couple many years of happiness, drove on to keep his appointment at the home of James Houghton where he would conduct a regular Sunday service. The Whites could well be excused for not accompanying him today.

At noon the Whites and Judkins sat down to a very delicious wedding feast. Rachel asked Philip to pronounce the blessing and he very graciously did so. They were all happy and hungry. The food that Rachel had prepared surpassed their fondest expectations.

Rachel said, "Well, Hannah, you certainly roasted them geese and them two hind quarters o' deer meat th' best I ever tasted. I aint had a mouthful of anybody else's cookin' fer so long, you can't imagine how good it tastes t' me."

"If anyone can make a better strawb'ry short cake than this one, I'd like to know who 'tis. How handsome it looks there, like a great white mountain all covered with the beaten cream! You didn't need to have a professional wedding-cake maker, for you can do a better job than any one I ever saw," said Hannah.

Sam was not too accustomed to carving a goose; so he asked Philip to do it while he worked on the roast venison, which was more in his line. They ate for an hour. There was not much food left on the table when Rachel asked the bride to cut the short cake and passed her twelve mulberry blue plates on which to serve it.

"That's part of a set my mother give me when I was married, and I now give them to you."

A sob rose in her throat preventing her finishing the statement.

But Sam said, "This would of been pretty nigh a perfect meal, if Marm hadn't been s' stingy with her elderberry wine." But all

(170)

he received in return for this remark, was a sniff from his wife.

Philip and Sam attempted to discuss the possibilities of invasion from the eastern part of the Province, but Rachel advised them to speak only of cheerful things at that dinner, saying, "we aint heard nothin' but war for years. Let's try 'n' forgit it fer a little while."

"Ye're right, Marm," said Sam. "We certainly have worried ourselves 'bout t' death. Sometimes we had cause 'n' sometimes we didn't. That summer o' 1812 we all lost s' much sleep, our eyes looked like burnt holes in a blanket, and we walked 'round here jest like we was a-dreamin'. When we weren't woritin' 'bout Injuns, we was a being pestered by catamounts."

Sam related their experience in losing the ox, and Philip asked what they did with old Star, the mate.

"Oh! We swapped him off for a pair o' young steers with Barrett who lives over there at the side of that mountain. I b'lieve they call it "Hurricane Mountain" he said as he pointed east across the lake. "Ye know that Barrett had a nigh ox break his leg, got it ketched between two rocks. He could use old Star. An' we swapped even for th' steers. They're provin' good, too. I cal'late by another year they'll be just as valuable t' me as the yoke was. But I tell ye, Philip, for a while I didn't even look to'ds th' tieup where them cattle had stood. It made me so lonesome, I was glad when we tore that old hovel down. Godfrey Mighty! Philip, I did wish you was here t' help build th' barn; but I tell ye now, we've got some good jiners right here on this side th' pond, and this man, James Sweat, c'n make th' best wagon wheels ye ever see. Ye know I've ben haulin' in my hay', 'n' grain every summer on my old sleds; but I've decided t' have some wheels made so's I c'n have a wagon. Our ro'ds aint very good yit, but we work on 'em a little whenever we can, 'n' wont be long 'fore we c'n have ridin' wagons."

Soon after two o'clock, Philip arose, and expressed his regret that he and Hannah could stay no longer, but assured them a return visit would soon be made. He invited them to come to Greene at their earliest convenience, and urged Sam to make every effort to have a mail route established from Webb to Dixfield, also a school house should be built on the west side and all roads in the Plantation improved.

Hannah and Philip waved goodbye to them all, happy in the

knowledge that they were leaving their son in good hands in his log house at the side of the beautiful lake.

Philip's conversation with Sam had convinced him the war was near its end, and Sam felt confident that Judkins would soon be able to leave Greene and come to Webb to join with him in the great logging project they had so long contemplated.

Chapter XVI

UNBELIEVABLY HAZARDOUS TRAVEL CONDITIONS IN 1814.

One morning soon after the wedding a man came to the door of Sam's barn, said his name was Gideon Bowley, said he had come to make plans for building a road starting at Sam's place, going south along the side of the ridge, continuing down the bank of the river about a mile to his saw and grist mill. As there were now a good many families settled on the west side of the pond, this road would accommodate them as his mill was nearer to most of them than the Holman mill a couple of miles above the head of the lake. Bowley pointed out the fact, that when Sam was ready to build his house, it would be far more convenient for him to have his lumber sawed at the mill on Webb River.

The idea seemed a good one to Sam and his sons and they gladly agreed to help build the road. Other west side settlers joined in the work and before long it was a common thing to see ox teams drawing loads of logs over the new road to Bowley's mill. In due time the same teams returned laden with boards and other house lumber. The settlers now took courage. Sam White spread his spirit of optimism among the men he met, never missing an opportunity to drop a cheering word.

The crops were extra good that year. Every one raised more than ever before. The last of September Sam took a trip down river, happy at having good news to report to his friend Philip. First there was the new road, then there was a school in the neighborhood taught by Abel Holt at his home. No school house had been built yet, but this would come in time; but there was a chance now for Naomi and Phenewel to learn the things their mother could not teach them. She had done her best each day in the short time she could devote to it, but with a paid teacher it would be right and Sam realized the value of an education, even though his own had been limited. He with several others had done their best to arrange for a Post Rider to come from Dixfield to Webb weekly; but so far had no success. He felt confident however that it would come before long.

When Sam reached Luddens where he planned to spend the night and where he was heartily welcomed by his friends, he learned how all summer the British had carried on with high hand along the Penobscot. Now they were attacking all ships around the West Indies. Many of our coastal towns had allowed their captains and crews to risk their lives and valuable cargoes in these troubled waters. Many ships never returned to home port. Again Sam felt he was happier at home in the wilderness where he could have no news of the outside world, and felt like returning at once to Webb; but his desire to talk with Philip spurred him on and the morning found him on his way. This time he spent several days in Greene. With three sons to protect his home and family, he decided he was justified in taking a little vacation. While he was with Philip, they called on the Parkers. He was charmed with lovely Hannah and her children, her third child having been born about a month earlier. It now slept peacefully in its cradle beside the chair of grandmother Rebecca. Sam had never before seen any of this family and he and Benjamin soon learned they had many things in common. Benjamin appreciated a joke as well as Sam and many were the tall tales they told. In spite of the fact that Great Britain had a large army quartered in the east and might any day start an invasion of the remainder of the Province, it did not seem to greatly dampen the spirits of these two optimists. Benjamin had experienced much worse than this and the British were not winning sea battles as in the past.

As they smoked their pipes and drank the spruce beer of Rebecca's brewing, for which she was quite famed, Benjamin told Sam and Philip of a recent experience.

"There's a man lives up river a piece and he's inclined to be a little light-fingered. I have t' watch him every time he comes into the store. You know I keep a pile o' cod fish on th' counter where they're handy, and I've been a-missin' one or two now and then, and I kind o' mistrusted he was a-takin' of 'em; but I couldn't seem t' ketch 'im. But t'other night he come in, and th' fust thing he done was t' sidle up t' that pile o' cod fish. He hung round there fer a spell, 'n' I watched th' best I could; but I was pretty busy, when all of a sudden he started out th' door in quite a hurry. 'Hold on' Rufus, I says. 'What's yer hurry'? He turned round 'n' faced me and there was 'bout four inches o' cod fish's tail a-showin' below his co't. "What ye want, Benj'min?" Sez 'e'.

"I don't want wothin'," sez I; "But I thought I'd tell ye, hereafter ye better either wear a longer co't er steal a shorter codfish."

"Speakin' o' cod fish," said Sam, "reminds of an old feller down Lisbon who kep' a store and he was powerful pious, always prayin' 'n' preaching, but never done much practicin'. He took in a little boy that some skunk put on th' town, and said he'd give 'im a livin', for what he would dew t' help him round th' store. One mornin' early, one o' th' neighbors went into the store and stood there waiting for th' boy t' draw some molasses for him. The old feller lived upstairs and didn't know there was anybody down in th' store. So he hollered from th' stairs—'John, have ye watered th' rum? Have ye sanded th' sugar? Have ye sprayed the cod fish? Well, then come up t' prayers' ".

The day before Sam thought he must return to his home, Philip suggested they cross the river and go up to see John Staples on the Turner side. Sam was agreeable to this idea as he had never seen John and wanted to ask him about his halfsister who had gone up river so long ago and never been heard from since. They rode up river a few miles till they came to an old raft, partly hidden by the bushes, where it was tied up. It was the only available means of crossing, so they managed to pole themselves over, then climbed the hill to the Staples homestead. They found John and Betsy with their two little children busy and happy. John was making shoes and after examining them, Sam gave him an order for a pair for himself. Said he could make shoes, but hated the job.

"I never seem t' git th' time for it," said Sam.

They had a pleasant afternoon discussing affairs of the day, the possible invasion from the east. John said Seth had made them a flying visit the week before and warned them to be prepared for this at all times. Said Portland people were making every preparation for defense. Sam and Philip had previously felt there was no immediate danger, but after hearing this report he grew quite alarmed. As usual Sam had a strong urge to start for home. He ate a hurried lunch at Philips and started up the river.

Chapter XVII

END OF THE WAR AND ADVENT OF WOLVES TO CENTRAL MAINE

The menace from wolves was growing daily. This, added to the possibility of the British coming west from the Penobscot, created a growing uneasiness. People who had traveled with one loaded gun, now carried two when possible. "One for the British and one for the wolves," they said.

As winter approached, the wolves became more plentiful and ferocious. A man and his wife, living a few miles up river from Parker's, drove one morning to Lewiston in their sleigh. While there they bought part of a bolt of cotton cloth that had been brought into town from Boston to sell to the highest bidder. The cloth was called "Copper Plate" and was considered very beautiful, as it was brilliant with many colors and quite different from the drab homespun worn by most women of the Androscoggin Valley. The travelers remained longer with their friends in Lewiston than they had intended, and so it was rather late in the afternoon when they started for home. These Lewiston friends, fearing for the comfort of the woman, persuaded her to accept the loan of their foot warmer, which they filled with live coals and placed at her feet. After wrapping themselves with blankets and fur robes, the couple started homeward. As they rode toward Greene in the snappy twilight, feeling warm and secure, their horse suddenly started running with all the speed he possessed. Looking behind them, the man saw in the half light, two stealthy forms creeping nearer and knew at once they were wolves. Taking his gun from the bottom of the sleigh, he fired, but missed. The loathsome creatures continued to gain on them. When they were within twenty feet of the sleigh, with his second gun, he fired again. This frightened the wolves and caused them to hold back for a little time.

"If we could only strike fire with my flint, we could set the robe afire and thus keep them off until it burns. We'll have to try it anyway. It is our only hope. There's no powder to reload the guns."

The wife was now thinking fast and said, "Pull out the bolt of cloth and set the end of it afire on the coals in the foot warmer and hang it over the back of the sleigh. When that's all gone, we'll set the robes afire. Blow on the coals, man. Blow, and it will blaze quicker."

"Oh, you do it wife. You do it and let me drive the horses."

With her quick fingers she managed to do this just in season, for the wolves were now close upon them, when the flaming cloth dropped over the back of the fine new sleigh. With a whine, the wolves slowed up and the woman watched the gleam of fire in their evil eyes as she unrolled the burning cloth, which fortunately was not entirely consumed until they thankfully drove into the settlement at Greene. A dozen or more men were sent out on the road in pursuit of these hungry beasts and each man carried either two or three loaded guns and extra ammunition, but very few were successful in killing a wolf.

Something must be done at once. Nobody had seen a deer or even a fresh track for weeks. The places in the woods known to be winter yards, where they lived on "browse", were empty; but there was plenty of evidence to show where many deer had been killed by wolves. The condition grew more alarming each day. Towns called special meetings and appointed men to do nothing but hunt wolves. Poisoned meat was left in the woods in the hope it would be found by wolves and aid in their extermination. Ammunition and compensation was furnished the wolf hunters by vote of the people. Reports from Fryeburg, Norway, Bethel and Rumford began to pour in of the destruction of deer. It was no longer safe to allow sheep or cattle to remain outside, even in barn yards, unless under armed guard. The settlers of Webb were having these same experiences. The Whites, who had lived so sumptously on deer meat, were now dependent upon fish for their main dish. Now and then a veal calf was killed for food, where formerly such creatures were reared as steers or bulls.

In August, a huge British fleet under the command of Admiral Cockburn and with a complement of several thousand soldiers, commanded by General Ross, sailed into Chesapeake Bay, where they landed and marched upon Washington some twenty miles away. General Winder was ordered to force back the invaders.

He was a brave commander, but his troops consisted mainly of untrained farmers, carrying only shot guns. The British forces numbered more than five thousand, while the Americans numbered only thirty-five hundred. A wanton destruction of the partly finished capitol followed. At the order of Admiral Cockburn all government records and papers were burned. The President's House, Treasury Building, Arsenal, Soldier Barracks, hotels and private homes were destroyed.

Next occurred a great battle in the Harbor of Fayal on one of the Azores, where the British were defeated. Their second defeat came soon after in New Orleans, where Andrew Jackson was in command. Here breastworks thrown up for defense, proved the undoing of the British on January 8th, 1815. Never had they been so soundly defeated, with twenty-six hundred killed and wounded. General Jackson's loss, only eight killed and thirteen wounded. The people said "Surely the Lord is on our side". This proved true for at Ghent, Holland, on December 24th, 1814, had been previously signed the Treaty of Peace between the United States and Great Britain. Word of this, however, did not reach New York until February 11th, 1815. A courier on horse back rushed to Boston with the glad news, arriving there in thirty-two hours. Another courier immediately started north informing the inhabitants along the way. People went wild with joy, shouting and throwing their hats in the air. Church bells were rung unceasingly, drums were beat, women and children marched the streets, pounding on pans and kettles. Parades, both civilian and military, filled the streets. Flags were flung from every window, fireworks lighted the skies by night and in the churches continuous services of thanksgiving were conducted. In Portland, Bath and all coastal towns and throughout the whole Province, public celebration was observed. Dancing was carried on in every public hall from the largest city to the smallest country town. Some of the New York and Boston ladies even danced with British officers from war vessels at anchor in the harbors. England at last had learned her lesson, she was no longer "Ruler of the Sea".

Chapter XVIII

"EIGHTEEN-HUNDRED-AND-FROZE TO DEATH."
PLANS COMPLETED FOR THE GREAT DRIVE

A son or father had gone out from many families of the Province of Maine, never to return; but the end of the war brought such general relief, nearly every one was happy. Almost every house on the Androscoggin had some one coming home again to it. Returning service men were daily passing the Parker homestead. People now began to feel they could really live again, could accomplish any task that might confront them. Mountains now became mole hills. They could scarcely wait for spring to come when they could begin their planting. All had the same idea, to raise the largest crops possible for the great profit they felt would be theirs. Up and down the river and throughout the Province, large fields of corn, wheat, oats, beans, peas, potatoes and all other vegetables were planted. As the returning soldiers reached their homes, their one object seemed to be to work early and late to raise crops.

Old Benjamin was so happy these days, he told his wife, "I don't know how to act. I'm 'spectin' any minute to see William and Jacob come up th' ro'd. Aint you, Becky?"

"Ye'us, I am. God willin'.."

Hannah added, " I hope Nathaniel will be with them." But she never saw her brother again. He had given his life for his country up there with the Northwestern Army a year earlier.

Benjamin decided to go to the next farm to see Philip. After enjoying an hour together discussing their future plans, at Philip's suggestion, they crossed to the Turner side and rode up river, walked up the hill to the Upper Street and there found John and Betsy with their four children. John Babson, their first child whom they now called "John B", a sturdy fellow in his eighth year, was pounding the door sill of the cobbler's shop with his father's shoe hammer. He was large for his age with the dark complexion of his father and with one black eye and the other blue. Little Betsy, six years old, "Lively as a cricket", Benjamin said.. Then came Ezra, four, and Christopher, not quite two. Philip complimented Betsy on her fine family, and said, "I see you are raising up a lot of boys to help your husband, and I guess he's going to need them all. When did you last hear from Seth?" Betsy replied that a letter had come that day, saying he expected to be discharged very soon.

"Well, I'm glad to hear that," said Philip.

Seth had always served in the defense of Portland when he was not training men in Turner. He had been very fortunate in never having received an injury. John went to the cellar and drew a pitcher of cider, while Betsy brought from the pantry a large plate of doughnuts which the three men enjoyed. Philip and Benjamin, both veterans of the Revolutionary War, went home after their call on John Staples and his family, in a happy frame of mind. The world again looked bright to them in spite of their years.

Philip said to Benjamin, "Well, we've lived through two wars and I, for one, hope I shall not see another."

"Well, 'taint likely we will," replied Benjamin.

One evening as John and Betsy were about to retire for the night, a gay voice hailed them from outside, and in walked Seth. He was the picture of health.

"Never got a scratch. And, Oh! how glad I am to be home," he said as he kissed Betsy and gently patted the sleeping babies. He and John grasped hands and looked long into each other's eyes.

"Well, its over, Seth, an' yer back for good this time."

"Ye'us, John. For Good."

"How ye been anyway? Are ye ready t' start hayin' t'morrer?" inquired the enthusiastic Seth.

"I'm ready t' start anything, now you've come and this war's over, Captain Seth Staples."

"I'm through with that 'Captain' stuff for ever I hope. All I ask, on this earth, is a chance t' live right here in Turner for th' rest of my days. 'Course I might marry some time, ye know," he said, grinning at Betsy.

"I should think 'twas 'bout time ye had some such idee. Why don't ye look round a little?" asked Betsy.

"Well, ye don't think I've been racing up here from Portland

(180)

with my eyes shet, do ye, Sister? I'll tell ye somethin' now. I've got one of th' best girls in the United States waitin' for me this minit, right over crost th' river down in Greene. So ye needn't worry for fear I'll be an old batch'. If I was, I'd be th' first one in the Staples family," replied Seth.

"Well, who in the world is it?" asked Betsy.

"She's got th' same first name's you have—Betsy."

"Betsy—who, for the Lord's sake?"

"Betsy Judkins. Queer ye hadn't heard."

"Queer? Queerer t' me when ye ever got a chance t' court 'er," said his astonished brother.

"Oh! I found time evenin's, after drill was over," confessed Seth.

"Well—I'll be cow-kicked!" said John.

In about a week Jacob Parker came smiling home. He limped as he dismounted. Said he had received a wound in the leg but not a serious one and that it was practically healed. He had been made a Captain and rode a fine horse. He had been able to purchase it from the Army at a low price, due to the necessity of his needing transportation home from New York State. From his general appearance, one would judge he had been spending a pleasant holiday at some summer resort; but when William arrived a week later, he told his father that Jacob had seen much hard fighting and had spent many months in a hospital before returning to Greene.

"But he don't want mother to know this, so don't say anything about it."

Hannah felt she was the happiest woman in the world, now that William had come. Hereafter there would be nothing to worry about she told Rebecca; but the mother knew life better than that and hoped, at least there would be a short respite from their troubles.

'Early to bed and early to rise, Makes a man healthy, wealthy and wise', was the only slogan the people of the Province now knew. They lived it days and dreamed it at night. Everywhere up and down the Androscoggin crops were being cultivated. The clanging of hoes against the rocks, the swish of cythes, and the "Whoa! Hish!" of the ox teamsters as they hauled in their hay, was sweet music to the ears of these returned veterans, who had listened to the thunders of war for the past three years.

In Webb, as in all other Province towns, the farming industry flourished during the summer of 1815. With the war ended, they could look forward to the bright prospects they felt sure were ahead.

Sam White, with his two sons and son-in-law, entered into all kinds of crop raising with renewed vigor. The same condition prevailed in all other families in the Plantation. The land on both sides of the pond was now nearly all under cultivation. The roads were being steadily improved, most of the settlers now owning farmcarts, the wheels for same having generally been made by James Swett, whose business had grown sufficiently to warrant his bringing his family from Brunswick to Webb to settle permanently.

During the fall of 1814, young Ebenezer Newman had left the settlement, gone down to Billerica, married a distant cousin, Judith Dowse, and brought her to Webb. Nehemiah Storer had married Lucy, daughter of Nathaniel Kittredge.

In June, 1815, the people of Webb petitioned the General Court to allow their Plantation to be incorporated as the Town of Weld. The petition was granted February 8th, 1816. Caleb Holt paid twenty dollars for the privilege of naming the town in honor of his friend, Benjamin Weld.

Young Sam, engaged to marry Lydia Whitney, decided he must go elsewhere in order to earn sufficient means to pay for the land he now determined to own, before marrying. At the suggestion of his friend Ebenezer, he decided to go to Billerica or some town nearby and find work on one of the large farms in that locality. So helping his father in the fall to harvest their more abundant crops, then working through the long winter on his clearing, he set out on foot for down river. It had been over four years since he went with his father to visit at the home of Philip Judkins when he tried to persuade Betsy to become his wife. It all seemed like a dream to him now; but at the time, he had felt sure that happiness would never again be his. Now he realized his mistake and thought he would call on the Judkins as he passed through Greene. But on second thought he decided to cross the river on the ice at Dixfield and go down on the west side through the towns of Peru, Canton and Turner, thus avoiding the scene of his former unhappiness. He was a boy then, but now being a man, he put away such thoughts and walked steadily on. The weather was unusually cold for late March, so he was obliged to find shelter each night at farm houses on the way. He looked anxiously forward to the time when he would reach the coast where his parents had said it was much warmer. He had known and suffered so much cold weather, the thought of a warmer climate gladdened his heart.

He was nearly two weeks on the road to Billerica, where he finally reached the home of Ebenezer Newman's relatives. They made him welcome and found work for him the day following his arrival.

Back home and throughout the Province, people were beginning to wonder what was causing April to remain so cold. Snow melted a little through the middle of the day; but at night everything froze solidly. The last week of the month was a little warmer and the farmers took courage. But on April 30th a foot of snow fell. May was no improvement on April, as another foot of snow fell on the tenth of that month. On high ground, conditions were some better and owners of such land planted a few crops; but although they started to grow, they were killed by the heavy frosts of June. A second crop planted later shared the same fate. People were now becoming greatly alarmed. Those who had raised large crops in 1815, could spare seed for a second planting; but those others, who were not as fortunate and whose farms were on the low lands, began to realize they would have no wheat the coming winter unless they bought it at the price of two dollars or more per bushel. There were many who did not have the funds to purchase at even half the amount asked, and so their families began to experience the effects of undernourishment. Some people ate the frozen, half grown wheat heads, which they cooked and served with milk. James Masterman of Masterman Hill. Jacob Coburn on Center Hill, Daniel Storer and Robert Potter on their great hill in Number 4, the dwellers on the hills of Mexico, Dixfield and Upper Street, Turner, raised a small amount of grain. What they could spare, they sold at the going price.

July, August and September proved no exception in their extreme unseasonableness. Ice formed every month of that year 1816 and it was afterwards spoken of as "Eighteen hundred and froze to death", or "The Cold Year". Water left inside barns at night would have a coating of ice in the morning. The temperature remained so cold that the ground never warmed all summer. The snow lay in spots in the woods, where people were obliged to drive their cattle, hoping they would be able to subsist on "Browse" like the deer. Many cattle and sheep died of starvation. Wild animals were very numerous, particularly catamounts, that lay waiting outside barns at night to devour any possible prey.

Winter came on in earnest in November, further discouraging the people. So that the next April, many men with their families migrated to other States believing the climate in the Province would always be the same. With no grain and very little deer meat, they decided it was impossible for them to live, so thousands of them left for Pennsylvania and Ohio. Those who stayed, managed to use as a substitute for deer, the meat of racoons which flocked around farms and probably helped to save the lives of many a starving family. There were those who believed the coons were sent to them by God, like manna from Heaven. At the time, they did not realize the deer were being driven from the country by wolves and it would be many years before they would return in sufficient numbers to furnish a source of meat supply. From that time until about 1860, moose and caribou were the only wild animals the pioneers could depend upon for food. These animals were large and capable of defending themselves from the wolves. In winter, like the deer, they lived in "yards" in th woods, where the hardwood growth furnished them with browse and kept them alive. The carcass of a big bull moose would often weigh one thousand pounds, thus supplying meat for a long time for a family. Moose meat is coarser grained than that of a caribou or deer and resembles beef in flavor, while that of bears is much the same as of sheep.

The summer of 1817 was not as pleasant and warm as desired and scanty crops were raised; but the courageous people of the Province, who had decided "to stay and see it through", were finally rewarded by a fine, hot summer in 1818. The general depression throughout the country which followed the war, was still on; but not growing worse. As soon as the people of the Province began to have sufficient food, their thoughts turned in another direction.

The Embargo Law of 1807, the War of 1812 and the severe climate of 1816-17, nearly ruined the industrial life of the State; but the "never say die" people who remained within its borders, squared their shoulders, tightened their belts and went on with the fight for livelihood.

Philip Judkins, had never faltered, never doubted a day would come when his schemes could be carried out. Now in March, 1819, he began to actually plan the ways and means for undertaking the great lumbering project that he and Sam White had dreamed of for so long.

First he went to Bath to learn conditions there. Word had come to him from various sources that ship builders were planning work on several ships in the near future. So to ascertain the truth of this, he set out on horse back over the road once so familiar to him. His first contact with a ship builder, a relative of Deacon Larrabee's, furnished the information he sought. This was, that a scarcity of lumber suitable for ship building was facing them and particularly a lack of tall trees for masts. There was talk of sending men to Georgia to cut pine there for this purpose.

During his journey home, Philip's mind dwelt almost continually on the work ahead; but he also thought of the privations and struggles he and Sam had endured since 1808, to make possible each year the payment of high interest on the Weld timberland to Jacob Abbott. Mr. Abbott now lived in Brunswick where he had moved in 1812. Philip said, "Its been a hard row to hoe; but we have lived through it, and we'll weather the next year or so. Then all will be plainsailin' for us, the Lord willin'."

That night after reaching home, he and Hannah sat long by the fire making their plans. It would be hard to leave that comfortable home in Greene for quarters in Weld that they knew would be entirely opposite. Their lives from now on would be very different from what they had known.

"But if all goes well, we shall enjoy the fruits of our labors there a hundred times more than we ever have here, my dear," Philip said. Hannah replieid she could leave the old home with much less regret, now that Betsy was married to Seth Staples and gone to a home of her own. Their little girl, Isabella, two years old, was a joy to her grandparents and Hannah and Philip would miss her very much; but they consoled themselves with the thought of the happiness that would be theirs, when they reached Weld and could see each day the two children of Philip and Rachel, whose names were Eastman and Mercy Ann. Hannah could hardly wait for that day.

Philip's sister, Mary, was not able to enthuse over the change of residence. Her experience with the wolves in the woods of Lewiston had killed any pioneer spirit she might previously have known, but she really had no choice in the matter. Seth and Betsy had offered her a home with them on the Upper Street in Turner where they lived near John and Betsy, but Mary's love for her brother Philip, was sufficiently strong to draw her with him wherever he went. She had cast her lot with him and Hannah, and with them she would stay.

Time had brought great changes in traveling conditions and the moving of Philip's effects to Weld, would be done on wheels and not on runners. They would not start out until the last of May when the roads would be well-settled. They would stop over night at taverns along the way, never remaining on the road after sunset. By so doing, Philip assured Mary, she would be safe from wolves on this trip although they were still numerous. Philip planned to engage Jacob Parker to go with them to help with driving the oxen and also as a further protection against wild animals.

"Jacob can shoot as well as I could in my best days. He has a gun, much more modern than any of mine, that he can reload in a jiffy. And that's what you need in these days. I'm goin' over tomorrow mornin', and see if William still wants to buy this farm. Maybe he has lost interest, havin' to wait so long. William might be willin' to go along too with us, for all I know."

The next morning when Philip walked into Benjamin's door yard, William was just coming through the kitchen door, a young baby in his arms. When he saw Philip, he handed the child back to its mother, while six other children were striving lustily to get through that door, all at the same time. Their exit resembled the overturning of a basket of kittens, for they seemed literally to pour down over the steps.

"Mornin', Philip," said Williaim, as he managed to step over a pair of twin boys.

"Mornin', William. I have lately heard that your family has increased so rapidly in the last ten years, that you contemplate makin' an addition to your house, and so I thought perhaps to save all that trouble, you might like to buy a bigger one, like mine, for instance."

"You mean that, Philip?" shouted William.

"That's what I said. I said it years ago. I meant it then, and I mean it now—if we can come to terms."

Men of that day did not hurry through important deals. They took their time. A slogan of Philip's was 'Make haste, slowly'. These two spent several hours discussing every detail of that very important transaction and in the end reached an agreement satisfactory to both. When Philip said his price for the farm was five thousand dollars, William smiled and said he had felt that was what it would be and had saved that amount during the years. He could now own that land along the river that he had coveted so long. From his jacket pocket, Philip took the carefully worded deed of transfer of Lot 236 from Philip Judkins to William Parker, who after slowly reading it through lifted a brick from the hearth, ran his hand down under the edge of the floor and brought out a long bag filled mostly with gold coins. He emptied its contents on the table and together they counted it twice.

"We'll go 'cross the ro'd to Uncle Stephen's and have him witness this. He's a Justice, y'know."

Before Philip left the Parker house, both William and Jacob gladly agreed to go with him to help move his family and belongings to Weld.

When word of Philip's leaving Greene reached the people of the town, much regret was manifested by his friends he had so faithfully served through the years. Many were the tears shed by Hannah's friends as they gathered that morning to bid her God's speed, to press into her hands little gifts and to urge her to return often to visit them.

The night before their leaving, Betsy and Seth had come to say good bye, bringing a large basket of delicious food Betsy had cooked for their journey. There was a smaller basket filled with muster ginger-bread and half a cheese that John and the other Betsy had sent. Now there were two Betsy Staples, it was hard to distinguish between them, so they were called "Betsy John" and "Betsy Seth".

At Monroe's Tavern, the Judkins caravan caused much excitement. Abijah was delighted to again welcome Philip and glad to meet Jacob and William Parker. Mrs. Monroe loaded the table with her best food, urging them all to take more till they felt it would not be safe to eat another morsel.

At the end of the second day, our travelers were at the door of the hospitable Amos, who now felt it a privilge to entertain his friends from Greene. He and Philip with the Parkers, talked for hours. Like most men who had spent years in the service of their country, William and Jacob had little to say of their experiences; but the subject of separation from Massachusetts furnished ample grounds for lengthly conversation. All agreed it was of vital importance and felt their independence from Massachusetts was very necessary to the development of the District of Maine.

Mrs. Trask invited Hannah and Mary into her own private sitting room, where they spent a pleasant evening together. Hannah requested Susan Trask to tell Mary of the bears' visit to the room of her little daughters years before. After this recital, Mary related the fearful experience with wolves while returning from Charlestown, New Hampshire. Many other experiences of friends and relatives were retold, the latest fashions discussed, as well as new recipes for pound cake, cookies, pies, pudding and syllabubs. Susan informed Mary of the building of the fort at Weld when Indians had been expected. Never before had Hannah heard this fearful tale. Philip had avoided the subject, fearing it would add to her worries and cause the idea of establishing her home there not too safe and pleasant a prospect. But Mary was the only one effected by it, for Hannah was the kind who never allowed things of that sort to upset her.

They reached the west side of Webb Pond before dark the third day without a mishap. There was great rejoicing when they drove into the White place. The women embraced, the men wrung each others hands. The only live stock Philip had brought were the four oxen, two horses and one cow, hitched to the back of one of the loads. Benjamin Parker had loaned Philip his horse and wagon in which Mary and Hannah had comfortably ridden all the way. This team would provide return transportation for William and Jacob. It was with some difficulty that Sam found room in his barn for Philip's animals; but he managed to get them safely inside from all night prowlers. Young Philip was happy to have his dear parents with him once more and justly proud to display to them his two fine children. The adoring grandparents had for a long time looked forward to this day. The men slept in the barn that night, giving over the use of the cabin to the women and babies.

At an unbelievably early hour Rachel and her girls had a hearty breakfast spread for the thirteen people, including the two small children. Where all the food came from was a mystery to Hannah; but knowing Rachel, she was not surprised. This morning, Sam was a happy man again. He could hardly stop singing long enough to eat his breakfast. The day which he had so long awaited. had come at last. The moment the Parker boys drove out of sight, on their return trip, Sam said to Philip,

"Come out t' th' barn where we c'n talk"—and it was there they made their plans.

Philip said, "First thing to do is build another barn where I can house my stock. Next thing is another log house where we can live. After that we must get some crops planted and later on we can build shelters for the oxen we will need for the logging, and camps for the men. I have brought quite a quantity of grain, mainly corn, wheat and rye to plant. I don't know how many acres Philip has that can be planted this year; but we'll need a good many."

Sam replied, "For years, I've worked with this thing on my mind. Of course in sixteen and seventeen we fell behind on th' grain; but last year we made up for it with interest. We've worked hard t' clear every foot o' land that wasn't covered with valuable timber on this tract o' ourn. Sam bought extry, of his own, over beyent here t' th' west and lately he has worked on that mostly; but he has given me a good many days o' hard work. Ye'us, he has. He foots it every spring t' Billerica an' works fer a big farmer. Then winters he comes back here and works clearin' of his land. I miss 'im, Philip. Godfrey! how I miss 'im; but he's gittin' along to'rds thirty and he plans t' git married afore long; but James sez, he shan't wait till he's an old man. He's cal'latin' t' marry Sophronie Holman."

By the way, did ye notice they's quite a number 'o' log houses down ther near Berry's? Some folks things they's goin' t' be more business down there later on than they ever will up here."

"Well, I did notice Berry has built a pretty good lookin' mill down there and it looks as though there was plenty of power to run several more. Any amount of water was coming over the dam yesterday," said Philip.

The arrival of Philip and his family added to the courage and enthusiasm of the people of the locality. They now felt there would be plenty of work for the men with their ox teams and horses, and this would mean money for them all.

As soon as word spread through the settlement that logging operations would begin immediately after harvesting, there was a stampede among the farmers, each vieing with the other to see who would begin work first. Probably there was never seen before or since in that vicinity such extreme activity as went on that summer.

Sam and Philip lost no opportunity in engaging men in Weld and down in District No. 4 to work for them and begin as early as possible. There were those who managed to work several days each week building camps, also hovels for the animals for the coming winter. In an amazingly short time, the side hill assumed the appearance of a log village through which ran the Bowley Road, now become quite a thoroughfare. A bridge had been built across Webb River at Bowely's Mill. Log cabins were being replaced by houses built of finished lumber. Both saw-mill operators were doing a thriving business. A three room house was valued at two hundred twenty-five dollars and a finished barn, fifty feet square at fifty dollars. There were now about a dozen frame houses and plans for more.

Dr. LaFayette Perkins had settled on the east side of the lake four years before where he built a good home. The town had voted to clear for him ten acres of land each year for three years as an inducement to him to take up residence there. His coming added a great feeling of security to the inhabitants.

There were now three schools in town. Abel Holt was teaching on the west side, James Kittredge at his home about a mile above the head of the pond; the third school was on the east side. Amaziah Reed and Lemuel Jackson, ministers of the Baptist faith, had lived on the west side of the lake since 1803. Jackson had organized the Baptist Church of about fifty members nearly all of whom lived on the west side. In 1818, he left for the west. Reed joined him six years later.

The settlers on the east side were largely Congregationalists, the organization having been started in 1809 with eighteen members. Both religious societies flourished. William Bowley built the first frame house in town. Jonathan Pratt built the first two-story house and was becoming well to do. He was later considered the wealthiest man in town.

With the number of frame houses increasing in Weld each year, modern improvements were also being introduced. In log houses with one window, possibly with two, over which thinly scraped sheepskins were stretched to admit a little light, windows of glass were beginning to appear. With Philip's goods from Greene, he had brought several dozen panes of glass and as soon as he could find an opportunity from his other work, James Swett would begin making window frames and sashes. Hannah and Philip insisted that Rachel should have the first three windows put into the log house, two in the main house and one in young Rachel's bedroom. It would be difficult to express the sheer joy and appreciation felt by those two women when the windows were installed. They were now living in a new world, a world of sun light. No longer must they work huddled and cramped over the light of a tiny candle. Sunshine flooded the rooms, making their work a pleasure. They had no longer to strain their eyes to find a small object dropped upon the floor; and to sew a seam now was such a pleasant pastime. Their whole outlook on life had changed in a day. The furnishings of the home now seemed lovely.

Rachel said, "I don't know how we ever got along without these winders. Jest think of it. Ten years we have lived in this dark room, 'n' t' tell th' truth, I never realized it afore."

Ebenezer and Sarah Newman came to call the first Sunday afternoon following Philip and Hannah's arrival. Ebenezer was anxious to hear all Philip could tell him of the night spent at the home of his brother, Benjamin, in Washington, New Hampshire. Philip elaborated on the account of their hospitality and dwelt at length and with considerable detail upon the fine home they maintained.

He said, "It is my ambition to build a home some day that in some respects will resemble that of your brother Benjamin's. If Sam and I do as well with this lumbering scheme as I think we shall, we both should be able to build fine homes."

Ebenezer confided to them he too intended to improve and enlarge his home in the near future. He also told them his son, Oliver, had bought land in District No. 4, down river a mile and a half below Berry's, where he wished to later make his home. Had already built a log house there and went as often as he could to clear land.

"He has worked three summers in Turner for Isaiah Leavett, saved his wages and paid for the most of his farm. He wants to have Silas Barnard of Dixfield run the lines. He's the best man round here to do that job," said Ebenezer.

"Yes, so Sam tells me, and we're goin' to have Barnard come up here and lay out our lots and do some estimating on this timber before we go any father," said Philip. l

"Has Oliver got a girl that makes him in sech a hurry to settle a place for himself?" asked Sam.

"Oh, I guess not. He's jest ambitious. He's gettin' to that age, you know how 'tis after that," replied the smiling Ebenezer.

The three wives exchanged knowing glances, but had nothing to say.

"Well, I don't suppose you've heard there's been a weddin' in this family this morning?"

"Who was married and where, Sam?" asked Sarah.

"Wall, our Naomi and Si MacLoughlin went up to Elder Reed's and got hitched. Rachel wanted 'em t' be married here and let us make a good weddin' for 'em, same as we did for Rachel 'n' Philip; but Naomi wouldn't have it so. Said there wa'n't no room nor no time for any sech thing. I sorta 'greed with her, that she'd used up about all th' time she oughter, a-gittin' married. Godfrey! She's been an old maid for more'n a year."

Just then observing the expression upon his wife's face, he realized he had said too much about old maids with Mary Judkins in the room and stopped short. Rachel deemed this a suitable time to serve some of her elderberry wine and seed cookies. This little gesture of his wife's caused Sam to swell with pride and also in spite of himself, to "Ah, Dum Dee' several times while Rachel was pouring the wine in blue cups without handles and daughter Rachel was carefully placing the seed cookies on one of her grandmother White's pewter plates. After partaking of the refreshments provided by Rachel, the women eagerly sought their knitting and the men lit their pipes from a blazing strip of dry cedar handed to them by Philip's wife. The afternoon passed pleasantly, even lonely old Mary decided Weld was a pretty good place after all.

Monday morning, young Philip rode to Dixfield to engage Silas Barnard to come at his earliest convenience to survey the Weld timberland. During his dinner hour at the Tavern, he met Isaac Stanley who had lately come to town. There were several other men around the Tavern with whom young Philip now felt well acquainted. He found the men of Dixfield were generally very sociable.

When Stanley learned Philip was looking for Silas Barnard, he said, "If all I hear of him is true, this Silas is a hard man to find. You never know where he'll be or how he'll be. Last week he went up the road here to work on the meadows. He owns some land up there on the flats near the river. He was clearing and burning brush and t'was pretty hot. So he took off his clothes and laid 'em on the ground and worked through the hottest part of the day as naked as a new born babe. When it began to grow cooler, he looked for his clothes, but failing to find 'em, finally decided he had burned them along with the brush. The mosquitos were pretty thick, so he had to keep slapping himself with branches till he was about worn out. When it became very dark, he started for home, keeping well to the side of the road so he could dodge under cover should any one come along. At twelve o'clock that night, his wife, Aunt Lucy, who had sat all evening waiting for him, heard a slight noise in the shed, followed by a light tap on the door, which she opened a little to behold her lord and master standing stark naked waiting for admitance. Probably it wouldn't be well to repeat all she said to him. They also tell of his starting out to walk to the home of Ben Leavitt, who lives at the top of the long hill just beyond here across the Webb River in the town of Mexico. When Barnard reached the grist mill he saw a friend of his just hitching his horse by the door and asked if he might borrow the steed to ride to the home of his friend Leavitt, on Eustis Hill. Said he was coming right back and would return the horse in an hour or two. The friend waited patiently one hour, two hours, three hours. His patience exhausted and desiring to return to his home, he decided to go to the Barnard house and tell Mrs. Barnard she could inform her husband when he came, that he should expect him to return the horse to his door that night without fail. He could also bring money to pay for his hire. The friend pounded none too gently on Barnard's door, and to his tremendous surprise was smilingly greeted by Silas himself, who upon seeing his friend, remembered he had ridden his horse to Ben Leavitt's house, put it in the barn and later walked home without it. He has the reputation of being the most absent-minded man in this town; But he is also called the best surveyor in this part of the country.

He is called to run lines all over both Franklin and Oxford counties and even goes to other states to do this work, I am told."

Philip had good luck in finding the illusive Silas who promised to go to Weld the following day and remembered to keep his word. During his stay in the town he proved to be most efficient in his work and a very enjoyable guest at the White homestead where he spent the nights. Many were the interesting tales he told them of his experience, not only in the District of Maine, but in the vicinity of the Great Lakes. He was not only a surveyor, but an explorer as well. He could estimate the amount of growing timber with a surprising degree of accuracy. His method was to go to the highest hill in the vicinity, where he would climb the tallest tree by falling a shorter tree against it, thus providing a means whereby he could reach its first branches. From the tops of these tall trees he was afforded a fine view of the forest and could thereby locate and estimate the standing pine, which was the only timber of any value at that time. His thorough knowledge of the topography of the entire district made valuable his suggestions regarding the stringing of booms in places along the banks of Webb River, where it emptied into the Androscoggin. Barnard carefully described the various meadows along the way where timber would float into many little creeks and lagoons and said,

"Unless the entrances to these places are securely boomed, half your timber will be lost before you get to Dixfield."

Philip and Sam gratefully accepted the advice of their new friend and as soon as possible made preparations to follow his instructions.

Philip at once began plans to build a boat that would prove to be indispensable in the spring when the log driving began. He knew exactly how to make it of spruce lumber, a flat-bottomed dory type boat, twenty feet long and six feet at its widest part, which would be sufficiently ample for holding extra ropes that Philip had already arranged to procure from the ship yards at Bath. Also it would carry other necessary equipment, and transport the men from one scene of action to another. There would always be several yokes of oxen for use in hauling along the banks or on roads that ran near the river, extra provisions for men and beasts. These ox teams would be a timely aid in moving logs stuck fast in the banks or to pull them away from rocks and prevent "jams" building up.

Young Philip assisted his father in the boat building. It was completed and ready to use in transporting their supplies and light equipment. The crew required for this work would be small. Sam and Philip and their three sons, young Ebenezer Newman and his brother, Oliver, with Collins Pratt, would make the party. It was a jolly crowd that started down river one early morning. There were two men rowing whose places would later by filled by two others in turn until all had taken their turns. No man would be overworked on the trip. For the first five miles the banks were high on both sides of the river. When they were about a mile below Berry's, Oliver pointed ahead to a high bank on the west where a small log house stood in a sizeable clearing that ran back toward the hills. He loudly announced,

"That's my place, boys. I own 'bout thirty acres up thar 'n' soon'll own some more."

There was much talking and speculating on the value of the soil, how rocky it would prove further west, when they suddenly observed the river had abrupty turned north.

"Is it gon' back t' Weld?" someone asked.

Oliver answered, "No, its jest takin' a turn up 'round my property. It'll soon flow south again. I call the land inside this little freak of th' river 'th Ox bow'. Don't you see it has the same shape?"

From then on for about a mile, the land on the west bank grew lower until it all became a meadow through which flowed a sizeable brook. Philip and Sam thought it best to fell a few trees across the mouth of this stream and at several other places which seemed to need guarding. Half a mile below the first meadow they came upon a second which required the rest of the day to boom. When this was completed, they camped for the night. The weather was perfect for such a trip and they enjoyed every hour of it.

To their surprise on the second day out, they suddenly came upon a miniature falls in the little river. They decided to make a landing and investigate. Soon after they were back on the stream, they sighted the "big meadows" of which Barnard had warned them. Now, trouble indeed had come. There were long stretches of this low land, along both banks of the river—booms must be strung—and more booms—seemingly no end. The type of boom called "sheep-shank" which they used was made by tying logs together with ropes. Two half hitches were made on each log leaving a foot of rope for slack between them. It required a great deal of rope and many logs to protect both banks the length of the two long meadows. Two whole days were necessary to complete the booming of the last stretch.

There was a saw and grist mill at Dixfield and Philip said he would soon make arrangements with Sam Parks to string a side boom in the early spring, for the lumber, to prevent its becoming mixed with his logs when they came through with the drive.

It was quite a different matter to take the boat and eight men back upstream; the distance from the meadows to Weld seemed twice as far as it had coming down. They arrived at the outlet of Webb Pond on the evening of the fifth day, happy and satisfied with their accomplishments. With the river banks guarded as far as Dixfield, they now felt secure. Barnard had said there were very few places along the Androscoggin where the banks were not of sufficient height to hold the logs from going astray and these places had already been boomed by former log drivers.

This done, the lines of the timberlands run, the corner posts plainly marked, Philip and Sam now felt they could begin the work of cutting down trees. Every day new men appeared from all directions with their ox-teams. Most of them brought their grain, and some men also brought their hay. The great log camp for the men was ample and comfortable; the hovels for the animals were as good as any of that day. For two weeks, young Philip and James had been hauling provisions from Dixfield. Chains, ropes, axes, saws, cant-dogs, a grindstone for sharpening tools, whet-stones and many other articles useful and needful to the big logging job had been sent by ox-teams from Bath.

Hannah and Rachel decided they wished to try to do the cooking for these lumbermen. Mary and young Rachel could do all the work at the White log house. If these two older women could accomplish the gargantuan task of feeding twenty-five or thirty men, it would saving hiring a man cook and cookee. Probably the cook would expect a dollar a day, and his helper half that price. Besides, men were much more extravagant than women. So, after much argument with their husbands, the women won out, and were allowed to try it for a month.

Chapter XIX

GIANTS IN TRANSIT

The first step in a "loggin' job" is "swampin' ro'ds". This means that after the big boss had laid out the job, or planned the operation, the roads must be built on which the logs will, later on, be hauled. Generally there is a center road running through the entire tract, and if sufficiently large to warrant it, many other roads will be built leading to it from both sides. All timber, after it is cut down, is either hauled to the nearest road, where it is rolled over "skids" onto "yards" or to the river bank. Efficiency of operation and keeping costs at the lowest possible level, entirely determined the success of an undertaking of this kind. Good roads were a very material factor. First, the smoothest places must be selected, then the rougher, rocky spots were made more passable by laying down logs of varying lengths, providing a substantial track over which the long timber could be drawn. This process is called "skidding". In many instances, bridges must be built over brooks or deep gullies. Over these long girders are laid, then floored over with logs of equal diameter and of sufficient strength to bear any weight.

"Yards" are built at sides of roads of long base logs running lengthwise toward the road. The cut timber is rolled onto these in huge quantities. These yards are generally built four or five feet higher than the road, which is very helpful to the men who roll the logs onto their sleds, to haul away later.

In cases where hills or ridges are covered with desirable timber, if the grade be high and too steep for oxen or horses to safely haul down the decline, oftentimes the trees are "sluiced" down. A "Sluice" is a narrow lane prepared as smooth as possible extending down the side of a hill or mountain, down which logs can slide. Sometimes, where the amount of lumber warrants, huge log troughs are built for this purpose. The timber on the back side of the hills has to be hauled around, if possible, as it cannot be hauled up. To retard the speed of a loaded team descending an icy hill, "medda hay" (poor hay grown in a meadow) is spread on the road in generous quantities. Another method is to fasten logs with chains to the back of the load to drag behind, and are called "snubbers".

To the "walkin' boss" fell the responsibility of road building and the removal of timber to the river. This was Sam's business. While the workmen were practically all neighbors of Philip's and Sam's and never used any title when addressing them, they did think of Philip as the boss and of Sam as the "walkin' boss". Young Philip was the clerk and his duties were many. First, he must keep a strict account of all hours worked by the men and their teams, all supplies bought from the "store", which was mostly tobacco, now and then a little rum, but the latter was not encouraged by Philip and Sam, for they knew it was an extravagance they could not afford. Molasses and salt were the principal commodities, the men of that locality raised whatever else they used.

Sam was an unusually good blacksmith, and had taught his sons to become nearly as efficient as he. It was arranged to hire young Sam to work at the shop for them as soon as he should return from Billerica. The price paid for this work was ninety cents a day, generally, but forty-five if "found". Philip and Sam were satisfied to pay fifty and found. This being twice as much as young Sam could earn on farms in Massachusetts, they felt sure he would be happy to accept this position offered him. It was no small task to build an "ox sling". Sam had a good one in his blacksmith shop at the log house, but the logging camps, hovels, etc. were more than a mile south of Sam's residence, so it seemed necessary to build another complete outfit. Sam and Philip went about the building of it with careful forethought, as they did with all the construction work. The strength of an ox is tremendous. Sam well knew this fact and built the tie-up in that first barn so strongly that poor Broad was unable to free himself when attacked by the wild cat, years previous. Had he built the sides of his barn with the heavy timbers, as he did the frame and "stantial" posts, the destructive animal could never have forced an entrance. The timbers of a blacksmith shop must be adequate to support an ox sling. This is built of heavy oak timbers like the frame, and suspended by iron hooks which are fastened to great logs lying on the floor above. Into this cage the ox is driven where a very broad belly band is placed around him. Straps at each corner extend up over his back and are fastened. To a stone post with an iron ring in the top, provided for this, the head of the ox is secured. In the chamber above a large wooden wheel is arranged with heavy rope in windlass fashion, connecting with the ox sling below. This wheel is turned by a wooden crank at the will of the blacksmith, who when all is ready carefully raises the huge animal a few inches from the floor, securing his legs to the four low corner posts of the cage, and begins his work. The great weight of an ox prohibits allowing him to stand for any length of time on three legs, as this always causes strain which has a very injurious effect upon the animal. Then the forge and bellows must be constructed, iron for making shoes must be obtained, oxen having cloven hoofs require two shoes for each foot, so there must be plenty of material on hand. Philip had a sufficient amount sent up from Bath. And last, but by no means least, there must be a large quantity of charcoal for this use. Sam had a goodly quantity of this already, and could borrow more from Jonathan Pratt if necessary. It was a task in itself to make charcoal. The people of the Province generally used alder wood for the purpose. After removing the sods from a good-sized area, a great mound of alders would be stood on end with a small space in the center forming an inverted cone. Over this they solidly placed the sods leaving a small opening at the bottom where a fire would be built and the whole thing allowed to smoulder for many hours, or until the wood had become entirely charred.

On October first, the first tree was felled. The Weld men descended upon that great forest, axes in hand, grim determination in their minds. If the Bath Ship Building Company, through Judkins and White, could furnish the money, they could supply the work necessary to clear that tract of trees. This forest was a perfect example of the survival of the fittest, for there were practically no poor trees; all were giants, towering their heads to the heavens in defiance of everything earthly, only paying their homage to the God above. The ring of the woodsmen's axes sounded over that ridge like a symphony in silver bells and it was the sweetest music Sam had ever heard. He never once thought of joining his voice with that sylvan orchestra. He lifted his eyes, that were now shining with tears of thanksgiving, toward heaven where he believed his God heard and answered prayer. But instead of his usual outbursts of enthusiasm, when things pleased him, after waiting eleven years, he could feel he really glimpsed success.

"Praise the Lord for His goodness to the children of men."

Then closing his eyes poured out his thoughts, "Dear good Lord, ye did hear my prayers, didn't ye? And I dew believe ye'll stand right by us 'til we land the last stick of this timber in Merrymeetin' Bay. It did seem sometimes, Lord, that I should never live to see this day. But I have 'n all my folks with me; 'n Philip 'n all his, even to his old maid sister, poor old thing. I wish ye'd find some way to brighten her up a little. I feel almost condemned for being so happy when I think of her sad little wizened up face. I ain't a-tryin' t' tell ye yer business, Lord, but, forgive me if I just hint that a husband would be the best Christmas present ye could give her. That is if ye would feel justified in hitchin' any o' yer male subjects up along side o' her. I ain't got no suggestions, mind ye, but I sorta pity th' poor forlorn critter. So far I ain't never been able to spot her a real suitable mate. My wife claims I'm always meddlin' this way for somebody, but men is scurce round here. Wal, here I am a kinda gittin' off th' beam a little, also takin' your valuable time t' listen. I'm askin' ye once more t' let this lumber job pay us big. Don't let no accidents happen to our men, they'er all such good fellers. Ye know it, Lord, 's well 's I dew, and ye know how their families need 'em. This is a rugged country, Lord, and ye know that too for ye made it, and ye know us folks have t' be rugged t' live here. Now, Lord, I won't bother ye agin t'day. Amen."

All the way down over the hill and into the cool woods, he hummed his Ah—dum—dee, stopping only when he met Philip, who was hurrying from one set of choppers to another as they surrounded themselves with the great trees they had already felled.

"It won't be long before we shall need to start working with our oxen, Sam. We shall have to get these trees twitched round into line a little, for I plan to have the main road run right over through there, past that tree Collins Pratt is limbin' out now, and on a straight line to the river. I tell you, Sam, these men we have hired know how to fell trees. I'd have been satisfied if they'd done half as much. Look around here. See what a lot of them are down waiting to be hauled. You see, there is almost no small stuff.

All the trees are big and they land just where the choppers plan. No little trees to bother, there'll be very few get lodged, in this section, anyway," said Philip.

That noon when the men went to camp for dinner, they found everything in readiness. Rachel and Hannah, with the help of James Swett, had converted that bare logging camp into a comfortable dining room. A great saw-buck table with benches running along each side would accommodate thirty men. Right now there were only ten outside of the two families, making sixteen in all to eat, as Mary, young Rachel and the children would live at Sam White's house. A great fireplace built of logs with a long lug pole provided ample cooking accommodations. Beside this an arch had been built over which the great iron kettle was placed. This would provide gallons of hot water for dish washing and could be used as it was today for cooking a "boiled dinner". To make this, in the morning there were placed two pieces of beef, each weighing five or six pounds, slices of salt pork of equal weight. These were allowed to boil slowly until about ten o'clock when two or three handfuls of salt were thrown in. Soon after this, a peck of carrots, cut in strips, four or five large turnips sliced, at least fifteen pounds of cabbage, cut in thick slices were added and allowed to boil another hour or two. About three-quarters of an hour before serving time, a peck of peeled potatoes were put into the pot, the whole covered. On the tick of noon, all was ready to pile on great platters which would be edged with slices of beets that had been cooked for several hours in a separate pot. The meat platters would be placed alternately with plates of brownbread, butter and the steaming vegetables on platters. Indian pudding, served either with cream or butter was the usual dessert served with a "biled dish" as this vegetable dinner was often called. Some generous housewives added twisted doughnuts and cheese, but no man ever left Sam White's table hungry and no man ever had cause to grumble at the fare furnished by his partner, Philip Judkins.

The cold days of November were beginning to cast a gloom over the hillside, spits of snow had been falling all day, when tired, but full of courage, appeared young Sam. The sights and sounds that greeted him when he walked down the road from Holt's were very satisfying, also aroused his curiosity. His father's suggestion that he take over the entire work at the blacksmith shop at such magnificent wages nearly transported him to the skies. Now he could marry Lydia, for he had nearly enough money in his pocket right now to make his last payment on his farm. Through the winter he would earn the remainder and after this great lumbering project was over, he would have plenty laid by to build a home.

Much sooner than either Philip or Sam had dared hope, the choppers had accomplished so much it was thought necessary to send for all the ox teams. About two feet of snow had fallen by the second week of December making it possible to start hauling the logs to the river bank. This meant twenty men drove the cattle, and added to the ten choppers, filled the great table. Rachel and Hannah now had thirty men to feed besides their husbands and sons. This was indeed a task. Three times daily the faces of those thirty hungry men faced the two women well past middle age. At four o'clock each morning, Sam raked back the coals that had been buried in ashes during the night, piled dry cedar kindlings on them and in no time a great fire was blazing; dry maple logs would soon produce the required amount of heat to enable Rachel and Hannah to cook breakfast, which was generally of baked beans, brown bread, doughnuts, cheese, "rye 'n' Injun coffee", with sometimes seven or eight mince or pumpkin pies thrown in for good measure.

At night when the last dish had been washed and put in its place, the menu planned for the following day, these two wonderful women sat for a few moments nursing their tired feet and aching backs. They would cheer each other with the thought of how much money they were saving for their husbands. Then they would tumble into their bunks beside their already sleeping mates, mumble a prayer, which was sometimes never finished because they fell aslep too soon. The morning would find them dressed and bustling about the fire before Sam could hardly finish its building. All this, by the light of half a dozen candles sputtering their defiance from their iron holders, making eerie shadows along the white newly-peeled ridge pole, or behind benches, syrup pitchers, salt shakers.

In less than an hour from the time Sam stepped out of his bunk into the frigid atmosphere of the camp to dress and make his fire, thirty sleepy, but hungry men filed past the bench where they made a pretence of washing their faces and hands in warm water and the soft homemade soap provided. Rachel would see to it that they at least took a lick and promise, all drying themselves on a coarse linen towel.

Sometimes she would say to one, who might linger over his task, "Hustle up there, you can wash off the rest of it Saturday night."

After a few swallows of hot "rye 'n' Injun coffee" or a few mouthfuls of steaming porridge, or beans, or red flannel hash, these men would begin taking long breaths, showing their stiffened limbs were beginning to relax, and for the rest of the meal would really enjoy themselves. This wasn't for long, as fifteen minutes was about the length of time it required for them to bolt down their breakfasts, light their pipes, and with an "all together now" push back their benches from the table and go outside into the frosty darkness.

It was Sam's job, as soon as he had built the fire, to make sure every man who owned an ox team was up and feeding his cattle so they'd be ready to start out as soon as their owners were.

Young Philip, who slept in the log house with his family, a good mile away, must be in the "store" ready to serve anyone who wished to buy tobacco for himself or grain for his oxen before he left camp for his day's work. Young Sam must also be prepared to do any work necessary that could be accomplished in the blacksmith shop. Four o'clock was the hour set for them to "pile out" and pile out they did. Being late was not to be tolerated in the Judkins and White camp.

As the winter wore on, and they settled comfortably into the routine ways of their bosses, these sturdy poineers became the last word in efficiency as each vied with the other to become a little the best.

Philip told Sam one evening in March, as they sat before the fire, allowing themselves a few moments of comfort, with their long-stemmed pipes, "It's almost unbelievable, Sam, the number of trees that are waiting to be rolled into the river. I don't really dare to estimate the thousands of feet that we have. This drive will be difficult on our little river, for the logs are all longer than the river is wide. They tell me in the spring there is always a tremendous rise of water, though. Course you have seen it all these years, but there are some ugly looking rocks between here and Berry's Mills."

"But it's no use to borrow trouble. We wunt cross th' bridge til we git to it, Philip, 'n' I feel mighty sure we'll make it some way," said the king of optimists.

"I have been watching some of these men with an eye to finding a good foreman on this river driving. I like the appearance of the Masterman boy they call Luke. He drives a big pair of red cattle, and I believe he's the most powerful man I ever saw work. He uses his head. As far as that goes, they all do, pretty much. There's another fellow they call Mac. I don't know what his name is."

"David McLaughlin."

"Well, he's another giant, and those two fellows from cross the pond, Abe Russell and Jim Houghton, when they take holt of a log, she goes up."

"Good Lord, Philip, I guess that's right. A man that can carry a hundred pound grindstone on his back through the woods ten miles and never turn a hair can lift the end of a log. Ye take him 'n' Houghton on one end 'n' Duke and Steve Webster on th' tother 'n' that log's goin' t' move a piece, I c'n tell ye that. This Eben Hutchinson is no weakling either. Oh, they're all stout men. I ain't got no fault t' find with any on 'em."

"Great Caesar, Sam, here it is nine o'clock and we up here losin' sleep."

"Good-night, you old owl," said Sam as he raked the coals and pulled his back-log into place.

The last week in March the weather turned warmer. It began to rain, the logs were now on the river bank, or along the shore of the pond close to the outlet. For three days and nights it poured, the roads grew soft, no oxen or horses were taken from the hovels, it was difficult for men to walk without snowshoes, everywhere they slumped through the deep, wet snow, which was settling fast. Young Sam was the only really busy man in the whole outfit, as many of the oxen needed new shoes made or repaired. When Sam wasn't doing this, he was making pick poles, or sharpening cant-dog bales, and doing all sorts of other repair jobs. Some of the men became restless and went home taking their oxen with them. Others fearing accident to their cattle due to the soft condition of the roads, preferred to stay in camp until conditions improved. These men played cards, whittled, wrestled, jumped, lifted weights, vying with each other as to the one who could hold "at arms length" the greatest number of horseshoes or any old iron heaped into a bucket. A man who couldn't "hold out" sixty pounds weighed on young Philip's scales, was considered more or less a "lardhead". All these things they did while it rained and rained. Several times each day some restless soul would venture forth when there was the slightest evidence of clearing, wet his finger in his mouth and hold it toward the skies to determine if the wind was changing. Disgusted to find it still coming from the northeast, he would return to camp.

"No sign of its veerin' round to'ds the west," he would say. Then all the men would turn to whatever occupation they could find.

One Sunday morning young Philip didn't appear at the wangan till after daylight. He cheerfully informed the men that the wind was changing and prophesied,

"Fore night it'll back round by the south and clear off, and besides there are great black places on the ice where it seems to be settling in the pond. It's goin' to break up fore long. We shan't have t' set round here much longer."

During the night, the wind changed into the northwest.

The following day the sun came out bright and warm, melting the remaining snow and ice like a fire. Sometime during the previous night the ice in the river had broken up and started in great cakes to float downstream.

"It's only a matter of time now before the pond ice will give way and go out, and we can start rollin' in the logs," said Philip.

"Oh happy day, happy day, Ah-dum-dee, A-dum-dee," sang Sam.

That night Rachel was awakened by peculiar faraway sounds, deep thuds broke the stillness. These unusual noises had never before reached her ears. She spoke to her sleeping husband, who listened for a moment then proclaimed in a loud voice to his friend Philip in the other bunk,

"The ice is a-goin out. Hear th' great cakes a-bumpin' into each other? Godfrey mighty, Philip, what was that crash?"

"It's the log pile. She's started. Hear them rollin', Sam, they're on their way. God Almighty has begun our drive for us. May it please Him to continue with us until the end." So saying, Philip sank to his knees beside the bunk, offered a silent prayer to his God.

Sam bowed his head where he stood, adding his own supplications, remembering, "Whatsoever ye shall ask in my name, that will I give you."

Philip said, "Amen," rose from his knees, immediately Sam started humming and all was action again.

Philip went to the door of the sleeping-camp, and in a stern, commanding voice, ordered, "Wake up, men. The ice is leaving the pond, do you hear the logs bumpin'? There are many thousand feet of timber to be rolled in during the next few days. Up and at it, my boys."

Such a commotion as these few words caused! The men, who for a week had been like drones in a hive, snapped into action like the now released ice-bound waters of the river. They tumbled over each other, almost fighting to be the first to get through the door of the hovel and get outside to do whatever was necessary.

Inside the "cook camp" Rachel and Hannah hardly touched the pole floor with their feet. They were so elated they flew from one task to another. Food appeared on that table like magic. Rachel spoke never a word if a man failed to take a lick and a promise at the wash bench. They rushed past her and settled themselves at the table. This morning her own strength seemed limitless.

"Oh Hannah," she said, as she lifted a tremendously heavy pot of beans and started pouring them into bowls to push along down the table. "Ain't it good to be alive!" "Think how many there be that ain't" said Hannah. God's bin good, we ain' never seen a sick minute since we started in 'n' think of the money we've saved. Course now it's bout over, I wish we was capable of goin' on 'n' cookin' for th' drive, but o'course we can't. Least, Sam says we can't. After this I b'lieve two o' th' Pratt boys is goin' to take over. Their mother told me they were good at it. They have done it several winters for their father. He owns big timberlands over to th' east. Young Philip is goin' t' have charge of th' wangan, 'n' it's goin' t'be no small job."

Hannah replied, "I wouldn't be surprised if the hardest work lies ahead. Philip has been greatly concerned all winter about the delivery of this timber, especially where the river is so narrow and full of rocks from heer to Dixfield. After that it will be easier in the big river. Of course, there are still timber pirates on the Androscoggin that lie in wait to cut booms and steal the logs, but I think our husbands have a pretty sound plan for avoiding that. There will be plenty of guns in their outfit. You and I know our men know how to use them. We don't need worry but that any man on that drive will be able to shoot straight and quick."

"I guess they'll manage that part of it. It's goin' t' be a long wait for us back here till our men get that drive through t' Bath. There won't be nawthin' for us t' do after they go."

"Oh, I think we'll find something," replied Hannah.

Thursday morning, Rachel and Hannah served their last breakfast to the crew which numbered in all, including the family, twenty-two men. The Pratt boys had previously built a makeshift camp down near Berry's Mills where they ate their supper and spent the night. This camp was not comfortable like the one in which they had spent the winter. From now on, comfort was the last thing to be considered. Food was paramount. The men's stomachs must be filled often to give them strength, for they must wade to their armpits in icy water half the time. They would be slipping on treacherous rocks that lay hidden just beneath the surface of the water. When night came they must lie down in their soggy, wet clothing on a poorly-made bough bed, covered by a coarse blanket which they must share with at least one other. And as the night advanced, grow so cold and stiff they could hardly turn over to ease their aching limbs. The first few days of this sort of life told the story. There would always be one or two who couldn't endure such hardships and would leave the crew, but there was a certain fascination in it. And those who were sufficiently determined to stick, gradually became toughened to the life. Few men caught cold. The idea that going to bed in wet clothing saved them from this was largely shared by all. Most men took their allowance of rum at night. It was always provided by the boss and no man was ever criticised for enjoying this privilege. Sometimes from his own private stock, a river driver would indulge during working hours and would invariably take a dip in the deep black water which would have an extremely sobering effect. If any man, through skillful planning or expert log riding, managed somehow to keep dry through the day, his fellow drivers would sometimes see to it that he was rolled in before he retired. But if a man was not honest in his work, found a secluded spot on the river bank where he could lie in the sun in comfort while others toiled in the frigid waters, it was an unlucky day for him if discovered. He'd certainly be forced to pay the penalty and lucky if he wasn't half drowned in the performance.

Philip tolerated no inhuman treatment of his men, expected them to be honest and do their work faithfully. If they failed, they were "sent down the ro'd" and that ended it.

Many were the trying situations faced by Philip and Sam. Those jagged rocks were not only a pitfall for the men, but great logs would catch on them and soon a jam would start building up. Crews of several men were sent far ahead to avoid this, but it wasn't always possible to accomplish. When once started, the swift rushing water would carry the great logs on to pile up faster and faster, until they became like mountains in the river bed. It required men of great courage, judgment and strength to start "picking a jam". One log, called the key log, generally held the whole pile. This was often in the center and some man must go to the middle of the jam and start picking away the logs. This was a dangerous piece of business. Sometimes a boat crew would row up in front of the jam and manage to pull the right log out. The whole jam might start and lucky the crew if they escaped in season. The jams could sometimes be picked loose from the sides. This was often a long, tiresome process.

The crew now working well-down, toward the eating camp, would be glad when night came to be near their food and bed. The midday meal was brought to them, also luncheon in the middle of the forenoon. Now they must move the wangan down river and so save the men walking too far after work. Sam and Philip disliked to see these tired men taking an extra step if it could be avoided. Sam conceived the idea of building another wangan camp on the river where it flowed through the second meadow; but their next stop could be at Berry's Mills. He hoped they might find lodgings in some of the farm houses there. This comfort would add greatly to the courage of these fellows who were giving their all to the cause.

Along that crooked river, for two miles, Philip rode on horseback ahead of the drive, while Sam generally stayed at the rear looking after supplies and making sure no logs were left behind. As Philip neared Berry's Mills, he dared hope things would go easier after this. But to his surprise he found a bridge had been constructed near the mill and it appeared to almost touch the water. The logs were coming thick and fast now, soon they would reach the bridge, but would they pass under? He jumped from his horse and ran to the bridge frantically calling for help from any of the men who might hear. Duke Masterman happened to be the only man near enough to sense the danger. In his hand he carried a long pick pole and with all his strength began to guide the fast moving logs between the piers of the little bridge. His power was almost superhuman, but it could not cope with the rushing water that hurled these logs against the abutments of the frail structure and started piling one on top of the other. Soon there was a tremor along the whole bridge, then the sound of breaking wood. Philip and Duke suddenly realized the floor upon which they stood was moving.

"Jump, Duke! Jump for your life. The bridge is going out," yelled Philip, as he ran to the nearest end. Duke ran, but not in season to step on land like Philip in safety. His pick pole had stuck in a log and he waited too long trying to save it. He glanced both ways trying to see a place on the shore where he could jump. But the little bridge was being lifted in the air by those monster logs. They seemed to have gone wild, crazily throwing the manmade structure first one way, then the other. What held it intact was past the understanding of any man. Now it was rising again. Up, up, higher it rose till it reached the first limbs of the elm tree along the bank. One of these branches brushed Duke's head and in a split second he grasped it. Would it hold? He held his breath and prayed. On the bank Philip prayed also and he too held his breath as the bridge dropped from its dizzy height and broke up into many small parts and mingled with the logs beneath it, soon crushed beyond recognition as it rushed on downstream. People came out from their houses to watch the helpless Duke still hanging in the branches of the tree. Philip, on the opposite side of the river, was unable to do one thing to help. If Duke could only drop into the river, there were several men on that side who could pull him ashore. But the logs were coming so fast he would be hit by them before this could be done. The strength in Duke's powerful arms was beginning to give away. He knew he must soon drop. If he could only hold on until there was a little space between the onrushing timbers, he might save his life. He watched for this chance. It came. He dropped. Down he went, it didn't seem possible the little river could be so deep. Would he ever touch bottom? He felt as if it were a mile down to where his feet touched the muddy river bed, then he started up—up with a rush. When he reached the surface and opened his eyes, a great white-ended pine dripping with pitch was within a few feet of his head. Instantly he dove under just in season to escape the impact.

"This time I'll use my head," he said, swimming under water, and this time he made it. Two men grasped his arms and dragged him up on the bank where he received every kindness the neighborhood could provide. On the opposite shore Philip stood watching, tears of thankfulness running down his cheeks, as he murmured, "Surely the Lord is good, His mercy endureth forever."

Every home in Berry's Mills opened its doors to the Judkins-White river drivers, some men even climbing the hill to stay over night with Daniel Storer.

Philip and Sam sat late talking that evening with Tom Berry. He had done considerable river driving on the Kennebec before he came to Number Four and was glad to learn that the inlets and meadows along the river had been well boomed the previous fall. He was very considerate in his demands for what Sam and Philip should pay him for the loss of his bridge, assuring them twenty-five dollars would rebuild it. With Daniel Storer's help he would soon have it reconstructed.

"And this time, very much higher. By the time you gentlemen return from Merrymeetin' you can ride your horses over it with safety," he said.

Philip felt concerned regarding the rock river bed half a mile below.

"I very much fear the logs will jam there during the night. Probably they"re piled a mile high right now."

The next morning showed he was correct. Such a sight as met Philip's eyes when he reached the "rips." Hundreds of long logs had piled one upon the other and stuck fast upon the jagged rocks and more were fast coming. Philip quickly turned his horse, galloped back to the Mills and sent Duke to the rear to gather all the crew along the way and order them to begin work on the jam. Half a dozen men, including Oliver, were sent ahead to see to it that the hundred-foot logs floated around the "oxbow" without getting caught on the banks. Oliver's curiosity led him to run far ahead of the others over to the bow and watch the great timbers as they rounded the bend and started again toward Dixfield.

The jam below Berry's did not prove a serious affair and noon found the men ready for their dinner which they ate at the mouth of the brook at the first meadow, later called Staples' Meadow.

That night they slept in the camp on the second meadow. The Pratt boys had made it as comfortable as possible and their food was plentiful and good.

The third day the logs began going over the little falls and started jamming soon after, but were not allowed to pile up for long. The middle of the afternoon found them at the head of the "big meadows".

"Now I s'pose our fun begins, 'specially if our booms don't hold," said Sam.

"Well if they don't I'll eat them," answered Philip, but there was no need for this. Hundreds of pine logs floated slowly along carried by the black waters of the now greatly enlarged little river. Men were stationed at every point where there was a question of th inadequacy of the booms. On moved the great pine monsters, seeming almost alive and anxious to join others of their kind far ahead in the big river beyond.

True to his promise, Sam Parks had collected all his logs into a well-made permanent side boom, allowing the Weld timber to go down over the dam and into the Androscoggin. Half the men of the village stood on the banks of Webb River to watch the first log drive go through into the deeper waters which would bear them to the coast.

Chapter XX

"SAFE IN THE ANDROSCOGGIN"

Several men of Dixfield expressed the desire to join the driving crew of Judkins and White and they were engaged. That night, when Sam "brought up the rear" and the last log had gone out into the broad expanse of the Androscoggin, there wasn't a river driver in sight, except those of Sam's crew, four in all. To Sam's delight, he found his friend, Silas Barnard, was waiting for him and it seemed a proper time for them to renew old acquaintances at the inn of Amos Trask. The taproom was well patronized by Sam's Dixfield friends and there they spent the evening in a manner pleasing to them all.

Philip, who had gone on to the first camp built on the banks of the big river, enjoyed a good supper and turned in early. If Sam and his crew were a trifle tardy the following morning, Philip guessed why and said nothing. He was too pleased and thankful to be at last on his beloved river headed toward the shipyard he knew so well. They had been very successful in getting logs down through this far, and Philip felt much credit was due Silas Barnard for his timely advice; and if Sam felt disposed to entertain him at the tavern, Philip was entirely agreeable to the idea.

Driving logs on the Androscoggin was a simple matter compared to that on the little river. Five days found them opposite Turner Village. It was some distance to walk up through the fields over the hill to the Upper Street. Philip, greatly desired a few minutes conversation with his friend, John Staples. Since leaving Livermore, he had thought of going up there if only for a few moments. but when he reached the place in the river where he had crossed on a raft more than once, there in a boat was John and beside him John B. The Staples had been watching for two days for the drive to make its appearance, and young John B. had seen the first log as it floated by. From the top of the hill he had seen with his keen eyes, one black and one blue, Philip's

(212)

horse as it had appeared up-river, more than a mile away. He listened to every word Philip said about the great wilderness farther up river and vowed in his heart to some day try his luck in the lumbering game there. He wished he could talk a long time with this Philip Judkins and learn more about Weld and all those other places along the river. As he listened to the conversation between his father and this tall dark man, the idea came to him to ask his father if he might join the river drivers and go through to Bath with them.

He said, "I would be willing to work for nothing if I could go. Please, father, let me go."

John looked questioningly at Philip, who nodded his head and asked, "Can you swim, young fellow?"

"Swim? He could swim almost before he stopped wearing clouts. His swimmin' would be the least of my worries. But if he gives his word that he won't go off explorin' around and leavin' the crew, I donno but I'd let him go. That is, if ye want to bother with him."

"How old are you, John B.?"

"Well, I'm comin' thirteen, but I weigh a hundred and two pounds on father's scales. I'm five feet and five inches tall, and if you'll let me go, I promise not to make any trouble for anybuddy, and I'll do what I'm told."

"All right, John B., you're hired, to do what you're told. You will be paid ten cents a day and get your board thrown in," Philip said.

"You'd better skip back to th' house and get a change of close from your mother. Mebbe she won't let ye go, but ye c'n find out," said the father.

"Tell your mother your work will be mostly with the wangan" called Philip to the boy who was fast disappearing up the hill.

At Philip's order, the Pratt boys built a small leanto on the river bank near the home of William Parker in Greene. This was for cooking, and housing supplies. William had offered the use of his barn as a place for the men to sleep. Philip was to stay in the house he had himself built and in the room he and Hannah had for so many years shared. Hannah Parker had insisted upon his taking this privilege. When he, with John B. arrived rather late for supper, they were given special privileges by the Pratt boys, Collin and Seth, who smiled a little skeptically when Philip told them he had brought them a valuable cookee, who would do as he was told. He added, as he winked at Seth, "I always contend it's a darned good man that does as he's told."

At break of day, John B. opened his eyes on a new world. He had slept well there beside Seth on the hay and felt ready for most anything. The feeding of twenty-five men at such an hour, from the few cooking utensils considered necessary at that time, was a revelation to the boy. Those mis-mated eyes of his didn't miss a trick. He soon learned what was required of him, did it quickly and well. Seth confessed later to Philip that he hadn't really expected the boy to do much, but said,

"It's a good show to watch that fellow wash dishes and get around here, for he's quick as a cat."

"Where is he now?" asked Philip.

"Up to the house, playing with the Parker children. There's a boy there about his age, I guess, and a girl a little younger, and a dozen or so younger still. I'd say these Parkers were obeyin' the Lord's commands all right, a-multiplyin' and a-replenishin' th' earth. Ain't that a fine pair of twin baby boys?"

John B., with considerable regret, left the Parker place the next forenoon, but luncheon must be served several miles further on. Collins had gone ahead with it in two great baskets, leaving Seth and John B. to bring the blankets, dishes and all the provisions. They left everything clean and in order at the Parker place where they had been so well accommodated. They must make all possible time and join Collins with their load of supplies at the new camp he would have ready for them several miles down river.

John B. had enjoyed himself with the Parker children more than at any time in his life that he could remember. The fact that he was a year older than Anslem and had a job on the river was enough to make him feel quite important. Lois, ten years old, was quite impressed with this boy. "Mother, he is the strongest boy you ever did see. He's ten times stronger than Anslem."

"Well, he ain't, Miss," snapped Anslem.

"Well, I notice he got snapped into line pretty quick by his Uncle Seth when he went on his first explorin' trip 'cordin' to his own story."

"What's that?" inquired the amused but interested mother, Hannah.

"I don't call it any great of a story myself, 'n' I 'spect he made up half of it anyway, but he said about a hundred thousand years ago, his father's brother and sister ran away to a Dead River somewhere, but I 'spect he meant the Dead Sea."

"Anslem Parker, he didn't say any such thing, a hundred thousand years ago!"

"Didn't he say his name was Noah?"

"Ye'us, he did," admitted Lois.

"Wall, then, I heard father say one time that Noah lived thousands and thousands of years ago."

"Oh, Anslem, this was not that Noah."

"Who's tellin' this story, I'd like t' know."

Hannah suggested that Anslem go on with the account of John B.'s travels and Lois should not further interrupt him, so he proceeded.

"John B. had heard so much about this Uncle Noah and Aunt Isabelle, with all their children being carried off by the Indians up there in that old Dead River country that he decided to take his father's hoss and his Uncle Seth's sword and gun, with a bag of grub and go up and find all them folks and bring them home. But he only got part way to North Turner when his Uncle Seth caught up with him and took that shiny sword and gun he had in the war, yanked John B. off his hoss and warmed his backsides. Then he sent him home, and I'l bet that took some of the quirks out of him."

"Mebbe it did 'n' mebbe it didn't, for ye know he said he was goin' t' wait till he had a hoss of his own 'n' then he was goin'. He is good and mad at his father for not trying to find his Aunt Isabelle. Said his father didn't seem to take no interest in her and said she was probably dead years ago, and as for Noah, he guessed he could shift for himself."

Grandma Rebecca, who had quietly listened to the conversation, later on remarked to Hannah that John B. was just like his mother Betsy. She was glad to learn that he was not the "ailing kind" like his father.

CHAPTER XXI

SAFE IN THE BATH BOOMS

Left back in Weld, the men and women of the Judkins-White drive were wasting no time. There was much to be done and few to do it. James was the only man in the White family who stayed at home. Sam considered he could better be spared from the drive than could young Sam, and with Phenewel now twelve years old to help, the two could carry on the farm work until the drive was over. Rachel and Hannah were capable of managing fairly well, even if no man was with them. But neither Philip or Sam were willing this should be. Also young Philip was quite reluctant to leave his young wife and two small children in that country which was still little more than a wilderness. So affairs moved on as usual.

Three years before, Sam had realized old Carlo was no longer a protection to the family or much help with the cattle. He had been a very faithful friend and aid in many ways, but during the last few years had grown very deaf. Now beginning to lose his sight, Sam decided he must find a new shepard dog to take his place. This he did and soon after, one morning when he went to the barn, he found old Carlo had gone to sleep by the door and would never waken. Faithful to the last, he had died at his post. The new dog, a powerful black and tan, part shepard, part beardog, weighing about seventy-five pounds, was all to be desired. No longer did they find bear tracks by the log-roofed pig pen. Prince was always on the spot. His hearing perfect, he could detect the slightest noise. When he did, his loud barking immediately warned, not only the White household, but the whole neighborhood. James trained him to get the cattle home at night, also to watch them in case any trouble threatened. The bull had shown defiance on one or two occasions, but decided to avoid those sharp teeth.

With the family now smaller, Rachel and Hannah decided there was ample time to do some extra sewing and offered to start making some clothes for the children. Cloth being so hard to obtain and neither Rachel nor Hannah having a loom on which they could weave, it was necessary and generally the custom, after a garment was partly worn out, to take whatever part remained in fair condition and make it over for smaller children. After careful consideration, it was finally decided to use young Rachel's old red dress to make over for little Mercy Ann. Young Rachel proudly related to Hannah the account of her first dance with Philip, told her of the wonderful meals served by Sarah Newman, of the napkins and forks, which they were afraid to use, of how well Philip danced and how handsome he was. Her mother ventured to remind her that she didn't look out o' place beside him. Hannah was very fond of her daughter-in-law, and always encouraged her to tell of her experiences there in Weld.

Finally the little red dress began to take shape. Each time it was put on to Mercy Ann for a fitting, it became more difficult to remove. The little girl had never before worn a red dress. Like her mother, all her clothes had been dyed butternut brown, or indigo blue. Now with this beautiful red dress fastened on for the last tryout, she determined no one should take it from her again. As quickly as any little mouse could, she scampered away from them all, out over the steps and down the side hill, apparently intending to join James and Phenewel, who were plowing in a field some distance below the house.

Young Rachel called to the child, but she only answered, "Uncle James" and ran on. In order to reach the field where the boys were, one must go around the end of the pasture, where the cattle were feeding. Grandma Hannah, feared the child would race thru the pasture, not remembering the ugly bull.

Young Rachel sensed the danger and ran like the wind, but old Hannah was far ahead of her. She reached the bars too late to grasp the little red skirt. It slid through and the child ran on with all her might toward the herd where the big Durham bull had already sighted her. He now began to paw the ground, making the dirt fly. With his head lowered, a fearful roar came from his throat as he started toward her. Mercy Ann was attracted by the sound and hesitated a moment. Hannah, whose breath was now coming in painful gasps, prayed that she might reach the child in season. She did not dare to call to her for fear that she would run the faster.

The bull was slowly advancing seeing nothing but the offensive red dress and growing more infuriated each minute. Hannah knew he would soon reach the point when he too would begin to run. Now she could only think a prayer. Somehow through the mist that was now coming before her eyes, she saw and reached the tiny red splotch. She ripped the dress off the baby girl and flung it with all her might to her right. The charging bull met it with his great bellowing, snotring head.

As Hannah fell forward with the child safe in her arms, she glimpsed through her blurred eyes, a black and tan object dashing past toward the bull who was tossing the red rag on his horns and making horrible hollow sounds in his throat. Grandma Rachel, a little behind her daughter, had had sufficient presence of mind to call the dog who had run furiously barking toward the bull. He moved him, with the rest of the herd, to the farthest end of the pasture.

It was several days before Hannah entirely recovered from the fright and fatigue caused by the episode of the red dress. It was several years before any member of the family could comfortably look upon a piece of red cloth.

Down on the Androscoggin, a little distance above the great falls, Collins built a leanto sufficiently large to house the provisions for the men and oxen, also provide space for bough beds for the men. Long before Seth and John B. reached the place, the heard the roar of the falls. John B. had never heard this before and the sight of all that tremendous water rushing over the rocks and flowing out below on each side, giving the appearance of a river twice as wide as it really was, proved a great revelation to him. He was so fascinated by the sight, he could scarcely leave it long enough to do his work.

Once, Seth was obliged to call to him rather sharply saying, "Where is our man that does as he's told?" This brought John B. up with a jerk and was sufficient to keep him on the job after that.

Work on the Great Falls proved to be the most difficult they had encountered. It hadn't been easy taking the drive over the falls at Livermore, but they were not to be compared with these. Here the black water flowed with terrific force down over the ledges which extended about an eighth of a mile. The hundred-foot logs would sometimes shoot straight out of the water or stand on end, then suddenly drop out of sight to reappear hundreds of feet ahead. Philip believed without the great depth of water it would have been impossible to ever take logs of such length over this mountain of rocks. No man would dare venture far if a jam should start. But with the water higher than the old river had been in many years, the logs raced on. If one dared jam, the force of the rushing torrent tore it from its rocky hold and sent it plunging dizzily on. The sound of these great pine trees knocking against the rocks reminded Philip of the booming of distant cannon. All day and all night the cannonading continued making it impossible for the men to sleep. Although the logs were still coming in great numbers, Philip and Sam decided it was best to move on with the wangan the second day and spend the coming night farther down river where the tremendous noises would not bother them. This decision was quite disappointing to John B., who told Seth he loved the noise and would like to live beside the falls forever. A few miles further on Collins built the next camp. Here they stayed several days, while they waited for Sam to finish "cleaning up the rear".

Sam who was fully as anxious as anyone to reach the town of Lisbon, came on as fast as possible. He told Philip, when he finally reached him, "Godfrey mighty, Philip, have I worked t' git here. I tell ye, I have, jest like a beaver. While I wouldn't swap my old loghouse in Weld for the best place in the town of Lisbon, it does somethin' to a fella t' come back t' th' town where he brought his new wife and where most of th' children was born. 'Course I can't see White Hill from here, but I know jest where she stands. I know jest how th' sun shines there in th' early morning 'n' jest how it looks when it sets. I know jest how th' crickets chirp at night, 'n' how th' whippoorwills sing in th' evening."

Hesitating for a moment, he added, "Wal, p'r'aps it's jest as well if I can't see White Hill from here. I'll soon be a'seein' th' hill on th' west side of Webb Lake, an' fore long everybody will be seein' our new houses."

Philip replied, "Yes, Sam, seein' the old home again does do something to a man. I'm not quite sure whether it's a good idea. A few nights ago, I slept in my old home in our own old room. I say I slept, at least I tried to, but I shall never do it again. As you say, it does things to you."

"Ye'us, I guess it does, Philip. I had thought mebbe I'd borra yer hoss 'n' ride up on the old hill some mornin' when we get down 'bout opposite my old place. I kinda wanted t' see Hinckley, but after all's said 'n' done, I guess I shan't dew it. How much longer d'ye s'pose it'll take us t' git th' last old pine tree into Merrymeetin'?"

"Ten days ought to finish us up I'd say, but sometimes it's hard to tell. We are pretty close to our goal, Sam."

"Ye'us, I'd say we was pretty nigh."

When the wangan team, Collins, Seth and John B. finally reached the spot where the Androscoggin River joins the Kennebec, the Pratt boys casually mentioned the fact to John B. little realizing how interested he would be.

"Seth, do you tell me that water across there is th' Kennebec?" he exclaimed.

"That's th' Kennebec, John B. That's th' river Benedict Arnold followed with his thirteen companies of about eleven hundred men back in '76. Y' know they left Cambridge in th' middle of September and sailed from Newburyport up th' river t' Gardiner where they'd had some boats built during th' summer. At th' end of th' first month after wadin' through mire to their knees, their backs loaded with salt pork and every other kind of thing, they finally reached th' Forks 'n' started up th' Dead River———"

"The' Dead River, did you say, Seth? How far is that from here?"

"Oh, I dunno—hundred miles or so. Why? What in th' world d' you care how far it is? Yer eyes are stickin' out like ye'd seen a ghost. Whatever is ailin' of you, John B.?"

"There's no great thing ailin' me, but as soon as I'm twenty-one, that's where I'm goin'."

"What in heck you goin' off up there for? I've heard that's th' very last place in th' world, and if a fella ever gits up there, he never comes back."

"How come ye heard that, Collins? Who told ye bout that?" demanded John B. so excited now one would be certain both his eyes were black as coal.

"I heard about a fella that went up there once years ago 'n' he ain't never come back as far as I've heard."

"How d'ye spose I know? No, prob'ly they didn't. Prob'ly jest a story."

"Of course, it's jest a story, John B. Don't be puttin' sech ideas in his head," said Seth.

"He didn't put th' idee in my head, Seth, it's been there a long time. Long fore I ever see you."

"Wal, we won't talk about it any more now or I shan't sleep a wink t'night," said Seth.

At last the tall pine trees from Weld found themselves in a permanent boom accessible to the Bath shipyards. Sam had joined Philip and together they entered the office inside a building owned by the ship·builders. where materials of all kinds were stored and where Philip had gone for his pay each Saturday night for so many years. Philip now carried in his breast pocket the papers on which the scale of the pine lumber had been made by Silas Barnard before it left Weld. At the office of the Bath Ship Building Company, they were extremely grateful to get these logs and said they were the longest ever brought into the Bay, to their knowledge. They also told Philip and Sam that the demand for long pine timbers for masts was now so great that they had already sent a crew of two hundred men to Georgia to cut pine for the Bath ship builders. This would later be brought to them in ships. He bargained with them to bring more of their trees in the coming spring. Philip reminded him that he was now seventy years old and Sam only a few years younger and perhaps another year would find them unable to cope with such a task, saying,

"You know, my friend, this operation from start to finish has been no child's play. But if we can't do it again, perhaps our sons can, now they have had the benefit of our experience." Eighty percent of the amount due them was paid, with the promise of the remainder in six months.

Sam was humming under his breath before they stepped from the wharf to mount their waiting horses. They were carrying more money than they ever dreamed of owning and he said in a subdued voice, which Philip had never heard before,

"I'll be goldarned if I b'lieve I am Sam White. Me with more than five thousand dollars packed into my boot legs 'n' round me in spots. It jest can't be me at all. Tell th' truth Philip, I'm scairt t' go 'n' I'm scairt t' stay. I don't b'lieve it's safe fer us t'ride home with all this money on us."

"Sam, we aren't goin' home alone. Our sons—three of them—and Duke Masterman will go all the way to Weld with us. Besides, Jake Parker will go as far as Greene. I'm not worried, we are armed and so is every one of the boys."

The ox teams, still hauling supplies, had already started toward home. Any of the men who wished to do so, could follow along with them, staying overnight at the camps along the way that had been made for their use as they came down river. Most of them, however, were anxious to get home to their families as quickly as possible, happy with what seemed to them a great deal of money that had been paid them by Judkins and White for their long days of hard work. This was generally fifteen dollars a month and found, and was a large wage compared with that usually paid for farm help.

The oxen lumbered along with their loads of left-over provisions. There were two teams now—the Pratt boys and John B. with the food team, Mac and Oliver with the other, hay and grain for the oxen. Philip had sold the boat to an old friend still working on the yard. He appreciated Philip's workmanship and neeedd a boat of that size, as he lived on a nearby island.

When these teams reached the Great Falls, Collins said to John B., "When we come down here, I intended t' tell you an Injun story but you was s' busy watchin th' falls I didn't git a chance."

"What is it, Collins? Go ahead ye slowpoke."

"Wel, th' story, is years ago when the very first settlers come in here th' Injuns was good to 'em. But after a while they began t' see th' white men was gittin' their land 'n' what was worse learnin' where all th' best fishin' grounds was. They thought t'was about time they got rid of 'em, so they had a pow-wow."

"What's a pow-wow?" asked John B.

"Oh, a kind of a meetin' t' talk things over 'n' git a little madder, 'n' make plans t' fight. So they set a night t' sneak up on 'em, but one old Injun wiser than th' others said, 'It wouldn't be safe t' go down river in th' dark so near th' falls on account of goin' over.' So they agreed to have one of their tribe build a fire on th' riverbank far enough above th' falls so th' water wouldn't be too swift, 'n' where they could land in safety. Then they planned t' walk from there down t' th' settlement 'n' start their butchery 'n' burnin'."

"Go on, quick, Collins, what happened?"

"Wal, there was one good Injun in that tribe, yessir, one good Injun."

"What made him good?"

"I guess twas cause one o' them white settlers had given him some grub two or three times when he was hungry. Anyway, he hated t' see all them white folks killed or scalped. So he sneaked down river 'n' told his friend, th' White man, about how they was goin' t' attack 'em. Also bout th' plan they had t' build a fire on th' bank t' show 'em where t' land 'n' keep 'em from goin over th' falls. So he said, when he saw a fire up-river he'd know they was comin' 'n' could git out their big guns 'n' drive 'em away. Now this Injun wa'nt no fool, but he hadn't stopped t' think how easy twould be t' put out that fire 'n' build one down near th' falls. So when they got down that far th' water would be so swift they couldn't land 'n' would go over th' falls. But th' white man thought of it 'n' that was just what he done, so when th' Injuns come along, over th' dam they went hellity larrup."

John B. had little to say after the recital of this tragedy. As soon as they reached the fields opposite Turner, John B. would have to leave them, a fact he greatly regretted. Oliver looked forward to a few days' visit at the home of lovely Julia Leavitt in her father's tavern, somewhat beyond the Upper Street settlement, where Oliver would cross on the ferry at North Turner.

They spent the last night out for John B. at William Parker's in Greene. Here John B. made quite an effort to impress the Parker children with accounts of the great sights he had seen, even th' Kennebec; and he scornfuly refused to enlighten these young people to any great extent on the historical facts concerning Benedict Arnold. He made a pretense at telling them a little of Arnold's struggles as far as the Dead River. After that, the story lost substance and when prodded by Anslem for more, he disdained to go further with the tale, saying,

"I guess it didn't mount t' much after that."

He was rather thankful to Seth for just then calling him to bed, for he hadn't remembered anything told him beyond the Forks.

When they were all settled on the hay now, Collins asked John B. if he knew this was their last night together and tomorow they would have to leave him there at the crossing opposite the Upper Street.

John B. said, "Ye'us, I know, and I tell ye I feel a hundred times worse about it than you do. I plan t' see ye agin some day, I don't know when. Y'see, I spect t' live up that way when I'm a man. I'm goin' t' git into th' lumberin' business myself someday."

"Oh, I thought ye said ye was goin' t' Dead River t' settle."

"Not t' settle, you lardhead. You said yourself it was th' end of nowhere. I am goin' up there t' git my Uncle Noah 'n' my Aunt Isabelle 'n' bring 'em back home."

John B. was soon fast asleep, but Collins and Seth remained awake until well into the night, thinking.

Many good-byes were shouted from the Parker dooryard to the men with the two ox teams, as they slowly disappeared up the road toward Turner.

Oliver was considerably older than John B. and so far during the trip had seen little of him, but now, on the road together, he found him quite interesting and admired his energy and enthusiams. Drawing the boy into conversation, he learned he was very anxious to go up-river and some day engage in the lumbering business.

Oliver said, "You know I don't live in Weld all the time, for I have a cabin and thirty acres of land in Number Four, fiive or six miles down river from where Judkins and Whites live and where my father, Eben Newman, lives. I think the land down there where I am is full as good as that on the west side of Webb River. Why don't you come to Number Four and settle?" (District No. 4. was later called Carthage.)

"I can't go anywhere to settle until my father and mother get ready to make a change. My mother says she wants her children to have a chance to go to school and she will never go any further up river till we get our education. She claims they don't have any good schools up there."

"Wal, I guess she's more than half right, but some day they will be better. I tell you what I'll do, John B., I'll make this bargain with you. In less than ten years, I expect to own a fine farm. I am goin' to get married in a couple of years to Julia Leavitt. She's used to havin' a good home and I plan to give her one. By the times your brother gets through goin' to school, probably your mother will be willing to make a change. If you play your cards right, maybe you can persuade your folks to come to Number Four. I'll agree to give you all the work you want. You know, you'll have to work for somebody part of the time, unless your father needs you every minute. There is a great chance for a young man like you, who wants to get into the lumber game, for there are so many acres of pine land up there it don't seem possible that it can ever be cut. I have seen enough of you, my boy, to know you like to work, and so do I. So, John B., lay your plans to come up river soon's you can. There are acres and acres off west of my place that you can buy cheap and the sooner you buy them the cheaper they'll be. Save every dollar you can from now on—that's what I did, and I'm gettin' ahead."

John B. looked Oliver straight in the eye, stuck out his chubby, grimy hand towards his new friend who grasped it and asked, "How bout it, John B?"

"I'll be there, Oliver."

They didn't say good-by, they didn't need to, but the Pratt boys spent considerable time telling John B. how well he had done and they seemed quite loath to leave him at the bank of the river.

Seth finally said, "Oh well, maybe we'll meet again."

"Torment it all, course we'll meet again. I'm goin' up river fore long myself. I'll be a neighbor o' yours someday."

Oliver and Mac, with their ox teams, were some distance ahead of the Pratt boys. But when John B. reached the top of the hill, he turned to watch their teams and was cheered to see Oliver waving his cap across the fields, far up the road. He watched both ox teams till they finally disappeared, then he ran for home with all his might. He rushed into the house on Upper Street where he was hugged, kissed and questioned by his mother, then asked to repeat the story of his river driving experiences to his father, who came from the cobbler's shop to listen. Soon, Uncle Seth walked in to get his share of information and John B. felt so puffed up with his own importance that his mother said later,

"I guess we shall have to hoop him, or he'll bust."

Philip Judkins had paid him three dollars, a full month's pay, when he hadn't worked but twenty days, and Oliver Newman's offer to hire him every day he could be spared from the farm, made him now sure they would some day own land in Number Four. He was the happiest boy in the town of Turner. He had a great desire to keep the three dollars as a nucleus toward buying that farm, but felt he should give the money to his father. Besides this, he had decided not to mention the pact he had made with Oliver until later on. Something seemed to tell him to wait a while, so he enthusiastically described some of the affairs at the Parker's the night before. Betsy, John and Seth laughed until tears ran down their checks at John B.'s recital of some of the tall tales told him.

"Anslem tried to show off," John B. told them, "Cause his father goes to sea and he said, 'My father was in Calcutta when, what do you think he saw—a man with a basket full of snakes and one of them had two heads. And he wan't a mite ascairt of it, put it right around his neck. And he had another basket, a big one, and he put his little boy into it, put on the cover and then stuck his sword right through that basket more than a dozen times. A little while later, who should come a-walkin' to'ds the crowd from up the ro'd but that same little boy without a mark on him.' 'That's nawthin' says Lois, 'I saw a man the other day that had five heads 'n' he could talk out of all five mouths 'n' sing a different tune out of each mouth all at the same time, by jiminy.'"

"What kind of a girl is this Lois? Does her mother allow her to tell such lies as that?" asked Betsy.

"No, her mother don't 'low her to do any sech thing, but you see, she don't hear everything her youngones say, she's too busy taking care of the smaller ones inside th' house. You know there's nine of them now with th' twins, but Anslem looks after th' older ones best he can. N' by cracky, he took some o' th' wind out o' Lois' sails after she told her whopper. He grabbed her by one o' her long yaller braids 'n' marched her into th' house 'n' told her mother. 'Twant long before we heard her stompin' up th' stairs t' bed. But th' first thing we knew she poked her head out o' th' chamber window 'n' stuck out her tongue at Anslem, called him a tattle tale 'n' spit on him. 'Bout then, Mis' Parker appeared 'n' took her by th' ear 'n' marched her off into th' back room where I guess b' th' sounds she warmed her out good."

"Is Lois pretty?" asked Betsy.

"I donno as I noticed how she looked, cept her hair 'n' that's uncommon thick 'n' long 'n' just th' color of a punkin blossom. She's a terrible little thing for her age, n' her feet don't look big enough t' hold her up, but by th' way she snakes them babies round, one under each arm, I jedged she was pretty strong. 'N let me tell you, she can run faster than I can or any o' her brothers, them little feet o' her'n can jest fly over th' ground. We had a spellin' match that evenin', before we started tellin' stories; 'n' if you think she can't spell, you jest oughta hear her. You know, there's a boy a year or so younger than she is, his name is Ami

(226)

and even he can spell better than I can."

"John B., I'm ashamed of you!" exclaimed Betsy.

"Wal, I'm 'shamed o' myself, but I tell you now, before I go down t' Parker's again, I'm goin' t' spell better'n I do now. You see, these Parkers set great store by learnin'. Mis' Parker 'n' Grandmam Betsy both team them youngones up to the table right after supper 'n' they spell 'n' do sums in their heads for quite a spell before they c'n play, 'n' you talk about doin' sums in your head, that Anslem is th' boy for that! He can add like lightnin'. He works in th' store some 'n' Lois said, 'I want you should understand there can't nobody cheat him.' Seth told me all th' family was money-getters. This Anslem is talkin' all th' time bout goin' t' college. He says he wants t' go down t' Brunswick 'n' get an education. We saw that college when we went down through t' Bath, they call it Bowdoin."

"What does it look like, John B.?" asked his father.

"Oh, no great t' look at, just a big buildin' somethin like a barn."

"Would you like t' go t' Bowdoin?" asked Uncle Seth.

"Wal, I ain't particala bout it. I'd ruther go into th' lumberin' business."

"You'll need to go to school a lot before you c'n do that," said his mother."

"All right, 'n' you c'n bet a four dollar bill I'm goin' t'. I ain't goin' t' have no boy a year younger'n I am stand right up 'n' reckon fractions in his head when I don't know enough to do it with a pen. Why, even that Lois can say her multiplication tables arse end fo' 'most."

"Do you mean backward, John B.? If you do, you can say so. Don't you ever let me hear you say 'arse end foremost' again. I guess I had better start you youngones in doin' your sums after supper. I don't plan on havin' th' Parkers outdo my folks. What did you tell 'em for a big story? I hope you didn't lie like they did."

"No, marm, I don't lie. That's one thing I don't do, 'n' I don't b'lieve Anslem lies, but as for that Lois—wal, o' course she's only ten years old 'n' she didn't cross her heart when she told it."

"Wal, let's hear what you told," said the father.

"I asked them if they ever heard of th' miracle Jesus Christ did. Some of them they'd heard of 'n' some of them they hadn't. They knew about th' Lord curin' th' blind man, and th' leper, but they didn't seem t' know much bout Lazarus bein' raised from th' dead. And Lois didn't act as if she believed it, so I said, 'Don't you know th' Lord c'n do anything he wants to? He could even jump right over this house.' 'Mebbe he could, but I'll bet you five cents my father could twitch him right out of his boots,' Lois said."

Betsy wasn't certain whether she should reprimand John B., the instigator, for what might seem a sacrilegious conversation with the Parker children, but she finally decided there was no such thought in the minds of any of them, and she had better pay no attention to it. Later, she remarked to her husband that they had best be thankful their own little daughter Betsy was no tomboy like Lois Parker.

"Strange she is such a little popinjay, for her mother is always so gentle. I have never heard her raise her voice," said John.

Riding along together, they were fast approaching Berry's Mills when Philip said to Sam,

"I suppose we're goin' to ride over Tom's new bridge before long. We must pay him his twenty-five dollars, you know."

"So we must, 'n' here's my share, Philip, 'n' I don't begrudge him a cent of it, dew you?"

"No sir, I don't That's cheap enough. God knows. There is some more to be paid to Abbott, also—about two hundred dollars, but it isn't due till fall and we'll get it from Bath before that time comes. I tell you, Sam, we are pretty well fixed financially. If we can keep up this lumberin' business a few years more, we shall be rich. We came up here just the right time and we certainly took that timber to Bath just the right time. Those ship builders will eat out of our hands for a while, my friend."

"Ah-dum-dee," was all the reply Sam made, he was too happy to do anything but sing. He was still singing when they rode down over the hill. The old familiar tune was the first Rachel heard to inform her of her husband's return.. She was noisily enthusiastic in greeting her Sam, while Hannah was exactly opposite. But both these men realized the joyful satisfaction in the fullfillment of their ambitions through the long years of waiting. The long hours of arduous toil that had filled each day of each year was as nothing now. Now they would enjoy the fruits of their labor. Now they could build their fine homes and take their families from the dingy loghouses where they had spent the last

(228)

several years. Their sons and daughters could do the same. Beside this, they had established a business that could be carried on by their sons many years after they retired or were called to the Better Land.

Chapter XXII

"TICK-TOCK, OLD CLOCK"

In the spring of 1836, John and Betsy Staples, with their sons John B., Ezra C. and Christopher Y. started for Carthage or District No. 4. They had sold their farm on Upper Street in Turner against the advice of their neighbors who said, "Y'll starve t'death in Carthage. There's nothin' to do up there t'earn a livin' but shave shingles."

"Well then," replied John B., "we'll shave shingles."

John bought a small house in Carthage with fifty-six acres of land and settled down to pioneer life again.

True to his word, Oliver Newman, who lived on the other side of the "ox-bow", gave young John B. all the work he could do. He was tireless in his efforts to accumulate property. He built a fine home and married Lois Parker which he had determined to do when he first saw her in Greene. His mother questioned the wisdom of this and had thought probably when he was older he would forget the "yaller-haired" girl. This was not the case and as he grew older he often found excuses to go to Turner by the way of Greene.

Betsy-John's mother was an expert spinner but when she left Turner she gave her fine spinning wheel to her daughter Betsy who had recently married Sullivan Hale and had settled on a hill not far from the Upper Street. Now, after living in Carthage a while, the mother wished she had a good wheel and some yarn to spin. John had bought a few sheep and there would be plenty of wool in the coming spring.

At the breakfast table one morning Betsy told her men-folks she didn't have enough to do in that small house to keep her busy and missed her spinning. Wondered if there was anyone in Carthage who could make a spinning wheel? John B. always ready to do anything his mother asked said, "I've heard there was a man up in Weld by the name of James Swett who makes fine spinning wheels; anything in the line of wood-workin' for that matter.

Father, let's drive up and get him to make a wheel for Mother." John agreed it was a good idea and they started out to find the home of James Swett.

"Oliver said he lived on the left side o' the ro'd not far from where his father Eben lives."

They drove up through Berry's Mills, turning off at the left toward Weld, and finally reached a good looking two-story house. John thought it was rather a pretentious place but John B. said, "Swett is a carpenter and of course he has a fine house."

As they went into the yard a tall, thin woman came to the door.

"James Swett live here?" John B. asked.

"No," was the reply." He lives down the ro'd a piece 't the next house. Jonathan Pratt lives here. Has for a good many years, 'smatter o' fact, ever sence we moved 'cross the pond when we come from Turner."

Old John had started to get out of the wagon when she mentioned Jonothan Pratt's name. He was slow in alighting and as he stumbled up the steps he cried, "Isabelle! my dear sister! is it you?" By this time John B. had clasped her in his arms fairly shouting, "My Aunt Isabelle! I thought you went to Dead River."

"My darling boy! Your Uncle Noah went to Dead River with his wife Ruth Bradford several years before we came up here." As is the way with reunions everybody began talking at once and nobody listened.

By this time they were all crying. Isabelle had her arms around both Johns. "Come see me often," she begged.

"I think I sh'll be up here tomorrow'n bring m' mother," John B. said as he gave her a hug.

True, to his word, he and his mother started out in the morning, taking the Old Tall clock as a gift for Isabelle. It was an old family heirloom. When Isabelle saw that clock she really began to cry. It was a toss-up which made her happier, the sight of it, or Betsy Staples whom she had never seen before, having left Turner when John was a small boy. "John and I were married in front of that clock," Betsy said, Isabelle nodded in understanding. John B. and his mother went home that night so full of stories it took way into the night to retell them to old John.

In the summer of 1840, as they sat on Philip's ample porch overlooking the lake, smoking their long pipes, and enjoying themselves generally, Philip asked Sam if he liked the sermon at church the previous day, and if he believed it had been good judgment to move their house of worship from Coburn Hill to the lower village.

"Most new-comers are takin' up lots down nearer th' pond. They have built a school house on the knoll a little below where the road runs up there and a store just this side of it. Looks to me as though the main settlement will be down on this level."

Sam said, "I always thought it would be over here on this westside, but mebbee I'm wrong. But there's a good many families settlin' all around here-must be twenty-five or more. I was talkin t' day with Eben Schofield. He was tellin me what he had done here in little over twenty years. His boys, William'n Lafayette, are young, 'n I declare I was astonished t' hear him tell what they could do. Y'know that's a beautiful spot there on th' hill where his place stands, one of th' prettiest places in this town. His two oldest children are girls, but they're bout as strong as any boys I ever see, 'n' can they work. Built for it, y'know. Tall 'n' straight as saplings, just as healthy as they are good lookin'."

"I agree with you, Sam, those two girls. Octavia and Julia are pictures of health. I wish Philip's Mercy Ann was like them. I sometimes wonder if she's long for this world: presently Sam fell asleep, Philip sat beside him as he snored and wondered what he was dreaming.

"At least, they are peaceful dreams. It's true what he said, neither of us has cause to worry any more. We are old men, and of course the grim Reaper will gather us in before many years."

After a short nap, Sam awakened and these two elderly gentlemen resumed their conversation. They proudly discussed the prospect of their granddaughter's coming marriage to Christopher Staples, youngest brother of John B., now a prosperous farmer living in Carthage. He and his wife, Lois, already had two sons, Parker and John. There was nothing Sam better enjoyed than living over those days when he and Philip had come to District No. 5 in search of the tall trees, thirty-one years before.

One story led another, and as was generally the case, the younger members of the family gather round to hear the stories told by their grandfathers. Finally Sam III whom they called "the other Sam" and who was now quite a sizeable boy, asked Philip if he would tell them of his experience when he was taken prisoner by the Indians and carried off to Quebec in Revolutionary times.

(232)

Philip, as usual, seemed loath to comply with the request of the boy. The other Sam said,

"Well, you must have had a mightly hard time."

"Yes," answered Philip, "I had a very hard time. I have known many hardships in my life, but I have never seen the righteous forsaken, nor His seed begging bread."

Everyone eagerly listened to hear what this venerable man would say, but there was a long pause. Those watching him, saw his grizzled old head drop forward on his chest. Young Philip slipped to his father's side, lifted his chin and said,

"Father."

But the ninety year old pilgrim had gone to the land where the tall trees grow on the banks of the River of Life.

END.